DEAD MAN'S DEAL

The Asylum Tales

JOCELYNN DRAKE

HarperVoyager
An imprint of HarperCollins*Publishers*
77–85 Fulham Palace Road,
Hammersmith, London W6 8JB

www.harpercollins.co.uk

This edition 2013
1

First published in the US by HarperVoyager 2012

A catalogue record for this book is
available from the British Library

ISBN: 978 0 00 752528 7

To all my peeps back on Finchley and Stevies.
You are missed.

Acknowledgments

WRITING BOOKS IS about dreaming big dreams while your eyes are wide open. It's about playing God and battling demons. With this book, I want to thank my husband for giving me the time and space to wage my wars and dream my dreams with Gage. He's brought me food, rubbed my shoulders, and listened when I needed to babble.

I also wish to thank my wonderful readers. You've followed me from a fiery vampire to a tattoo artist with attitude and a wand. Your outpouring of support and enthusiasm carries me through the rough days when Gage doesn't want to talk.

As always, a big thanks to my amazing editor, Diana Gill. I write stories because it's my thing. Diana is the reason I tell a damn good story. She guides and pushes me, and with a little luck and hard work, I learn to be a better storyteller. Thanks to my agent, Jennifer Schober. She's my coach, my friend, and my defender.

DEAD MAN'S DEAL

1

THEY WERE KILLING pixies.

I glared at the brown brick house with its neat little lawn and trimmed hedges. I wanted to storm inside and set the pixies free before I took a baseball bat to the head of whoever was running that slaughterhouse. Instead, I slouched in the passenger seat of Bronx's Jeep, thinking of all the ways I would love to kill Reave, but I was no closer to getting out of the car.

I couldn't set the pixies free and I couldn't beat anyone's head in. I was there to set protective wards on the house, not burn it down.

Bronx shifted in the driver's seat, watching the house as well. "You know we can't sit here all night."

"They're killing pixies," I said, glancing over at the troll. "They're making fix—killing not only pixies, but anyone who is stupid enough to take the drug. I can't put a protective ward on that house. I'd rather hand myself over to the Ivory Towers."

"Reave isn't going to let you out of your deal just because you have moral objections to his business pursuits."

"Fucking bastard."

Months ago, Reave discovered that I was a former warlock. Well, just a warlock-in-training, but the information was enough to get me killed. To keep him from selling me to the highest bidder, I had to work for him. And because I was an idiot, Bronx was stuck working for the dark elf Mafia boss as well. I needed to extract both myself and the troll from this mess, but I didn't have a clue as to how. So for now, here I was protecting drug manufacturers and helping them kill creatures for their livers.

Sitting up, I unbuckled my seat belt. "I warned Reave that I wasn't going to kill anyone for him. Protecting these assholes would make me an accessory to murder."

"Then we go back to Reave and we tell him that we're not going to do it," Bronx said as he reached for the key still sitting in the ignition.

"No," I snapped. I wasn't angry at the troll. I was angry at Reave and maybe even angry at myself. If it was just me, I'd tell Reave to shove his little task up his ass. But Bronx was in this mess too, and if I told Reave to fuck off, Bronx would get hurt.

Unlocking the door, I pulled the handle and rolled out of my seat to the sidewalk. Bronx climbed out of the Jeep at the same time and walked around to stand beside me. The large troll with the spiky blond hair scratched the stubble on his chin as he stared at the house. "Let's take a look," he suggested. "You should know what you're protecting. Things could go wrong, through no fault of your own, if you don't know what you're dealing with."

An evil grin spread across my mouth as I shoved my hands into the pockets of my baggy jeans and strolled down the block toward the two-story house. *Man, I loved his wicked sense of humor.* We were going to see what kind of trouble I could cause while maintaining a somewhat believable alibi. It was unlikely that Reave was going to buy any excuse that we came up with, but it was worth a try. If I taught the Svartálfar anything, it was going to be that you never backed a warlock into a corner.

A woman with a blue handkerchief wrapped around her greasy brown hair jerked the door open after we stood pounding on it for a couple of minutes. A cigarette was pinched in the corner of her mouth, while lines dug deep furrows in her face. Working for Reave wasn't helping her preserve her youthful vitality.

Slipping the cigarette between two fingers, she pulled it away long enough to blow a cloud of smoke in our direction before barking, "What do you want?"

"Reave sent us," Bronx replied while I coughed, gasping for some clean air.

"Oh. You're him, huh?" Her eyebrows jumped toward her hairline and her mouth hung open in surprise. Apparently I wasn't exactly what she'd been expecting.

"Yeah, I'm him," I said.

"You gotta come inside to do your thing?"

"It helps. Reave said he wanted this place thoroughly protected. If I don't know what I'm protecting, things could go wrong." I leaned close, flashing a wicked grin while struggling to ignore the gagging body odor rising from her. "Horribly, painfully wrong for anyone inside."

The woman jerked away from me, her dull brown eyes going wide. She pulled open the door and moved out of the entrance so Bronx and I could enter the house. From the exterior, it looked like a normal suburban house. You would have expected to see a tidy living room with upholstered furniture in floral patterns, neatly piled magazines on the coffee table, and maybe a stack of cartoon DVDs beside the TV in the corner. You would have been wrong.

The house was a lie. It had been chosen so it wouldn't draw any attention. The police didn't expect to find a lab for manufacturing lethal drugs in the middle of suburbia. They were looking for things like that in the slums on the other side of town.

The curtains were drawn over the front windows and the living room was lit by a single desk lamp resting on an old orange crate. A large man sat on a metal folding chair behind the crate, cleaning one gun while another was disassembled and resting on the crate. A small TV played in the corner, sound muted so he could hear our conversation at the front door. The guard watched us as we entered, but said nothing.

The stinky woman shut the door behind Bronx. She dropped her half-burned cigarette on the hardwood floor and crushed it under her stained pink house slipper before guiding us to the back of the house. We passed through an empty dining room and she started toward the kitchen, but I stopped her at the stairs leading to the second floor.

"What's up there?"

She shrugged her thin shoulders. "Couple cots. Bathroom. Reave don't keep any kind of furniture or valuables here."

"Where are the other guards?" Bronx asked. The woman narrowed her eyes and I held my breath. I didn't want her to whip out a cell phone and call Reave to check our story. I wanted to get in and out. "He needs to know. Otherwise your own guards could be locked out."

"Oh, that makes sense," she murmured, and it was hard not to laugh because Bronx was just piling on the bullshit. "The other two are picking up dinner. There's usually only three guards here, plus me and my husband. Except on delivery and pickup days. Then Reave sends over four more guards."

We continued to the kitchen, where we found all the counter space covered with take-out containers and greasy fast-food bags that desperately needed to be thrown out. The trash was overflowing with empty beer bottles and more rotting food. This place needed more than extra security. It needed a cleaning service, but then both the people I had seen so far also needed a few lessons in personal hygiene.

At the back of the house, the woman pulled open another door and we descended into the basement. This wasn't one of those nice finished basements with a big-screen TV, minifridge, and pool table. This was an old-fashioned basement with cold stone walls, concrete floor, and exposed pipes overhead. All the lights were bright bare bulbs and an odor of mildew hung in the air.

A man looked up from where he was leaning over a long table, his black eyes enlarged by his thick glasses. "Where the hell have you been, woman? I'm ready for the next batch," he shouted as we came into view. Along the wall behind him was another long table, but this one held a row of silver boxes and several glass containers with tubes coming out of them.

"Those men Reave called about arrived," she snapped irritably, waving one hand back at Bronx and me.

The man's eyes settled on us and his frown deepened. "Why they down here?"

"We need to see all of the premises so that the work can be done properly," Bronx said, but the man didn't seem to be as trusting as his wife. His frown deepened as his fists landed on his hips.

"Is that one of the new gravity convection ovens or are you still using forced air?" I asked, stepping around the woman to approach the table. The man straightened, his frown disappearing as he glanced over his shoulder at the row of ovens behind him.

"The two on the far end are forced air. I just got in the new gravity convection," he said slowly, sounding as surprised as Bronx looked beside me. Unlike a lot of tattoo artists, I had studied various methods of preparing ingredients used in potions. Most tattoo artists bought their ingredients prepared for them, while I liked to work with the raw materials. The result was that I knew a fair amount about the machines found in professional laboratories.

"How do you like it?" I asked, scratching my head as I looked over the ovens. "I've worked with the forced air for years and think they're great. I'm reluctant to change when I think something works just fine."

"The gravity is a dream," the man said with a chuckle, his whole demeanor relaxing as he imagined that he was talking to someone who was in the business as well. "It took me forever to talk Reave into getting me one, but it has sped up production. It's a lot more reliable than the forced air."

"You've got a great collection of desiccation jars, particularly the vacuum ones. I wasn't expecting you to use those."

He shrugged as he took off his glasses and cleaned the lenses on the hem of his dirty Black Sabbath T-shirt. "They come in handy if you get backed up. If we can't get the livers directly into the ovens after harvesting, they'll go into the traditional desiccators, but if we need to let them sit for a while after coming out of the ovens, we'll drop them into the vacuum desiccators. With all the moisture in the air down here, we have to be careful that the product doesn't get contaminated."

I nodded, pretending to be interested in his tools and gadgets when my stomach was churning inside. I knew the basics of how fix was produced. Pixies were torn open, their insides ripped out and separated. Their livers were used for the drug, but most of their other organs could be sold to vendors for potions and a few delicacies. The livers were thrown into laboratory-grade ovens and dried until they could be pounded into a fine powder, which was later snorted or injected by trolls, ogres, giants, and other large races. A smaller creature's heart would quite literally explode in its chest in a matter of seconds.

"Yeah, that's got to be a problem," I murmured before turning back to the man. "Do you keep the pixies on-site?"

"Have to. The product has to be fresh."

"Can I see the room they're kept in?"

The man's expression closed once again as he crossed his arms over his slightly bulging stomach. "I don't know why you need to see that."

At the same time I could hear the heavy thump of two sets of footsteps descending the wooden stairs into the basement. The men fetching dinner had returned. Excellent—more gun-wielding assholes running around this enclosed space. Three people with guns we might have been able to handle quietly, but five was getting tricky. The scent of salty fries and greasy burgers hung heavy in the air, adding to the uncomfortable gurgling in my stomach.

I forced an indifferent shrug. "Fine. Reave said to protect the house. It was my understanding that meant the most important parts of the house. I'll just do the upstairs. You can explain to Reave why I didn't protect the pixie storage room. You can also tell him that I'm not making a second trip. I've got better things to do with my time."

Bronx was expressionless as he started to follow me back toward the stairs. I didn't even reach the bottom stair when the man was anxiously calling me back.

"Look, man, I didn't mean nothing. If anything happens to the supply, it's my neck."

"I'm just trying to do a job," I said, still standing by the stairs as if I was going to bolt at any second. "The sooner you let me do it, the sooner I can get out of your hair." What this guy didn't know was that Reave hadn't said anything about protecting the pixies. I think he wanted me to put a quick ward on the front and back doors and drop a fireproof charm over the house before calling it a night. I had something better in mind.

"Here. The storage room is right here." The man scurried to a door in the far wall. He took an old iron key out of his pocket and unlocked the door while waving me over. I gave a quick nod to Bronx to hang back while I stepped over to the room. The man flicked on the light and there was no stopping my harsh gasp. It was a small room, barely larger than a walk-in broom closet. The entire back wall from floor to ceiling was covered in small cages made of fine mesh metal wires so the little bodies they imprisoned couldn't squeeze through the openings.

The small room was filled with the sound of rapidly beating wings like a thousand insects gathered in a single space. Over that, there were high-pitched cries. I couldn't understand what they were saying, but it was heartbreaking to hear. Unlike faeries, pixies glowed with an almost phosphorescent light from the inside, a variety of red, blues, greens, and orange. Their lights seemed dimmer than usual to me.

The man in the thick glasses grabbed a baseball bat from near the entrance and hammered on the front of the cages. "Shut the hell up! Nasty vermin."

The pitiful cries stopped, but not the sound of those desperately beating wings. It was all I could do to keep from ripping the bat from his meaty hands and using it on his skull. I kept facing forward, walking up to the cages with my hands buried deep in my pockets. Tiny hands reached between the mesh wires at me while wide, liquid black eyes held my gaze.

"How do you keep them from using magic on the locks?" I said in a rough voice, struggling to keep the anger from my tone. The people in this house saw the pixies as animals, or worse, something to be used up and thrown away.

"The inner workings of each lock are made of iron and each lock is opened with an iron key. Their magic don't work on iron."

I nodded. I'd guessed as much, but I had to be sure.

"So, you got a way of protecting them?" the man asked my back as I continued to look over the wall of cages.

I winked at the pixie hovering directly in front of me. "Yeah, I've got something that will protect them," I said. The pixie cocked her head to the side, looking a little confused for a second before a small smile lifted one corner of her mouth. Turning back to the man, I motioned for him to precede me out of the storage room. "I'll need you to leave the door open and stay out of that room while I work."

"How long is that going to take?" he demanded, looking over his shoulder at me.

"Not long. Few minutes at most. Go eat dinner while I work."

The man hesitated for several seconds before he walked over to the guards holding the food, his head shaking as he went. I smiled to myself and pulled some blue chalk out of my pocket. Time to go to work.

All around the door and on the interior doorjambs I wrote a series of symbols in blue chalk, murmuring a spell as I went. Each glyph briefly flared to life with bright white light as I finished writing it, then went out. The spell and ward combination was what I considered loud magic, like sending up a signal flare on a cloudless night for anyone who might be watching the magical currents in the area. There would be no escaping Gideon's attention with this, even using the excuse of defensive magic. Since leaving the Ivory Towers and turning my back on the warlocks and witches, I had been banned from using magic except in self-defense. This was *not* what they had in mind.

Gideon may have admitted that he wasn't opposed to my staying alive, but that didn't mean he was willing to risk his life and his cause in order to protect me. If it meant protecting himself and his family, the warlock would haul me in front of the Ivory Towers council in a heartbeat and let me be executed.

Stepping back into the storage room, I knelt down and started drawing more symbols on the sloped concrete floor. The sound of the beating wings had died down and the room was silent as the pixies intently watched me. The pixies held no love for the drugmakers, but I suspected that they liked the warlocks and witches even less. The Ivory Towers had been hunting them for centuries to obtain the magical properties found within their organs. We all knew that any good potion could be made even better with a little pixie heart. I was afraid that whatever trust they had put in me was dissolving before my eyes as I sketched each symbol, but it didn't matter. They didn't have to trust me. They only had to escape when the time came.

Standing again, I looked over the cages and smiled at the pixies before turning and leaving. The man and woman were seated at the end of the long table in the middle of the basement, inhaling some fast food, while a pair of guards stood watching over Bronx and me. On a patch of dry floor, I drew one more symbol.

"Stay out here for a few more minutes. I'm almost done," I announced while motioning for Bronx to accompany me up the stairs. The troll was silent, watching my back as I walked through the house, drawing on each door and on the floor before reaching the front door. No one questioned what I was doing. We had all been raised not to question the witches and warlocks. Hell, you never approached one if you could help it. People had been killed by the members of the Ivory Towers just for wishing them a good day.

Drawing one last special symbol on the doorknob, I pulled the front door closed as I whispered the last word of the spell. I chuckled to myself as I followed Bronx down the front steps to the sidewalk.

"Should I ask what you've done to the house?" Bronx asked while picking his way across the front lawn beside me.

I smiled up at him, unable to hide my excitement as I tucked the piece of chalk back into my pocket. "It's called the Spell of Defenseless Enticement."

"Reave is going to be pissed. You were supposed to do a protective spell." Bronx shoved one hand nervously through his hair as he turned back to look at the house. Everything looked fine, but that was part of the enticement. That so-called fine was only going to last for another second or two.

"I did. It's a very powerful protection spell, but to achieve it, you have to leave yourself completely defenseless. In this instance, all locks become useless. You can't lock a door, a window, or, say, a cage in this house."

As if on cue, screams erupted within the house followed by loud banging. We paused in the middle of the lawn and looked at the house. Lights could be seen being flicked on through the cracks in the curtains, followed by more bangs. A few sounded like gunshots, but I wasn't worried about the pixies. They were wickedly fast when they took flight. The humans were more likely to shoot each other than a pixie in that chaos.

"What's the protection?" Bronx asked.

"Oh, if you enter the house with ill intent toward the occupants, your feet become stuck to the floor," I said. I was still waiting to see the pixies escape. "A warlock has to release you, or you have to have your feet cut off to get unstuck again."

"That's pretty powerful."

"I've been dying to use it for years, but could never come up with a good excuse."

The front door was thrown open and the man I had spoken to in the basement and one of his guards came running out. They had their hands over their heads while screaming at the pixies, who were pelting them with what looked like scalpels. As they hit the warm night air, the pixies scattered in all directions, rising higher into the sky until they disappeared from sight.

"What have you done?" shouted glasses man. "They're all loose."

I gave him an indifferent shrug. "It's a protection spell. Unfortunately, it has the side effect of disabling locks. I thought you could handle the pixies."

"You've ruined me!"

The asshole grabbed a gun from the guard and pointed it in my direction. Bronx jumped in front of me, acting as a shield. Grabbing at the troll, I tried to shove him away. My magic was out in the open here. I could stop a damn bullet without risking harm. He couldn't.

"I don't think so," said a calm, irritated voice over the din. The gun exploded in the man's hand, leaving behind a bloody stub. He screamed, clutching his wrist as he fell to his back in the grass. The guard stood beside him, frozen and white-faced as he stared over my shoulder.

I didn't want to look, because I knew who I would find. There were things in this world worse than a pissed-off dark elf and his Mafia thugs. Like an irritated warlock with a chip on his shoulder.

Gideon stood behind me, glaring at the moaning man. Reaching into the left sleeve of his shirt, he pulled out a wand. With a quick flick of his wrist, the night was filled with an ugly gurgling before becoming completely silent. The man was dead and I was definitely fucked.

"TWO MONTHS," GIDEON muttered, shoving his wand back up his sleeve. "You couldn't go two full months before I had to track you down again."

"I missed you too," I said with a nervous smile. Mocking and irritating Gideon was something that I specialized in. However, he had never approached me before when others were around—the world wasn't supposed to know what I was. With Gideon's attention now on me, the surviving guard ran into the house and slammed the door shut, leaving us alone with the pissed-off warlock.

"Gage?" Bronx said softly.

I moved in front of the troll, not that my smaller body offered much protection. I didn't have a wand on me, which made any type of magical protection shaky at best, but I'd protect Bronx from Gideon the same way the troll had intended to protect me from the gun.

"It'll be okay. I've got this."

Gideon stopped in his pacing and arched one eyebrow at me. I didn't mean it to sound so challenging, but I needed to try to reassure my friend. Gritting my teeth, I tried to think of some way to placate Gideon. It was as if I was standing in quicksand, the earth slipping away from my feet the more I spoke. A smart man would keep his mouth shut. I wasn't always a smart man.

"This is a surprise," I started again, trying desperately to think of a way to defuse some of Gideon's anger. His mouth firmed into a hard line, proving that I was failing miserably. Warlocks and witches were a testy lot in the best of times. Gideon had proven that he was a good guy, or at least as much as a warlock could be, but he hadn't batted an eye at killing that fix producer. I didn't know whether it was because the dealer pulled a gun or because Gideon had been annoyed by the man's screams. Either way, dead was dead and I wasn't about to let that happen to Bronx.

"Two months, Gage," Gideon said, picking up his earlier thread of conversation, seemingly oblivious to the fact that Bronx and I were standing there waiting to see if our lives were about to come to a messy end. I watched, barely breathing, as he tugged on the cuffs of his blue, collared shirt within the dark gray business jacket he was wearing. He could have been a banker by all appearances, with his shiny shoes, Rolex, and blue-and-gray-striped tie. The only thing missing was the wedding band on his left hand, but then warlocks and witches weren't permitted to marry. I wondered if the missing ring bothered him, or his hidden wife.

"I seem to have fallen into a bit of trouble," I admitted.

Gideon's gaze drifted over to the house I had protected, his face expressionless. The occasional pixie slipped from its hiding place in the eaves to the nearest tree, thick with leaves that were only now starting to show the colors of autumn. "So I gathered. Your new job involves freeing pixies?"

"Not quite."

"I gathered that as well," he muttered, turning to walk toward Bronx's Jeep. "Come along. I'm not going to kill you or your troll."

I sighed, my shoulders slumping. Motioning for Bronx to accompany me, I walked over to where Gideon was standing beside the Jeep. It was somewhat larger than many of the vehicles people drove simply because it was one of several styles that had been enlarged to accommodate large creatures like trolls and ogres. The warlock peered into the passenger-side window, seeming curious about the interior.

"This is the one that works with you?" he said, straightening to look over my shoulder at Bronx. His expression was the same as when he was looking over the car, only mild interest but largely dismissive.

"Yes, he's a good friend," I bit out, but I stifled my irritation. The fact that he had deigned to notice Bronx at all was a compliment. In general, warlocks and witches considered any creature as beneath their notice. All the same, his manner was insulting.

"My name is Bronx," my companion said in a smooth, even tone, betraying neither fear nor anger.

Gideon said nothing, so I spoke for him. "And this is Gideon, a dear friend. You'll have to excuse him—the Ivory Towers don't teach manners."

"That would explain a lot," Bronx replied, earning a shocking, surprised bark of harsh laughter from Gideon. I turned to find that the troll was looking straight at me, the butt of the joke. *Ha. Ha. Ha.*

"You . . . you seem very protective of Gage despite what he is," Gideon said stiffly. "Are you worried about your job?"

I could hear the shrug in Bronx's voice when he spoke. "Jobs come and jobs go. There will always be others. Gage is my friend and there won't be others like him. I would prefer to keep him alive."

"He's a warlock."

"And I'm a troll. He's my friend not because of what he is, but because of who he is."

Gideon's tone grew hard, intent on pushing him. "He's going to get you killed."

Bronx smiled as he looked down at me. "Better him than cholesterol."

To my shock, Gideon was smiling when I turned back to him,

but there was a sad look in his eyes. "He reminds me of Ellen," he whispered. "She says she'd rather die because of her association with me than because of boredom."

My smile died before it could rise on my lips. Ellen was Gideon's secret wife. He had shown me a picture of a pretty blond woman and their daughter, Bridgette, two months ago. If the Ivory Towers found out about Ellen or Bridgette, all three were dead, but Gideon would be killed only after he had watched his family ruthlessly tortured to death.

"Are they all right?" I demanded. Gideon's eyes snapped to my face, as if he were waking from a dream. "Has something happened to them?"

Gideon wasn't someone I would dare to call a friend. We had similar goals and ideas and we had both been brought up in the Ivory Towers, but that was where the similarities ended. Gideon had been a thorn in my side for years, a shadow chasing my every step. Even so, I couldn't help but feel something for the man. Particularly since I had discovered that he had been protecting me.

"No, they're both fine."

"Safe?"

"Yes."

"Hidden?"

"Not unless you drop it," he growled.

I breathed a soft sigh of relief. "Then what are you doing here?"

"You mean other than because of your display?" he said, waving one hand at the house we had just left. Honestly, I had almost forgotten where we were and why we were even there. But then a pissed warlock standing in front of you made you forget about everything else.

"Well, you usually pop in, smack me around, threaten me, and then leave. This is an extended visit."

"I came to warn you."

And with that, all the joking was pushed aside.

Gideon was my main source of information on what was happening in the Ivory Towers. I may have left years ago, but I soon learned that I wouldn't be able to safely turn my back on the group. Many of the witches and warlocks of the Ivory Towers had wanted me dead for leaving, and it seemed that despite the passage of time, that was still the prevailing sentiment. Gideon's job wasn't so much to make sure I didn't break the agreement to not use magic as it was to come up with a reason to haul me before the council so I could finally be executed. Gideon was the only buffer I had between myself and death at the hands of the Towers.

"I might soon be removed as your guardian."

My knees buckled, but I didn't realize it until I felt a pair of large hands slowly lowering me to the ground. My mind was too busy trying to absorb the information that he had dropped on me. Gideon not my guardian? I was fucked. Totally, undeniably fucked.

Yes, Gideon was an asshole. He had taken pleasure in beating me and scaring me every opportunity that he had. But I wasn't an idiot. I knew that I had given him plenty of opportunities over the years to drag me before the council. Hell, he had the council's permission to kill me on sight if he caught me using magic. If anyone else had been tasked with watching me, I wouldn't have survived my first year away from the Towers.

I'd gotten better, severely cutting back on my magic use. I didn't absentmindedly flush the toilet with a wave of my hand anymore, but I still used magic and I would have to continue to use it until I got free of Reave.

"Why? What's happened?" My voice was hoarse when I could speak. Bronx released his hold on my arms, but was hovering close.

Gideon paused and looked over at Bronx.

"Trust him!" I shouted. "He's not going to run off and tell your secrets."

"The Towers are in chaos," he admitted in a rush. "While a body hasn't been located, the general consensus is that Simon Thorn is dead, and with few exceptions, all fingers are pointing in your direction."

Simon had been my mentor at the Ivory Towers. I'd left at the age of sixteen because of my hatred for their beliefs, and Simon wasn't pleased with my decision. He tried to kill me, but I survived by some insane stroke of luck. The council let me live and leave, but Simon had never accepted the decision. When an opening on the council recently popped up, Simon decided to kill me so the blemish on his past was eradicated. He had failed and was now buried under a residential street in an extremely shitty part of Low Town.

"I doubt you're going to find a body," I said, and then glared up at Gideon. "You can't tell me anyone is upset the bastard is gone."

He shook his head, looking tired. "No. Some are pissed that you managed to kill someone from the Towers. Others were simply reminded that you're still alive, and are focused on having you killed, legally."

Legally.

Now, that was the big joke. A witch or a warlock could come down from the Towers and strike down anyone they wanted with no fear of retribution from anyone. However, there were rules for killing a witch or a warlock. Problems within the Towers were brought before the council to be decided on and people were punished accordingly—most of it being a painful death sentence. Of course, there were exceptions: people who secretly took matters into their own hands. But I could guess why most wanted me put down *legally* and it had to do with the recent jump in the number of runaways from the Towers.

"And since you've not succeeded in bringing me back before the council for my inevitable execution . . ."

"They are considering replacing me with someone who will get the job done," Gideon finished.

"Does anyone suspect that you're helping me?"

"I'm sure someone does, but so far no one has dared to voice it out loud." Gideon paused and I could feel the weight of his gaze on me. There was something he needed to say, but was holding back.

"Spit it out." My nerves were already frayed with fear. I didn't like being pinned between the forces of the Towers and Reave's Mafia.

"I'm currently left with two choices. I think I've got a matter of weeks before they agree to replace me, if not less time. I can either find a reason to bring you before the council . . ." Gideon paused again, lifting one hand gracefully toward the house I had "protected." "Or I can let them replace me, leaving you to fend for yourself."

"Does the council still have an empty seat?" There were a total of thirteen seats on the council, but if there was one open, a tie vote would mean at least a temporary stay of execution.

"Yes, but with things in such turmoil, I don't think you'll get the tie vote you're obviously hoping for. You'll be dead within an hour of arriving before the council."

"Fuck." I sighed, dropping my head into my hands while resting my elbows on my bent knees. The Ivory Towers needed a scapegoat, someone they could use as a warning to the others who were training to be witches or warlocks. There was no escaping. There was only one way in the world—theirs.

Sadly it took me a minute to think of another angle. My head snapped up so I could see Gideon again. "Are you safe?"

"What do you mean?" Gideon demanded. His brow furrowed at the sharp question, casting his gray eyes in shadow.

"If they replace you, it's likely they suspect you're at least a sympathizer. It would put you in a dangerous position. You and your family. Are you safe? Are they?"

A ghost of a smile crossed his grim mouth. "They are safe for now, and I will manage. But if it comes down to protecting them and protecting you, I'm sure you know how I will choose."

With a grunt, I pushed back to my feet and brushed off the back of my pants. They were damp from where I had been sitting on earth soft from the recent rains. Unfortunately, I had bigger problems than a mud stain on my ass. "Yeah, I know."

"Have you spoken to any of the runaways?" Gideon suddenly asked.

I blinked, my mind struggling to keep up with the swift change in topics. "Not knowingly."

"Are you sure?"

"Look, I don't know who left the Towers. I didn't know any apprentices while I was there and you and Sofie are the only ones that I speak with now. If one stopped in the parlor, I wouldn't know it. Are you saying they're in Low Town?"

"Yes. My group knows they're in town, but rumors are starting to circulate in the Towers that they're here."

"And I imagine rumors are stating that I drew them here," I grumbled. "Damn it, Gideon! The Towers aren't even supposed to know where I am."

The warlock nodded. "Four more left recently. We've tried isolating the apprentices more than ever before, but it seems to be getting worse."

"Four? What's that make it? Seven here in Low Town."

He sighed, rubbing the bridge of his nose with his thumb and forefinger. "Five. Two were killed in their escape attempt."

"Wouldn't it be best if these runaways sought Gage out?" Bronx inquired.

"No!" Gideon and I said in unison. For a moment I had forgotten that the troll was even there, I had been so lost in a world that I had tried desperately to leave behind.

"But you've survived; thrived even. You could help them," Bronx suggested.

"Things were different when I left ten years ago." I looked down at my hands and tried not to imagine the blood that had been splattered across them during my short time living in the Towers. "I was the only one to ever consider leaving. An anomaly. They let me go, but with restrictions, and many are still calling for my head."

Gideon shifted, crossing his arms over his chest. "If the Towers can confirm that Gage has anything to do with the runaways, they will see it as a sign that he's attempting to lead some kind of revolution." The warlock frowned, staring at me. "It will be war, and the Towers won't stop until Gage and all the runaways are dead. I wouldn't be surprised if they chose to wipe out an entire generation of human children as a warning. It's been done before."

I leaned against the side of the car, my hands shoved in my pockets. Low Town was becoming a dangerous place for me and there wasn't much I could do about it. I was tempted to ask how well known it was in the Towers where I was located, but I bit back the question. Running would happen eventually, but not yet. I'd make plans, but I wouldn't leave yet. There were too many things I needed to get done here first.

"Thanks for the heads-up on everything," I said. My mind wheeled in endless circles, leaving me with more questions than answers. And the answers that I did have were pretty shitty.

Gideon nodded, his mouth quirking slightly as if he were trying to fight a smile. "I have to go. It's dangerous to be around and not try to kill you."

"You're not the only one who feels that way," I grumbled, glaring at the ground.

"But . . . I could use a favor," he said. He wet his lips, hesitating as if he was afraid I would instantly turn him down. That or he simply didn't want to feel like he needed me for something. "Find out who cursed Sofie."

"That was a long time ago."

Some of the tension eased from his face. "Afraid she forgot?"

"Not likely. You thinking of helping her?"

Gideon remained silent so long, staring off in the distance, that I thought he might not answer me. But when he spoke, my stomach knotted in pain for the man who wasn't my friend but was. "I thought if Sofie were human again, she might like to take on an apprentice. If I remember correctly, she had a gentle way with children."

My mouth fell open and some part of me wanted to say something comforting, but there weren't any words. Gideon must have known, because he stiffly nodded to me and disappeared. I leaned my head back against the roof of Bronx's car and closed my eyes. *Poor Gideon.*

"I'll admit that I didn't understand a lot of what you were talking about," Bronx said, drawing my eyes open again. "But that part about Sofie . . . why is he interested in her? Is he trying to get her to go back to the Towers as a spy?"

"No," I said, straightening. "Let's get out of here. Now that he's gone, I'm sure the cops will want to descend on the house."

Bronx nodded and punched his key remote to unlock the doors. We got the hell out of there, letting me sink into silence for a minute and get lost in the rambling thoughts.

The Ivory Towers were the ultimate rulers of this world, deciding life and death (well, mostly death) for its inhabitants, but when they weren't around, the cops tried to maintain some semblance of peace. The fix maker's death would be chalked up to a DBW—death by warlock/witch and the book would be closed. Naturally, they would search the house and find the drug-manufacturing equipment. The house would be confiscated, but I knew better than to hope that it would be tied back to Reave. He was too smart for that.

It wasn't until we reached the highway that I felt some of the tension that was threatening to choke me start to ease. Bronx didn't turn on the radio and I was content to listen to the sound of the car cruising down the smooth concrete while the streetlamps flashed overhead. As dire as my own situation was becoming, I found my thoughts centering on Gideon and his young daughter. She would be turning seven soon.

"You asked about Sofie," I started, and then stopped. Bronx patiently waited while I attempted to organize my thoughts. It wasn't so much that I was trying to censor myself, but that it was simply better if he didn't know certain things. Swearing softly, I reached up and touched the ceiling of the car while whispering a quick word, creating a protective bubble over the car so no one could magically overhear me. Damn, I was getting paranoid.

"Gideon has a daughter," I confessed after another lengthy silence.

"Is that a bad thing?"

A smile quirked the corners of my mouth. "Witches and warlocks aren't permitted to marry or have children. It's seen as a weakness and a liability."

"What does Gideon's daughter have to do with Sofie?"

"His daughter has either exhibited some magical talent or he's afraid she will. If so, she has to be trained, and he can't send her to the Towers. They would know in a heartbeat that she was his daughter."

"And Gideon, his daughter, and eventually his wife would be killed," Bronx concluded.

"Yes."

"But if Sofie was changed back to human, would she stay here or would she rather return to the Towers?"

I stared out the passenger-side window and frowned. "I don't know."

I had known Sofie in human form only briefly while I was living at the Ivory Towers during my apprenticeship to Simon Thorn. She had been nice and motherly, albeit a little meddlesome. Somewhere along the way she had run afoul of a witch or warlock, and had been turned into a big Russian-blue cat. As far as I knew, she couldn't return to human form until the person who cursed her died. After spending several years as the pet of an elderly woman, she was now living fat and sassy with Trixie.

Unlike Gideon, Sofie gave no indication that she didn't approve of how things ran in the Ivory Towers. The only reason she had left was that she felt more vulnerable in cat form. Her ability to use magic had been severely limited. I feared that if Sofie were human again, she would happily return to the Towers, which would be of no help to Gideon and his daughter.

There wasn't much I agreed with when it came to the beliefs of the witches and warlocks of the Ivory Towers, but I thought they were right when it came to training all human children who possessed magical talent. It was for the children's protection and those around them as much as it was about spreading knowledge. An untrained child who could unconsciously tap magical energy was a serious danger. In moments of fear or anger, people died around the child without the child intending it to happen.

Gideon knew that. If Sofie couldn't train his daughter, he had few options. He couldn't do it himself without risking others finding out. Training was an intensive, full-time gig and Gideon was already working for the council as a guardian. But if Bridgette wasn't trained, she'd have to be killed.

I closed my eyes against the ugly thought but it was still there. For a brief second I thought that I could at least teach her a few basic things about control and protection, but I crushed the thought before it fully formed. What the fuck did I know about caring for a seven-year-old girl? I was an outcast former warlock-in-training now a tattoo artist who moonlighted nights doing odd jobs for the local mob. Not a great role model. Sofie was the best choice. I'd have to convince her of it.

"As much as I hate to ask after all the fun we've had tonight," I started, shoving my thoughts back to my most immediate problem, "but what are the chances that Reave doesn't know about tonight's events?"

"Oh, he knows," Bronx said as he took the exit ramp off the highway. "He definitely knows by now."

"Retribution?"

"Oh, yeah. Expect pain."

I leaned my head to the side, hitting it against the window. It was my fault. Bronx had nothing to do with my decision to free the pixies but I knew that Reave would punish him along with me. "Damn it! I'm sorry."

"For what? The pixies?"

"Yeah."

"Do you regret it?"

"No."

"Then don't apologize," Bronx said. He slowed the car to a stop at a red light and glanced over at me. "You saved lives tonight, and if you didn't do something, I would have."

"Thanks."

He shrugged. "It's been a rough night. You want me to drop you at Trixie's?"

"You think it's safe?"

"Reave's going to need time to realign his distribution network after tonight's escapade. We've got a day or two. Besides, I'm sure he knows about Trixie and you. Staying away won't protect her if he wants to attack you from that side."

"Then Trixie's would be great," I said with a sigh. "You can come up too. She won't mind."

Bronx chuckled. I knew that trolls were naturally solitary creatures, but sometimes I worried about him feeling lonely even if my worry was unrealistic. "I'll be fine. I've had enough fun for one night. I don't need another session of strip Chinese checkers burned into my brain."

I gave a snort of laughter. "We don't have to play that. Trixie said she's been working on a way to make a drinking game out of *The Princess Bride*."

The troll rolled his eyes, one corner of his mouth quirking in a half smile. "Let's save it for this All Hallows' Eve. Go spend some quality time with your girlfriend."

Smiling, I relaxed in my seat as we got closer to Trixie's apartment. Beautiful green eyes. Musical laughter. A soft touch that soothed the tears in my heart and the holes in my soul. Tonight, I would fall asleep holding Trixie and I would deal with the rest of the world tomorrow.

REAVE SURPRISED US as we reached Trixie's apartment complex. Escorted to a large, dark warehouse in a not-so-nice part of Low Town, we stood in an open area with large wooden crates lining the far walls. Reave's black clothes and liquid black hair allowed him to nearly disappear into the shadows. Streetlights leaked through the dirty second-story windows, but he avoided the light for the most part.

To say that Reave was pissed would be an understatement. The Svartálfar wasn't raving and stomping around the room while intermittently throwing things at us. Dark elves, like their Summer and Winter Court brethren, didn't show emotion like that. But the telltale muscle spasm at the corner of his eye and the constant fisting and unfisting of his hands said it all.

"Why do it, Gage? That's all I want to know," Reave said in a low, even voice. He almost sounded reasonable.

I shrugged, fighting to not look over at Bronx. "I'm not sure I know what you're talking about. You wanted the house protected from intruders. I protected it."

"While destroying my supplies in the process." Each word was ground between clenched teeth. "There are consequences for every action."

It happened too quickly for me to react. Two pairs of hands roughly grabbed my arms, jerking me away from Bronx while at the same time turning me so I could easily see him. Five large trolls stepped out of the darkness toward Bronx and began beating on him. He fought back for a few seconds, ducking blows and swinging his meaty fists, but they were too many and too strong. Trolls can take a beating, but even they will start to fold under so much abuse from their own kind. As Bronx was knocked to the ground, I increased my struggles against the hands holding me while screaming at Reave until I was hoarse as they kicked Bronx in the ribs and stomach.

The dark elf jumped from the shadows; a long curved blade winked in the faint light before it was pressed against my throat. The sharp edge bit into my skin, sending a trickle of blood down my neck.

"Easy, warlock," Reave snarled in my ear. He was taller than me, forcing him to bend his head down and press it against the side of my head so that I could hear his ragged breathing. The knife sawed into my neck while he crowded close, but my eyes were locked on Bronx as he tried to regain his feet under the punishing blows. "Hold it together. We wouldn't want any accidents."

"Let him go, Reave!" I shouted. "You know he had nothing to do with what happened at the house. It was me. Punish me."

Reave chuckled in my ear, tilting the blade so that it slipped a little deeper into my throat, sending more blood down my neck. "Does it really feel like you're not being punished right now? If you want to break a man, you hurt the ones he loves first."

"Stop it! You've fucking won!" I couldn't pull my eyes from Bronx. He had stopped moving and was lying on the dirty warehouse floor, curled into a fetal position as he tried to protect his head and gut.

Reave pulled the blade away and smiled at me as he stepped into my line of sight. "I won months ago. You're just slow to realize it."

As he turned from me, he snapped his fingers. The trolls stopped beating Bronx and stepped away while the hands on me fell from my arms. Pressing one hand to my throat to slow the bleeding, I hurried over to Bronx and knelt beside him. What I could see in the darkness wasn't good. His face was bloody and swelling so that he could barely see out of either eye. I couldn't tell if his nose was broken because it had always looked somewhat broken to me, but I figured it was a safe guess that it was by his labored breathing through his mouth.

"I warned you, Reave," I said in a low voice. "I warned you that I wasn't going to do anything that would hurt someone else. I'm not going to kill anyone for you, and leaving that house as it was would have meant killing pixies. I don't regret what I did. And if I find another one of those fucking fix houses, I'm going to do it again."

"And risk putting Bronx in danger again?" Reave asked lightly. His voice echoed across the warehouse, dancing through the shadows. He was walking, but I couldn't see him.

Energy crackled around me as I grew angrier with each passing second. I wanted to burn away every shadow and dark corner in that room so Reave had nowhere to hide. I wanted to run him to ground and beat him the same way Bronx had been beaten. But I did nothing because I couldn't afford to draw the attention of the Towers, and Reave knew it. "No. This was the last time you'll ever touch Bronx. I promise you."

Reave laughed. The sound was like razor blades across my back, leaving me gritting my teeth until my jaw ached. "You're right. I'll leave Bronx alone. You've got plenty of other people in your life that you care about."

I kept my mouth clamped shut, fighting the urge to warn him off of Trixie. He knew about her. There was no reason to prove my feelings for her even more, deepening the danger. My jaw throbbed from my clenched teeth while I mentally repeated to myself, *If you use magic, the Towers will kill you.* Everything was insane right now in the Ivory Towers, and they would jump on the opportunity to string me up in hopes of reining in the chaos. Gideon wouldn't be able to protect me.

My death meant that Bronx would be trapped working for Reave. A dead Gage meant that Trixie was in danger and on the run from the Summer Court. If I kept my temper and was smart, I could stay alive and help my friends.

"If you have no more use for Bronx as leverage, then release him from your little organization," I said when I had my emotions somewhat under check. "You only need me."

Bronx groaned softly. "Shut up, Gage."

"The troll is right. Shut up, Gage. I have plenty of uses for Bronx. I'd hoped that he might be a voice of common sense for you, but he has failed at that endeavor. I guess I'll have to find something else to do with him."

"You've got plenty of others to do your dirty work. People who want to be here. Let him go."

Bronx shifted beside me, slowly uncurling his body, but still remaining on his side so that his back was to Reave. "I work with Gage or not at all."

The dark elf stepped close, moving away from the shadows to the edge of a square of light. His expression was blank as he stared at Bronx's inert form. I tensed, waiting. If Reave did anything more than breathe, I would jump the bastard. My friend had been hurt enough because of me. I wasn't about to let Reave inflict more harm.

"Fine. Rein him in," the dark elf bit out. There was an "or else" left hanging in the air. We both knew that if I crossed Reave again, Bronx would be killed regardless of whether he could stop me.

He paced away, brushing his hands against each other as if wiping away the distasteful business that had brought Bronx and me to his doorstep that night. I wished he would leave so I could work on healing Bronx. A handful of healing spells could fix the worst of his wounds, but he would still need to get home and rest. The cold concrete floor that he was currently lying on didn't seem like the best option.

"Now then, since my first task seemed too difficult for you to handle, I've got a new job for you," Reave began, as if he was content to wipe away all the previous unpleasantness. I frowned, keeping one reassuring hand on Bronx's shoulder. I wanted to tell this asshole where to shove his new job, but I kept my mouth shut. Obviously Reave was done trying to get me to cooperate through beating me. He was going to drag in one person I cared for after another and beat them until I agreed to his terms.

He paused and turned to look at me, waiting.

"What job?" I asked through clenched teeth, earning a grin from the dark elf.

"I'm so glad you asked." Reave chuckled and resumed his pacing. "I have someone that will be doing an important errand for me and he needs some added protection. Unfortunately, he can't travel with the usual assignment of muscle. It's too conspicuous. As a result, you will be giving him a tattoo that will provide him with the needed protection."

It seemed too easy and it appeared as if it would be legal as well. "What kind of protection does he need?"

"I think that will best be decided by you."

"How can I do that? Who am I protecting him from? What's this job that he's doing for you?"

"Delivery." I waited for Reave to elaborate, but he didn't say anything else. I sighed, running my free hand through my hair, leaving it standing on end. It was turning out to be a long fucking night. "Fine. Am I to meet this person somewhere or will he come to my shop?"

"He'll stop at your tattoo parlor for the work."

"When?"

"Soon," Reave called over his shoulder as he started to walk out of the warehouse with his flunkies following behind him.

"Hey! You never told me his name!" I shouted, lurching to my feet.

"You'll know him when you see him." Reave's comments were soft as they floated across the empty expanse toward me.

I stared at the door that slammed shut behind the last thug as he exited the warehouse, leaving me alone with Bronx. My heart thudded in my chest and a chill crept down my spine. *I'll know him when I see him.* Yeah, that sounded bad. I knew a lot of guys who were involved in some shady shit, most of them being tattoo artists. But as far as I was aware, none of them had these kinds of dealings with Reave and his sort. I wanted to pretend that Reave hadn't found another way to strike at me, but even *my* imagination wasn't that good.

Bronx groaned as he rolled onto his back. The pain left him panting heavily and I could see sweat—or blood—shining on his wide brow in the faint light.

I knelt at my friend's head and hastily pulled off my light jacket. Fall was just settling on the city and the nights were still warm, but I had grabbed it more out of habit than real need. I rarely remembered to glance at the weather report most days and I had learned from experience that weather in Low Town was unpredictably strange on the best of days. I placed my hands on either side of Bronx's face and angled his head so that he was staring straight up at me. He winced at the movement, but didn't make a sound. Quickly folding my jacket, I gently placed it under his head.

"Where's the pain?"

"My body," Bronx grunted.

"A little more help, please."

"Get me home. I need some rest." His words were labored between bursts of heavy breathing. Each breath was wheezy and slightly liquid, making me think that one of his lungs had been punctured, possibly by a broken rib or two. If I had to guess, he had internal bleeding from several organs and broken bones, and a concussion. From what little I knew of trolls, they weren't the quick-healing type like shifters or vampires. If I didn't do something, Bronx would drown in his own fluids.

"You need a lot more than rest, but you don't seem the take-me-to-the-hospital type."

"Go to hell, Gage." Bronx gasped as he tried to move, clenching his eyes shut.

"Already there," I said, but my mind was elsewhere, focused on setting up the cloaking spell I needed in order to do my work. I was planning to do a whole lot of loud magic and I wasn't stupid enough to do it right out in the open to draw the attention of every Merlin and Morgana in the Ivory Towers. Gideon might not have been actively hunting my ass, but that didn't mean others weren't watching for me to fuck up.

The cloaking spell wasn't without its defects. No one would be able to see what I was doing, whether they were using magic or not. To the naked eye, we were invisible. When I was using magic, a warlock or witch would simply see us sitting on the warehouse floor, but at the same time there was an energy void around us. Voids were anomalies created by magic spells, which would raise questions should a warlock or witch stumble upon us. My plan wasn't foolproof, but without the cloak, my healing spells would be like fireworks in a frigid winter sky.

"You using magic?" Bronx asked.

I sighed as the cloaking spell fell easily into place with a wave of my hands and a couple of whispered words. "Just a bit."

"Don't. You've . . . got enough problems."

"Stop talking. You don't want to distract me," I said, earning me a low growl. "Got to heal you. I'm not carrying your heavy ass to the car."

"Fucker."

I smiled and closed my eyes as I placed both my hands on his shoulders. "Just a warning: this might not work. I've never tried it on a troll."

Bronx stiffened under my fingers, sucking in a ragged breath. "Great."

Truth was that I had never tried this healing spell on anyone but myself. Warlocks and witches were more concerned with their own survival. Hell, when we were learning to heal wounds, it was always the hard way. Our mentors beat us until we were barely conscious and then left us alone in an empty tower. You learned to heal yourself or you died overnight from a ruptured kidney or drowned in your own blood as it poured into your lungs.

Focusing on the spell, I sent a wave of energy coursing through Bronx's body, kicking off the first phase of the spell. Organs were mended so that they were no longer losing vital fluids and were returned to normal functioning levels. They were still battered, bruised, and extremely sore, but no longer in danger of failing him. As the spell moved through him, I could feel each organ as it healed. One lung had been punctured and flooded with blood, the other bruised. A kidney had been badly damaged and it looked like his spleen was on the point of rupture. A few blood vessels had been crushed, but were now open again, sending blood through his body.

As the energy exited through my hands, I sent in a second wave. This was the painful one. Each broken bone was set back to rights, causing a sickening echo of snaps and clicking through his body. Bronx groaned loudly as the spell took effect, causing him to arch off the ground while trying to pull away from my hands. I rose up on my knees and pressed down, holding him in place. The spell needed additional time for the bones to properly set and harden again.

The second phase lasted less than a minute, but there was nothing I could do about the pain, leaving both Bronx and me covered in sweat and breathing heavily. The energy flowed back to my hands and I sent the final wave through. This one knit together any cuts in his skin, stopping any additional bleeding while urging his body to speed up the process of creating fresh blood to replace what he'd lost. There weren't many cuts and the final wave returned to me after only a few seconds.

I fell backward, sitting on my ass on the cold concrete, trying to get my breathing to even out again. I was exhausted, but Bronx's life was no longer in danger from his wounds. I looked down at my friend. He breathed evenly without the sickening rattle and squish I had heard before.

"What the hell did you do to me?" Bronx asked. He had yet to move and I was glad for it. He needed time to recover. You didn't walk away from a troll beating even if you were a troll.

"Heal you."

"Then why the hell do I still feel like shit?" he growled.

I laughed, my head dropping back so that I could stare blindly up at the ceiling. There was nothing but blackness broken by dirty light filtering through a grime-encrusted skylight. "The spell fixed broken bones, stopped bleeding, and mended organs. You're still badly bruised and battered. Time needs to heal that. I don't have the energy in me to fix it all."

"You didn't have to do it," Bronx murmured.

"Yeah, I did." My eyes fell shut as the memory of his beating rose back to the forefront of my mind. He wouldn't have been touched if I had protected the house like Reave had ordered. *Fuck.* Bronx wouldn't have been in this mess to start with if I had killed Reave two months ago when he first threatened me with exposure.

But I was clinging to the idea that I wasn't a killer. Warlocks were mindless, empty killers who thought nothing of taking a life. Witches were heartless killers. I chose to leave the Towers. I chose *not* to be a killer.

Simon's laughter picked that moment to rattle through my brain like the Ghost of Christmas Past. I had killed Simon, but it had been self-defense. Right? I had to kill Simon or he would have killed me.

"Gage?" Bronx said, jerking me from my thoughts. Silence had stretched between us, but I didn't know for how long. Had he been talking to me, waiting for my response? I had to let these doubts go. Fuck you, Towers. I wasn't one of you. And fuck you, Simon Thorn. I hoped you liked your new job as ferryman to the dead.

"I had to heal you," I said, my voice picking up strength as I returned to our conversation. "It was either leave you to die or carry your fat ass to the car. Do you know how hard it is to find a good tattoo artist to work in our part of town? Not that easy."

Bronx chuckled. His normally deep voice was even deeper from the pain that lanced through his body. I rose and offered him a hand while bracing my legs to help pull him to his feet. It took a couple tries and we were both puffing heavily when it was over, but Bronx was standing without help. The troll was roughly triple my weight. There wasn't much I could do if he couldn't walk to his car on his own.

I waved my hand in the air, dispersing the last of the cloaking spell before bending down to scoop up my jacket. My back protested and my knees were stiff from sitting on the cold floor. I needed to get back to the gym. I had been trading off my usual trips there in order to spend time with Trixie before going into the parlor. Maybe it was time to find a little balance. I was beginning to think that I needed to be in shape if I was going to keep up with Reave and his band of thugs.

"Now what?" Bronx asked around another wince of pain as he hobbled toward the door.

"Home. Shower. Bed," I listed, keeping pace beside my friend. "We'll deal with tomorrow when tomorrow comes."

"Not Trixie's?"

Trixie's place felt like some distant dream, an oasis in the wasteland my night had become. I would have given anything to see her and settle in her soft arms, but I shook my head. "Home."

Trixie didn't need to see me when I was in this mood. She would have argued otherwise, but our relationship was still too new for me to be dumping the weight of my past into her lap while I grumbled the last of the night away. She would try to help me forget and move on, but the only thing that would help me was sleep. In sleep, there were no memories to haunt you and no doubts to chase you. There was just the cool bliss of nothingness.

A SOFT CHIME tinkled through the parlor as the front door opened. At the same time magic prickled lightly across the bare skin of my forearms. Someone had activated the antiglamour spell upon stepping into the shop. The feeling passed, but I picked up my pace as I walked from the back room to the front lobby. I set a worn clipboard on a stack of papers and glanced at the surveillance monitor to see Trixie crossing the lobby. The elf in human disguise smiled at me as she moved around the front counter and stepped into the tattooing room.

To the world, she appeared as a lovely brunette human with soft features that included brown eyes, lush lips, and a heart-shaped face. But I was able to see the real her through the glamour she wore as protection. The sexy elf with acres of blond hair and crisp green eyes still managed to make my dick twitch when I saw her for the first time every day. She had only recently started to tone down some of her outfits now that we were officially dating. Bronx joked that he had told her to cool it or I was going to kill the next man who looked at her, which wasn't too likely but wasn't impossible either. I wondered if she had only dressed like that to catch my attention, but shoved the thought aside. My ego wasn't that big.

Today she wore a somewhat sedate outfit. A black halter top

hugged her breasts, revealing the perfect expanse of her back complete with a sparkling butterfly wings tattoo. Her snug jeans rode low on her hips, revealing a narrow strip of her stomach and belly button, which contained her newly acquired belly-button ring. Yet another thing to make my dick twitch. She had exchanged her usual belly-button ring for a red gem that winked in the overhead lighting.

Trixie's throaty chuckle caused me to jerk my head up while a surprised blush lit my cheeks. She had caught me staring. Fuck, she was lucky that I didn't have to pull out the mop to clean up the drool. What this woman saw in me I didn't have a fucking clue. Brown hair, brown eyes, and barely her height when she was in heels, I wasn't that much to look at. My body wasn't bad. All lean muscle, the result of frequent trips to the gym, but you wouldn't know it under the baggy T-shirts and faded jeans I wore. Maybe it was my charming personality. Not. Fucking. Likely.

"Seen enough?" she teased.

I closed the distance between us, wrapping my arms tightly around her so that I could feel every inch of her soft body pressed against mine. Of course, that meant she knew exactly how happy I was to see her, but I didn't mind. We were still early in our relationship. If we weren't screwing like rabbits every chance we got, I'd be worried. Her mouth found mine as if drawn to me, her lips already parted. She tasted of strawberries and something sweet and intoxicating that was uniquely her. Her hand drifted down my back, bunching in my T-shirt so that it pulled up my back as she held me close. A soft moan slipped from her throat and I was ready to go. The parlor was empty. The counters could be resterilized.

Someone called my name in an angry and plaintive voice. I jerked my head away from Trixie, breaking the kiss but not releasing her. I heard it again and groaned as my dick throbbed in frustration. We weren't alone. This time, Trixie blushed as I stepped backward and looked down at the forgotten cat carrier in her hand. She had brought Sofie in to work with her.

"Sorry, Sof," I muttered, walking to the opposite side of the room in hopes that the distance would get my hard-on to pass. Her only response was a soft growl while Trixie set the carrier on the floor and unzipped the opening. Trixie brought the cat into the shop a few times a week so she had a little variety in her day. Trixie's apartment was smaller than Sofie's previous home with an elderly woman named Mae. It also didn't include a balcony, limiting Sofie's time outside. I didn't mind since she spent most of her time lounging on the glass counter or sitting in the front window, watching the people walk by.

"I still can't believe you let her put you in that thing," I said as the large Russian Blue jumped from the floor to the tattooing chair at Trixie's station. The cat gave a little shudder and rubbed against the arm of the chair a couple times as if to put mussed fur back into place.

"It's not bad so long as you don't distract her when she walks in," Sofie grumbled, sitting in the middle of the chair.

"Sorry about that." I flashed Trixie a smile that wasn't at all apologetic. She shook her head as she turned and shoved the cat carrier in an empty cabinet.

I walked over and scratched the cat's head in greeting, trying to once again suppress the thought that Sofie was a witch and not some weird talking cat. You didn't rub the head of a witch. Sofie never complained and I had heard her purr a few times, but I didn't want to think too hard about any of it.

"I'm worried that you're not getting enough exercise; getting a little soft around the middle from letting Trixie put you in that carrier."

Sofie growled and took a swipe at me with a lethal set of claws. I jerked my hand back, but she caught my middle finger, tearing a thin red line along the side.

"Hey!" I yelped. "I know a couple good vets who can take care of those claws."

"And I know a couple good ways to make you a soprano," Sofie threatened. I stepped back over to the counter I had been standing at earlier, sticking my wounded finger in my mouth.

"Gage!" Trixie sank gracefully onto her stool. Sofie jumped into her lap and curled up while Trixie proceeded to stroke the witch/cat. "You know better than to tease a woman about her weight. Sofie is the perfect weight." Trixie lowered her head and rubbed her forehead against the top of the cat's head while cooing at her. Under those noises, I could hear Sofie purring.

"She knows I was teasing!"

Trixie looked up and frowned at me. "That's no excuse."

My eyes fell shut as I swallowed a sigh. Sofie was a witch. She had been born human, and despite the fact that she walked around as a cat, she was still a witch. It seemed wrong to treat her as a cat, but Sofie didn't balk at any of Trixie's attention, which was more than a little disturbing. Maybe Sofie had spent too much time in the form of a cat and it was starting to affect her sense of self.

"You didn't stop by last night," Trixie said softly.

I opened my eyes again, watching as she lifted her head from Sofie. Her expression was filled with questions, but she didn't say anything else, leaving it up to me as to whether I would tell her anything of my adventures with Bronx and Reave's little organization.

The sigh I thought I had swallowed rose back up and escaped me. I would have to say something since I wasn't completely sure that Bronx would be in to work that night. He would need time to heal and it was very likely that he would still be feeling like shit when the sun set.

"Things didn't go too well. I wasn't in the greatest of moods when we were done and I didn't want to drag that over to your place last night," I said with a frown. "Also, Bronx might not be in tonight. I'm going to call him in an hour or two to check on him."

"Not in? How bad did things go last night?"

Leaning against the counter, I crossed my arms over my chest and stared at the floor. While the lobby had a nice old hardwood floor, the main tattooing room was covered in this crappy yellow linoleum that was cracked, chipped, and lightly stained with splatters from dropped ink containers. "I was sent to protect a fix-production house." Trixie gasped and I clenched my teeth and chanced a peek up at her. Pixies weren't directly related to elves, but it was my understanding that they were at least seen as some kind of distant cousin—a lot closer than humans were believed to be. "I relieved them of their supply in the process of protecting the house."

"Thank goodness," she breathed, her shoulders slumping in her relief. But they stiffened again as her mind traveled along the next natural conclusion. "Is that how Bronx was injured?"

"Sort of. We got out of the house fine, but Reave decided that I needed to be punished to make sure that I didn't try anything like that again."

Trixie's brows furrowed, meeting over her petite nose as she looked at me. "So Bronx was hurt?"

"Reave knows that the best way to handle me is to threaten the people I care about. I'll take whatever beating that he can dish out, but I break when he threatens my friends. I guess we all have to have a weakness, right?"

Trixie opened her mouth to say something, but never got the chance. Sofie jumped out of her arms and back onto the tattooing chair between Trixie and me. "Absolutely not!" she snapped. Her tail flicked back and forth as she paced along the chair. If she had been human, I think she would have smacked me.

"You are a warlock, Gage! You do *not* have weaknesses. You do not allow ordinary, weak-minded thugs to control your actions through threats. You take care of them and continue on your way."

I gave a little snort. "This coming from a witch trapped as a cat for the past several years."

Sofie primly sat in the middle of the chair, facing me. "My condition has no bearing here. You are a warlock!" Her chest puffed up as she added that last bit, as if it was supposed to instill some kind of latent pride.

I shrugged. "I'm not a warlock. I never finished."

"You became a warlock the minute you were taken to the Towers. Doesn't matter if you finished."

"No. I'm not a warlock. I don't kill."

I didn't know it was possible, but Sofie managed to arch one little cat brow at me in mocking question. Fuck. Simon was haunting me.

"That was self-defense," I said slowly through clenched teeth.

"You're saying that you didn't go there intending to kill him?" Sofie pressed. While it didn't show now, I could easily imagine the smug expression on her human face.

I looked away, glaring at the wall. I could argue that I didn't go across town looking for Simon because I had been looking for answers from my old tattooing mentor Atticus Sparks. But deep down, I had always known that it would all lead back to Simon and that matter came down to killing him before he killed me.

"Does Reave know about me?" Trixie asked, breaking into my train of thought.

I jerked my gaze over to her and stiffly nodded. I wasn't going to lie to her in an effort to leave her feeling safe when she wasn't. It would be better if she at least knew to look over her shoulder on occasion, not that I wanted to add to her worries. She was already looking over her shoulder in expectation of seeing another elf hunting her. We might have earned a reprieve from her people, but neither one of us trusted it.

"I won't let him touch you," I said.

"Why? Because you'll kill him?" Trixie's words were soft and gentle, possessing a wealth of sadness for me and this life I was trying to live.

I pushed away from the counter and walked over to the doorway so that I could look across the lobby and out the front picture window to the street beyond. Shoving my hands into my short hair, I leaned my elbows against the doorjamb and stared at nothing.

"No, he won't touch you because I'll do as he asks until I think of some way to take care of this problem."

Trixie slid her arms around my waist and laid her head against my spine. I flinched. I hadn't even heard her move from her seat she was so quiet. "And sell out your morals and beliefs in the process. Things like that damage the soul."

"Who says that I've got any soul left to damage?" I teased, but dark truth underlay that comment. I was already missing a piece of my soul. Simon had stolen it and I failed to get it back before killing him. After all the decisions I had made, I was beginning to wonder if I wasn't missing more than that one piece.

"Your soul is beautiful, Gage, if a little tarnished." I didn't say anything. I wanted her to believe this if only so that she would keep her arms around me for a little longer. "This Reave deserves to die for what he's done to the pixies and everyone else he's hurt. I won't mourn him if you decide to get rid of him. Just don't kill him with magic. You've already lost one year."

I closed my eyes against that horrible reminder. That little fact woke me up from a deep sleep on more than one occasion, scaring the shit out of Trixie during the few times I had slept over at her place.

Magic had some strange rules. There had to be a little give for everything you got—particularly for the big things like killing someone. For the most part, you simply moved energy that already existed in the air, directing it to do your bidding. But killing someone with magic was another matter. You were ending a life, removing a big source of that energy from the earth, and that unbalanced things. The price was that you lost one year of your own life for each person you killed with magic. And it wasn't one of those crappy years off the end. No, you could be twenty-five, healthy and happy in the prime of life, and fall dead while walking down the middle of the street with no warning. You'd be dead for exactly 365 days and then wake up as if nothing had happened; assuming that those around you were nice enough to preserve the body so that it could start up again

I had killed Simon with magic. He was dead and I owed magic one year of my life. I didn't know when it was going to happen, but I was terrified that it would happen before I could help Trixie solve her problem with the Summer Court. I was terrified it would happen before I could get Bronx free of Reave. I was terrified that it would happen and the Towers would discover my body helpless and unprotected. I was terrified of Lilith, who was waiting for me with a chunk of my soul on the other side.

Forcing my eyes open, I drew in a slow, steadying breath before dropping my hands down to cover Trixie's where they rested on my waist. "It'll be fine. I'll find a way to deal with Reave before he even thinks about bothering you."

"It's not me that I'm worried about," she said against my back.

Turning, I smiled at her. "I'll deal with Reave before he even thinks about bothering Bronx again."

Trixie made a sound of disgust as she shoved away from me and returned to her workstation. It wasn't what she meant and we both knew it, but at least my comment succeeded in removing the concern from her eyes.

"Do you have any appointments?" I asked, redirecting her thoughts.

She glanced up at the clock on the wall and shook her head. "Not for another hour and I've already done the prep work."

"You mind keeping an eye on things for a little while? I've got a couple things I want to check on downstairs."

Trixie gave a little wave of her hand as she sat back on her stool, leaning against the counter behind her. "Go for it."

"Thanks." I flashed her a quick smile before I turned to look down at Sofie. "You care to join me in the dungeon?"

"Fine with me," the cat replied, jumping off the chair to follow me. "I've been waiting to see your stash of goodies for a while now."

I gave a soft chuckle as she trailed me down the narrow hallway to the back room. I closed the door behind her, but didn't lock it. Trixie wouldn't enter unless it was an emergency. She knew of the dangers associated with my private storeroom.

"Hang back until I call you," I said as I knelt and pulled up the trapdoor in the floor. Out of the corner of my eye, I saw Sofie give a little nod as she sat a few feet away, her tail softly swishing across the floor.

The basement was one of the reasons I had chosen this building when I decided to open up my own shop. After living several years with Sparks, I had been eager to get out on my own and a part of it had been because I thought I could set up a secret place to practice a little magic. I had been stupid. It was only recently that I discovered that Gideon had always known about my secret spot, though I was hopeful that he didn't know about everything it contained.

I paused while descending the stairs as a thought struck me. If Gideon was no longer the guardian who kept an eye on me, I would need to close this spot down or whoever was assigned as my parole officer would drag me in before the council in a heartbeat. I'd have to get rid of everything, or get Gideon to help me hide it better.

The warped wooden stairs creaked under my feet as I continued to the dirt floor. I walked to the center of the pitch-black room and blindly reached up, feeling for the beaded metal cord that hung from the only light. I had been in the basement a thousand times, knew it blind, but my stomach still churned the first few seconds after entering. I had already checked it once when I first arrived at the shop, but it was only after I turned on the light and saw that nothing had been touched that I started to relax.

Lifting my right hand, holding the open palm toward a symbol spray-painted on the far blank wall, I murmured a few words and directed a little energy toward it, disarming the protective spell.

"It's clear," I called, leaning toward the stairs and the opening in the ceiling.

A second later, Sofie poked her head in the opening, peering down before delicately descending the stairs on silent paws. She stopped halfway, the hair on her back standing on end. The cat gave a little shake, settling her fur back while narrowing her eyes on me. "Goodness," she said, sounding a bit breathless. "You've got some powerful magic down here."

I smiled a bit stiffly at her. This was the first time I had allowed another witch or warlock to come into my secret dungeon. I felt the heaviness of the energy too, but I had grown accustomed to it after so many trips. I even felt it when I was on the main floor, but only slightly. I wondered if Sofie did as well.

"I've got some dangerous items down here."

Sofie started to come down the rest of the stairs, but abruptly stopped when her eyes fell on the black symbol that covered the only blank stone wall in the room. Every muscle in her body had gone stiff and I could almost hear her heart pounding in her chest. "That's a very strong protection spell." Her voice was tight and barely above a whisper, as if she was afraid that the slight sound would awaken the dormant spell.

"Like I said, I've got some dangerous items down here." Sofie continued to stare at the wall, unable to move. "Sof, I wouldn't invite you if I couldn't properly shut down the spell. You're safe."

"But it's not shut down. I can see it . . . moving . . . underneath the paint."

I squinted at the symbol, but didn't see anything. It might have had something to do with the fact that she was looking at it through the eyes of a cat, but she was right. It wasn't completely shut down. I could feel the energy humming around it. "I mean, shut down against you, me, and Trixie. You're safe." To prove my point, I walked over to the stairs and gently picked her up. She growled at me, but didn't move, her eyes locked on the symbol.

Sofie was right. It was a dangerous spell and not very discerning. If the spell lashed out at her, it was going to get me as well. When someone entered the room who wasn't supposed to, it attacked violently and the results were always lethal. If anyone entered while I was away, I wouldn't find a dead body at the bottom of the stairs. I would find mangled body parts and a lot of blood.

I had installed the protection spell when I was younger and didn't know as many spells as I should have. It was the most dangerous and strongest spell I knew. I had picked up a few others over the intervening years, but I had never bothered to change it simply because this one, while frightening, was still the best.

With a half smile, I picked Sofie up and cradled her against my chest while rubbing my knuckles gently against her cheek. Slowly, the muscles in her body started to loosen and her breathing evened out.

"Better?" I asked.

Sofie took a deep breath, rolling one shoulder and then the other. "You're insane, you know that?"

"Have to be to try to escape the Towers and expect to live," I said. "Do you want me to put you on the floor or on the table?"

The cat tore her eyes from the wall to look around the room, taking in the three walls of cabinets and the makeshift, chest-high table against the far wall. "Table."

Keeping her close, I carried her to the table and set her on the flat surface amid the random flotsam I had collected over the years. There were bits of twigs, half-burned candles of every imaginable color, a row of old baby-food jars holding pieces of chalk arrayed in a line of colors, feathers, and a few dead animal parts—magic, as with potions, wasn't always the prettiest of things to watch. Crystals of different shape, size, and color hung from leather thongs along the back wall.

There was also an old, wooden box at the back edge of the workbench. I could hear it humming as if resonating in time with some silent song that rose from my soul. The locked box held my wand. I had told the council that it had broken in my battle with Simon. I had even shown them the remains of a wand I had used a couple times and then snapped. I knew that if they allowed me to leave the Ivory Towers, I couldn't let them take my wand. Regardless of what sanctions they put on me, I knew I would need my wand in order to survive a witch or warlock attack. I rarely took it out, rarely used it. The risk was too big.

Now I prayed that Sofie didn't notice the box, couldn't hear the humming. Sofie and I were friends, but I knew better than to try to push the friendship too far.

"Nice collection," the cat said as she picked her way across the table. She leaned down, sniffing here and there, but always careful not to touch anything. "Albeit a little messy."

"I don't exactly have a housekeeper doing rounds down here," I muttered. Rolling my shoulders, I forced my jaw to unclench and relax. I told myself that I didn't have anything in common with other warlocks, but it was a lie. I didn't know of another witch or warlock who was comfortable with someone else touching their collection. It was like letting a stranger rummage through your underwear drawer while reading your diary. "I don't get to spend much time down here."

Sofie paused and glanced over her shoulder at me. "That is probably for the best." She continued on, stopping at the end of the table, where I had a large stack of black hardback journals. "What's this?"

"Notes. For the most part, it's potions that I've come up with for one thing or another."

Sofie jumped up and sat on the top journal while staring at me with wide eyes. "And the parts that don't fit in your 'most'?"

Leaning against the table, I crossed one leg over the other and smiled at her. "Take a wild guess."

"Gage," she said sternly.

"Oh, come on, Sofie!" I angrily waved one hand at her and the journals. "Did you expect me to quit? I can't. I can't quit magic any more than I can quit breathing. At first, it started out with me making notes, listing all the curses, wards, enchantments, and charms that I learned while I was with Simon. It wasn't about learning anything new. I didn't want to forget anything that I had learned."

"But . . ." she prompted when my voice died off.

I shrugged, my eyes dropping to the sundry bits on the top of the table. I picked up the severed leg of a raven. The claws were turned inward, still looking as sharp as the day I found it in a potion ingredients shop. "I started remembering things that Simon did, but didn't necessarily teach me. With a little time and thought, I pieced the spell together. Others, I thought of on my own, so I made note of them. Sometimes, magic comes easy to me. A lot easier than tattooing ever has."

"Why did you leave?" Sofie shook her head at me. There was a sad note to her question. She lay down on the top book, tucking her paws in at her chest. "Learning magic would have made you so happy. You've got such raw, natural talent. You could have been great."

"And I can't be great now, as a tattoo artist? I could only achieve greatness as a warlock?" I teased, but Sofie wasn't amused as her ears flattened a little against her head.

"I don't know what a tattoo artist can achieve, but I know what you could have done as a warlock."

"I loved learning magic," I admitted. "When I held my wand for the first time, it was like all the buzzing around in my soul and along my skin settled and found a direction, or like music notes lining up into a symphony. But I couldn't be a warlock if it meant being like Simon or any of the others that I knew, and I had to do that if I was going to survive in the Towers."

"You don't know that."

"Yes, I do. If you want to be a warlock, you have to be willing to kill. You have to kill other warlocks and witches to get ahead. You have to kill other creatures to use their organs in potions and spells.

You have to kill innocent people or risk them not fearing you. The Towers survive on two things: power and fear. To achieve both of those, you have to be willing to kill."

Sofie remained silent when I finished talking. She was staring at the far wall, looking at one of the cabinets with the glass-and-wood front. There were locks on each of them. If someone managed to get past the protective spell, I didn't think the locks would stop them. They let me sleep better at night.

"How did you do it?" I asked softly. "You were there for years, but you were the only one I ever saw who didn't beat the shit out of an apprentice if they failed to cower before you. You seemed nice."

The cat sighed heavily, closing her eyes. "At first, I was no different than you described. I killed, constantly and indiscriminately. I think that might be how I stayed a little sane while there. Young and old. Helpless and powerful. I killed them all without blinking an eye, and nearly all were for no reason. I told myself that God didn't need a reason to kill any of them, so why should I? But when I reached my second century, I started to mellow. I killed less, though when I did, there didn't need to be a reason. I no longer had anything to prove to anyone. That may be why I seemed nicer than the others when we met."

I tried to smile at Sofie, but the corners of my mouth weren't working properly. I didn't know if she was any saner than the ones who lived in the Towers. She had found a way to deal with the violence that that life required, but her way wasn't the answer. Gideon was closer to the middle ground, but I felt his underground movement was progressing far too slowly. The Ivory Towers had to stop. Stop being overlords for the world. Stop demanding abject fear and total obedience.

Magic wasn't about being powerful and controlling the world. Magic was about tapping into something beautiful and about becoming more than a fleshy meat bag if only for a couple seconds.

"Would you go back if you had the chance?" I asked.

Sofie cocked her head to the side as she looked up at me. "What do you mean?"

"If you were human again, would you go back to living in the Towers? You weren't exactly escorted to the door. You could go back now if you wanted and no one would stop you. If you were human again, rather than a cat, would you go back?"

The cat stood and arched her back, stretching while extending her claws briefly to scratch along the rough surface of the book. "It's going to be a long time before I see skin again, if ever."

"But if you could?"

"I don't know." Sofie sat on the book and looked at me. "It's been several years since I was last there. I've lived with a human that I depended on for several years. I've lived with you and Trixie for a while now. I honestly don't know if I could return to that life. I've changed and I feel like I'm too old now to change back to the way I was when I was living in the Towers."

"I'm glad," I said with a smile. It was a good answer. It was one Gideon could accept. If he could get Sofie changed back to a human, he would have someone safe who could train his daughter if she proved to have magical talent.

Sofie made a noise. She was either scoffing at me or coughing up a hairball. I prayed it was scoffing. "You make me sound soft."

"No, just a good person."

Sofie wouldn't look at me. She jumped down from the table to the dirt floor. The air directly above her seemed to grow a little hazy. I stood and looked over at the symbol, but the protection spell was quiet. As I looked back at the cat as she crossed the room to peer in one of the cabinets, the misty haze above her solidified slightly so that it looked like I was seeing a ghost. But it wasn't a ghost. It was a misty image of Sofie as she looked when she was human. She was right. There was a lot of powerful magic down here.

"Who cursed you, Sofie?" The cat or the ghost didn't look over at me, but I could see her stiffen. It was the first time I had ever asked her that question. Sofie didn't talk about the attack and I respected her privacy, but I had someone who might be able to help her.

"It's none of your business, Gage," she said in a low voice.

"I know, but tell me anyway."

"Why the sudden interest?"

"Because I know of someone who may be willing to help you."

Sofie jerked around and quickly padded closer to stand in the middle of the room. The freaky thing was that I could see hope scrawled across the face of the ghost as she peered at me. "Who?"

"Gideon."

"You've spoken to Gideon?" The ghost's mouth hung partially open and it was only then I realized how much I had gotten accustomed to trying to discern Sofie's moods by her tone of voice and the expressions presented on a cat's face. I was beginning to think that I was wrong . . . a lot.

"Yeah, we're not exactly mortal enemies, though I can't say that I would trust him with my darkest secrets. He's indicated to me that he could help you if he knew who cursed you."

Sofie moved away from me. She sat and then stood as if she meant to pace around the room, but she didn't move. "Her name is Victoria, though I liked to call her Vicki to piss her off."

"It worked." I snickered.

"*That* wasn't why she cursed me."

"I hope not. I don't want to think about this lunatic running around using magic. Last name?"

"Tremaine."

"I don't remember her."

"She didn't spend much time in the Tower you were living in. You wouldn't have met her."

"Would it help Gideon if he knew why she cursed you?"

The ghostly Sofie frowned at me. "If he needs to know, then he can talk to me."

I threw up my hands and smiled at her. "That's fine with me. I don't need to know."

"Why is Gideon doing this? Particularly now after all these years."

"That's something you'll have to discuss with him, but I will give you the same warning that he recently gave me." I shoved my hands in my pockets and leaned back against the table. "Things are getting bad in the Towers. Lot of unrest and anxiety, from what he tells me. I'd keep your head down as much as possible."

"What does that mean for you?"

I sighed, my shoulders slumping. "Nothing good. As it stands, I'll most likely lose Gideon as my assigned guardian soon unless he hands the council my head on a pike. From there . . . well, I'm sure you can imagine the shit storm that's going to follow."

"I'm sorry."

I shrugged helplessly. There wasn't anything I could do about it. "Thanks. I would appreciate it if you could keep this info to yourself. I don't want Trixie worrying yet. You know how slow the council can be at times. It may be months before anything happens."

"Or days."

"Even so, she has her own problems, things that we can do something about. For now, we have to sit with our thumbs up our asses until something is decided in the Towers."

"Agreed."

I pushed away from the table, stretching my arms above my head. "Thanks, Sof. We better get back upstairs before Trixie comes looking for us."

Sofie started to walk beside me then paused. "I thought you had some things you needed to do down here."

I stopped with one foot on the bottom step and smiled down at her. "I did. Gideon wanted me to talk to you and I didn't think you'd want to discuss this in front of Trixie."

Sofie purred as she headed up the stairs. "You always were a smart boy."

I snorted at her, but kept my mouth shut as I followed her. For such a smart boy, I seemed to be in a hell of a lot a trouble with few ideas on how to get out. As soon as the cat reached the main floor, I waved my right hand at the symbol on the wall and, with a little push of energy, reactivated the protection spell. One thing at a time. First, Trixie and the elves. Then, free Bronx from Reave. And if there was anything left of me after that, I'd find a way to wipe my memory from the Towers.

Yep. I was in big trouble.

5

AFTER LAST NIGHT'S clusterfuck, I was relieved to find that to-night was quiet at Asylum. Sofie had settled on the glass counter at the front of the shop, lounging between the cordless-phone charger and the framed article proclaiming Asylum the top tattoo and po-tion parlor in Low Town for 2012. It was the third year in a row we had won the local award. We didn't get anything for the title besides a nice certificate and an increase in business. I preferred to display the article rather than the certificate, since it contained a cheesy photo of Bronx, Trixie, and me sitting in the lobby of the shop.

Business was steady, but far from hectic. Trixie finished up her appointment with a banshee in a matter of minutes. From what I overhead of the conversation, the death wailer had recently gotten a job at a nursing home. Unfortunately, she had been bemoaning the dying so much that she had gotten a sore throat, which was threat-ening to give way to laryngitis. Instead of a tattoo, Trixie gave her a mixture to be steeped with tea daily and advice to get a job at a day care.

From there, I tattooed a drake with an antiseasickness potion. Apparently the cannibalistic ogre was going deep-sea fishing with some friends off the coast of Florida in a few weeks but was having problems managing boat trips. I kept my mouth shut for most of the tattoo. Drakes, who are not related to dragons as many people believe, are more likely to take a bite out of you than hit you if you piss them off. Trixie enjoyed lightly teasing this one despite my glares, but then a pretty girl could get away with so much more than a guy.

Trixie then handled a pair of goblins wanting matching tattoos to express their love for each other. At least they didn't want to get each other's name tattooed on their shoulders. But I wasn't being fair. From what I heard, goblins were among the few races that were good at relationships. Once they bonded with a mate, it tended to be for life and they were happy with each other the whole time. Humans couldn't even come close to understanding something like that.

I was finishing up a tattoo on a young werecat when Bronx came in. The werecat had wanted a tattoo on her hip that would keep her from getting pregnant for the next five years. She'd still go into heat every season, but the ink would protect against pregnancy. There were special waivers required for that particular tattoo since I didn't want to be sued in case something was off. I had yet to have that one come back to haunt me, but I wasn't taking any chances.

The troll settled onto his stool with only the softest of grunts. The swelling had gone down in his face and there was only a slight discoloration around one eye. Otherwise, he looked normal. He was moving a little slower than normal, but most wouldn't notice it.

"You know you could have stayed home tonight," I said after the last client left the shop.

"So you said yesterday," Bronx grumbled. He set up his station with his usual meticulousness, checking to make sure that he had all the supplies he had put aside the previous night.

Trixie flit across the room and wrapped her arms around his shoulders, laying her head on top of his. "How are you feeling?"

"I'm fine," Bronx said, patting one of Trixie's hands.

"I knew that Gage would be trouble. I don't think you should hang out with that bad influence any longer," Trixie continued in her best doting-mother voice.

At that, Bronx finally smiled. "Yes, Mother, but he's my only friend."

"No, dear, you'll always have your mummy," she said, earning a bark of laughter from me. Trixie kissed Bronx's cheek and then walked over to where I was lying back in the tattooing chair in my station. She put a knee between my legs, a little too close for comfort. "What are you laughing at? I'm old enough to be a great-great-great-grandmother to both of you. Sometimes I think I need to take you over my knee, spank some sense into you."

I placed my hands on her hips and tried to pull her closer, but she grabbed the top of the chair, halting her descent. "I could be up for that."

"Good grief," Bronx muttered under his breath with no small amount of disgust. I laughed. For the most part, when Bronx was in the shop with us, Trixie and I maintained a somewhat professional atmosphere. Well, as professional as it ever was before we started dating. Every once in a while I let something slip to make Bronx shake his head.

The chime for the front door sang through the lobby as someone walked in. "Saved by the bell," I said, starting to push Trixie back.

"So it would seem," she said with a glare before easing into a smile. "Stay. I'll get it."

I nodded and then watched her walk toward the front. Turning, I found Bronx relaxing on his stool, his back leaning against the counter behind him. He looked tired, both physically and maybe even a little emotionally. I opened my mouth, but he held up his hand, stopping me.

"Apologize again and I'll hit you."

"I can't help it."

"If you hadn't done something, I would have and I'd be feeling worse if not dead right now."

My eyes hardened on his face while my hands clenched the arms of the chair I was sitting in. "I'll get you out of this."

"You'll get us both out," Bronx corrected, his eyes drifting closed. "I'm not leaving you alone with Reave. Both or none at all."

I nodded in a sharp, jerky motion as Trixie's heels thudded across the floor toward me. I looked up and forced a smile on my face. She'd talk to Bronx after I left for the night and then again to me when we met up after her shift. There was no hiding the Reave business from her now, but I didn't want to worry her while we were in the shop.

Trixie motioned toward the front with her head. "He's asking for the owner."

"Problem?"

"I don't think so. Doesn't seem angry. I don't remember ever seeing him before, so I don't think we've tattooed him."

"Got it." I pushed to my feet and gave her hand a quick squeeze as I stepped around her and walked to the lobby. I hadn't heard any of her conversation with the customer because my attention had been on Bronx. I hadn't heard his voice, but I wished I had.

Stepping behind the counter, I felt as if someone had punched me in the stomach, forcing all the air out of my lungs. The blood drained from my face as I stared at the man. He was older than I remembered, but it had been more than ten years since I had last seen him. His blondish-brown hair was longer, brushing against his shoulders, but it was the same brown eyes.

"Shit! Robby?" I gasped when I found my voice.

The man's brows snapped together as he stared warily at me. He even backed up a step. "Yeah, it's Robert. Robert Grant," he said slowly. He looked like he was about to bolt for the door, but he paused, squinting at me. "Ja—"

"Yeah, it's me," I said, cutting him off. "Baby brother."

"Holy fuck!" Robert shouted as I came around the counter. He pulled me into a rough hug, thumping hard on my back several times. I hugged him back, laughing. I hadn't seen my older brother in a decade. What were the insane odds that he'd walk into my shop? I didn't care. I had my brother back; didn't matter if it was for an hour or for the rest of our lives.

Robert pulled away, holding me by the shoulders as he looked me over. We were about the same height. I was leaner in build, while Robert had become stockier, with a thick chest and neck. There was a small scar on his chin that hadn't been there when I last saw him and more worry lines stretched around his eyes, but he was the same.

"You've changed," he said, seeming to talk mostly to himself. I smiled, running one hand through my hair. When last he had seen me, it had been longer, stretching past my shoulders. And pale blond. "You dyed it?"

I shook my head, my smile changing to a cocky smirk. "Tattoo."

"Then you're not wearing contacts either?"

I shook my head again. Stepping from his grasp, I turned and pulled up my T-shirt to reveal the tiger tattoo that stretched across my back. It was my only tattoo and it had taken three months to complete. Woven throughout it were a series of potions that tweaked my appearance and the way people remembered me. It was as much for their protection as my own. "The tattoo permanently changed my hair and eye color to brown."

"Must be easier than having to dye your hair once a month," Robert joked as I pulled my T-shirt back into place. I turned to face him and he clapped me on the side of the head, pulling me close so he could press his forehead to mine. "Doesn't matter. You're still the same old Ja—"

Again, I had to stop him. "It's Gage now." I pulled back so I could see his smile fading and sadness enter his eyes. The Ivory Towers had come between us. He was trying so hard to bridge that gap, but it was crumbling under his feet. First, I no longer looked like the brother he had known, and now my name. There were other things, I had no doubt, but I wasn't going to let him slip away. Grabbing one shoulder, I thumped him hard on the chest, right over his heart, with my fist. "I'm the same in here. They couldn't change that. They didn't take that away."

"Yeah," he said, then continued, his voice gaining strength. "Yeah! My brother. Gage?"

"Gage Powell," I said with a smile as I released him.

He nodded. "Gage Powell. I guess it'll do. I can't believe this. How long have you been in Low Town?"

"Ten years." I shrugged. "It's where I ended up after leaving Mom and Dad's. It seemed far enough away. Big enough to get lost in, small enough to avoid notice."

Robert chuckled. "You think like Dad."

"What do you mean?"

"They moved here eight years ago. They live up in Shadybrooke."

I felt my knees start to give out. Somehow I stumbled backward, so that I ended up sitting on the bench that ran the length of the back wall rather than sitting on the floor. Shadybrooke was one of the suburban outskirts of Low Town near the north side of the city. Nice if you don't mind bland and monotonous.

"Here? Why? They loved Vermont."

Robert plopped down next to me on the bench and clapped a hand on my shoulder. "Don't worry about it. They're here and they like Shadybrooke." He then cocked his head to the side as he looked at me. "I'm guessing you haven't seen them."

"No, not since I left." I shook my head, lost in a sad memory for a moment, when my brain checked in with a thought. "Wait! When did you last see them?"

Robert grimaced, looking down at the hardwood floor. "Been a few years."

I bit my tongue hard to hold in the questions. I had a feeling that I wouldn't like the answers and I didn't want to start a fight within five minutes of seeing my brother for the first time in ten years. I'd save the fight for when I was sure there was going to be a later. "What about Meggie?" Inwardly, I prayed our younger sister was a safe topic.

Robert's smile returned, softening his features. "She's in Romania, teaching English and French." His hands dropped into his lap, where he loosely threaded his fingers together.

"She didn't go vampire, did she?" I asked hesitantly. Romania was heavy vampire territory.

"No!" he said with a laugh. "Well, not since I last heard from her, which was about six months ago, and she didn't sound like she had any plans to. She's teaching a couple night classes for the vamps." His smile faded and a frown returned to his eyes. "Though it does sound like she's fallen in with some Gypsies. In her last e-mail, she was bragging about getting good with her hands. I thought it was best not to ask too many questions."

I chuckled, scratching the back of my head. Yeah, that was our mom's influence on us. She always seemed to know when it was best to pry into our lives with questions to put us back on the straight and narrow and when to let us run wild. "How'd she end up in Romania?" When I had last seen Megan, she had been twelve years old with blond pigtails, freckles, and a glare.

Robert relaxed on the bench beside me, stretching his legs out while rolling his eyes toward the ceiling. "How do you think? Some guy." I laughed at the disgust in his voice, but he wasn't serious. "You know, our sister didn't turn out half-bad-looking. Good thing she was the one in the family that also ended up with the brains. As soon as she finished college and got her teaching certificate, she ran off to Germany with this guy she met."

"She still with him?"

Robert snorted. "Lasted three months."

"And she didn't come home after that?"

"Would you?" He arched one brow at me, mocking. I shrugged. Truth was, the Ivory Tower I had lived in was in Europe and I'd seen most of the hot spots in Europe by the age of fifteen. They were nice, but I liked living in Low Town.

"She lasted in Germany for another few months, then ran off to Austria, Croatia, Uzbekistan—don't ask me why—and then Romania. I doubt that's everywhere, but our dear sister has been kind enough to censor her e-mails to me."

I smiled at his tortured expression, leading me to believe that our dear sister wasn't censoring her letters enough for Robert's comfort. I held on to the smile, pushing down a nagging feeling. By my guess, Megan had been traveling Europe for a couple years and Robert hadn't seen our parents in a few years, so who was watching over them? When I left my family the second time after escaping the Ivory Towers, I had consoled myself with the thought that my parents still had my siblings.

There was one other bothersome question nagging me. Why had they left Vermont? It could have been nothing, but I doubted it. I pushed the question down with the other and looked at my older brother. It could wait. He was living in Low Town. We had found each other again, and if I was careful, we could safely stay in contact without the Towers ever getting wind of it.

"You know that leaves only one important question," I said.

Robert stiffened a little as he looked at me. "What's that?"

"What the hell are you doing here? I mean, of all the tattoo parlors in Low Town, how did you end up here?" I laughed.

The tension instantly flowed out of his body and he lounged against the bench again. He waved one hand at me and smiled. "Oh, that. Reave sent me."

I DON'T RECALL getting to my feet, but I suddenly found myself standing in the middle of the lobby, barely holding together the rage that was burning through my brain. That fucking bastard! Reave had my brother. My older brother was working for that low-life Mafia scum. The dark elf had found a way to get even with me. I thought it was over when he had ordered Bronx's beating. I had been punished and I thought we would be starting fresh, but Reave had shoved the knife a little deeper into my gut.

The Svartálfar was using my brother for whatever horrible job he needed done, putting him in danger. It was the perfect way to force me to do exactly what he wanted. I had to protect my brother. No matter what he was doing or how he was involved, I had to protect my brother.

"Reave?" I demanded in a rough voice when I could get my teeth to unclench enough so I could speak. "You work for the fucking Svartálfar bastard Reave?"

Robert pushed to his feet and pointed one finger at me, his expression losing all its earlier lightness. "Watch what you say about Reave," he warned. "He's my boss and he's been good to me."

I pressed my hands to my temples, my fingers threading through my hair as I swallowed a scream of frustration. It had suddenly become hard to breathe, as if the air had been sucked from the room. Squeezing my eyes shut, I tried to block out the sound of blood pounding in my ears like a tribal drum. Energy sizzled against my skin. The magic was building, pressing against the seams of the walls. With a push, I could blow the entire building down. I could rip it apart like a twister blowing through a trailer park.

Trixie's voice was suddenly there. Soft, breathless, and desperate. Her pleading penetrated the fog, so that I could feel her gentle hand on my cheek and the other arm wrapped around my back, her slim fingers digging into the side of my waist.

"You have to breathe, Gage. Just let it go," she was saying. "Let go of the magic. If they catch you, they're going to kill you. They'll kill us all."

Another, larger hand landed on my shoulder opposite to where Trixie was pressed against me. Strong and firm. Bronx. "Let it go, Gage."

Overhead, soft popping followed by the tinkle of glass echoed through the shop. The lightbulbs hanging from the ceiling were exploding and the glass was falling inside the protective containers that surrounded them. I opened my eyes to find that the parlor was black except for the light coming in the front window and door from the street. Robert was standing with his back pressed against the far wall. There was no missing the terror on his face.

Fresh pain lanced through me. I flinched and Trixie pressed closer, holding me a little tighter as if she could absorb the pain. Robert was working for the devil but he was looking at me with fear in his wide eyes—as if I would ever hurt him. We had had scuffles as kids, but I didn't hurt him and I had *never* hurt him with magic.

"He's got my brother," I whispered in a rough, broken voice. My world was breaking apart around me, but Trixie and Bronx continued to press close.

"We'll fix it," Trixie murmured in my ear, and Bronx's hand squeezed my shoulder.

Dropping my hands from my head, I dragged in a deep breath in an attempt to relax the muscles that had tensed throughout my body. The energy dissipated. The soft snap and crackle faded to nothingness and the air seemed less thick. Trixie loosened her grip on me, but remained close.

Bronx waited for a nod from me before dropping his hand. He looked up at the darkened light fixture above us. "I think we've got some spare bulbs in the storage closet. I'll go get them and the step-ladder."

"It could have been worse," Trixie said, drawing our gazes. "It could have been the front window . . . again."

Bronx shook his head as he left the room. I tried to smile but couldn't quite manage it. Trixie was trying and I appreciated it. "I've yet to break the front window. That's Bronx."

Trixie dropped her arms from around me and grinned. "It's not like you didn't want to." She was right. Less than a year ago, a customer Trixie was tattooing had hit on her hard. She was polite but it was obvious that she was becoming uncomfortable with his persistence. Bronx gave the asshole one warning, but he didn't listen. A minute later, he was flying through the front window.

Trixie tried to step away from me, but I grabbed her wrist, holding her in place. "Trixie, this is my older brother, Robert," I started, looking at my brother. He was still pressed against the far wall as if he were trying to sink into the plasterboard rather than be in the same room with me. The fear was gone from his eyes, but so was the easy laughter. "Robert, this is Trixie. She's a tattoo artist here, and she's . . . my girlfriend." The last two words fumbled from my mouth, but then it was the first time I had ever introduced her as such.

Trixie shot me a smile before turning to face Robert. She extended a hand toward him and he hesitated before quickly shaking it. "It's nice to meet someone from Gage's family."

Robert mumbled something that I didn't quite catch before

sinking back against the wall. Trixie turned to me and gave a little roll of her eyes. She wasn't afraid of me and I loved her for it. Bronx wasn't afraid of me, and in my own way, I loved him for it, though I was grateful that I didn't feel the need to kiss him like I needed to kiss Trixie.

She wrapped her long arms around my neck as she snuggled close. "Get out of here. Your shift's done. Spend some time catching up with your brother."

"I'll see you later tonight."

"You're stopping by?" she asked, going for innocent, but the wicked light in her eyes ruined it.

"Oh, yeah. Gonna need to."

Trixie gave me one last lingering kiss that managed to put a different kind of tension into my body before gracefully sauntering from the room. I glared at Robert when I saw his eyes following her. My older brother opened his mouth, but I stopped him.

"Watch what you say or I will give you a reason to be afraid of me," I warned.

Robert glared at me. "She's hot," he said as if daring me to argue with him.

I snorted and shook my head. "Yeah, I'll give you that one. Let me grab my jacket and we can get out of here."

"What about the tattoo Reave said you'd work on?"

Rage flooded my veins once again, but I kept my head this time. It wasn't as much of a shock as it had been the first time. "I doubt what Reave has planned is something I can slap on in a few minutes. We'll need to talk and plan. And drink." The drinking probably wouldn't help much with the planning, but it would help me from exploding again—safer for all those around.

Using the dim light from the front window, I walked into the main tattooing room to find that Bronx had already lit some candles and was in the process of setting up the stepladder so he could replace the fluorescent bulbs I had destroyed.

"I'll be upstairs in case you need anything," I announced. I crossed to the far cabinet and knelt down as I pulled it open.

"You taking the Mordred?" Bronx asked from the stepladder in the center of the room.

A little shudder racked my frame. "Absolutely not. I need to mellow out, not get stupid. I've got a bottle of Jack that should get us through without killing each other." I may have hated Reave and held no love for the entire Svartálfar race, but by all that was sacred and pure, they knew how to make a damn good whiskey. Mordred was fucking hard to get your hands on if you weren't Svartálfar and like liquid fire going down, but damn, it was good.

"I can take your keys to the shop. Protects against intoxicated tattooing," Bronx offered.

"Fuck you," I grumbled with no real venom. The last time Bronx and I had drunk Mordred together, the results were not good. Suffice to say, Bronx had tattooed an incubus, resulting in an outbreak of mass fornication that needed to be stopped.

I grabbed the liter bottle and stood, shutting the cabinet with my knee as I scooped up my jacket off a nearby chair. "I'll talk to you guys later."

Robert was out in the lobby when I returned, looking as if he wished he had left but was afraid to after my temper tantrum. He followed me out the front door of the parlor, but paused when I started down the alley beside the shop.

"Where we going?" he demanded, stopped at the mouth of the alley.

"Somewhere we can talk and drink." I held up the new bottle and gently shook it back and forth as if trying to tempt him. Or hypnotize him. I'd take that. He frowned, but started to follow after me through the alley to the back of the shop and then up the wooden stairs to the second floor of my building.

After Asylum took off, I managed to buy the entire building from the owner instead of renting. I had lived in the second-floor apartment for a while, but had moved out a few years ago so I could get a little space in my life from work. The apartment above the parlor was kept empty for times like these, when it was better to deal with matters here rather than drag anyone into my home.

"This your place?" Robert asked as he shut the door behind him.

I shook my head. "Just somewhere I crash on occasion." Setting the bottle on the scarred coffee table, I walked into the tiny kitchen and grabbed a couple plastic cups that I kept there. I paused, staring at the disposable plastic cups. It had been a while since I had gotten plowed in this apartment with a friend or two. Was I mellowing out too much? Getting old? I rolled my eyes and wandered back into the living room with its cracked beige walls and stained carpet to find Robert sitting on one of the sunken cushions of the couch.

Sitting on the other end of the couch, I poured us each a healthy shot of whiskey and sat back. "All right, talk."

Robert took a big swallow and winced as it went down. Definitely not as smooth as Mordred, but it would get the job done. "I don't have to tell you shit."

"You're going to talk and tell me every fucking thing I ask for. I deserve that if I'm going to protect you from whatever Reave has got you involved in." I set my own glass down without drinking. It was like talking had triggered all the emotions that I had managed to get a handle on. "Why are you fucking working for Reave? You're not an idiot. Fuck. How could you do this to Mom and Dad?"

"Do this to Mom and Dad?" he repeated, looking at me like I had lost my mind. "I'm not doing this to them. I'm helping myself, and what the fuck do you care about Mom and Dad? What the fuck do you care about any of us? You left!"

"Of course I left!" I shouted, jumping to my feet. Robert pushed to his feet as well so I wouldn't tower over him. Whatever fear he was feeling toward me wasn't there now—we were both too pissed. "I had to leave if I wanted to protect you and Meg and Mom and Dad. The Towers might have let me go, but they weren't going to let me live happily ever after. I've had warlocks and witches hunting me for years. You think they wouldn't have tried to use you or Meg as leverage to get me to do what they wanted? Fuck! I left because I had to."

"You should have never come back in the first place!" Robert roared. I took a step back, my anger instantly melting away, but Robert didn't notice. Apparently there was something on his mind that he had been itching to vent. "When you disappeared as a kid, we told the world that you had been killed in an accident. You think we could tell anyone that you became *one of them*? We would have been lynched in a heartbeat. But no! You came back, destroying everything. Dad tried to make up stories, like you were a distant cousin, but no one believed him. They knew you had been taken to the Ivory Towers. They knew you were a warlock, and everything changed."

Robert paced a couple angry steps away from me and then turned back, his face twisted with pent-up rage and pain. "You want to know why Mom and Dad moved to Low Town? Because of you. They left Vermont and New Hampshire and Pennsylvania and West Virginia because they were trying to outrun the rumors that they had given birth to a warlock. They came to Low Town to hide!"

I collapsed on the couch behind me, staring blindly at the wall. Whatever anger I had felt only seconds ago about my brother being a part of the Low Town Mafia evaporated. My chest ached and there was a lump growing in my throat threatening to cut off my breathing. In my lifetime, I had been burned, stabbed, poisoned, shot, and had a chunk of my soul ripped off. This felt worse. It hurt to breathe. It hurt to move. It hurt to think, but I couldn't stop my mind from churning over the same thought. *If I had never returned home after leaving the Towers, my family would have been happy, healthy, and safe.*

I had been sixteen when I left the Towers and I couldn't think of any place I wanted to go more than home to my family. I hadn't seen them in nine years, but they still represented the only happy memories I had in my life. They were laughter, warmth, and love wrapped in a modest middle-class home on an old tree-lined street in Vermont. I had nowhere else to go and nowhere else I wanted to go. I knew that it was only temporary; I didn't trust the council's promises and reassurances. But I needed help and my feet set. I was only sixteen.

When I walked in the front door, Mom cried. She held me so tight and cried tears of joy. She cried for four days every time she looked at me. Dad cried too, his arms wrapped around Mom and me. No one asked questions. We hugged, cried, and were happy to be together. I could only guess that was before anyone started to think about how the rest of the world would react to my miraculous return from the dead.

I should never have gone home.

"Gage, man," Robert whispered beside me. The couch shifted as he sat down again, but I was still staring straight ahead, my body so stiff that muscles ached. I was afraid that if I moved, I'd shatter. I had destroyed my family. I destroyed them by being a warlock and by returning home to give away their secret shame.

"I didn't know." My voice was rough and low like I had been gargling razor blades, and it was starting to feel that way as well.

"I know. They didn't want you to know and, man, I'm a fucking idiot. I'm sorry. I shouldn't have said anything. It's not your fault."

A short, bitter laugh escaped me as I looked over at him through narrowed eyes. "Yeah, not my fault that I was born a warlock, but it was my fault that I came home."

"We never felt that way." I frowned at him, not needing the lies. Robert squeezed my shoulder and smiled. "Well, okay, so maybe I was pissed at you for a year or two right before I dropped out of college, but then I got my shit together. Mom and Dad never regretted you coming home. Not once."

"I ruined their lives. I'm guessing I screwed up yours pretty badly as well as Meg's."

Robert gave my shoulder a shove but didn't let go when I started to look away from him. "It's not your fault. Blame it on the assholes in the Towers. Hell, better yet, blame it on the assholes that ran us out of New England. They only focused on the fact that you'd been born a warlock—which could have happened to any one of them just as easily. They should have been focusing on the fact that Mom and Dad raised a kid who was smart and brave enough to fucking leave the Towers."

I nodded, trying to breathe. "Thanks."

Robert dropped his hand back to his lap while reaching for his drink with the other hand. I did the same and we both finished our first glass before either could speak again. The alcohol would numb the worst of the pain. There was truth to what Robert had said, all of what he said. It wasn't all my fault, but by the same token, I should never have gone home when I was a teenager.

"You should go see them," Robert suggested. He reached across the table and snagged the bottle, pouring us both a new glass.

"Mom and Dad?"

"Yeah. I know they'd love it. They miss you."

I sat back against the couch and stretched out my legs, trying to ease the tension crawling through my frame. "I don't know if it would be safe."

"I think they would argue that it's worth the risk." Robert took a drink and smiled at me. When he spoke again, his voice was rough from the whiskey burn. "Do you honestly think it's ever going to be safe? You're wasting time."

"You could always go talk to them first for me. Warn them that I'm in town, what I look like now so it wouldn't be such a shock if I showed up on their doorstep." Robert frowned at me and remained silent. Yeah, I wasn't exactly subtle. I wanted to hear why he was no longer talking to our parents. "Did you fight?"

"No, not really."

"So . . . what? You just stopped seeing them? Stopped answering the phone when Mom called?"

"Pretty much."

I set my cup on the table and waited. Robert sighed before downing the last of his drink and placing his empty cup next to mine. "Things didn't work out at college," he started.

"Because of me."

He shrugged. "Part of it, but I think I was looking for an excuse. I was tired of school, wanted to be doing something. I made some friends here that I probably shouldn't have, started helping them out on the occasional job. I knew the business they were in, but I told myself that I wouldn't get drawn in." He stopped and stared down at his hands.

"But you did."

Robert looked at me with a little self-mocking smile. "Reave came to me and offered me a job personally. Said I was good. He offered me a lot of money and I took it. I told myself that I wasn't hurting anyone, so it was no big deal."

I clamped my mouth shut. People were getting hurt by the things that Reave was into. Robert might not have been the one to pull the trigger or wield the blade, but anyone who supported Reave was only adding to the body count.

"Did Mom and Dad find out what you were doing?"

"No. Well, I don't think so." He stopped and threaded a loose strand of hair behind his ear. "They had such hopes for me at college and getting some big job in an office building wearing a tie and carrying a briefcase. Every time I went to see them, I had to see those hopes. Got tired of it, so I stopped going."

I stared at the bottle of Jack on the table, a part of me wishing that I had brought up the Mordred. Numb and stupid would have felt a lot better than what I was feeling right then. After leaving for Low Town, I didn't let myself think about my family much because

I knew that I couldn't go back, but I told myself that they were all happy and safe. Unfortunately, happy and safe were extremely relative terms, I was learning. All I knew was that they weren't the kind of happy and safe that I had imagined.

"I'll get you out," I said in a low voice.

"What?"

I looked over at Robert, meeting his confused expression. "I'll get you out. Get you free of Reave. I'm stuck with him holding threats over my head, but I'll get you out when I get out."

"I don't want out," he said. "Didn't you hear me? The pay is good and I'm good at what I do. It might not be legal but I'm not hurting anyone. I don't need you to rescue me."

I sat speechless for a minute, staring at him. Between Bronx and me wanting out so badly, I had naturally assumed that Robert would consider himself trapped as well. But he wasn't trapped. He was exactly where he wanted to be and . . . I was being an asshole. I might find Robert's line of work distasteful, but I couldn't judge him because he had chosen to color outside the lines. There was a good percentage of my own work that was off the books because it wasn't exactly legal. Well, that and the whole warlock thing, which wasn't illegal but it wasn't a crowd pleaser either.

"Sorry," I muttered, feeling like an ass while, at the same time, finding a whole new reason to hate Reave.

"No problem. Are you still going to help me? Reave said you would."

I nodded as I moved to the edge of the couch. Snagging the bottle, I filled up my cup and Robert's. I had a feeling that I was going to need this. "Keep you safe? Sure. What's Reave got planned for you?"

"Nothing too major. I'm just a package boy." Robert shrugged, but there was something in his expression that wasn't quite modest. He might have been a package boy, but there was such a thing as a valuable package boy based on intelligence, courage, and resourcefulness. "He wants me to deliver some information to a buyer."

"What kind of information?" Robert was silent so long that I finally looked over at him to find him frowning down at his whiskey. "You have to at least give me some kind of hint if I'm going to be able to protect you effectively. It will give me an idea of whom I'm protecting you from."

"You don't think we'll be overheard here?" Robert asked, lowering his voice to a whisper.

It was a struggle not to whisper as well. "By who?"

"*Them.*"

Fuck. What the hell was Reave dealing in that my brother was worried about drawing the attention of the witches and warlocks? We all worried about the Ivory Towers, but for the most part, we didn't worry about them listening in to our conversations. They pretty much ignored the fact that we existed until we stepped on something that did interest them. Apparently, Robert had stepped into something big.

Putting my cup on the table, I stood and quickly tapped the energy floating around in the air. It only took a couple of seconds and a brief wave of my hand to summon the silencing spell that was becoming a regular part of my repertoire recently. For someone who had chosen to break away from the Towers, I was frequently in the midst of things that would most interest them.

"Don't move," I said, flopping back down on the couch. "I created only a small bubble—attracts less attention. No one can hear you."

Robert looked at me a bit skeptically. "I didn't see you do anything but wave your hand in the air."

"The best spells are the subtle ones. Now talk."

A smile peeked out for a second. "I still can't believe you're a warlock. My brother . . ."

"My brother, the warlock. Scourge of all that is good and just in the world. Yeah, yeah," I said a bit irritably. When I lived in the Towers, I was told that I was being reborn into godhood. When I moved back among the "mortals," I became the bane of their existence. Such a fall back to earth tends to bruise the ego. "Now, what does Reave have you transporting?"

Robert's smile faded. "I don't know how he acquired this information, but Reave knows the exact location of all the Towers."

My heart stopped and then started again, pounding away like a madman on crack. I lurched to my feet, wanting to put some distance between my brother and his words as if I was expecting a bolt of lightning to strike him, but I remained rooted to the spot. I couldn't move outside of the spell without disrupting it and I definitely needed to do a little venting that wouldn't be overheard.

The first of the Ivory Towers was built before the Great War, but the warlocks and witches forced everyone after the war to work on building others—one on every continent plus a secret eighth so that they could tighten their hold on all the peoples of the world. As each Tower was finished, the memory of everyone was altered and powerful spells were placed over the Towers to hide them. No one but the warlocks and witches knew where they were, and I believed it to be for the best. If you couldn't find them, then you couldn't start shit that was going to get everyone killed.

Reave was going to get us all killed.

"What the hell is he thinking?" I yelled.

"Maybe that he's tired of being under their thumb," Robert snapped.

"We all are!" I shouted simply because I couldn't stop shouting. I dropped back down onto the couch and put my head into my hands, trying to learn to breathe again. When I spoke, my voice was low but not particularly calm. "I don't want to know what he's planning. That's the least of our problems. If they find out he's got that information, they will come down off the Towers and kill us all." I glared at my brother. "You don't know them like I do. If they suspect anyone has that information, they won't bother to hunt down you or Reave. They will destroy the entire city, every living creature, to make sure the information has been silenced."

Robert tried to smile. His mouth moved in the right direction, but it was strained, while his eyes flickered with fear. "Then I guess you better come up with something good."

"Has he told you yet? Do you know the locations?"

"Just one. He said it was insurance so that you wouldn't try to 'rescue me.' He also said that if you tried to erase the location from my memory, he'd kill me." Robert didn't look particularly disturbed by the threat, probably because he knew that I would do everything within my power to protect him.

My teeth were clenched so tightly that my jaw had begun to throb. I was going to kill Reave. I wasn't a killer, but this dark elf was driving me to it. My brother might not have wanted out, but he needed out because Reave was shortening his life substantially by putting him in the path of the Towers.

"I need time to think and prepare." The words were stiff and hard when I spoke. "When are you scheduled to make your delivery?"

"I get the information in three days. You'll have one day to tattoo them on me—"

"What?"

"Reave is giving me the locations as coordinates. I can't memorize seven sets of exact coordinates and he doesn't want paper or digital copies traveling. He wants them tattooed on me, and you have to include a spell to protect the information."

Sitting back against the couch, I rubbed my eyes with my right hand against the pain that had started there. There was some small relief that he said seven—even Reave didn't know about the secret eighth Tower. Hell, even I wasn't completely sure where it was. All the same, I could feel the strands of the web Reave was weaving around Robert and me tightening, entrapping us so perfectly. It seemed as if he had thought of everything, tying my hands so I couldn't free my brother.

I needed to think. This was more than protecting Robert and all of Low Town from this information. The Towers had become a powder keg of unrest, and Reave was creating a human torch out of Robert. If the Towers and Robert collided, the war that ensued would make the Great War look like a playground scuffle between third-grade girls.

Unfortunately, I couldn't turn to Sofie or Gideon for advice. They would have only one answer. Kill Robert. Kill Reave. There had to be another way. I had to figure out what the hell it was.

7

IT WAS DARK. The world had been reduced to shapes lacking definition so that everything took on a menacing demeanor. My eyes strained, desperately trying to give meaning to my world, but it was useless. Any light that crept into the room was quickly swallowed up in the great maw of blackness that enveloped me.

I stretched out both hands, determined to use my remaining senses to figure out where I was, how I had gotten there. My fingers hit cold, damp stone. Dirty grit crusted under my fingernails and embedded itself in the fine grooves of my fingers as I slid them along the rough surface. The wall beside me was composed of giant stones, while the floor beneath my feet seemed to be made of the same uneven rock. The room curved slightly, as if it were circular rather than square.

There was no sound beside the soft scrape of my fingers along the stone wall and the scuff of my feet on the floor. My heart pounded in my ears, frustrating me. Was I alone in this room? Was someone else here, tracking me by my thudding heart and shuffling feet? Would it kill me? Help me?

Footsteps broke through the silence. I froze, waiting in the stillness as they grew steadily closer. The tread sounded even and familiar. A friend? The footsteps stopped close, followed by the clang of metal on metal and then scraping, like a key turning a rusted lock.

Light surged into the room, blinding me. I fell back against the wall, throwing my arms up in front of my face to protect myself from the sudden invasion. Shrinking back, I squinted and blinked, willing my eyes to adjust to the brightness rather than stay frozen and helpless.

"Come along!" snarled an angry voice that chilled the blood in my veins.

I moved shaking hands from my face, praying that I was wrong, but I wasn't. Simon Thorn stood in the open doorway, a magical ball of white light hovering above his shoulder. This wasn't right. Simon was dead. I'd killed him months ago. Simon had to be dead.

But if Simon was dead and trapped in the underworld, did this mean I had died as well? Had I passed during the night, called by Lilith to pay the year I owed magic for killing Simon? I couldn't be dead. I could feel my heart pounding in my chest and the cold seeping from the stones through my thin shirt. I wouldn't feel these things if I was dead, right? Was I dreaming? Remembering? Both?

In the bright light, I stared down at my hands to find them smaller than I remembered. My arms and body were smaller and thinner, while Simon was taller. It all seemed wrong, but my mind kept stumbling as if the wheels in my brain were slipping as they tried to puzzle out this problem.

"Now, boy, or I'll drag you by your hair," Simon said, pulling me from my internal struggles.

As if willed by some unknown force, my body obeyed his command and I pushed away from the wall. On shaky legs, I crossed the small stone cell and followed my mentor down the long, narrow hall marked by other heavy doors in front of silent rooms. There were others behind those thick doors, huddled in the darkness, cold and wounded.

At the end of the hall, we turned left and walked down a wider hall until we came to a large circular room. There was more light here, created by torches and little balls of magical light. A pair of witches and a warlock stood near the back of the room, silent and grim. I stopped just past the threshold and looked around, taking in the bleak gray walls. This room was familiar, creating a cold chill in my mind. I'd been here before and it hadn't been a pleasant place.

Simon roughly grabbed my shoulder, his thin fingers biting through the ragged cloth of my shirt to pinch muscles and nerves. "Get in there," the warlock said. He gave me a hard shove and I fell into the shallow circular pit in the center of the room. My knees hit the hard compact dirt, sending a sharp pain down to the bone.

Placing my hands against the dirt floor, I pushed back to my feet and my eyes fell on Bryce. *Oh God.* Now I remembered why this place seemed so familiar. The young boy lay on his side, his breathing ragged as the air slipped between split lips in short, quick gasps. Dirt and blood crusted his face. His clothes had been taken away, revealing an all-too-thin frame covered in ugly bruises and long, festering cuts. Pain glazed his eyes, making me wonder if he was aware of where he was and that I was near him.

I backpedaled until my back slammed into the wall of the dueling pit. Turning, I looked up at Simon. My hands were on the chest-high rim, ready to climb out of the arena. I couldn't do it. I knew why I was here and I couldn't do it.

Simon stepped directly in front of me, blocking my escape. "This is your third and final chance to finish this. You kill him and we will move on with your training, or we will keep him alive indefinitely, locked in constant pain. Kill him or I kill you." Placing his foot on my shoulder, the warlock shoved me backward, away from the wall and into the center of the pit.

I stumbled, but managed to stay on my feet. Swallowing back the bile in my throat, I looked down at the wounded apprentice again. Three days ago, Bryce and I had been placed in the dueling pit. We had both been learning curses used in fighting, and our mentors had decided that the best way to prove we were proficient was a duel to the death. I won the duel, but refused to kill Bryce. I had been locked in a cell, while Bryce had been beaten and tortured as they waited for me to submit to their wishes.

Shaking my head, I tried to backpedal again when I heard Bryce give a little whimper. His head moved so that he was now looking up at me. Pain cut heavy lines through his young face, sweat glistened on his brow. His lips moved, forming the words *Help me* but he lacked the strength to put sound to it. There was only one way to help him, to remove the pain and the fear.

My hands were trembling when I raised them, gathering together the energy I needed. I kept repeating in my head that if I did it quickly, Bryce wouldn't feel more pain, he wouldn't have a chance to be afraid.

"No!" Simon's harsh voice sliced through the silence. A wave of energy swept through the room, pushing the magic I had pulled from my fingertips. I twisted around to look at my mentor in confusion. "You had your chance to kill him with magic and you threw it away. You'll kill him with this."

Simon reached into his trouser pocket and pulled out something that he tossed into the pit. I looked down and my stomach lurched. At my feet was a small wooden dagger. The tip was sharp, but the blade was dull. There would be no saving Bryce from pain.

Slowly, I bent down and picked it up. It was incredibly light and smooth. It didn't feel like a weapon, but a toy I might have used when I played pirates with my brother in the backyard so many years ago. You couldn't kill someone with a toy. It wasn't right.

"Do it! You have until the count of three or I will kill you!" Simon shrieked, his voice cracking in his growing rage. "One!"

"Gage." A woman's voice gently drew my attention back to Bryce.

My head jerked up and I saw Lilith lying on the ground next to the pain-filled apprentice. She was on her side in a languorous pose with one arm curled around his head. "Send him to me, Gage. He's in such pain. Set him free."

"Two!"

"Set him free, Gage. Help your friend."

"Three!"

I screamed, my voice hammering against the cold stone walls as I charged across the pit toward Bryce. The wooden blade was jerked over my head as I fell to my knees next to his prone body. All I saw were Bryce's brown eyes widening in terror so that I was nearly drowning in them as I brought the knife down. The boy screamed in pain as the blade broke through his chest, but I had to bring all my weight down on the knife to push it through his heart.

Blood splashed over my hands and I remember thinking that it wasn't as warm as I thought it would be. I couldn't take my eyes off him as I watched the light fade from his wide eyes.

A cold hand cupped my cheek and I looked up to stare into the dark pools of nothing that composed Lilith's eyes. She was smiling at me. "I'll be coming for you soon, Gage. And you'll set me free."

I screamed, the sound ripped out of my throat like a banshee's wail. Something shook me hard and I jerked upright to find myself sitting on my bed with my brother kneeling on the edge, his hands braced on my shoulders. He said something, but I didn't hear it past the pounding in my ears. As I gasped for air to scream again, my stomach lurched.

Shoving him aside, I jumped off the bed only to get tangled in the sheets. I fell to my hands and knees, but managed to crawl the final few feet across the room to the small wastebasket before I started heaving my guts up. Bile burned its way along my throat and my lungs locked up, crying out for air. I couldn't purge my mind of the memory, but my body could purge the contents of my stomach. Tears streamed down my cheeks, but I doubted it was because of the vomiting.

When the spasms stopped, I wiped my mouth with the back of my hand and fell to my side near the basket. I sucked in deep breaths, willing the shakes to stop as I lay there with my eyes closed. My skin was clammy and covered in a cold sweat, while my entire body hurt as if I had pulled every muscle.

I hadn't had a nightmare about my time in the Towers for years, and never one about Bryce. I had suppressed that bitch of a memory until I had forgotten about it completely. I had been thirteen when Simon first took me to that damned dueling pit. Bryce looked like he was no more than ten or eleven at the time. We had never met before that day, but I could still remember that nervous smile he had flashed me before we found out what we were expected to do. I remember thinking that he seemed like an okay kid and that if I had met him at home, he would have been someone I would have ridden bikes or played wiffle ball with. Instead, I killed him.

Looking back nearly fifteen years later, I wasn't sure what had spurred me on to kill him. I wanted to say I had been saving him from more pain and torture. *Oh God, I wanted that to be the reason.* But a slick and horrible voice whispered in my ear that I had killed Bryce because I had been afraid to die.

"Gage?"

I flinched at Robert's voice despite its soft and gentle tone. The old wounds were suddenly fresh and the memory was raw in my mind. I was having trouble climbing back into the present, where I was free of Simon and the Towers.

"What time is it?" My voice was rough and hoarse as it escaped my injured throat. I lay on the floor with one arm thrown over my eyes, blocking out the world a little longer. I wasn't ready to look at my brother when I could still see Bryce's wide brown eyes in my mind. Even more, I didn't want my brother to look at me.

"A little after one."

"Could you start some coffee? I've got to jump in the shower before I head to the parlor."

"Yeah. Yeah, I got it." He didn't move for several seconds and I think he was debating whether to ask me something, but he must have decided against it because he left my bedroom without speaking.

When I was alone again, I moved my arm from my eyes and looked around my messy bedroom. The heavy curtains were pulled over the two windows, blanketing the room in a thick darkness that was broken only by light pouring from the open door. Clean and dirty clothes were strewn everywhere along with all the other bits of flotsam accumulated in the normal course of a life. The familiar helped to push back the swell of ugly memories from the Towers and the pain dulled to a throbbing ache that sank in to become a part of my soul.

Around three in the morning, Robert and I had come back to my apartment, where we watched a movie before he crashed on the couch. I made it to my bed, where I slipped into a sleep that left me dead to the world and the trouble that was brewing.

Wincing, I shoved to my feet, but paused as my eyes caught on the bed. I rarely dreamed about the Towers and that was the first time I had ever dreamed about Lilith. Was it a nightmare brought on by the stress of Robert's news? Maybe my mind demanding that I confront something that I refused to think about—my dwindling time until I paid my debt. Or was the nightmare a warning? Was my time almost up? Would I soon have to pay for the year that I owed magic?

Shaking my head, I grabbed a pair of clean boxers, jeans, and a T-shirt without looking at them and headed for the bathroom. Fear curled in my queasy stomach. It wasn't that I didn't want to leave Trixie and Bronx in the lurch if I suddenly died. If all went well, I'd be back in a year. I was afraid of facing Lilith for that year in the underworld. As keeper of all visiting souls, she was going to make my year an undead hell unless I found a way to set her free so that she could visit the land of the living on a more permanent basis.

And this world had enough to deal with. It didn't need someone like her running around.

Stripping off my dirty boxers, I turned on the water and jumped into the shower, not giving it time to warm up. The cold water cleared away the last of the fog and got my brain working past the old memories and horrors. If Reave was threatening to bring the world to war and put my brother in the dead center of it all, I needed to be thinking clearly. The only problem was that I didn't have a fucking clue as to what I was going to do, but I needed to figure it out fast. Preferably before the Towers learned that the puny mortals were plotting something.

As the water warmed up, I grabbed the shampoo and lathered my hair, wishing I could wash my mind clean just as easily. The bathroom door opened and I stilled for a second before ducking under the spray to rinse away the soap.

"Gage?" Trixie's voice rose above the rush of water, pushing away the last of the tension.

Wiping the water from my eyes, I pulled the curtain back and forced a smile on my lips. "Want to join me?" I teased, but I had no interest in sex. Just the sight of her helped to ease the pain in my chest. For once, I simply wanted to hold her and let her presence chase away the last of the ghosts from my past.

She shook her head, smiling at me, but I still saw the worry in her eyes. "Not this time." Leaning forward, she gave me a quick kiss before stepping away so that I couldn't pull her into the shower with me.

I closed the curtain again and grabbed the soap. "Give me a minute. I'm almost finished."

"It's okay. I just stopped by to tell you something."

There was a long pause and I froze in the process of spreading soap over my chest. Her voice didn't sound like it was going to be a happy something.

"You're here to tell me that you're pregnant and want to run away with me so we can be broccoli farmers in Montana," I said, trying to get her to laugh.

"Do they grow broccoli in Montana?"

"I have no idea."

Another long pause twisted in my tender gut. I dropped the soap and jerked the curtain back again. "Are you pregnant?"

Trixie scowled at me. "No, I'm not pregnant."

"Oh. Good." I closed the curtain and quickly finished rinsing off. "Then what's up?"

"The Summer Court is in Low Town."

I turned off the water and jerked the curtain completely open. Trixie's eyes skimmed over the entire length of my naked body before rising back to my face.

"Nice," she murmured with a grin.

It was my turn to scowl at her. I grabbed a towel hanging opposite the shower and started to dry off. "Have you spoken to your brother?"

"Not yet."

"Have the king's men made another grab for you?"

"No."

I stopped drying off and stared at her in confusion. "Then how do you know?"

Her lovely mouth twisted up into a frown. "I just . . . know. It's a feeling. I can't explain it. Summer elves know when the Court is near. This isn't just a few of my people. Both the king and the queen are in the area."

I nodded, wrapping the towel around my waist before stepping out of the shower. "Fine. Then we have to be careful."

"I trust my brother. He'll be fair about this. He'll send word as to whether the queen will meet with us before he comes after me again."

"All the same—"

"All the same," she interrupted with a knowing smile. "I'm going to stay with Bronx this afternoon until my shift and then I'll be at the parlor with you until we go on our little adventure tonight."

"Shit! That's tonight?" I groaned.

My nightmare had completely wiped my memory of the fact that I was scheduled to conduct a little larceny with Trixie this evening. I wanted to strangle the king of the Summer Court. He had been hounding Trixie for three centuries, trying to force her to be his consort after it was discovered that he and his wife couldn't have children. If he made another grab for her, I was afraid that Trixie would bolt and I didn't want to think about living without her.

"I'm going, Gage," she warned. "I'll agree to extra precautions, but I won't stop living because of the bastard. So you can get that look off your face."

"What look?" I tried for innocent, but knew she wouldn't believe it.

"The one that says you plan to lock me in a room and guard it with a thousand trolls."

I grinned at her. "That's not a bad idea."

Trixie leaned up and pressed a quick kiss to my lips. "I'll see you tonight and I'm still going." The elf quickly slipped out of the room before I could grab her, leaving me with only the haunting scent of her floral perfume.

With a sigh, I finished getting ready and met Robert in the kitchen, where he was pouring himself a cup of coffee. He stepped out of the way as I grabbed a mug and filled it.

"Everything good?" he asked from the doorway as I took my first sip.

"Yeah," I said with a sigh as my grumbling stomach accepted my peace offering of heat and caffeine. I'd appease it with actual food when I made my way to the parlor.

"How long have you two . . . ?"

Robert's voice drifted off and I smiled. I had never let myself imagine this day. I never thought I'd see him standing in the kitchen with me while we drank coffee. I never thought we'd talk again.

"I've known Trixie for a couple years, but we've been dating only a couple months."

He grunted and took another drink of his coffee. Last night he'd told me that he was divorced and had no kids. We had learned odd facts and collected strange stories about each other's life, but there were big gaping holes in his past that I was waiting to have filled in.

"I want you to stay in my apartment," I said before draining the last of my coffee.

"Why?"

I walked over to the faucet and rinsed out my mug before putting it in the sink. "It's safer. I don't know who else knows about the information Reave's trying to move or if anyone knows you're involved. We need time to think and plan. No one knows we're related, so they won't think to look here."

Robert frowned at me, looking as if he was ready to argue.

"Just for a few days. It won't be bad. I've got cable, Internet, video games, and food in the fridge. You can spend the day eating, gaming, and watching Internet porn for all I care. Just stay here."

"Can I at least go back to my place and get some clothes?"

"Fine. Be quick and don't make any calls. Okay?"

"Yeah, sure," he grumbled, leaning against the counter across from me.

I pulled open a drawer and grabbed a spare key to my apartment. Tossing it to him, I walked out of the kitchen and into the living room. "I'll be at Asylum until dark and then Trixie and I have to run an errand. I should be back here near midnight," I said as I picked up my keys, wallet, and cell phone from the coffee table and shoved them into my pockets.

"Anything else, Mom?" he asked with a sneer.

"Yeah, don't do anything stupid."

Robert flipped me off, but he was smiling when he did it. I flashed him dual birds in return and then headed for the door. I needed to get to Asylum. I did my best thinking in the parlor.

"Hey, Gage."

Robert's voice stopped me as I pulled open the door. I turned to look back at him and frowned. He looked genuinely uncomfortable and for a moment I thought he was going to tell me to go on.

When he spoke, his voice was gruff and halting, as if he was afraid to speak. "That nightmare you had. Was it about when you were in the Towers?"

I quickly glanced out into the hall and was relieved to find it empty. My nosy neighbors didn't need to know I was an ex-warlock.

"Yeah," I said on a sigh.

"Was . . . was it bad there?"

My eyes fell closed for a second. Robert and I had never discussed my time in the Towers. I never discussed it with anyone. They were dark, ugly memories, for the most part filled with pain and screams and someone somewhere dying.

"Yeah, it was bad."

"I'm sorry. When you were taken, I made all kinds of plans on how to rescue you. But I guess after about three years, I finally figured out that I couldn't rescue you. No one could."

I smiled weakly at my brother. He was leaning against the wall, his hands fisted at his sides as he stared at the floor, lost in the pain of an old memory. "The Towers are a bad place, but I don't entirely regret it. If I hadn't learned to control my powers, I could have hurt you or Meg without meaning to. I could never have lived with that."

Robert nodded, but remained silent. I waited, not sure if he had anything else to say. I felt like we were both treading on eggshells. A sigh escaped me as I started to leave again.

"When I came in, you . . . you kept saying 'Bryce.' He a friend?" Robert asked, stopping me.

"No," I said, looking away from my brother to stare out into the hall. "He was a kid I knew a long time ago."

"I'm sorry."

His words cut like razor blades across my flesh rather than the balm he meant them to be. I grunted and then pulled the door shut behind me. By his tone, Robert knew Bryce was dead. But he'd never know that his baby brother had killed the boy.

If there was any justice in this world, Bryce was at peace, away from all the pain, fear, and misery. And if he was, a little part of me envied him and hoped he forgave me.

WITH EVERYTHING GOING on with Reave, my brother, and the Towers, it wasn't the best time to try to break into a walled-off private garden, but the growth cycle of the rare Asian Moon Lily couldn't be altered simply because I was having a bad day. I was irritated by the distraction from what I needed to be doing, but in truth, I had to get away from the shop and all the building insanity so I could clear my head. And what better way to clear my head than to do a little trespassing and larceny?

Trixie was settled beside me in the tree, seeming more ghostly apparition in the moonlight than flesh and blood. It was the first time she had accompanied me on this excursion and I was grateful that she had chosen sneakers instead of her usual heels and leather.

"I can't believe you do this," Trixie said as she sank into a new crouched position in the large maple tree we were sitting in. We had been up in the tree for nearly a half hour as we waited for the last of the lights in the house to go out. Our legs were starting to cramp and grow stiff, but I wasn't willing to move yet. "You know they sell this stuff at most potion-supply stores."

Looking up at her, I smiled. "You know how expensive that stuff is? Crazy. This is easier."

"And dangerous."

I shrugged. "Maybe, but it's certainly more fun."

About three years ago, I had entered a pool with five other parlor owners in the area. We had found the only grower of the Asian Moon Lily in the region and decided that we would liberate one flower when it opened. The catch was that the Asian Moon Lily only opened at night once every twenty-eight days. As a result, it was my turn to pluck a flower once every six months, which was an agreeable schedule.

"I don't think we even need the flower," Trixie continued with a frown. "None of us have used it in the shop lately and the flower remains good for one year when stored properly."

"We don't, but that's not the point." It was rare that any group member needed the flower. We all had enough stock after the first three months of the agreement, but no one had wanted to stop. It was too much fun.

A few days before the run, e-mails were sent around so the runner knew who needed a piece of the flower. Any pieces left over were usually sold. For my run, I had only two shops needing a supply. Since we had learned to divide it evenly six ways, that meant I had four portions to sell for myself.

The other catch was that the previous runner never told the next person if the garden owner had made any changes to his security. Since we came regularly every twenty-eight days, the owner knew when we would show up and regularly implemented new security measures to stop us. Nothing lethal, but enough to get you caught if you weren't paying attention. And who wanted to go to jail for stealing a fucking flower?

I glanced over my shoulder at the elf as she stared over the eight-foot wall toward the garden. "Look, if you're going to suck all the fun out of this, you can stay here."

"I'm trying to be sensible. I'm not sucking the fun out."

"Oh, I definitely feel some suckage going on." Trixie glared at me, but I could see the hint of a smile she was fighting to hold back. "I thought you'd want to spend some quality time together."

"Not exactly my idea of quality time."

I looked back toward the garden, shifting on the large branch as I tried to get some circulation back into my legs. "You know, there's more to life than sex."

Trixie smacked me on the back of the head. "No, there's not."

I opened my mouth to tease her some more, but the light we had been waiting for went out on the second floor of the house. The owner was settling into bed and it was only eleven. Early for him considering what night it was. He had something new he was planning. In all my visits, the man had tried motion-sensor lights, glass shards in the top of the wall, moving the flower inside the house, dogs, and even a couple hired thugs. From what I heard, the dogs had lasted one month, if not less, as I believe the type of dog he acquired also liked to dig. New security items came and went without warning so you were never quite sure what you were faced with.

"I don't understand why you don't . . . you know . . ." Trixie broke off and waved her hands in the direction of the garden.

I fought back a smile, playing dumb. "What? Flap my arms like a chicken?"

"You know what I mean!" she said in a harsh whisper.

"You mean the stuff I'm forbidden to do?" I pointedly asked, arching one brow at her.

"Like that's stopped you."

With a shrug, I looked at the garden wall again. "I like to think the forbidding part has at least slowed me down. I can't rely on something that I'm not supposed to be using in the first place."

"True," Trixie murmured, and then fell silent for several moments. "How do you want to do this?"

"You don't have to—"

"Oh, I want to. I was just making sure that you wanted to do this."

I chuckled. This woman was insane and I loved her for it. Pushing the thought roughly aside, I focused on the garden before us. This might not be a dangerous task, but I still didn't want to get caught for sneaking in to steal a flower. "Careful and quiet. With the weather remaining relatively warm at night, the six pots should be in the center of the garden next to a fountain. He's been turning off the fountain at night so we won't have the sound to muffle our movement. We take one flower. No more. You have your bone knife?"

"Got it."

Asian Moon Lilies were extremely temperamental. They were notoriously hard to grow and the flowers could be cut using only a knife blade made from bone. Anything else would instantly destroy the magical properties of the bloom. From there, the flower had to be stored in a brown paper bag in a dark space.

Glancing up at the house one last time to make sure there was no movement that I could see, I jumped down from the tree and headed across the yard to the garden gate. I peered through the iron bars at the garden in the full moonlight. All was quiet, with no sign of a dog or thug. In the center of the garden in a circle around a silent fountain were six terra-cotta pots holding large bushy plants with showy white blooms. Only two of the six plants were blooming tonight. The others would bloom within the next few days.

Reaching into my pocket, I pulled out a lock pick that I had used for nearly three years on the gate—one of the few things the garden owner had never bothered to change. With a soft click, it swung open without a sound. I hesitated. Nothing moved in the garden. There was no breeze to stir the leaves, no nocturnal animals flitting about. It looked empty and safe, but my stomach churned as adrenaline pumped through my veins. I was missing something. There had to be more. Unfortunately, the only way for me to see anything was to step farther into the garden.

With my left hand, I waved once behind me, motioning for Trixie to approach while I stepped into the garden. I moved toward the house, peering into the darkened windows through slits in curtains and in between slats in blinds. My eyesight was no better than any other human's in darkness, but I saw nothing within the house. Turning back toward the garden, I watched as Trixie soundlessly moved between the plants along the little stone path to the center. The moonlight glided over her, caressing her curves. The small bone knife in her hand seemed to glow as she raised it to one of the flowers.

As she came away with a bloom cradled in her hand, I approached the center of the garden. Trixie tucked the blade away in her pocket and looked at me with a mocking expression. "You made this sound difficult."

I shrugged. "Some months are. He may not have had time to play tonight." Lifting one hand to cup her cheek, I leaned in to kiss her, but my body froze less than an inch from hers when I heard an out-of-place click. Trixie stiffened under my fingers as she heard it as well.

Fuck. We had company.

The click that came from one of the garden doors to the house was followed by a much louder *chunk* from a shotgun as a round was chambered. Lifting my hand from Trixie's face, I held both hands open and out to my sides as I turned around.

A little old man with a bald head and a wrinkled face like a bulldog frowned at me as he held a shotgun pointed at me and Trixie. His skin was a nice chocolate brown, while his dark eyes were lost in the night. "Brought some help this time, didn't ya?"

"A shotgun, George?" I said with a sigh. "Do we really need a shotgun over a flower?"

The old man glared at me through thick glasses balanced on his round nose. The end of the gun trembled slightly as if he was already getting tired of pointing it at us. "This shit is getting old. Sneaking into my garden, stealing my flowers. I thought a gun would show you that I mean business this time."

"Fine. Then let my associate leave unharmed and we'll discuss it." Trixie bumped my back with either her hand or elbow, I couldn't quite tell. She wasn't exactly pleased with my suggestion. Didn't matter. Bringing Trixie along for a silly romp through a garden at night was one thing. Letting an old man point a gun at her was entirely different, and I wasn't good with that.

"And let her leave with my flower? Not a chance?"

I clenched my teeth in my growing frustration. My fingertips tingled as the urge to draw in the energy to cast a protective spell was nearly overwhelming. "She'll leave it here."

"How did you catch us?" Trixie interrupted.

George graced her with a smug smile and he lowered the gun slightly. "I had a new laser grid installed last week. When you entered the center of the garden, it set off a silent alarm inside the house."

"Nice," Trixie purred, winning her an even wider grin from the old man. "But how did you get downstairs so fast? We watched the light go off on the second floor."

"The light was on a timer. I was on the first floor the whole time, waiting."

"Fabulous," I muttered. The old man was getting crafty and I was getting sloppy. Lesson learned? Don't bring your sexy girlfriend along on a clandestine mission because you'll get distracted thinking about taking her clothes off when you should be worried about infrared laser grids.

Unfortunately, things were about to get more complicated as I spied a moving shadow to the right of the old man. I stifled a curse. Apparently I wasn't the only one who didn't care to have a shotgun pointed in Trixie's direction. As the shadow lunged at the old man, I pivoted on my right heel and plowed into Trixie, tackling her. Before we hit the ground, a shot echoed through the silent garden while buckshot ripped through plants directly overhead.

I raised up enough to look down at Trixie, her expression stunned. "He shot at us," she gasped.

"More likely the gun accidentally went off when he was knocked to the ground. Old George might be pissed, but he isn't the violent type. Are you okay?"

"Yeah. I crushed plants instead of hitting concrete. What about my brother?"

"I'm sure he's fine," I said in a growl.

Eldon's timing was impeccable, leaving me to believe that the elf had been following us for quite a while. Not a good sign. As my problems with Reave grew more complicated, I didn't want to worry about Trixie and the Summer Court as well.

Pushing back to my feet, I extended a hand to Trixie, helping her up as I looked over my shoulder. Eldon was kneeling over George's body. I didn't think he'd kill the old man, but then this guy had been hunting his sister for centuries to turn her over to a man she didn't want to be with. There was no telling what Eldon was capable of.

I caught Trixie's arm as she tried to move around me toward Eldon. "Cut a new flower and get out of the garden. I'll be right behind you."

"But—"

"Please. Eldon's not here to cover our asses. He'll follow. We've got to go. I'm sure the cops are on the way after the neighbors called in that gunshot."

Trixie frowned, but still turned back toward the Asian Moon Lilies sitting serenely in their pots, watching this little play unravel. I jogged over to where Eldon was getting to his feet. He was frowning as well, but I never expected the elf to be happy to see me.

"Dead?" I asked.

"Unconscious. Are you done endangering my sister?"

I grinned, wishing I could put my fist into his pointed nose. "I would say she's safer with me than in your hands, considering your plans for her."

Even in the darkness, I could make out the flush that filled his pale cheeks while his eyes widened. "Life as consort to the king of the Summer Court is far preferable to a life as a . . . a . . . common—"

"Shut it, Eldon," Trixie snapped as she came up behind me. As my smile grew, she turned her glare on me. "You too. We need to get out of here."

Trixie led the way out of the garden, a brown paper bag clenched in one fist as she silently walked across the wide lawn to a stand of trees. I had parked my car on the other side a couple streets over. Eldon and I followed. No one spoke, mostly because neither Trixie nor I wanted to hear what had brought Eldon back to Low Town.

"Trix, wait," I called as she made it to the tree line. We were away from the house and hidden enough that we wouldn't draw the attention of the cops when they arrived. I couldn't put it off any longer.

When she stopped and turned back to face her brother, I could see tears glistening in her wide eyes. She was scared, but then, so was I. Three centuries ago, Trixie had left her home with the Summer Court and gone into hiding because the king was determined to take her as a second wife. She had changed her name, changed her appearance, and was in constant hiding as she turned her back on her people and her family. Sadly, her brother was a member of the royal guard, and had spent the past three centuries pursuing his sister in hopes of dragging her home against her wishes.

Grabbing Trixie's hand, I pulled her close, wrapping one arm around her waist. I needed to hold her, to feel her against me. If Eldon had come to take her back to the Summer Court, I had to hold her one last time because I knew that I'd either have to kill him or Trixie was going to run out of my life forever in hopes of staying out of the king's clutches.

"What's the news?" My voice was rough as I struggled to push aside my growing panic.

"Rowena, I'm hoping that this break has given you the time to think about your situation," Eldon began. I flinched at hearing

Trixie's real name, brutally reminded of the long life she had lived with her people before she had been forced to run to protect her freedom. "Come back to your people, where you belong."

"No! She's not returning so she can be a plaything for a selfish asshole!" I shouted.

"Selfish? The king is trying to protect our people by selflessly putting aside his desires so that he can ensure the continuation of our people."

"Bullshit! He's a pompous prick—"

I never saw Eldon's fist, he moved so quickly. Pain exploded across my jaw, snapping my head around and knocking me off balance. I recovered quickly, swinging two fists at him. He dodged both, but the kick to the stomach caught him by surprise. I slammed my fist into his chin, knocking him to the ground.

The elf rolled back to his feet and started to charge when Trixie jumped between us.

"Enough! You're acting like a pair of idiots."

I stepped back, breathing heavily, my eyes locked on Eldon. If he touched Trixie, I was going to be all over him again. Trixie's brother didn't appear to be winded at all, but at least he was rubbing his jaw.

"You're not the only one being hurt by your decision, Rowena," Eldon said in a low voice. "What remains of your family is hurting. My daughter is hurting. Come back, and you can start to make it right for everyone."

Pain slashed across Trixie's face at his words and I growled, ready to jump over Trixie to get at him. "You know I never meant to hurt you or our family. But what he wants, what he's doing, is wrong. Let me fix this, my way."

Eldon took a stiff step backward, his face becoming a blank slate. I didn't know what the elf thought. He was ready to hand his sister over to the king to be used as some kind of brood mare. Yes, I could understand trying to protect your people, but what about the happiness of your own flesh and blood?

"Do you have any news or are you here to harass Trixie?" I demanded, breaking the thickening silence.

Eldon glared at me for a second before he spoke. "The queen has agreed to meet with you. Tomorrow at noon at Mirror Lake."

"Anything else?" I said when he started to walk away.

"Don't be late."

Trixie reached out, catching his shirt with two fingers, halting him when he would have turned his back on us. "Eldon."

His shoulders slumped and he shook his head before looking at his sister. I wasn't sure who was older. They both could have passed for midtwenties, even though I knew that Trixie was more than six hundred. They both had green eyes and blond hair, but Eldon's features seemed hard and cold to me, where Trixie was soft.

"Don't get your hopes up," he said, breaking the silence. "After the king's betrayal, I was lucky she didn't have me killed for seeking an audience with her."

Trixie gasped beside me, her fingers fisting around his shirt. I frowned. This wasn't a good sign. "Do you think she'll try to execute Trixie when we show up?"

"Possibly. But I think she's more interested in you."

"Then I take it she knows what I was?"

Eldon smiled at me; a cold, evil thing that made my skin crawl. "*Was?* You don't ever stop being one of them no matter what you do. And, yes, she knows what you are."

"Thank you, Eldon," Trixie interjected, trying to defuse some of the tension. I kept my mouth shut rather than adding to it. There wasn't much I could say. Witches and warlocks had brought the elves close to extinction during the Great War; not exactly something that is easily forgiven or ever forgotten. I may not have been the one killing elves, but I was counted as one of that race and that was condemning enough.

"You know you could avoid this need to meet with the queen," Eldon said, looking over at his sister.

"I'm not going to him. There has to be another way."

"I don't see it if there is." He started walking into the woods, his shirt pulling out of Trixie's grasp.

"How's my niece?" Trixie called in a voice that slightly wavered.

Eldon didn't look back as he continued to walk away. "Waiting to meet her aunt."

Trixie laid her head against my shoulder and sighed. She was in a shitty position. Leaving the Summer Court had made her an outcast among her people. She'd never seen her only niece and she'd been at odds with her brother for centuries. Adding to her problems was that she'd chosen to align herself with a warlock—the most hated of creatures in this world. Even if she did win her freedom from the king, it was highly unlikely her people were ever going to welcome her back. Certainly not with me hanging on her arm.

I squeezed Trixie's waist, pressing her tightly against me. "We'll figure this out," I whispered against her hair. Trixie looked up at me and nodded, but there was no accompanying smile. I had a sick feeling that her thoughts were traveling in the same direction as mine, which didn't bode well for our relationship. I couldn't blame her. Bronx and I were family and friends as much as we could be, but blood ran so much deeper.

Well, at least that was true for everyone but witches and warlocks. We didn't give a shit about each other beyond how we could use one another. But there was a comfort in having something in common with another people. Whether I wanted to admit to that comfort was another matter altogether when it came to the Ivory Towers.

"Let's get going," I said, releasing her so we could walk between the trees to the car.

I followed her through the thin strip of woods toward the car, both of us silent as we remained lost in our own thoughts. I wanted to think of something brilliant that would fix all of this, but the wheels in my brain kept slipping. The stress of dealing with Reave, trying to think of a way to free Bronx, protect my brother, and extricate Trixie from her problems with the king of the Summer Court had left me with a brain that felt like mush.

As the car came into view, Trixie slowed her step as she reached into her back pocket and pulled out her phone. She had put it on vibrate after we left the car and started walking toward George's house.

"Hey, Bronx," Trixie greeted when she answered the call. "Everything okay at the shop?" Her voice sounded weary to me, but there was a little relief in it, as if the promise of moving her thoughts to Bronx and the shop seemed to lighten the load on her mind.

I pulled my keys out of my pocket and clicked the remote to unlock the doors, only half listening to Trixie's side of the conversation. I wasn't expecting much to happen at Asylum. I had put in my usual shift and I had pulled Trixie out only a few hours early. Bronx was supposed to have a light load for the rest of the night and he was accustomed to working alone.

"We're getting to the car now and heading back toward you. You need us at the shop?" I stopped beside Trixie as she paused in the act of reaching for the door handle, a frown pulling at her lips as her eyes jumped to my face. "He's right here with me. I'll tell him. Thanks."

"What's up?" I asked as she ended the call.

"Not sure. He said to turn on the radio immediately and call him if you needed anything."

I stared at Trixie for a second, my face twisting in confusion. "Is everything okay at the shop?"

"I guess so. He didn't say."

I started walking around my SUV to the driver's side. "Did he sound like he'd been drinking?"

"Oh, come on! You know better."

I shrugged before pulling open my door. "Yeah, but Bronx isn't usually this cryptic."

I let it drop as we settled into the car. Slipping the key into the ignition, I only turned it enough to get the radio on. I had a sick feeling that I didn't want to be driving yet.

"What channel?" I asked, reaching for the tuner. I think Trixie was going to tell me that Bronx didn't say. She opened her mouth, but the words never came out, as they were stopped in her throat by the announcement coming across the radio. Bronx hadn't needed to give a station—the news hitting the airwaves was on all stations.

> . . . skies are filled with smoke and the flames can be seen for several miles away from where the city had been. As far as we know, there was no warning that this strike was coming and no explanation has been released since the strike. The president has sent both the National Guard and members from all branches of the armed forces to do rescue and reconnaissance. While there are no official news reports coming out of the city, it is believed that every living creature within the confines of the Interstate 465 loop has been destroyed by members of the Ivory Towers. Our prayers and thoughts go out to everyone who had family living within the confines of Indianapolis.

OH, SHIT! THEY KNOW.

The words kept ringing through my head while the radio announcer's voice became a dull buzz in the background. My hands gripped the steering wheel so tightly my knuckles ached and turned white. Muscles were rigid throughout my whole body while air was pulled into my lungs in sharp, harsh gasps. All those people . . . dead. Thousands gone in a flash of fire and destruction that I was sure had completely leveled the city and surrounding area.

The witches and the warlocks had struck, and I knew it had to be because they suspected that someone knew the Tower locations. I don't know how they found out, but Low Town was no longer safe. Gideon's warning that the situation was bad in the Towers only made this tragedy worse. They were going to be quicker to act, quicker to strike out to protect themselves as their panic increased.

I looked over at Trixie as she sat silently beside me, staring straight ahead. One trembling hand was pressed to her parted lips while tears traced down her pale cheeks. She looked over at me, horror filling her wide eyes.

"Why?" she whispered, her voice shattered. "Why would they do such a thing? We've done nothing to antagonize them."

"I . . . I'm not sure," I replied. I had a guess, but I couldn't be sure. I needed to talk to Gideon. And I needed to beat the shit out of Reave.

Reaching for the key in the ignition, I hesitated. Where was I going to take her? If this was about the Tower locations, Low Town wasn't safe any longer. Hell, I was surprised they hadn't attacked the city already because of their animosity toward me.

Sadly, the first safe place I could think of was the Summer Court. The Towers weren't going after the elves and they stayed out of the cities for the most part. But I couldn't bring myself to make the suggestion. Even if I could convince Trixie to go, she'd be alive but miserable as the consort to the king. That wasn't a life.

Sending Trixie off to the Summer Court might save her life, but what about Bronx and Sofie and the thousands of other people that called Low Town home? What about my parents? The only way to save Trixie and everyone else in Low Town was to stop the Ivory Towers from striking here. I didn't have a clue how to do that without risking the life of my brother as well.

Taking a deep breath, I grasped the key and turned it, starting the engine. I wasn't going to solve anything sitting in the car, staring blankly through the windshield. The first thing I needed to do was talk to Gideon and find out if this had to do with the information that Reave possessed. If I was lucky, it didn't, but I wasn't a lucky kind of guy.

As I pulled away from the curb, I hit the radio knob, silencing the announcer. He was repeating the same horrific information over and over again, adding to the sickening feeling in my stomach. It would be a couple more hours before they could provide details about the damage in Indianapolis. I had no doubt that everyone was dead. The witches and warlocks were thorough when they decided to kill.

"Gage." Trixie's soft voice shook me from my dark thoughts. "Is this the beginning of something new? The start of another war with the Ivory Towers? Because I don't think I can go through another Great War."

Her words cut through my heart, leaving me feeling wounded and bleeding. I had never thought about it. She was over six hundred years old. She had lived through the Great War the warlocks and the witches had waged against the world for dominance, while I had only read about it in books—most written by the Towers. Millions had been slaughtered, leaving at least two races extinct and many others on the cusp of extinction. The elves had come close. At the time of the war, Trixie had been on the run. Every day must have been a torture, never knowing if the people she loved had been killed.

I reached across and grabbed her hand in mine, tightly squeezing it. Her fingers were cold against my palm as the horror filled her. "I will do everything within my powers to stop it from reaching that point. This world can't survive another Great War."

Out of the corner of my eye, I saw her lift her head and look at me. "If you did know what was happening in the Towers, would you tell me?"

I flinched and I knew she felt it because I was holding her hand. She captured my hand as I tried to withdraw it, holding it with both of hers. "I honestly don't know," I said. "I've got a couple ideas as to what's going on, but I don't know anything definite."

"But you still won't say."

"I think it's better if I don't."

"Because you don't trust me?"

I jerked my hand free while struggling to keep the car on the road. "What the fuck? How could you even ask that?" I exploded. Growling, I found an open spot on the side of the road and pulled over before I got us both killed with my distracted driving. I threw the car in park, tore off my seat belt, and twisted to face her. There was fear, pain, and a lot of uncertainty in her wide eyes, causing my anger to disappear.

Slowly, I reached up and cupped her cheeks, wiping away her tears with my thumbs. "I love you, Trixie. I have loved you for so long that I can't remember a time when I didn't. I love your smile, sarcasm, and that brilliant mind of yours. I love how you mother Bronx and Sofie like they're a pair of lost children. I love how you laugh and I love every time you tear into me because I'm a fucking idiot. For almost two years, the worst days of the week were Sunday and Monday because I knew I wouldn't see you. And every day since I told you about my past I wake up in a panic, terrified that you're going to come to your senses and hate me because of what the Towers did to your people." I paused and licked my lips, my heart pounding in my chest. I hadn't planned to tell her any of this now. I didn't know if I ever planned to tell her. I could be pushing her further from me, but it didn't matter. With the world teetering on the brink, she had to know.

"There is no one in this world that I trust more than you," I whispered. "I wish I could tell you everything, but I can't. It's not a matter of trust. It's because I'm a coward. I'm afraid if you know everything, then you'll leave. I'm afraid that you could be hurt because of what I tell you. Short of pulling out my wand and killing anything that comes near you, keeping my mouth shut is the only way I know to protect you. I'm sorry."

The pain had eased from her eyes as I spoke but she still looked sad. She reached up and laid her palm against my cheek. I could feel her wipe away something wet, but I refused to think she had made me cry as well as admit that I was a coward. The League of Men was going to come confiscate my balls at this rate. But it didn't matter. Trixie was worth it.

"Oh, Gage, how could any woman hate you?" Trixie asked in a broken voice.

"Talk to Sofie or Bronx. I'm sure they could provide examples," I joked but I couldn't hold the smile on my lips. It wasn't exactly the response that I was hoping for, but at least she wasn't getting out of the car and walking out of my life.

I dropped my hands from her face and started to turn back in my seat to face front when Trixie tightened her hold on my cheek. She pulled me closer while she leaned across the remaining distance. She kissed me hard and I hesitated only a heartbeat before I kissed her back, getting lost in her soft lips, the warmth of her mouth. She broke off the kiss before I could pull her into my lap.

"First, I'm not happy with you but I understand your reasoning for keeping secrets," she said in a hard voice. "Second, you're not a coward. I've never known anyone braver than you. And third, I will never hate you because you're a warlock. You weren't one of the bastards hunting down my people. You chose to leave rather than be like them."

I smiled at her, some of the tension easing from my chest. "There doesn't happen to be a fourth thing you want to tell me?"

Trixie frowned and I pulled away from her, struggling to keep the teasing smile on my face. Yeah, I was definitely pushing my luck. It was enough that she wasn't leaving. It was enough that she didn't hate me.

I was reaching for the shifter when Trixie's laughter rang through the SUV, jerking my gaze back to her face. "For fuck's sake, Gage," she said between giggles. "I feel like I've been throwing myself at you for almost two years. How could you not know that I love you?"

Releasing the shifter, I grabbed Trixie with both hands and pulled her into my lap. It was cramped and uncomfortable, but her mouth on mine made me forget about everything else. She wrapped her arms around my neck while I pressed her as close to me as I could. The world was burning around us, but I had Trixie in my arms and I would keep her safe even if it meant taking apart each Tower with my bare hands.

Trixie pulled away, her breathing heavy, but a smile was on her beautiful face. "How can you be so smart and so stupid at the same time?"

"I lose ten IQ points anytime we're in the same room."

Trixie arched one thin eyebrow at me. "That's all?"

"Well, twenty points when you're wearing leather."

She chuckled again as she nuzzled her cheek against mine. "I love you, Gage. Don't ever question that."

I squeezed her, some of the tension easing from my chest. I didn't know what this meant for us. I had never uttered those words before and I had never received them in return. For now, it meant nothing more than that someone was going to stick beside me through the mess that I was faced with, and I was grateful for it.

Trixie leaned back so she could look at me. "What are we going to do about the Towers?"

I jerked back as if she had hit me. The anxiety that had so nicely flowed away rushed back, squeezing my heart with fear. "*We* aren't going to do anything. It's the Towers, Trix. What could we or even I do about the Towers?"

She frowned. "You're telling me that you're going to huddle in Asylum and pray that it blows over? I don't believe that for a second."

I wanted to shake her. She knew me too damn well despite my tendency to keep secrets. "We aren't doing anything. I am going to try to contact a couple of people and see if I can get a little inside information. Besides, I think we've currently got our hands full with our meeting with the queen tomorrow."

Her expression crumpled as she was reminded of her own plight, which didn't look much better than my own when it came to the Towers. We were in a world of hurt and we needed to start digging our way out of it if we were going to not only survive, but also have something that resembled a normal life again.

"What are we going to do?" she murmured, resting her head on my shoulder.

I gave her a hard squeeze. "We're going to take this one day at a time, one problem at a time. I'll try to get some information about tonight's attack and then we're going to get some rest ahead of tomorrow's meeting. I have a feeling I'm going to need to be sharp for this little parley with the queen."

Trixie snorted softly before pressing a kiss to my cheek. "And then some." She slid across my lap and sat in the passenger seat. I immediately missed the feel of her against me, her warmth and wonderful weight, but I kept my mouth shut and tried to focus on what she was saying.

"You have to be very careful with the queen, Gage. She's . . . tricky, and I imagine that after everything that has happened, she's probably more than a little bitter. I'm not sure that she's going to want any help that you have to offer. The truth is, I'm not even sure as to why she agreed to this meeting."

I shook my head as I reached for the shifter on the steering column. "Doesn't matter. We'll meet and figure out the next step from there." I threw the SUV into drive again and pulled back out into traffic. The ride back to the shop was silent. We didn't bother to turn the radio on again, though I was sure that we would be flipping on the news when we were back at our respective apartments. Neither of us seemed ready to be bombarded by the reality that thousands of people had been slaughtered in the blink of an eye and Low Town could be next on the hit list if the witches and the warlocks decided to strike again.

Of course, we weren't the only ones stunned by the destruction of Indianapolis, as the roads were mostly empty on the ride to Asylum. It was as if all the inhabitants of Low Town had scurried into their homes to protect themselves from the dark gaze of the Towers.

When we reached the parlor, Bronx was sitting at the glass counter while Sofie was stretched out along the top. He had a news radio station turned on rather than his usual MP3 music. The lines on his face seemed to ease when we walked through the front door.

He rose as Trixie rushed across the lobby and around the case so that she could embrace him in a fierce hug.

I gave him a stiff smile while I placed the brown bag containing the Asian Moon Lily flower on the case. My hand drifted over Sofie's head, trying to reassure her that everything was okay. It didn't feel that way, but for a moment we all needed the reassurance, whether it was the truth or not.

"Do you have any more appointments tonight?" I asked when Trixie released the troll.

Bronx returned to the stool he had been sitting on. "I've got two more that haven't canceled."

"Why don't you call them and reschedule? I don't think they're going to come in tonight and I'm sure you'd feel better if they were already on the calendar for another time."

"Closing early?"

"No one is out right now. They're all home, glued to the news. We could keep the place open until dawn and we wouldn't see anyone. We'll call it a day and start fresh tomorrow. I have a feeling people are going to be looking for a little extra protection after this."

"Is there anything we can do for them?" Trixie asked. She stood behind the case opposite me and stroked Sofie's fur.

I stared down at the case, my eyes drifting over the random books filled with old pictures of tattoos as a sense of helplessness settled into my bones. "No, not really. We have to keep people calm and help them where we can." There was no good defense a tattoo artist could offer against the Towers. But then, neither could the president and he had the various armies and warheads at his disposal.

Pushing that dark thought aside, I looked up at the troll again. "Bronx, would you stay with Trixie tonight?"

Both looked surprised by my question. "Are you expecting trouble?"

I paused before I answered, weighing my fears. "No, just being cautious. I can't be there tonight and I might get some sleep if I know you're there."

"Where are you going to be?" Trixie demanded.

"At my apartment, waiting for some answers. My contacts are unlikely to talk to me if anyone else is around." Both of my friends frowned at my comment and I couldn't blame them. It certainly didn't sound safe. "Don't worry. I'll have Sofie with me."

The cat made a sound of disgust as she rose so that she was sitting on her hind legs. "So it's like that, is it?"

"Sorry, Sof. You know I'd go myself if I could."

The cat muttered something under her breath in what sounded like Russian. She hopped down off the case and walked over to the front door, which opened for her as if manned by some ghostly doorman who waited on her pleasure. A faint smile touched my mouth as I watched her go, the door shutting behind her. She had been expecting my request, but then I had a feeling that she was also anxious to get the inside dirt on why Indianapolis had been unexpectedly leveled. This was the first big strike that the Towers had made in years and the first that Sofie had not been privy to before the event. Curiosity had to be eating away at her.

Of course, I was itching to put my hands around Reave's neck and keep squeezing until his eyes popped from his skull, but I couldn't overreact yet. There was a slim chance that the destruction of Indianapolis had nothing to do with him gaining the locations of the Towers. But I wasn't counting on it.

"Where's Sofie going? Will she be safe?" Trixie asked.

"She's off to make contact for me. She'll be safe. It's me the Towers hate, not her."

"I'll get on those calls so we can get going, Trix," Bronx said, breaking the lingering tension. Trixie didn't argue, as I doubted she wanted to be alone. I wished it could be me in her apartment all night, keeping her safe, but it was more important that I understood what was happening in the Towers. The elf absently patted Bronx's arm before she turned and walked into the tattooing room, where I could hear her settling into one of the chairs.

"Thanks for this," I said as I started around the counter. It was no small thing for Bronx to agree to spend the night at Trixie's. It would mean that he would also be stuck there during the day, as he couldn't go out in sunlight without risking being turned to stone. And unlike gargoyles, this was a permanent state for trolls. If anything happened to Trixie's apartment building during the day, such as a fire, he was trapped.

I had been to Bronx's house a few times and it was heavily protected so that he would be safe during the daylight hours. The small ranch-style house was plain and austere on the first floor, but the windowless basement level was loaded with large comfortable chairs, an entertainment center, several bookcases filled with books, a sweet gaming system, and a fully stocked kitchen.

"No problem. Just try to stay out of trouble and away from Reave," he warned in a low voice.

I flashed him a quick grin. "Got to. Trixie and I have a date tomorrow that I wouldn't miss for anything in the world."

Bronx shook his head as he picked up the cordless phone before walking back into the tattooing room, where he kept his personal schedule.

Shoving my hands in the pockets of my jeans, I wandered over to the large picture window that looked out onto the street. The sidewalk was empty and there wasn't a car in sight. Low Town, like most of the world, had closed up shop. People were clustered in their homes behind closed doors with the blinds tightly drawn against the world. They were sitting around their televisions and scanning the news sites on the Internet, trying to digest this latest development.

Wars happened every once in a while between two countries, but the battle lines were neatly drawn in most cases and the deaths of innocent bystanders were infrequent. The United States had been lucky in that we hadn't seen any battles fought on our own soil in a long time.

But this was different. The Towers had been quiet on a large scale for decades. We had convinced ourselves that if we kept our heads down and ran when they appeared, we'd be safe. We told ourselves that they wouldn't have a reason to attack us. We could live in peace if we ignored them. We were wrong and thousands died because of it.

Tonight was a time of grief and overwhelming fear as people searched for a reason behind this unexpected attack. The long-lived races would be gathered, trying to figure out if this was the start of another Great War and what they should do. They would remember the horrors of the last war, the devastation to their races that were even now struggling to pull away from the brink of extinction.

Tomorrow, grief would be replaced by boiling rage. The creatures with shorter life spans, shorter memories, would shake their fists in the air and call for arms against the Towers, regardless of the fact that they didn't know where to go to strike at their enemy. Regardless of the fact that they didn't have a hope in the world of winning.

I was angry for all the lives that had been senselessly wiped out in a matter of seconds by a handful of witches and warlocks. I was angry for all the years of violence and bloodshed. But more so, I was afraid. I was afraid for the people of this world if we were forced to go to war again. And a bit selfishly, I was afraid for myself.

Despite my petty claims of leaving the Towers and turning my back on that lot, I was still a warlock. If we went to war, I wouldn't side with the Towers, but what could one warlock-in-training do against them? And would the rest of the world even welcome my help if we went to war?

No. This had to be stopped before it came to that. The mess with the Towers had to be sorted out before anyone else had to pay the price.

10

A BAD FEELING followed me back to my apartment that night, making me grateful that I picked up a few items from my secret hoard in the parlor's basement. Along with my wand, I grabbed some colored chalk, a couple crystals, and a handful of various herbs. I didn't know when Sofie was getting to my apartment and I definitely didn't know if or when Gideon was going to show up. In the meantime, I needed to be protected.

It didn't help that the number of people who knew my dirty little secret was growing due to my recent association with Reave. I couldn't trust his flunkies to keep their mouths shut. While the unwashed masses might not know where to find the Towers, my aging apartment building, less than twenty minutes from my tattoo parlor, wasn't difficult to locate.

Before reaching my place, I stopped at a gas station and bought a small bag of sunflower seeds. Breaking open the bag, I scattered the seeds outside my front door. My landlady wasn't going to be pleased if I didn't vacuum up the mess the next morning, but at least I was protected against a bunch of OCD vampires for the night.

My stomach twisted as I discovered that my apartment was empty. There was no note and no text telling me when Robert had left, where he'd gone, or when he'd get back. *Asshole.* How the hell was I supposed to protect him if I couldn't fucking find him? He'd mentioned something about getting clothes from his place, but I'd expected him to have done it in the afternoon. Unfortunately, I couldn't wait. I needed to protect the apartment.

As soon as the dead bolt slid home, I grabbed a piece of chalk out of my pocket and drew a series of symbols on the plain wood door and along the doorjamb. Each symbol briefly flared to life and then faded again as the protective wards were locked into place. When I was finished with the door, I pocketed the chalk and hurried to my bathroom, grabbing a bar of soap. Going through the apartment, I drew symbols with the soap on each window and on the sliding-glass doors that led to the balcony. I hesitated, looking at the balcony. I thought about scratching a few symbols on the concrete floor, but decided against it. If someone went to the trouble of climbing to my balcony, the wards on the sliding-glass door would stop them. This would give me a glimpse of my would-be attacker before I sent the bastard packing.

Dropping the soap and chalk on the coffee table in the center of the living room, I bent and pulled my wand out from where I had shoved it into my sock before collapsing on the sunken sofa. With my wand tightly clenched in my right hand, I lay back and draped my left arm over my eyes while kicking off my sneakers. It was only now that I was alone in the suffocating silence of the apartment that I realized how exhausted I was as well as sore.

Business at the parlor had been steady, but not hectic. While the little adventure at the garden hadn't been particularly clean, it had been successful. At some point tomorrow, I'd have to divvy up the flower and call my buyers, but for now, it was safe in the shop in its little brown paper bag.

It was the chaos that was brewing with Reave and the Towers that felt like a fucking gorilla sitting on my chest. I hadn't talked to my brother since leaving the apartment that afternoon and it hadn't been the happiest of partings. But then anything that had to do with the Towers was a big downer.

I felt bad for my brother. Not only had my being born a warlock fucked up his life, but I knew that when he looked at me, he saw someone damaged, broken beyond repair. Who wanted that in the family? I didn't know what happened to the families of warlocks and witches. Never thought about it. I knew the families were instructed to tell the world that the kids had died, because they never expected to see them again. But what if the world found out they gave birth to a great killer? I can't imagine there are that many support groups out there for them. Were grieving women sneaking off to Mothers of Warlocks/Witches Anonymous?

Sleep settled over me for a short time, so that my mind wasn't churning about in useless circles. My thoughts slipped away and a blissful blankness cradled me, but it didn't last long. At least, it didn't feel like I'd slept long.

An intense buzzing ran over my arms, as if electricity had jumped from the nearest outlet and was trying to burrow into my flesh. My hand reflexively tightened on my wand, but I didn't lower my arm from my eyes as I continued to lie on the sofa. I strained with all my senses, trying to place the feeling that had jolted me awake. Someone was using magic very close to me. I guess that answered the million-dollar question as to who was going to arrive at my apartment first.

There were no sounds beyond my own uneven breathing and the distant hum of the refrigerator. Whoever was using the magic had yet to enter my apartment. I lowered my arm from my eyes and looked around the living room. Only the light in the kitchen was on, spilling through the rest of the apartment. Thick shadows crowded around the living room, but I was alone.

As I sat up, the buzzing feeling that I had felt upon waking returned. A second later, the front door exploded inward as it was blown off its hinges. The warped plank of wood hit the opposite wall and was left partially blocking the hallway to the bedroom and bathroom. A woman with a wand clutched in one hand lunged into the room and screamed, her body instantly wrapped in a white net of energy. She shrieked and writhed where she stood, unable to move her arms so she could use her wand. Her mind was locked in a fog of pain, leaving her powerless to remove the spell that held her.

I couldn't stop the smile that rose to my mouth as I stood. I loved it when those arrogant pricks underestimated me. Gideon didn't, but then Gideon was smart enough to watch me; smart enough to know that if I survived several encounters with my former mentor, then I obviously knew how to weave a spell or two. This bitch assumed that since I left the Towers when I was a teenager, I didn't know shit about protecting myself. She easily blew through the first ward guarding the door, but didn't bother to check for anything else before entering my apartment.

Raising my wand to banish her from my place, I shouted when the sliding doors exploded, covering me in glass. I didn't risk looking around to see who else was knocking on my door. Diving forward past the witch, I rolled until I hit the cracked and stained linoleum of the kitchen. My heart was pounding loud enough in my ears that I could barely hear anything else. There were now two magic users in my apartment. I was in serious shit.

When I had battled to leave the Tower, I had faced only Simon. Of course, Simon was a master warlock of considerable power, so beating the bastard had been no easy task and I had no illusions about the fact that luck had played a large part in my final victory. But now I was faced with two and I was beginning to have some serious doubts about the likelihood of my survival.

With my back pressed against the cabinets, I peered around the edge of the wall to see a warlock with bright blond hair taking a slow step across the balcony toward the glassless doors. Yeah, warding the balcony was starting to look like a good idea. I quickly waved my wand and lifted my empty left hand. The glass shards that littered my living room rose up into the air and turned toward my newest guest like thousands of little daggers. With a whispered command, the shards shot through the opening at the warlock, attacking him again and again. They wouldn't kill him, just buy me some time.

Turning my attention to the witch, I frowned, struggling to think of something that would be effective in getting her out of my hair without killing her. Of course, even if I managed to send her away, there was still a good chance that she would only return at a later date. If the inhabitants of the Towers were anything, they were definitely single-minded. With a grunt, I gave my wand a short wave in the air, wrapping the energy net tighter around her so that it sizzled as it bit into her skin, sending her screams even higher in pitch and volume. A second later, she disappeared from sight and I gave a quick sigh of relief. If the spell I had woven was correct, she was now sinking to the ocean floor near a reef off the North Shore of Oahu.

Could this kill her? Sure. If she was stupid enough to come after me without knowing some basic escape and underwater breathing spells, of course she could die. Was she going to die? Most likely not. Warlocks and witches were harder to kill than that. The only plus in all this was that if she did die, I wasn't going to get dinged again. If she died, it would be because she drowned, not because of magic. It might seem coldhearted, but the witch bitch had been here to kill me first and I wasn't about to owe Lilith a second year.

The air crackled again with pent-up energy. I jerked my head back, pressing against the cabinets as a bolt of magic shot through the entrance into the kitchen and slammed into the wall, leaving behind a black scorch mark. Apparently the warlock had gotten free of my little glass entanglement.

"What the fuck do you want?" I shouted from the kitchen. I stayed back, unwilling to stick my head out and give the asshole a target. I could hear the muffled crunch of glass underfoot as he stepped onto the living room carpet.

"Your head for treason," snarled the warlock.

Before I could stop myself, I leaned around the doorway so I could look at him. "What?"

He didn't speak but snapped his wand in my direction, sending yet another blast of green energy in my direction. I raised my left hand before my face, calling up the appropriate countercurse to shield myself. A grunt escaped me when the energy pummeled my shield, knocking me back. Cracking sounds filled the air, sending my heart pumping in fear. The energy stopped for a second only to be followed by another blast. My defensive shield splintered and I was thrown to the back of the narrow kitchen.

Pain exploded down my spine and radiated through my ribs as I slid down the wall and fell on my ass. Fuck. This bastard was strong. He would have given Simon a run for his money. Were the witch and warlock the next in line for the open seat on the council and they thought killing me would give them a leg up?

Breathing in short, ragged gasps, I couldn't get a lungful of air. I was also having trouble clenching my wand in my hand as my fingers had started to tingle.

With a wave of my left hand, all the drawers in the kitchen slid open. A second later, the utensils hovered in the air, and more knives jumped from the butcher block on the counter. I smiled. This would keep the bastard busy for a bit. With a nod, all the objects hovering in the air flew through the doorway into the living room, seeking out the only other living creature in the apartment.

I pushed to my feet with a groan and grabbed the handled knife sharpener out of the butcher block. It was little more than a dull silver rod about the diameter of a Magic Marker that came to a sharp point. I could barely grasp my wand in my right hand, but this weapon was held firmly in my left hand.

Charging from the kitchen, I dodged a wicked steak knife that was slashing at the warlock and used my wand to knock aside his wand as he attempted to focus on me while ducking the downward blow of a stainless-steel ladle. I plunged the knife sharpener into his chest just below his heart. He stiffened, his eyes going wide with pain and surprise. At the same time several knives hit home, burying themselves in his arms, legs, and stomach. As he crumpled to the ground, I waved off the spell that was controlling the silverware, allowing the utensils to fall harmlessly to the ground.

The warlock gasped, blood gurgling up his throat and spilling out the side of his mouth. On shaky legs, I kicked his wand away from his reach. I hadn't killed him, but he was dying. He could heal himself without the wand, but he could use the wand to kill me. My stomach clenched to look at him. I needed to finish him off, put him out of his misery. Right now he was in so much pain that he couldn't concentrate enough to use magic to heal himself or even take himself back to the Towers. I could pull the silver rod out of his chest, heal him, save him. But wouldn't he come after me again?

"What the hell?" thundered a deep voice.

Spinning toward the front door, I raised my wand but stopped myself before I let loose the bolt of energy I had summoned. Gideon stood in the open doorway, his hair mussed and shirtsleeves rolled up to his elbows. It was the most unkempt I had ever seen him. Yet it was the sight of Sofie bloody and limp in his hands that nearly stopped my heart.

"Sofie! What happened?" I cried, lowering my wand.

Gideon walked into the living room, his sharp gaze taking in and assessing the damage. "I found her on the landing of the stairs as I came up. She must have been caught on her way back." The warlock's frown deepened as he looked down at the mortally wounded warlock. "Why isn't he dead yet?"

"I hadn't . . . decided . . ."

"Damn it, Gage! You have to kill them!" he shouted, losing his temper. With a growl, he shoved Sofie at me. "Heal her. I will take care of him."

I didn't question it. As I was kneeling down to gently lay Sofie on the floor, I saw Gideon pick up a long boning knife from the carpet. He knelt beside the warlock and stabbed him straight through the heart, ending his pain and the threat he presented.

"Holy shit!" Robert cried from the open doorway, popping my head up again. My older brother stood white-faced and frozen on the threshold, a pizza box in one hand and a six-pack of beer in the other. This was not the side of my life my brother needed to see—a warlock kneeling over a dead body, me kneeling over a nearly dead cat, and my apartment trashed from a magic fight. *Perfect!*

Gideon raised his wand, his body twisted toward my brother as he prepared to sling whatever attack that had come to mind.

"No! Don't! He's with me!" I screamed while throwing a protective shield in front my Robert with my free hand.

The warlock's wand halted, but I could see the thick muscles in his forearm tensed and ready to strike.

"Please, he's my brother," I said.

Gideon's gray eyes jumped to my face, filled with shock. He knew I wasn't in contact with my family. It wasn't safe, as evidenced by my thoroughly trashed apartment.

"Please," I repeated, a little firmer and a little calmer.

With a frown, Gideon lowered his wand and looked back at my brother, waiting. I dropped my shield and waved my brother into my apartment. Damn, I needed to get that front door back in place before a neighbor wandered by.

"What can I do to help?" Robert asked, his voice a little wobbly as he gave Gideon a wide berth as he approached me.

"Nothing."

"Gage, it looks like you're in pretty deep shit here. I can help."

I smiled at Robert, touched more than I wanted to admit that my brother, who was obviously scared shitless, was ready to wade in and watch his little brother's back. A part of me wished I could let him help, but this was a mess best handled with magic. Lots of magic. "Just go hang out in my bedroom while we clean this up. And save me a couple beers."

Robert frowned as he looked at Gideon and then nodded. "Got it." He stared down at me for a few seconds and I don't know what was passing through his mind, but it didn't seem to be abject horror, which was surprising. "You need anything, you shout. Anything at all." And then he shimmied past the broken door into the hall to my bedroom. Under his breath, I could hear him muttering that he should have bought a fucking case of beer.

Turning my full attention on Sofie, I found that her lovely bluish-gray fur was now dark and matted with her blood. There was a large wound in her abdomen and her breathing was shallow. She was fading fast. With a deep breath, I drew in as much energy as I could hold. As I exhaled, I sent that energy streaking through her body. It was a similar spell to what I had used on Bronx nights ago, but stronger. I was afraid of her dying before I could heal her. This spell tied her soul to the energy in her body. As long as I maintained the spell, her soul was trapped.

Despite the smallness of her frame in comparison to Bronx, it still took several minutes for the worst of her wounds to heal. I was vaguely aware of Gideon using magic around me. I could hear the tinkle of broken glass and the clink of silverware while a heavy breeze swept by me as the door flew to its place at the front of the apartment and the lights clicked on. I kept my eyes closed, straining to keep as much of my focus on Sofie as I could.

When the beat of her heart was strong beneath my fingers and her breathing was even, I started to unravel the healing spell, pulling the energy out of her body. Sofie shifted and I thought I could feel her purring. I opened my eyes and took a deep breath, relief making my hands shake as I pulled them away from her. Sofie was an annoying, meddlesome old witch, but she was *my* annoying, meddlesome old witch and I'd be damned if I was going to let some fucking witch or warlock kill her because I had been stupid enough to send her into danger.

I sat on the carpet, leaning against the nearest wall, and dropped my head until my chin nearly hit my chest. Both Sofie and I had nearly been killed by a witch and a warlock. I was exhausted down to my soul and my body hurt in more places than I wanted to think about. I didn't want to move, didn't want to breathe, didn't want to think, but I still had to do all of the above because Gideon was here and was going to want some answers. He also had some answers that I desperately needed.

Something nudged my elbow. I looked down, lifting my hand. Sofie crawled into my lap and curled up. She didn't speak, only purred as she snuggled close. I gently ran my fingers over her wet, sticky fur, soothing away the last of the trembling and terror that had gripped us both. I had almost lost her. A lump grew in my throat and my chest ached with a pain that had nothing to do with physical injuries. The Towers were picking apart my life no matter how hard I tried to escape. I'd left my family to keep them safe from the Towers and now the bastards were trying to claim the lives of my friends. There had to be another way.

"You're better than I am at that particular healing spell," Gideon said. "I think I would have been able to save her, but she wouldn't be as strong as she is now."

I wanted to smile, but I was too tired. As I looked up at him, I found that my apartment was back to its prebattle state with both doors fixed. The dead warlock was gone along with the bloodstain in the carpet. All that was left were a few stray pieces of chalk and my own bloodstained hands.

"Good to know I've got at least one skill," I said, scratching Sofie on the top of the head and behind her ears.

"If you're fishing for more compliments, I'd stop."

"Wouldn't dream of it. Why don't you tell me what the fuck is going on? And by that question, I mean for you to start with Indianapolis, cover Sofie's injuries, and finish with the two fucknuts who popped by to rearrange my apartment."

"I'll start with the easiest and the rest should fall into place," Gideon said on a sigh as he sat heavily on my couch. He looked as exhausted and as rough as I felt, but without the bruised and cracked ribs. "I didn't get to talk to Sofie, but I did see her briefly in Dresden. I assumed that you sent her in hopes of drawing me back to Low Town."

I stared down at Sofie in my lap. "You went all the way to the Tower?"

Sofie gave a wide yawn. "You aren't the only one who wants answers. And it was the only place I was guaranteed to get them."

I suppressed a shudder at the thought. She had walked into the lion's den. The European Ivory Tower wasn't in Dresden, Germany, but more to the north of the city in some forestland called Der Loben near a series of lakes. Everyone referred to it as Dresden because that was the closest big city. And for roughly nine years, the Dresden Tower had been my home.

"As I was saying," Gideon continued a bit irritably. "When the meeting broke up, I had already lost sight of Sofie, but I gather someone else was following her. They took care of her once they were sure they had your location."

Sofie rubbed her head against my hand. "Sorry, Gage. I didn't mean to lead anyone back to you."

"As long as they didn't tell anyone else where they had found me, it doesn't matter. Any idea who they were?"

Resting his right elbow on his knee, Gideon leaned his forehead against his right hand, scratching his scalp in thought. "The warlock on your floor was Neil Wilson. If there was a witch with him, it was most likely his apprentice. I think her name is Leanne, or maybe Lenore. He usually called her Useless Clod. Did you at least finish her?"

I looked away from the warlock, unable to meet his gaze. "Don't know. Sent her fishing off the North Shore. She might have escaped." Gideon remained silent so long that I had to look back. He frowned at me and I could feel his disappointment. For the first time, my claim that I wasn't a killer like him sounded weak and pathetic. An excuse rather than a principle.

"I get that they were here to kill me," I said, breaking the silence. "But do they have a new reason to be here?"

"For both our sakes, I fucking hope not," the warlock snapped, surprising me with his choice of language. He flopped back against the couch and dropped one foot on the top of my coffee table.

"You want a drink? My brother's got some beers," I said with a smirk.

Gideon hated me most days and the feeling was more than mutual. He was a pompous, arrogant, controlling asshole who liked to make my life hell, but I had to stop there because I also knew that he had done a lot to protect my life. Regardless, he had never looked quite so human as he did slouched on my couch with hair standing on end and shirt wrinkled. If his state didn't scare the shit out of me, I would have laughed.

"God, that would be nice." He sighed and shook his head. "No, Ellen will worry."

"You go home every night?"

"I try, but it's not always possible. After Indianapolis, I have to."

Yeah, the whole world was in a state of shock and terror. His wife would definitely need a little reassurance tonight from her warlock husband. While the news reports were offering little information beyond horror, a warlock could provide a better view of why the world was close to burning.

"Speaking of which, what happened with Indianapolis? Is the renewed attack on me tied to it?"

"Yes."

My head dropped back against the wall and I closed my eyes. Fear coiled in my stomach and that drink was starting to sound better by the second.

"Things have been bad in the Towers for a couple of years now. Between Peter's death, Simon's death, and the runaways, everyone has been on edge. It all exploded this afternoon when rumors hit New York that someone managed to get exact Tower locations."

My heart stopped and my breath froze in my chest. I could even feel Sofie stiffen in my lap at this news. Apparently she hadn't heard this bit yet despite her quick trip to Germany. The world was teetering on the brink of destruction and I now had a hand in it. To make matters worse, a key figure in this growing debacle was sitting in the next room eating pizza and drinking beer. May whatever forces there were in the cosmos please take pity on me and let my brother stay in my bedroom with his mouth shut.

"All locations?" I asked, struggling to keep my tone steady.

"We don't know. I'm not even sure how true the rumor is, but it doesn't seem like most are concerned about the truth of it any longer. What I've heard is that two to three locations have been discovered. The ones that keep coming up are New York, Dresden, and Canberra."

"Where'd the information come from?"

"We are aware of several small resistance groups that have been working on trying to find the locations for the past few decades. It's been largely humans with a few ogres, trolls, and others thrown into the mix. No one strong in magic, particularly glamour, so we've left them alone. The guardians gleaned word a few months ago that they made a new contact and were excited. We watched but this person was very smooth. We never saw him or her, but when a couple representatives struck the enclave they were watching, nearly all were found dead."

"Their contact killed them?"

Gideon nodded. "One person was found clinging to life. He was squeezed, but we got only one last fleeting thought. Elf."

"Fuck," I whispered. This was a disaster.

"Yes, the one race that we've feared from the beginning. Those bastards know more about glamour than anyone else. We always worried they would crack the protective spells. The Towers hoped that the elves had been broken, that they wouldn't try to fight back, but apparently not."

"Stop. You don't know this is the elves. It could be one rogue elf acting alone. You also don't know if this is the elves or the Svartálfar. There is a difference."

Gideon arched one eyebrow at me. "Afraid for your girlfriend?"

"Don't push me, warlock," I said in a low growl.

Gideon's expression hardened, but he let the comment pass. Picking a fight now wasn't going to help anyone. "The guardians searched their headquarters and found stacks of maps. Only the ones for upstate New York and Germany held markings, but another for Australia had been pulled aside."

"I'm guessing their headquarters was in Indianapolis," I said mostly to myself.

"No, that was in Oklahoma City. Their contact had nearly cleaned them out, so the Towers didn't feel the need to raze the city. Unfortunately, the witch and the warlocks caught the scent of one other person who had escaped. He slipped into Indianapolis. They were afraid he would have a chance to talk to someone if they waited to ferret him out, so they leveled the city."

"They killed thousands to silence one person?"

"They were protecting our secret," Gideon said evenly.

"No!" I roughly lifted Sofie off my lap and placed her on the floor so I could push to my feet. I couldn't sit still any longer. The worst of the pains in my body had subsided, but there was a growing pain in my head as if it was going to split in two in anger and frustration.

"Don't tell me you side with them. That you agree with what they did."

"Of course not! And neither does the council." Gideon sat up, sliding to the edge of the sofa cushion.

His comment stopped me short, snapping my gaze back to his haggard face. "They were executed?"

He snorted. "Barely even a slap on the wrist. The council members, for the most part, cursed and shouted, but in the end, the attackers walked out of the hall with a pat on the back for doing what they had to in order to protect the Towers."

I shoved my hands through my hair, clenching my fingers around the short strands. Muscles clenched and unclenched throughout my body as I struggled to keep my temper under control. The Ivory Towers were locked into the same mentality that had persisted for centuries. They had to be the top dog. They slaughtered countless innocents to maintain that position. There was no talking. No negotiating. No looking for other options. For them, the best defense was a crushing offense.

"We're trapped, aren't we?" I asked, unable to raise my voice over a whisper. I turned back to Gideon, who had dropped his head into his hands. "The Towers, the witches and the warlocks, they've been like this for so long that they can't back down even if they wanted to. They're so locked into this sense of entitlement that they can't walk down the street like normal beings. Can't stand in line at the grocery."

"All were taken before the age of twelve and most by seven. I doubt there's one who remembers what it was like to be human, let alone wait in line."

"So I'm right. There's no escape. They're everywhere, suffocating the world with their hate until we all roll over and die."

Gideon lifted his head to look at me. "We're trying. We've found a few places around the world where the watchful eye of the Towers is . . . somewhat blind. It's a place where we can live in relative peace with others."

"It's a pretty idea, Gideon, but what about the rest of the world?"

"You want to save the world now?"

"Fuck!" I shouted. Balling up my fist, I slammed it into the wall, denting the drywall enough to create a small hole. "No! I don't want to save the world, but I don't want to watch it burn either. I don't want to see that look of terror in Trixie's eyes because she's afraid that the Towers are going to hit her town or attack her people again on a goddamn whim."

"I want a better life for our loved ones as well, but railing at the fates and punching holes in the wall aren't going to fix anything." Gideon's voice was calm, but there was a light in his eyes. I think he wanted to punch a wall or two as well, but he was holding himself in check. He was right. My temper tantrum was helping no one, but damn it, venting at least kept me from using magic to blow holes in things.

"Then where does that leave us? What do we do?" I snapped, struggling to rein in my anger.

"Survive," Sofie said.

I had honestly forgotten that she was even in the room. Had I said anything that I shouldn't have? I froze, my mind scrambling to replay my tirade. I trusted Sofie with my life. She was my friend, but I wasn't willing to trust her with the lives of Gideon's family. That was his choice.

The large cat made a sound of disgust in the back of her throat before she jumped up on the coffee table in front of Gideon. "You two think you're so smart and sneaky, but you're both babies," she said. "The softer edge movement started well before Gideon arrived in the Towers. I wasn't a part of it, but I kept an eye on it."

"Why? To crush it?" Gideon demanded, sitting up straight. His voice hardened. I had a feeling that if Sofie gave the wrong answer, he wouldn't hesitate to skin the cat right there. And of course, Sofie wasn't the type to back down from anything.

She laughed at Gideon. "No. I guess I was curious. At my age, I don't get curious about the actions of people much. I feel like I've seen it all. I might not have been at Gage's trial, but when I heard that Peter had assigned you to watch over him, I knew that you had found your way into the movement. I always knew your visits were a way of safely transmitting information to Gage. I might be stuck as a cat and out of the Towers, but I'm no fool."

The warlock frowned at the mention of Peter's name. I hadn't known him personally, and I had only seen him the one time when I stood before the council for my trial. He had been the one to cast the deciding vote to let me live. He had been the one to advise me to hide. Apparently, he had also been a part of the movement among the witches and the warlocks who wanted to live in peace with the rest of the world. It had been his recent death that created the opening on the council.

"I'm sorry if you feel that you were used," Gideon said stiffly. "We were never sure where your interests lie. I mentioned to Gage that you were in the area, and was pleased when he gravitated toward you on occasion as it gave me a chance to keep him abreast of changes."

Sofie gave a shrug of her small shoulders. "I didn't mind. I appreciated the visits from both of you and the information. I doubt that I'd agree with everything that your group believes, but I do agree with Gage's sentiment. Things need to change. I watched the Great War and the growing pile of dead bodies. I haven't the stomach to do it again." She looked up at me. Her expression was unreadable as a cat's, but I had a feeling that she was sad. "But for anything to change, the first thing you have to do is survive."

I waved one hand at her and paced a small distance away. I was getting tired of this you-have-to-stay-alive mentality. I had to do more, but I didn't know what. As it was, I had to find a way to help Trixie settle things with the Summer Court, get Bronx free of Reave, and extricate Robert from the mess he was tangled in before the damn dark elf got us all killed. There was no time to lead a fucking revolution against the Towers . . . and maybe that was the point.

"Fine. I stay alive," I said under my breath. "I've got enough to keep me busy for now. I'll leave the rest of the world to you."

"Staying alive is going to be harder than you might think," Gideon warned, drawing my gaze back to him. He drew in a heavy breath and stared at the table in front of him.

"What? You've been removed as my guardian? A new warden has been assigned?"

"Not yet. During the last meeting, your name came up a few times. There are some who are afraid that you could prove to be a source of information since you've defected."

I threw my hands up in disbelief. "They're thinking of this now? I've been out for roughly ten years."

"Some have voiced it before but I think they had trouble accepting the idea that you'd be disloyal to your own people. I guess some believed that you only wanted to get away from Simon, not the Towers. They thought you were still one of us."

A horrible sinking feeling filled my body so that it was like my heart was pumping sludge through my veins. "Someone thinks I have something to do with the information leak?"

"No, not this one. The spotlight is firmly on the elves. But I think they are now realizing that you're a risk. You and the other runaways."

"That was the reason for the hit squad on my doorstep?" I shook my head and then paced back to where he sat. "Someone found out that I was in contact with Sofie. I'm sure she never particularly hid where she was, so when she was located, they followed in hopes of locating me."

"Gage—" Sofie started, but I held up my hand.

"Don't, Sof. You didn't know and it doesn't matter. If they want to find me, they will. I'm sorry that you got hurt in the process."

"Speaking of that, unless Gideon has something else to reveal,

I'm going to jump into your shower. I never was a fan of the taste of my own blood."

I kept my mouth shut on that one. It sounded too much like she might not mind the taste of someone else's blood. Sofie might be a nice witch, but she was still a witch and that left the door open for all kinds of weird shit.

"Nothing much else." Gideon sighed as he relaxed slightly on the sofa. "They're searching for a sign of the elf that helped this resistance group. Their search is staying close to Oklahoma City, but it's branching out. No other cities are on the chopping block, but that could change in an instant. For now, they've decided to take out the Internet."

"For Oklahoma?"

"For the world."

"What?" I cried. "That's going to—"

"People will survive," Gideon said a bit irritably. "They lived centuries without it. They can go a little while without checking e-mail. We can't track digital transmissions with magic as easily as we can trace paper and analog trails. Taking down the Internet won't cover everything, but it gives us a hand in tracking down this bastard."

"Good luck with that," Sofie said before jumping down from the table and walking through the hall to my bathroom. She sounded less than confident about the Towers' chances of success. I wasn't feeling so good about them myself. Losing Internet was going to create a lot of angry and scared people.

"Are the Towers going to at least tell the world why they're doing this?"

Gideon shook his head. "Not yet. They seem to think that it will give them an edge. If people realize that someone knows the location of one or more Towers, they may decide to help him rather than help us."

"You think whoever has this information doesn't know you're

looking for him? The whole Indianapolis thing is a pretty good indication, you know."

"I'm not saying I agree with it. It's how they're handling it."

I bit my tongue, keeping my grumbling to myself as I walked around the table so I could flop on the couch next to Gideon. Leaning back, I stared up at the hole in the ceiling I had yet to repair. During the summer, I had hanged myself to gain access to the underworld. It had all worked out, sort of, but Trixie didn't appreciate the constant reminder that she had been the one to find my dead body.

We sat in silence for several minutes, listening to the water falling in the bathroom. Sofie had managed to get the shower going, which wasn't a surprise since she had managed to get to and from Germany with no problem. Good thing, too, since I had absolutely no desire to give a witch-turned-cat a bath.

There was also a low murmur of noise coming from the bedroom. Robert was watching something on my laptop. The Internet wasn't down yet.

When Gideon spoke again, there was a wariness in his voice to match his obvious fatigue. "Gage, I'm not going to ask if you know anything about who has the locations. Well, I'm not going to ask you yet." I tensed next to him, but said nothing. "I don't want to risk having you lie to me. Just think about it. You know I'm not one of them, but I think we both agree that the best way to protect this world is to keep that information out of the hands of the other races."

"I know," I said, closing my eyes. The knowledge hurt. I felt like a traitor to Trixie, Bronx, my family, and everyone who had suffered under the control of the Towers. I could rant and rave all I wanted about how the world had to escape the tight grasp of the Towers, but when the opportunity came, I turned my back on the world in the name of protecting it.

"Then I'm sure that you also know that if the shit hits the fan, I'm going to protect my family first. I'll try to get word to you, but Ellen and my daughter have to come first."

"I would expect nothing less." I opened my eyes and looked over at him. "You have to protect what's important to you."

"It's interesting that you say that since you're struggling with the idea yourself."

I sat up, staring over at the warlock who had hounded me for nearly ten years. There were moments when I felt like I knew him, and then there were others when I was sure I was looking at a total stranger. His expression was closed, but I could feel a warning in his words.

"What are you talking about?"

"If Neil had escaped and found out about Trixie or Bronx or your brother, there is no doubt that he would be striking at them next in an effort to get at you. That could still happen if his apprentice survived."

Frowning, I fell back against the sofa and glared out the repaired sliding-glass door. The sky was black and I had no idea what time it was. It felt like I should be seeing the sun rise, so much had happened.

"I'm not a killer. It's why I left the Towers. I'm not like them," I said, even as Bryce's battered face surfaced before my mind's eye. I was starting to sound like a broken record. On and on again, I was telling everyone around me, even myself, that I wasn't a killer. I wanted to think that maybe I wasn't very convincing, but I was beginning to wonder if maybe they all knew something that I didn't.

"No, you're not like them, but I'm not talking about being a heartless killer like Simon." Gideon paused and I looked back at him. "I'm talking about protecting the people that matter to you. The warlocks and the witches coming after you can't be reasoned with. They can't be convinced that they are in the wrong. If you let them live, they will keep coming after you and along the way they are going to kill that elf of yours, Bronx, Sofie, and your family."

I pushed to my feet and walked around the table to put some space between us. Out of the corner of my eye, I saw Gideon rise as well. "You don't understand."

"You're the one who doesn't understand," Gideon snapped. He grabbed my shoulder and spun me around so that I was forced to look at him. He leaned close, his sharp features becoming harsh in his anger as he slipped back into his role as my main tormentor. "It's time to stop clinging to these childish notions that you're above them, that you're better than them because you won't stoop to kill another person. You can't afford that luxury any longer."

"Easy for you. You—"

"It's not easy for me!" Gideon cut me off, giving me a hard shove, so that I was pressed against the wall. "When I am faced with someone, I ask one thing: is this person a threat to my family? If the answer is no, then they walk away. If it's yes, then I finish it quickly. And a threat to me is a threat to my family because it means I won't be around to keep them safe. It's time for you to get off your high horse and take a hard look at what's really important to you. This pretty idea you're clutching or that woman on your arm, because in this world, you can't have both."

Gideon turned away from me and started to walk back toward the couch, running one hand through his dark hair to push it away from his face. His shoulders slumped under his fatigue and probably from the weight of the life he was trying to lead.

"I'm done cleaning up for you," he said in a low voice. "Next time you handle it."

"Got it."

Gideon's head snapped up and he looked over his shoulder at me. I thought I could see regret in his eyes for a second, but it was gone before I could be sure. He made it sound like he killed with such cold, heartless ease, but it took its toll on him all the same. There was something about the hardness in his eyes, the stiffness in his shoulders, that made me think this life wore on him. I don't think he wanted me to have to live with the toll as well, but as he said, we didn't have that luxury in this world.

"I've got to go. I need to check on Ellen and Bridgette."

"I'm sure they're anxious to see you."

He nodded and started for the door.

"Did you talk to Sofie?" I said as he reached for the doorknob.

Gideon half turned back toward me. "No."

"She wouldn't tell me any details, but she said that Victoria Tremaine cursed her."

The warlock frowned, staring blindly at the floor as if lost in thought. "It's good to know. There's too much going on right now to worry about it, though, and Victoria's tricky enough that I'll need to be focused on the problem when I attack it."

"Good luck."

Gideon shook his head, a little half smile on his face. "Yeah. Don't forget to handle your brother."

I frowned at the weary warlock. He was talking about wiping Robert's memory of what he saw. "There isn't enough bleach in the world to scrub his mind clean."

Gideon gave me a little smirk I had never seen on his face before. "Run in the family?"

I rolled my eyes at him, fighting the urge to flip him the bird. We were having a good laugh. I didn't want to piss Gideon off, which would only push him into taking care of Robert himself.

"At least bury the memory a little. We don't need him accidentally mentioning the dead warlock on your floor to someone."

"Got it," I said on a sigh. I watched as Gideon started for the door again, a little amazed that I found myself in this moment with the man I had been sure was my greatest living enemy. "How old are you?"

He was stunned by the question, enough that he turned the rest of the way around to look at me. "I'm thirty-one."

Only five years older than me. "You seem . . . older."

Gideon nodded, not showing any surprise at my comment. "It might not show in our appearance, but this life ages you." He turned back toward the door and left without another word.

I leaned my head against the wall and tried to breathe. This life torn apart by the Towers was aging us all ahead of our time, and it was a crime. But whining about our fate wasn't going to change a fucking thing and neither was my reluctance to accept what was in front of me. It was time to grow up. If not for myself, then I had to do it for those who were depending on me.

11

WHY COULDN'T IT have been an overcast day? Sleep had not been an easy thing to find last night after Gideon left and Sofie was settled from her shower. After a couple slices of lukewarm pizza, a beer, and a quick memory spell on Robert, I had lain in bed staring up at the ceiling, my mind replaying the events of the day until I wanted to scream. The sun was peeking over the horizon when I drifted off and then it was only a short time later when Trixie called with plans to pick me up.

A cold shower got me moving, but I was still waiting for the coffee that I had been sucking on since I fell into her car to get my brain moving. Dressed in jeans and a mostly clean T-shirt, I knew I was underdressed to meet with the queen of the Summer Court, but I couldn't summon up the energy to care. The dark sunglasses weren't keeping out nearly enough of the bright, early-afternoon glare, and the world had this cheerful feel that seemed horribly wrong considering that the Towers had an itchy trigger finger and were gunning to take out more people.

It was a struggle to push my grumpy attitude aside. Trixie was strained with worry and fear. I was beginning to think that even in my sleep-deprived state, it would have been a better idea for me to drive. She was hitting the brakes at the last possible second, as if her mind wasn't fully aware that her body was driving.

"Did you have any problems last night?" I asked, causing Trixie to jump. We had been quiet since I'd slunk into the passenger seat, not even daring to turn on the radio.

"Nothing other than Bronx's snoring rattling the windows this morning," she complained, but there was no venom behind the comment. "We stayed up watching old *M*A*S*H* and *Great American Hero* reruns. I left him curled up in the shower with a pile of blankets."

I smiled at the image. It had to be a tight fit and couldn't be particularly comfortable, but the bathroom was the safest room in Trixie's apartment since it had no windows. I'm sure Bronx was fine though. The troll slept like the dead and probably wouldn't stir until sunset.

"After this meeting, we'll grab some food to drop off to him before heading into the shop."

"You think we're going to have any customers today?"

I sighed, placing my travel mug in the cup holder. "I have no idea, but we'll probably get busy soon."

Trixie paused, her eyes on the road in front of her as she exited the highway onto the off-ramp. "Did you have any problems last night?"

"A couple," I admitted, praying that she didn't press me for details. She already had enough on her plate.

"Did you talk to Sofie?"

"Some. She had a small problem herself, but she's fine now. Last I saw, she was sprawled across my bed like she belonged there. I swear, I think she's happier as a cat."

"Doubtful." She eased to a stop at a red light, her driving smoothing out as she neared our destination.

"What's not to love? She sleeps most of the day, has food brought to her, and everyone that sees her rubs her head. Hell, being turned into a cat is starting to sound pretty good."

Trixie narrowed her eyes at me, but I could see her fighting to hold back her smile. "If it happens, I'll be sure to have you fixed immediately."

"That's cold, woman! You should never talk about cutting off a man's balls."

The smile she had been fighting slipped forth as she pressed the gas, sending the car across the intersection. "I think it might be a good idea for the king and I'm sure the queen would agree with me."

I leaned forward and grabbed my mug. I drained the last of my coffee, grateful that the wheels were starting to turn a little. "I think I've got some pruning shears somewhere at the shop. Just a quick snip."

"For you or him?"

"Him," I growled, earning me a low chuckle that sent a ripple through my stomach. If we survived all this with the elves, Reave, and the Towers, I swear I was going to lock this woman in some secluded spot with me for a week, and when we were done, we weren't going to be able to walk right for a goddamn month. Trixie had a way about her that wiped every sane thought from my head.

Winding through the park to an empty row of parking spots, Trixie settled her little green hybrid between a silver minivan and a black sedan baking in the sun. She turned off the engine and dropped her hands into her lap as she stared straight ahead. I reached over and twined my fingers through hers on her right hand, drawing her gaze up to me.

"We're just meeting to talk," I said calmly, as I placed my sunglasses on the dashboard. "Get a little information. I'll be there the whole time and I'm leaving this park with you beside me."

She nodded, forcing a smile onto her lips. I took in her brown hair, brown eyes, and lovely heart-shaped face. She was putting on the glamour spell out of habit, whether she needed it or not. The human version of her was beautiful, but it rankled me at the same time. It wasn't Trixie. It wasn't the green-eyed vixen that I loved. "I think it's safe to lose the spell. I'm sure the queen would appreciate it."

Her smile wavered a bit, but with a blink of her eyes, the spell faded away to be replaced by a vision of blond hair and green eyes.

"We should get going. I'd rather not be late," she murmured as she leaned in and pressed a kiss against my cheek. I released her hand as we got out of the car, but grabbed it again when we started toward the park and the man-made lake with the geyser-like fountain in the center. The area surrounding Mirror Lake was open with neatly trimmed green grass and a scattering of flower beds showing off the last of their summer blooms. There were a few people jogging around the lake and a few others walking their dogs, but otherwise the park was quiet in the warm afternoon sun.

"The gazebo," Trixie said with a jerk of her head toward the far end of the park.

I squinted against the sun glinting off the water as we turned toward the gazebo. "It's been a while since I was here. I don't remember that." The small open building was painted white with a blue roof and was surrounded by a profusion of flowers. Within the shadows of the gazebo, I could see a few figures, but I couldn't tell how many.

"I wouldn't be surprised if she had it built for today's meeting. She is the queen after all."

"True." I gave her hand a little squeeze. "How many are here?"

"Other than the queen, twenty-three. All guards."

"I don't think she could fit twenty-three guards in that little gazebo with her," I said with a grin.

"There are three guards in the gazebo with her. The rest are spread around the park, hiding just past the tree line."

I suppressed a shiver, clenching my teeth. I couldn't see them and I wasn't even sure that I would be able to pick them out using magic. Elves were one of the few races that I hadn't had a lot of experience with. After the Great War, they kept a distance from the rest of the world, particularly warlocks and witches. I couldn't help but wonder if I had found yet another way to get in over my head.

Trixie's pace slowed as we reached the small stepping-stones leading up to the gazebo. She tightened her grip on my hand, her touch growing cold. The guard at the entrance to the gazebo glowered at us, his hand resting heavily on the short sword that hung at his hip, before he stepped aside. Gazing in, I found two more guards standing on either side of a lovely woman seated on a cushioned bench near the back of the structure. She was partially hidden in shadows thrown down by a nearby bank of trees.

As Trixie lifted her foot to the first of two steps leading up to the gazebo, I placed my free hand against her stomach, halting her. "Wait," I said under my breath as I sent a small spell swirling about the gazebo, checking for other spells the elves might have used while unraveling any glamour cast on the area. To my surprise, there was none.

"You don't trust us?" asked a melodious feminine voice.

"It's not that I don't trust you. It's that life has taught me to be cautious, Your Majesty," I said with a bow of my head toward her.

"That is fair," she said in an even voice. "Please, enter so that we may talk."

I dropped my hand from Trixie's stomach and allowed her to enter first. The guard moved back to the entrance behind me as I stepped before the queen. Seated on a bench with white and pale yellow cushions, she appeared to be quite young, with soft blond hair piled high on her head with jeweled clips. She had the same green eyes as Trixie, but the queen's were cold as they looked us over, while Trixie's seemed to twinkle with laughter. Her wispy dress was an ice blue, lending her a cold air. Was she as cold as she seemed?

Had she been like this before her husband had started chasing after Trixie? It would explain a few things.

Trixie deeply curtsied before the queen while I dipped into an awkward bow that caused her to give a little giggle as she picked up a delicate cup and saucer from a little table near her knee. "How refreshing! A warlock paying me court," she said before taking a sip of her tea. "I'd almost be willing to brush this all aside to have you wait on me every day for the rest of your life."

I clamped my mouth shut, tapping down a dozen different comments, ranging from informative to snide. None of them would help and Trixie didn't need more problems heaped onto her.

The queen took another sip of tea before placing the cup and saucer on the table again. She turned her gaze on Trixie, her eyes narrowing as she examined her from head to toe. Trixie had chosen to wear an ankle-length floral skirt and long-sleeved blouse that made her look extremely delicate and feminine. It was the most conservative outfit I had ever seen her in and she looked beautiful. Unfortunately, I didn't know if that would help or hurt her.

"You've gotten lovelier," the queen announced, folding her hands in her lap. "I think I shall take some pleasure in seeing my dear husband's face when I tell him that I not only saw you but that you've gotten even more beautiful since you were last with the court."

"Please, Your Majesty," Trixie said, tightly grasping her hands before her. "You must believe me. I don't want him."

"Oh, I believe you," she said with a cold little smile. "It's the only reason I haven't sent my own guards to kill you. Allowing you to live out of my husband's grasp is a far more exquisite torture for him than him believing you dead."

"Don't you think enough lives have been disrupted and destroyed by this little game?" I demanded before I could stop myself.

The queen looked up at me, her smile growing even frostier. "I bow to your wisdom on that point. Only a warlock would know what is *enough* when it comes to destroying lives."

I inwardly cursed myself, the Towers, and the elves. I should have kept my mouth shut, but it had become apparent that I was going to have to answer for the crimes the Towers had committed on the elves.

As the queen turned her attention back to Trixie, her smile dimmed. "You realize I did not have to agree to this meeting. I could have killed your brother when he requested it. When you arrived, I could have had you killed, and that would have ended my headache after too many long years. I still might."

"Ah . . . but you have agreed to the meeting," said a man as he leisurely strolled past the guards and into the gazebo. "And at such a horribly early time of day." I twisted to watch him walk behind Trixie and me before stopping next to the queen's little bench. His dark blue eyes drifted over me for only a second before settling on Trixie. He gave a small, distracted smile. "Hello, Ro."

"Hello, Lori," Trixie said with a soft catch in her voice. Tears shimmered in her eyes and it looked like she was struggling to stay standing still when she badly wanted to launch herself at the newcomer.

I took another look at him. He didn't look like an elf. While their paleness seemed healthy and glowing, his was powdery. His pale blond hair was fine, almost like feathers on the top of his head. He was also soft and round, where the elves were all slim and elegant. But there was a grace to him, as if he were trapped in perpetual slow motion. He wasn't an elf, but I was willing to bet that he was fey.

Despite the growing heat of the day, he wore brown slacks and a pale yellow shirt under a heavy green corduroy jacket, while a blue-and-black scarf was wrapped loosely around his neck. He was reminded of pictures of bohemian artists lounging along the Seine in Paris or even the descriptions of the old Romantics who were troubled with the same soul-weary ennui as Byron.

"It's good that you could join us," the queen said a bit frostily.

Lori shrugged, unperturbed by her mood. "When I heard that

little Rowena was stopping by, I knew that I had to get a peek at her." He tilted his head to the side a little as he looked at Trixie. "You haven't changed."

"Nor you," Trixie said, her voice growing firmer.

"You seem eager to help Rowena with her little problem," the queen interjected into the conversation, her crisp tone chilling as she fixed her narrowed gaze on me.

"Yes." I waited, wondering what price I would have to pay for the slaughter of her people by the Ivory Towers. And while she was busy taking her pound of flesh from me, would she punish Trixie as well for the trouble caused by her husband?

"Then, since I was so pleased with the feeling of you bowing to me, I think you will be my servant for the day," she announced with a growing grin. My eyes darted to Lori, weighing his sudden appearance at her side, standing close at hand like a servant waiting to do her bidding. Was that how he had gotten ensnared? Promising to serve the queen for a day?

When I looked back at the queen, her smile was positively sharklike, as if knowing where my thoughts were traveling. Trixie grabbed my hand, squeezing tightly, but she didn't argue. Not too reassuring, but at least I didn't have to fight anyone. "What are my tasks?" I asked.

"Nothing much," the queen said. Her small hand drifted back to her teacup, her finger sliding around the rim. "I've decided that I would like some mint for my tea. You will fetch it."

I nodded, stopping myself from thinking that the task sounded easy enough. "Fine. I know a shop not far from here that sells fresh mint. I'll—"

"No need to travel so far," she purred, her voice seeming to warm for the first time. "I have a friend who lives in a house at the edge of the park. She grows many useful herbs. You will fetch me some fresh mint from her."

I hesitated, meeting Trixie's wide eyes. My heart pounded at the idea of leaving her alone with the elves. She had spent so much time on the run from them, surviving on her own. I hated the idea of abandoning her in their midst with no one to watch her back. "And Trixie will be safe?"

"No one will touch a hair on her head while you are gone." The queen was too eager to agree to Trixie's safety, which only failed to reassure me. But there was nothing I could do. I had to play along with her little game if we were going to reach any kind of agreement that would end the pursuit of my girlfriend.

"Where's the house?" I asked.

The queen gave a little wave of her hand. "Lori will escort you."

The pale man sighed but ambled around the gazebo and down the steps. He paused, and stared up at the sky with a grimace at the sun before reaching into one of his jacket pockets and pulling out a folded, floppy straw hat. Plopping it on his head, he continued across the park.

I gave Trixie's hand one last squeeze before I followed after Lori. A couple jogging steps allowed me to catch up with him and then I had to reduce my natural pace since the man walked so damned slow. It was as if nothing in the world could make him want to rush.

"You've known Rowena a long time?" I said after several minutes of silence as we cut across the large open area in the center of the park.

"I saw her born," he said, and then smiled a little. "She was my student for a time. She loved watching the stars with me."

"You're an artist?"

For the first time, his features crumpled a little as he looked over at me. "Of course." He said this as if that was the only thing he could possibly be. His face smoothed out again like glass and his voice returned to its dreamy state. "She spent years drawing vines and curling leaves, trying to breathe life into her art."

"Are you an elf?"

"No. My people are called Lorialets."

"Fey?"

"Not really," he said with a slight shake of his head as he paused at the edge of the sidewalk. He looked both ways and waited for one distant car to pass us before he continued across the street. "But we prefer to be with the fey. They understand us."

"I've never met a Lorialet." But I had heard of them. I had thought they were a faery tale, a crazy myth. Lorialets were also called Lunatics, but with the current connotation of the word, I didn't think he'd take the other name as a compliment. Lorialets were supposedly the children of Selene and Endymion. They were moon gazers, dreamers, poets, musicians, and seers of the past and future.

"There aren't many of us."

"Because of the Towers?"

He paused in the middle of the sidewalk and tilted his head a little to the side in thought. "No," he slowly said. "There were never many of us to begin with, and the Towers have never taken much interest in us."

I could guess why. Every time he spoke, his voice was soft and distracted, as if his mind were only half on where he was at and what he was doing. He'd drive any warlock or witch insane within a few minutes with his slow, plodding ways.

"Will the queen keep her word and not allow Rowena to come to harm?"

"She has no plans to physically harm our little Rowena," he said on a sigh.

His choice of words didn't reassure me.

"At the moment," Lori continued as he stopped in front of a large two-story home of dark red brick with black shutters, "our lovely queen is telling Rowena who you are getting the mint from."

"You know whose house this is?"

"Oh, yes. Her name is Demoiselle Noire de Gruchy and I think you will find her quite interesting."

"I don't care about this lady. I need to get back to Trixie," I said in a strained voice, glancing over my shoulder toward the gazebo. Regardless of what Lori said, I didn't trust the queen.

"You should definitely care," Lori said. I looked back at my companion and there was something in his eyes as he glanced from me to the house that made me pay attention to my surroundings.

A cluster of magpies roosting on the roof and in the trees in the little front yard had grown silent the moment we stopped before the house. I could feel all their eyes trained on us, watching and waiting. The house looked like any other, but there was a faint tang of magic in the air. It was old, as if years of magic use had settled into the earth and danced on the wind like particles of dust.

Lori sighed and frowned. "She will not be pleased with me," he muttered to himself as he reached inside his trouser pocket. He pulled out a little glass vile with a cork stopper and handed it to me. "Dab a little on each eyelid. Quickly. Do it now."

I pulled out the stopper and sniffed the liquid. "Dandelion water?"

"Yes, please hurry." Despite the intensity of his words, his tone retained its usual dreamlike quality.

I spread a little over each eyelid, smearing it in so that it didn't drip into my eyes. Blinking a few times, I shoved the stopper into the bottle and handed the vial to Lori. As I looked around, I found that everything looked . . . exactly the same. Dandelion water was supposed to help you see through glamour and keep you from being ensnared by the fey.

"Nothing has changed," I said.

Lori smiled and gave his little shrug. "I am as you see me. Nothing more. But it will help with her. Don't tarry too long. The sooner you're back, the better it will be for everyone." I opened my mouth to ask about Demoiselle Noire de Gruchy but Lori held up a hand, stopping me. "I can say no more. I've already helped more than I should."

That's what I was afraid of. I was lucky that he'd helped me this much. His fondness for Trixie was forcing him to give me what little assistance he could, and I appreciated it. With a brittle smile, I turned down the walk and approached the house. The magpies watching me erupted into loud chatter, as if excited that a new fly had fallen into this mystery woman's web.

The lawn was neatly trimmed without a single stray branch or fallen leaf in sight despite the trees being full of birds. Mums bloomed in the beds along the house and the walk was edged with chest-high hedges. I paused before the front stairs, my right hand hovering over the hedge nearest me. There was a tingle against the palm of my hand and I almost laughed. Noire de Gruchy had hawthorn hedges. How convenient. My wand was made of hawthorn.

Kneeling down, I carefully reached in past the long thorns and broke off a branch. I quickly pulled off the excess shoots and thorns, before shoving the stick in my pocket. It wouldn't be half as strong as my own wand, but it would give me a little bit of a boost and more control, which I was sure would be helpful against whoever this bitch was.

Armed with a pseudowand and dandelion water, I mounted the stairs and knocked on the front door. A gust of frigid air swept out of the house and bit into my bare arms as the door swung open. I flinched, falling back a step. The day was warm for early September, but not warm enough to have the air conditioner cranked to late-July levels.

"Please, come in," said a woman's soft voice. She had stepped back and was hidden within the interior darkness and behind the door.

Wishing I had brought a winter coat along, I stepped into the cold foyer and turned back to face my host as the door closed. Blinking against the darkness, my eyes took a moment to adjust after my walk in the bright afternoon sun.

When my eyes focused, I felt like I had been hit in the gut. The woman standing in the golden sunlight pouring through the slender window beside the door was stunning. Her skin was pale but perfectly flawless as it stretched over high cheekbones on a lovely oval face. She had dark eyes that could have been either dark brown or dark blue, but I couldn't tell in the shadows. Her exquisite mouth spread into a warm smile when I realized that I had been staring, but even with that knowledge I couldn't stop myself.

A black silk tank top clung to her breasts and revealed long, white arms. Her black pants hugged her long legs and were molded to her shapely hips. Demoiselle Noire de Gruchy was not a thin, waiflike creature like so many that filled fashion magazines and action movies. She was lush and curvy, leaving me aching to fill my hands with her.

I cleared my throat loudly and jerked my eyes from her, if only so I could get the blood to flow back from my pants to my brain. "Are you Demoiselle Noire de Gruchy?" I asked.

"Yes, I am." Her voice was silky smooth and left a slow burn in my chest like good Kentucky bourbon. A part of me wanted her to go on talking, but the little sane part that wasn't my libido was screaming to never let her open her mouth again.

"I'm Gage. The queen . . . the queen of the Summer Court sent me."

"Oh, yes. She's in town, isn't she? Is she well?"

I closed my eyes and drew in a deep breath. There was a hint of something in the air. Almost like flowers. Soft and cloying. I couldn't identify it without getting a stronger whiff, but I didn't want to draw more of it into my lungs. Something was off in this house.

With my eyes closed, some of the fog was clearing from my mind and I could think a little better. I was becoming more aware of the slight tingle of magic in the air. It was nothing aggressive and may have been nothing more than a defensive spell or two, but I hadn't even known the magic was there when I had stared at the woman. I tried to focus on the feeling of the magic, see if I could identify the spell. Was the spell muddling my thoughts, making it impossible to think about anything beyond this woman and sex?

A whisper of fabric was my only warning that Demoiselle Noire de Gruchy had moved closer to me.

"Oh, you poor dear," she cooed in that intoxicating voice. "You've got something in your eyes." A hand as cold as ice slid along my cheek, chilling my skin while sending a fresh shot of hot lust straight to my dick, which was now rock hard.

I jerked away from her touch, slamming against the nearest wall. My breath exploded from my throat in hard, jerky gasps. She had been about to wipe off the dandelion water. Holy shit, if this was how I was reacting without falling under her glamour, I was totally fucked without it.

"Mint! The queen needs mint!" I shouted at her, sounding like an idiot, but I didn't care. I needed to get the mint and get the hell out of there before I lost control. I didn't know what it was. Her beauty, her smile, the sound of her voice, the scent in the air, the magic—maybe all of the above—but whatever it was, it was driving me toward one thing. Even with my eyes squeezed shut, all I could think about was pinning this woman to the floor and fucking until we both died of pleasure.

With some effort, I pulled up a pleasant memory of Trixie and clung to it like a life raft bobbing helplessly in the middle of the ocean. I loved Trixie. I wouldn't betray Trixie with this woman. Trixie was my happiness. Trixie was my sanity. Trixie . . .

Demoiselle Noire de Gruchy gave a little laugh, proving she wasn't disturbed by my idiotic shouting. "Of course. Come to my greenhouse and I'll get some for you." I wanted to tell her that I would wait outside on her front porch in the warm sunlight and fresh air. There were other things I wanted to do to give me some physical relief, but I didn't want to do them with her. Never with her.

Regardless of what my brain was screaming, I found my body

following her through the opulently decorated house to an open, two-story room filled with windows. Sunlight poured in, seeming to glint over her pale skin, but there was no warmth in this room either.

As she picked up a pair of pruning shears, I watched her out of the corner of my eye, but was careful not to look at her directly. My thoughts were sluggish, but at least my mind was working now. Despite my reaction of mindless lust, I knew she wasn't a succubus. I had a good friend who was an incubus, which meant that I'd met a few succubi in my time—I knew the difference. Noire de Gruchy was perfect in every way but ice cold to the touch. Both incubi and succubi were warm, their body temperatures naturally running a little higher than humans, like most shifters.

Standing beside the long table filled with a wide variety of potted plants, I noticed that the magic felt stronger here. If this woman was fey, it made sense, since the fey got the bulk of their power from nature. But this was different. I held out one hand toward the nearest plant, taking in the stronger feeling of energy, when the plant shivered.

I jerked my hand back, my heart pounding in my chest. Holy fuck! That plant was human. Unlike the low energy that comes off many plants with magical properties, this one had a pulse and consciousness. I could feel the slight hint of a soul.

Demoiselle Noire gave a little chuckle over the sharp snip of her shears. My eyes jumped to her face and the horror helped knock the lust back. She smiled at me and I could now see that her eyes were black, matching her lush, coal-black hair.

"Finally figured out what I am, have you?" she said in that same low sweet voice that poured over me like warm maple syrup. She could be talking about peeling my skin off with a cheese grater and my brain would imagine hot, sweaty sex.

"The plants. They're humans," I said roughly, tightly gripping to my horror as an anchor.

She placed the snippets of mint in a little white envelope and folded it shut. "They were." Turning toward me, she slowly approached. I backpedaled a step for each of hers. "Former lovers that I've grown tired of. So are the magpies on my trees." She paused beside a large yellow rosebush and gently caressed the glossy green leaves. The bush shuddered and I could feel the hint of intense pleasure from it.

She continued approaching until I was pinned against another wall. Stopping a few feet away, she extended the hand holding the white envelope with the mint. I stared at it, confused. That was it? No attack? No bitter struggle for freedom?

She laughed again and I clenched my teeth against the sound as it throbbed through my body. "Go ahead. Take it. No strings attached."

My hand was shaking, but it flashed out and snatched the envelope from her fingers before she could draw it back.

"I've promised the queen that I wouldn't kill you. The damage has already been done."

"What do you mean?"

"Rowena knows you were sent to me. She knows that no man has ever escaped me without visiting my bed. Even if I never touch you and you proclaim your sweet loyalty to her, she will always have a doubt eating away at her happiness in the back of her mind."

And thus the queen has her revenge on us both. Trixie would spend the rest of our relationship thinking that I had wanted someone else, and I would lose the person I loved most in the world.

My head fell back, hitting the wall behind me as my eyes closed. I had been afraid of the queen kidnapping Trixie, having her put to death, torturing her physically. Hell, I had expected some kind of physical attack on me. I had never thought of an attack of this sort and I had no defense against it.

"You know, if she's going to think you had sex with me, you might as well have the pleasure," Demoiselle Noire de Gruchy said.

Lost in my own misery, I couldn't put up any kind of defense. She plastered her body against mine in a heartbeat. I grabbed her left hand and held it out, while my other hand caught her shoulder as I tried to pry her away from me. Every nerve ending trembled as I struggled against both her and a host of angry instincts that were snarling for sex with this creature. The scent I had picked up earlier came back, thick and heavy, so that my mind was lost in the growing fog.

Straining, I managed to hold her upper body off my chest and keep her from kissing me, but her pelvis was pressed to my groin. She was icy to the touch, but I was putting off so much heat that I was confident that I could have melted an iceberg. Her leg slid up mine and a shudder racked my frame as she ground herself against my erection. This was not how I imagined I was going to die, but my heart wasn't going to be able to take much more of this.

Her free right hand slid over my chest, dancing over my pounding heart. I dared a glance down at her face and she flashed me a wicked smile. I sucked in a sharp breath before her hand slipped back down my chest and slid inside my pants and boxers. Her long, soft fingers circled my dick and I moaned at the exquisite feeling before I could stop the sound. My hips jerked once, sending her hand over the head and down along the length, pushing another long groan past my lips.

I tensed every muscle in my body as sweat beaded at my temples and dripped down the sides of my face in the strain. I was teetering painfully on the edge, but I refused to give in. This beautiful creature was a monster. She lured lovers to her bed, and when she had sucked them dry of all they had to offer, she turned them into plants and animals so she could remain in control of them. The pleasure she offered wasn't real. It was an illusion of magic. There was no love, no tenderness. Only Trixie could give me that.

"It's not real," I moaned, trying to gather the strength to push her off me.

"This doesn't feel real?" She squeezed my cock so that I nearly came.

"Trixie is real. I love Trixie," I said between clenched teeth.

"It's okay. She doesn't have to know. Just come for me now. You're so close. Give yourself that little release. It'll be our little secret."

"No!" I roared. Releasing her shoulder, I grabbed her right wrist and pulled it as quickly and carefully out of my pants as I could. When my dick was free of her, I gave her a hard shove across the room. I didn't see where she landed. Bending down, I grabbed the white envelope I had dropped and ran through the house. Demoiselle Noire's furious shriek sliced through the air, chasing on my heels. As I hit the hallway, I pulled the hawthorn branch from my pocket and waved it with a quick burst of power that blew the front door off its hinges. Charging down the porch stairs, I started to run across the sidewalk when a rush of power swept across the front yard. The hawthorn hedges shifted and shivered a second before long branches lashed out at me. All the magpies took to the air at once, filling the silence with their loud cries. Ducking my head down under my arms, I kept running, a scream escaping me only when one branch hit my back and dragged the long thorns across my flesh.

I barely missed being hit by a car as I darted across the street, but I didn't stop until I was back in the park. Struggling to catch my breath, I dropped to my knees in the soft grass before I fell on my face. Muscles screamed and my fucking dick was throbbing in time with my racing heart. You'd think with the pain burning in my back from the thorns that the damn erection would go away, but I had been so close that some part of me was still crying for sex. For half a breath I thought about stumbling into the nearby woods to finish what had been started, but why give the elves watching me a show? Instead, I dug the fingers of my left hand into a large cut on my right biceps, sending a fresh wave of pain through my body that in turn washed away the last of my erection.

The reasonable part of me knew that the queen had watched her people slaughtered by the Towers. I knew that she had to be hurting over the betrayal of her husband. I knew these things and that reasonable part could understand why she would attack Trixie and me like this. Yet the larger part of me that was in pain, and still trying to get over the horror that I had very nearly been raped by something evil, was pretty fucking pissed at the queen.

WHEN MY BREATHING had slowed to normal again and I was no longer worried about setting Demoiselle Noire's house on fire, I pushed to my feet and walked to the white gazebo beside the concrete lake. Anger bubbled inside of me, helping to dull the worst of the pains in my back and along my arms. Before entering the gazebo, I was of half a mind to do a little Tower-style threatening to get Trixie free of the Summer Court, but there was no need.

Trixie gasped. She was already pale with worry, but her wide green eyes filled with tears at the sight of me. I was sweaty and bloody, but for the first time in my life, my soul felt dirty. Logically, I knew that my body's reaction had been the result of magic and that I had been loyal to Trixie in my heart and in my head, but that logic failed to scrub away the gritty feeling on my soul.

She rushed across the gazebo, her arms open to embrace me. I opened my mouth to tell her not to touch me. That I was dirty. But the words never came up my throat. She crushed against me on a sob, her arms wrapping around my neck as she pressed her face into my throat.

"I love you," she cried. She repeated the words over and over again, teary and soft.

They were the balm I had been looking for, healing the cuts on my heart and washing away the filth covering my soul. My arms came around her like a vise, clutching her as tightly as I could.

"It's okay. I'm okay. Just had a little trouble with a hawthorn bush, that's all," I said in a light, teasing tone that was completely undermined by the ferocious hold I had on her.

"I love you," Trixie repeated.

I closed my eyes and let those wonderful words sink into me again. She didn't ask any questions. She didn't say anything besides those three words, because it was her way of showing that it was okay, that we'd get through whatever happened. Trixie knew who, or rather what, I had met, and by my appearance, she knew that at least I put up a fight. I wasn't sure if we'd ever talk about what occurred while we were separated, but I liked to think that she'd at least try to understand.

When I opened my eyes, I looked over Trixie's head at the queen. She was sitting stiff on her little bench, one delicate hand pressed to her open mouth while tears glistened in her wide eyes. She was also looking pale.

"I'm sorry," she whispered in a wavering voice. "I've made a terrible mistake."

Regret. Not because she had attacked a warlock and was now afraid of retaliation. She regretted what she had done because she had hurt two people who didn't deserve her venom. There were some people in this world who were born to be villains. They killed and tortured with no remorse. The queen of the Summer Court was not one of them. She had been carrying centuries' worth of pain and anger around. It drove her to strike out and now she regretted her action.

A frown tugged at the corners of my lips. Trixie's love and the queen's regret had cooled the last of my anger so that I was ready to block the event from my mind.

"I forgive you," I said in a rough voice as the words were lodged in my throat.

A thousand times over in my mind, I had thought that if the world was to ever find peace with the Towers, two things would need to happen. The warlocks and the witches would need to express regret and the world would have to forgive. How could I ever expect the world to do such a thing if I couldn't do it myself?

Trixie loosened her tight hold on my neck and pulled back so that she could look up at me. I smiled a little at her shocked expression before pressing a quick kiss to her forehead.

"Shall we continue with our meeting?" I asked.

Trixie released me and we returned to our places before the queen. Reaching into my back pocket, I pulled out the white envelope and dropped it on the little table holding her teacup and saucer.

"Your fresh mint, Your Majesty," I said.

With a slightly trembling hand, she reached forward and picked it up. Placing the crumpled, blood-streaked envelope in her lap, she gently ran her fingers over it while keeping her head down.

"What do you need of me next, Your Majesty?" I said, and her head popped up with a look of surprise. "I will do whatever task I must so that Rowena will no longer be pursued and barred from her people."

The queen looked down at her hands in her lap and her shoulders slumped slightly. For a moment she looked uncomfortable, but it passed and her shoulders straightened again as she lifted her narrowed eyes to my face. "I'm older than I look to you. I remember back centuries, to a time when the warlocks and witches didn't try to crush the races of the world. They were scholars and . . . healers."

I nodded. "It's sad that the Towers strayed from such a role."

"When I spoke with Eldon, he intimated that you might be willing to lend some assistance in exchange for some leniency toward Rowena," she said carefully.

"I would be honored to lend Your Majesty any assistance that I possibly can," I said with a slight bow that had me grimacing as the movement caused fresh pain to shoot through my back. "However, I must interject one thing. While you're correct in that I have a past with the Towers, certain choices I have made in that respect have resulted in . . . my hands being tied in a way."

Her lovely faced twisted as she frowned. "What choices? In what way?"

I shoved my hands in my pockets and sighed. "The Towers ruled that if I was going to be permitted to leave, I had to give up magic."

"But you . . ." Her voice drifted off as she motioned toward the gazebo entrance and a fresh look of horror slipped across her face. Yes, she had sent me to Demoiselle Noire de Gruchy with the idea that I would use magic to escape and now she was realizing that I had been in even more danger than she had believed.

I considered letting her twist with that thought for a moment, but tossed it aside. "I've found ways to do some quiet magic. It's the big stuff that's going to get me killed."

The queen sat back against the little bench and stared at me for several seconds, confusion written on her face as she tried to puzzle something out. "And if what I required was not such a little quiet thing, would you do it? Would you risk your life for Rowena?"

"Yes," I immediately replied.

"No," Trixie snapped at the same time. She turned and laid her hands on my cheeks. "No, this stops now. You're not casting any more spells, no matter what she asks."

I placed my hand over one of hers, rubbing my thumb over the soft skin on the inside of her wrist. "As she's pointed out, the warlocks and witches have done horrible things to your people. Isn't it time a warlock did some good for your kind?"

"Gage, you weren't one of the warlocks that hurt us. Damn it, you weren't even born yet!" she said, blinking against the fresh tears gathering in her eyes. "You don't have to pay for the sins of other people."

"Then let me do it for you."

Trixie's hands slipped from my face and she wrapped her arms around my waist, pressing close. I winced but held her, laying my cheek against the top of her head. "After all the hate and anger and fear, let me do this one thing out of love," I whispered.

"I can't lose you," she said, her voice muffled against my chest.

"You won't. I haven't agreed to anything yet. We're talking."

"You . . . love her, don't you?" the queen asked in amazement.

"Very much," I said, meeting the queen's cool eyes.

"You are a strange one," she murmured, bringing a chuckle from Trixie.

I smiled while hugging Trixie, easing the last of the tension that had been hanging in the air since my reappearance. "It's one of my many charms."

Raising her hands, the queen clapped loudly twice. "Chairs!"

I twisted around to see the guard at the entrance step aside as two elves entered carrying a pair of comfortable chairs, which were set before the queen. As the two newcomers left, she raised her hands again and made a little shooing motion. "Everyone leave me with my guests." The three guards hesitated for several seconds, staring at me, before leaving the gazebo. I had no doubt that if I made one wrong move, they were going to be on me within seconds. They were gone, but not far.

I ushered Trixie over into a seat before slowly sitting beside her. Muscles were sore and my back was killing me, but it felt so damn good to sit down. To my shock, the queen pulled a lace handkerchief from her sleeve and offered it to Trixie.

"Thank you, Arianna," Trixie murmured as she dabbed her eyes and dried her cheeks.

The queen chuckled at my confusion. "You will be further surprised to know that Rowena and I used to be close friends many years ago. When I could pull her away from her murals, she was one of my closest companions." The queen looked away, blinking back tears before she turned back to us.

"It's what made this mess an even bigger tragedy." Trixie's voice wavered. "I felt like I was betraying our friendship when I realized that I would be his choice for a consort. I had to run. Not just because I didn't want him, but I didn't want to betray you."

I slumped in my chair and ran a hand roughly over my face. Why either woman hadn't killed this asshole yet was beyond me. He throws aside his beautiful wife so that he could chase after his wife's best friend? I had heard of women shooting their husbands for less.

"But it doesn't look as if love has been any kinder to you," Arianna said, drawing my gaze back to her.

"What do you mean?" I said, a little more harshly than I had meant to.

She smiled. "An elf falls in love with the most despised creature on the planet, the scourge of her people. And to make matters worse, one who is despised even by his own kind. If I had to choose, I would keep my indifferent husband. He may not want me like he wants Rowena, but at least he won't get me killed."

"Arianna, please," Trixie said.

I frowned at the queen. I didn't need a reminder of the danger my presence posed to Trixie. "I believe you mentioned something about needing my assistance."

Arianna chuckled lightly, a soft, dancing sound that somehow pushed aside my anger and growing tension. She was smiling again. Some of the earlier cold I had seen in her had melted away, making her look even younger and lovelier. How had her husband so easily tossed her aside? Fucking moron.

"Then again . . . maybe he isn't such a bad choice."

"You can't have him," Trixie warned.

"I know. For better or worse, my heart has made its choice," she said absently, then turned her attention back to me, her expression growing serious. "As I'm sure you've been made aware, the reason my husband and I parted was that we couldn't have children. The royal line needs to be protected, or we will face a dire threat from both the Winter Court and the Svartálfar. That is part of the problem. The larger issue is that most of our people are having trouble bearing children, and we've not been able to determine why or even trace it back to see if it is an issue with the mother or the father."

Resting my elbow on the arm of the chair, I leaned my temple against my fist, trying to quiet the knots twisting in my stomach. "And you want me to help you conceive in hopes that it will result in helping the rest of your people as well?"

"It would go a long way to healing the wound caused by the Towers," she added.

I was out of my depth with this, but the request wasn't unexpected. Sure, I knew how babies were made. I was quite fond of that act and firmly believed in regular practice, particularly with Trixie, but all the other stuff that went into conception and whether it worked I didn't know. With magical creatures like elves, I had a feeling a little more went into it than introducing a horny sperm to a sexy egg.

"I'm guessing that you tried the usual route of potions, prayers, and special herbs," I hedged while I mentally dug through the knowledge I did have about childbearing.

"No, my husband and I didn't try everything as he wasn't interested once the difficulty was discovered," Arianna said stiffly, but then added, a little more softly: "But others have and they still are childless."

My eyes fell shut, blocking out the look of worry on her face. "I need some time to think, to research. I don't think this is something I can fix with a quick spell and I'm not interested in being there to hold together a spell while you try to make a baby."

Arianna gave me a smile that had me blushing a bit and Trixie clearing her throat. *Yeah, didn't need that mental image.*

"If you've got any notes or research your own people have done, anything listing what has changed since you could have kids, it would help."

The queen turned and reached behind a large pillow on the

bench, pulling out a white book that she handed to Trixie. "It contains all the notes we've made. The problem started shortly before the Great War. It's written in elvish, so Rowena will need to translate."

I nodded. I spoke several languages, both human and other. The only words I knew in elvish were what Trixie occasionally shouted during sex and I didn't think I'd find those in the queen's little white book.

"I need some time."

"Unfortunately, that's something I can't give you," Arianna said, her tone once again becoming cold and brisk. "It's now early September. In a few weeks, it will be the fall equinox. I will need to be with child before then so the baby can be born with the summer. My husband knows that I am meeting with Rowena. If something is not arranged soon, I am quite sure that he will make another grab for her."

"Fine. A few days, then. Leave us with some way of contacting you in case we find something," I said with an irritated wave of my hand. "I'm assuming that you have a . . . consort chosen should I come up with a solution."

"I will have someone." She was sitting up so straight that her spine could have been made of steel.

At the same time I slouched a little lower in my chair, balancing my left ankle on my knee as I turned over the situation. It didn't feel fixed to me, not completely.

"If I come up with a solution, your problem is solved, but I'm not sure Trixie's has been. Say you conceive with your consort. What happens to your husband?" I asked.

Arianna frowned a little. "He will remain king, but his line within the royal family will end. My consort's family will rise in standing."

"Would he be free to pursue a consort?"

"Yes."

"So you would have a child, and he would be able to chase Trixie." I shook my head. "I need a better fix."

Trixie sighed. "Short of his death, I don't see how we are going to get him to stop." Her head then snapped up and she glared at me. "Not an option."

I threw up my hands. "I didn't even consider it." Her frown deepened and I dropped my head back. "Okay, I didn't consider it for long. I'm trying *not* to destroy the Summer Court."

"There is one way," Arianna said softly, drawing my eyes back to her face. She hesitated as if she didn't want to say the words out loud. "If he was the father of the child, then he couldn't have a consort. We would be bound to each other again."

"You would take him back?" Trixie asked before I could.

"I would if I could be given some kind of assurance that his gaze won't wander. I know he doesn't love me and I can accept that, but I need the assurance that he will remain faithful to me."

Trixie looked expectantly over at me and I shrugged. "We could tattoo them with the infinity heart, binding them to each other." I looked over at the queen, whose delicate eyebrows had drawn together in question. "I've only ever used it on goblins, but it's a type of binding tattoo. It doesn't create feelings of love, but more of a deeper sense of connection and a need for unity. You'd both have to be tattooed for it to work. Just a small one on the interior of your left wrist."

"And he won't stray?"

"The thought would never cross his mind. Of course, you couldn't either."

"Very good. You will make it so that we can conceive and then you will tattoo us so that he will no longer pursue Rowena," the queen said with her regal tone as if she was handing down a royal decree.

"And when all this is accomplished, Trixie can come back to her people without fear? She can stay with the Summer Court and then would be free to return to her other life if she wanted?"

Arianna nodded with a small smile. "She would be welcomed back. She should have no fear of being harassed or fear reprisals for all that has happened."

Sitting up, I sighed with relief as I reached across and squeezed Trixie's hand. That was what I was hoping for. I wanted her to no longer feel like she had to hide when she was in Low Town, but I also wanted her to be able to return to her people if there was trouble in my world. I looked up to find Trixie smiling at me, but there was something in her eyes, a question that made me wonder if she saw the direction of my thoughts as well.

I looked back at the queen, who appeared to be relieved by all this as well. "We need to be going. I've got a lot to work on. But before I go, I would like to pass along this warning." I paused, licking my lips as I sorted through the information that I had. Arianna needed to know something, but I didn't want to start a panic. "I'm sure you're aware of yesterday's destruction of Indianapolis." Arianna had gone completely still to the point that I doubted that she breathed. "There is much I don't know, and what I do know I am not comfortable talking about yet. There is a belief within the Towers that secret information has been stolen and the Towers feel threatened. There is also a belief that an elf is the culprit."

Arianna became deathly pale before my eyes and I heard Trixie gasp as her hand tightened around my fingers.

"We've done nothing—" Arianna started, but I held up my hand, stopping her.

"I know that. But we both know that the Towers aren't going to concern themselves with details like finding the identity of the true culprits, whether they are members of the Winter or Summer Courts, or if this is a lone Svartálfar acting in his own interests. For now, they are searching for the real culprit, but if the search stretches too long, if panic sets in, they will start killing indiscriminately."

"What do you advise?" Arianna asked. The panic was gone from her voice, but she was still frighteningly pale as she clenched her hands in her lap.

"Stay calm and stay hidden as best you can. If you disappear completely, they will take that as a sign of guilt and will search in earnest for you. Until this is settled, stay alert and be ready to act at a moment's notice." I shook my head, feeling like shit. Her people were already struggling to survive, as they fought to simply bear children, and now I was dumping this in her lap. "I'm sorry that I can't help you more."

"You have already helped my people more than any other warlock by simply passing along this warning. I thank you."

I looked over at Trixie, who seemed to be digesting this information. "Do you have a way of contacting her quickly and safely?"

She gave a jerky nod. "Yes, I can contact her."

"Good." I pushed to my feet, pulling Trixie up with me. "We'll be in contact. I will try to find something as quickly as possible, but as you can see, I've got my hands full."

"I understand," Arianna said, taking a deep breath as she seemed to rein in the last of her emotions. "Gage, again I am sorry. I have sorely misjudged you."

I frowned down at her, taking in her quiet strength and elegant poise. "You're not the first, but you are one of the first to apologize, and I appreciate that." I started to turn away with Trixie, but stopped to look at the queen. "And for what it's worth, he doesn't fucking deserve you."

Arianna smiled at me while Trixie laughed. "Maybe so," the queen agreed coyly. "But nevertheless, he is a good king and cares for his people. If he had known there was a warlock who might help our people bear children, then he would have already spoken with you. Maybe not for the two of us, but definitely for our people."

With a smile, I gave Arianna another of my stiff and awkward bows before ushering Trixie out of the gazebo, her body pressed close to my side. She was safe for now from some of the Summer Court elves, but I needed to feel her close. The end of that conversation had only reminded me that while I was one step closer to helping her, we were also one step closer to the whole world going to hell in a big fucking handbasket.

13

AS WE STARTED across the parking lot toward her car, I could feel Trixie relaxing beside me. She had met with the queen of the Summer Court and walked away unscathed. What she felt like now, after running for nearly three hundred years, I couldn't imagine. Of course, we weren't out of the woods yet, but at least we were headed in the right direction.

"Are you going to ever tell me what Sofie told you about the Towers and Indianapolis?" Trixie asked in a deceptively calm voice. I cringed. I had known this question was coming but I'd been hoping that she would stay focused on her problem with the elves for a little longer. Did we need to heap the Towers on her list of things to worry about?

"What about that conversation we had about me not telling you everything because I wanted to protect you?" I said, flashing a hopeful smile at her.

She didn't smile back. "I said I understood your reasoning, not that I accepted it. You need to tell me what's going on."

I sighed. "I know." Pulling her close, I leaned over and brushed a kiss against the side of her head. There was a part of me that wanted to tell her. I wanted to pull open my chest and spill out everything that I had been hiding from the world all these years, but that desire to bare my soul was outweighed by a fear that the truth would send her screaming from me, as any smart person would.

"Well, isn't this a surprise!" declared a cocky voice from behind us. Trixie and I stopped walking and turned toward the speaker. My heart lurched in my chest as my eyes fell on the warlock standing a few dozen feet away in the middle of the parking lot with his wand pointed at me. "It seems we've found the elf we were searching for, and she's strolling with the one person who would most like to see the Towers fall."

"You're insane, Billy," I called back, shoving Trixie behind me. "You've got the wrong elf and you know it. I might not like the Towers, but I wouldn't be stupid enough to try to attack them like this. It's suicide."

My mind scrambled for protective spells that would shield both Trixie and me. I didn't have my wand on me and I had dropped the stick I grabbed from Demoiselle Noire's in the grass when I returned to the park. Fuck. I didn't even have a weapon. Heading to a meeting with the queen of the Summer Court armed to the teeth hadn't seemed a good way to convince her that I wasn't a threat.

"No one believed you to be particularly smart." The warlock laughed.

I ignored his taunts, focusing on drawing energy toward me. William Rosenblum was old, but not too old. Maybe in his fifties. We had had a few run-ins while I was living with Simon in the Tower. He was an arrogant prick and had never thought too much of me, which I was hoping to use to my advantage.

"Trix, when I tell you to run, I want you to head straight for the woods and don't stop," I said in a low voice.

One of her hands rested on my side, her fingers tightening in my ragged T-shirt, while the other pressed the edge of the white book she was carrying into my wounded back. "I'm not leaving you." Her voice wavered with fear. A couple months ago, she attacked Simon, but then she had been lucky enough to sneak up behind the old bastard while he was busy attacking me. This time she was staring down the wrong end of a wand with no defense.

"You have to. I can't protect us both. Now go!" I shouted. At the same time I threw a massive bolt of white-hot energy at Billy, sending it crashing against the shield he had barely created in time. The energy bounced off his shield and shot out, crackling through the air as it slammed into nearby trees and lampposts. Limbs crashed to the ground and sparks jumped. Out of the corner of my eye, I saw Trixie running for the tree line to my left.

Billy knocked away the last of the energy with a wave of his hand and shifted his stance so that he was facing the direction in which Trixie had run. I ended the first spell and quickly wrapped energy in my hands while shifting my thoughts to a second aggressive spell. I wasn't trying to kill him. Well, at least not yet. For now, I would be content if he would keep his attention on me, giving Trixie some time to put some distance between this bastard and herself.

With a grunt, I whipped the second spell loose. The energy caught up the wind, sending it scraping along the ground before it pummeled Billy so that he was forced to shield his eyes against the dirt and gravel that was thrown in his direction. His shirt and protective cloak flapped in the fierce wind, plastering against his thin, frail frame before dancing behind him like a pair of black wings. While I was good at it, I didn't like fucking with the weather. Spells like that tended to get out of control fast and cause massive amounts of collateral damage—not that the Towers were worried about a little thing like that.

I took advantage of his brief distraction to close some of this distance between us. My movement didn't go unnoticed because as Billy dropped his arms, the wind died and I was pummeled in the chest by a surge of energy. I rocked backward, struggling to regain my balance while I instinctively raised a new protective shield against another strike.

"What brought on the sudden decision to attack the Towers?"

William called while his hands moved before him, weaving strands of energy together as he cooked up a new spell to rip my face off. "You kill Master Thorn and then decide that it's now safe to take down the rest of us?"

A ring of fire sprang up from the concrete around me, the flames reaching more than nine feet in the air. The heat was intense, baking the air so that it was becoming hard to breathe and making it feel like my skin was melting off. Asshole. I hated fire spells. They weren't difficult, as aggressive magic went, and were, in my opinion, the lazy man's go-to magic when he didn't want to be bothered with something that took a little effort and originality.

"Come on! Don't even pretend that you're sorry Simon is gone," I said, forcing out a laugh. Sweat was pouring down my face, leaking into my eyes, so that it was becoming difficult to see. My body was screaming for me to get out of there, but my mind was torn between maintaining my protective shield and dissecting the fire spell. I had always thought that William was a decent warlock, so he had to be up to something else.

Just as I finished unraveling the spell and was dousing the flames, a pair of blades shot through the last of the fire. The first bounced off the shield while the second embedded itself in the barrier, stopping a bare inch away from my stomach. I grabbed the blade from where it hung in the air with my left hand.

William frowned to see me unharmed. "It's not about being sorry that Master Thorn is dead," Billy began a bit stiffly, as if insulted by my saying that he might be concerned about Simon's well-being. "It's that someone like you succeeded in doing him any harm."

"Yeah, should have lain down and died," I said while strengthening my protection spell.

"Exactly." William smiled as he switched to an ice spell. I had been expecting it. It was like he was thumbing through a teaching syllabus for a new apprentice. There wasn't an original thought in his little brain. I was beginning to wonder if he had come after me to earn himself some street cred in the Towers, because I couldn't imagine that he was all that well respected. Fucking puss.

With a wave of my hand, I blocked his new spell before it could jump from his fingertips and then smiled when a new sound entered the area. Gritting my teeth, I pulled in as much energy as I could before shoving it at William. The warlock's eyes went wide as the force hit him from the side rather than head-on as he was expecting. Still on his feet, he slid several yards to the right into the street and into the path of what turned out to be an approaching pickup truck.

Tires squealed as the driver slammed on the brakes before the sickening crush of steel hitting flesh and bone echoed through the park. Switching the knife to my right hand, I ran over to where Billy was groaning on the ground. The truck couldn't have been going more than thirty-five, so Billy wasn't killed by the impact, but he was in pain. Dropping to one knee, I raised the blade and hesitated. Could I do this? My gaze flashed to his blood-streaked face and in his eyes I saw blazing hatred—not fear. If I didn't kill him, he'd come back. He'd kill me. He'd kill Trixie.

The blade arced downward, fast and straight, plunging into his chest. Billy gave one last cry and died. Out of the corner of my eye, I saw movement. My hand flashed out and the figure was thrown against the side of the truck, trapped. When I looked up, I saw the driver watching me from where he was pinned against the side panel. The large man's face was sickly white and his brown eyes were so wide I was afraid they'd fall out of their sockets.

"You okay?" I asked, pushing to my feet while releasing him from the spell.

He nodded, cringing back into the crumpled steel. I paused to look at the front of his truck. It looked to be one of those diesel-guzzling monsters that sound like a semi. It took a little more damage than I would have expected, but then he hadn't had much time to stop.

"Sorry about your truck. Your insurance cover acts of warlock?"

He nodded jerkily, still looking dazed and terrified.

"Good. If you could wait a few minutes before calling the cops, I'd appreciate it."

"You're . . . a . . . a warlock?"

I frowned. "Yeah."

"You gonna kill me?"

"No."

The fear didn't completely ease from his face as his eyes jumped to Billy's body. "Was he a warlock?"

"Yeah."

"Are you sure he's dead?"

"Yeah."

"And you're not going to kill me?" he asked again, with no small amount of skepticism filling his deep voice.

"No, I think I've done enough of that today," I muttered as I started to walk to the parking lot and Trixie's car. Behind me, I heard the large man whisper a relieved thanks. I started to raise my hand to wave off his thanks, but immediately dropped it to my side. In this world, when a warlock waves his hand, everyone shits their drawers in fear of the spell. This guy had been through enough for one day.

I was sick to my stomach. It wasn't bad enough that I had killed another creature, but I had scared the crap out of another person when he had done nothing more than happen to be in the wrong place at the wrong time. To make it all the more sickening, I wasn't sure if he was thanking me for killing a warlock or for not killing him. How much longer could the world survive living on this edge of fear?

Stepping onto the sidewalk, I walked into the nearby grass, crossing to where the woods started. With a couple whispered words, I waved my hands as if scooping up air. Seconds later, water bubbled up. It drifted into the air until it collected into an orb about the size of a bowling ball and hovered about waist-high. I dipped my hands into the water, rubbing them together to wash away Billy's blood. I shouldn't have been performing magic, but after being forced to fight Billy with magic, I didn't care if I was being watched by Gideon. I needed to find Trixie, to hold her, but I wasn't going to search for her with another man's blood on my hands.

Lifting my clean hands from the water, I sent it dripping back to the earth while I wiped them on my jeans.

"That's a pretty neat trick," Trixie said.

My head popped up, searching the area until she stepped out from behind a large tree. I sighed with relief, my shoulders slumping. I was grateful that she had run, but I'd known down in my bones that she wouldn't go far.

"I've tried it with dishes, but I get water everywhere," I said, forcing a smile onto my face. My first instinct was to run across the remaining few yards that separated us and pull her against me, but I forced my legs to remain locked in place. I needed her to come to me. Every time this shit happened, every time she was faced with violent evidence of my past, I expected her to reject me, to run screaming in the opposite direction, because it was the smart thing to do. She hadn't . . . yet.

Trixie walked toward me, carefully picking her way over fallen limbs and brush to reach the edge of the trees. My hands were fisted at my sides and my teeth were clenched in the effort to hold still.

"Are you all right? Did he hurt you?" she asked, stopping just out of arm's reach.

"I'm fine. Not a scratch. You?"

She nodded. "Fine." But when she looked up at me, I could see the tears in her eyes. My willpower crumbled. I took a step forward and roughly jerked her into my arms while she wrapped hers around my neck, pulling my face down to her shoulder. A shuddering breath racked her body as she tightened her hold on me.

"I was so scared," she said in a broken voice. "I didn't know what to do. I couldn't help you. He could have—"

"I'm safe. We're both safe. He's dead and we're safe," I kept repeating, waiting for the reassurance to sink into both our brains.

"This has been the worst day ever," she said, wiping away her tears.

"Definitely."

"But I don't understand. What elf are they searching for?" Trixie asked, pulling away so that she could look up into my eyes.

Reaching up, I cupped her cheek with my right hand, wiping away a stray tear with my thumb. "We should get going. The cops are going to be here soon and I'd rather not have to answer too many questions."

"No," Trixie said sharply as she stepped away from me. "You're not evading this. This had to do with what you warned Arianna about. Why do they suspect elves of threatening them?"

My right hand fell back to my side while fear tightened in my stomach. She was right, but I was afraid to utter the words, afraid of her reaction, but if I couldn't trust her, then I had no one in this world. "It appears that a group has managed to locate the Ivory Towers," I said slowly. Her mouth dropped open and her breathing became heavy. "They chased one of the surviving members involved to Indianapolis but lost him. They were afraid that he would tell others before they could find him, so they destroyed the city."

"But I don't understand. Was he an elf?"

I shook my head. "They believe it was an elf who found the Towers, but they never saw him."

"What?" she cried. Her beautiful features twisted in anger as she paced away from me into the woods and then back again. "This is ridiculous! If they never saw the person, how the hell do they know he's an elf? They're using this as an excuse to continue to hunt my people."

"Trixie, the elves are known to be the best at working glamour and that's what's hiding the Towers. It makes sense. Without being a trained witch or warlock, elves are among the few races that could see through the glamour."

She drew close to me, rising up on tiptoes so she could glare at me in the eye. "How can you defend them?"

"It's logical," I snapped. "Logical and true."

Trixie gasped, jerking away from me as if I'd hit her. She stared at me through narrowed eyes before they widened with an idea. "You know," she whispered. "You know who found the Towers!"

"I have a strong idea, yes, and he's an elf. Technically, a dark elf, but the Ivory Towers don't see much difference between the Summer Court, Winter Court, and the Svartálfar. If they don't have their hands on the actual culprit, then they're going to start wiping out elves until they're all gone so they don't have to worry about this problem again."

"What are you going to do?" Her tone had softened as the anger seemed to seep out of her.

My shoulders slumped and I shoved one hand through my hair. "Find him. Either kill him or hand him over to the Towers in hopes of preventing anyone else from finding out what he knows."

"What?" She shook her head as she grabbed my arm. "You can't do that. You have to let him tell others. Tell the world leaders. Let everyone know where the Towers are."

"And then what?" I shouted, losing my grip on my temper as fear burned up the last of my restraint. "Let the world march on the Towers? Send their armies and bombs rushing toward the Towers? The only thing that will happen is that they will fail. All the soldiers will die and not a Tower will be touched by a bomb. And when the dust settles, the warlocks and the witches will come out of the Towers and then the real carnage will begin. The war that follows will put the Great War to shame."

Trixie shook her head in denial. She released my arm but I grabbed her wrist, holding her in place. "Do you know how many it took to destroy Indianapolis?"

"Gage . . ." she started in a strangled voice, but I didn't let her off the hook. I couldn't let her hold on to this thought of taking on the Towers with force.

"I know the spell. Not well enough to do it myself, but I know it. It would have taken no more than six warlocks and witches to destroy the city. Six! There are hundreds of witches and warlocks around the world. Do you think the armies of the world honestly stand a chance? Hell, the Towers wouldn't have allowed the countries to build them if they thought the countries could win in a fight against them."

Tears slipped down her face and she stopped trying to pull free of my grasp. "Then what are we supposed to do? We can't continue like this."

"I know," I whispered, releasing her wrist. She stepped back and I sighed. "Things need to change, but this way, taking on the Towers with force, isn't the way. It will only make things worse. If I thought we had a chance, I would have blasted the locations of all the Towers out to the world years ago."

"You know?"

I nodded. "I don't think it occurred to any of them until recently that I might tell someone. They knew I didn't like them, but I don't think they thought I was capable of betrayal like that. They don't think one of their own kind would do such a thing, and despite my separation, they still consider me one of them."

"Will they hunt you now?"

"Some." I shoved my hands in the pockets of my jeans to keep from reaching for her. "They'll keep coming until I give them a reason to stop."

"And that's handing over the elf to the Ivory Towers?"

Half of my mouth quirked in a smile. "Try not to feel too much sympathy for him. He's a real asshole and I think the world would be better off without him around." My half smile disappeared as she frowned. "I'm sorry. I want change as badly as you. Maybe even more so, but this way will only get millions of people killed and we'll end up in a worse place than we are in now."

"Then how do things ever change?"

"From within. It's slow and dangerous, but the fighting is unlikely to spread into the rest of the world. I know you can't tell, but it's happening. Things are changing in the Towers. It will get better. Maybe not in our lifetimes, but it will get better if they keep pressing forward."

Trixie looked up at me. A thin, fragile smile drifted ghostlike across her lips. "Things must be changing. You're here."

"Yes, and I'm not the only one. It will get better." I extended my right hand to her, holding my breath as I waited to see if she'd take it. I understood her need to strike back at the Towers and I held a great key that would help the world. I prayed that she understood that revealing the Tower locations to the world only led to death and destruction, not freedom.

Slowly, Trixie stepped closer and placed her hand in mine, allowing me to pull her into my arms. "I don't like it and my instincts say that the information should be shared, but I understand. So many of the people I knew when I was a child are dead as a result of the Great War. I can't go through that again. Maybe I'm a coward," she said against my shoulder.

"No. You're trying to fight smarter."

In the distance, I could hear the whine of police sirens drawing closer to the park. The truck driver must have called in the cops and it was time for us to get going. Pressing a kiss to Trixie's temple, I ushered her over to her car. As I placed her in the passenger seat, I took the keys and jumped behind the wheel. I was afraid that I'd have to work a little glamour of my own to get by the cops, and oddly enough it was more easily done while driving the car.

"So what now?" she asked on a sigh of relief as we jumped on the expressway without being stopped.

I reached over and tapped the cover of the white book that lay forgotten in her lap. "You need to read through that and make some notes for me. I need to know what changed with the elves before they started having problems. Diet? Magic? Sexual positions?"

Trixie gave a little snort. "I doubt Arianna had such things written down, but I'll make a note," she said sarcastically. She sighed again and I looked over to find her staring at the book she was now holding. "I honestly forgot about this. It all seems so . . . unimportant now, you know? Considering the mess with the Towers."

"This is important to me," I said firmly. "The Towers thing is fixable and so is this. It won't be easy, but we'll fix it."

"Thanks, Gage."

"No problem." I hit the turn signal and glanced in the mirrors before sliding over into the left lane. Afternoon traffic was light, and I was eager to get Trixie safely tucked away. "I thought of something else you could look into for me."

"What?"

"Have the elves ever consulted the Hearth Women?"

Trixie turned in her seat to look at me. "No, but then I thought they were just midwives and humans were their only clients."

I smiled. "You're right in that humans are usually their only clients, but a few other races trickle in here and there. They have skills beyond being midwives. Centuries ago, the Hearth Women were called the Handmaidens of Hera. Hera may have been the goddess of marriage, but she was often seen as a protector of the home, hearth, and childbirth. Could you ask them their opinion and advice?"

"Sure. If you think it will help."

"Thanks," I said. I had a feeling that they would be much more helpful to Trixie than to me, because much like their patron goddess, the Hearth Women didn't much care for men. "Oh, and a word of advice: don't eat or drink anything they offer. Also, don't let them touch you if you can help it. Be polite, but also try to keep a distance."

"Why? Are they dangerous?"

"Only if you don't want to find yourself extremely fertile," I grumbled under my breath. "I think we've got enough to handle right now and don't need to add to it with an unexpected bundle of joy."

Trixie sank a little lower in her seat as she stared out at the winding road as we got closer to my apartment. "Definitely."

For now, I thought it was enough that I had told Trixie that I loved her. She knew I was doing everything within my power to protect her from the Towers and help fix her problem with the Summer Court. We had never talked about the future and we never uttered the word *kids* beyond commenting on mixing up a potion to protect against conceiving any. When the world wasn't on the brink of exploding around us, our lives were good and neither of us was ready to take it a step further. At least, I didn't think so.

A QUICK STOP at my apartment allowed me to wash off some of the dirt, sweat, and blood. I dug up an old T-shirt and changed into it while Trixie went to speak to the Hearth Women. I wasn't fond of leaving her alone, but I knew she'd get more out of them if I wasn't hovering close by.

Somewhat clean again, I jumped into my battered SUV, ready to head back toward Asylum. I looked up after shoving my key into the ignition and paused as my eyes caught on a trio of teenagers as they darted across the parking lot. One hesitated at the edge of a building and looked back at me with cold eyes before disappearing from sight with his companions. The trio reminded me of the Tower runaways that were loose in Low Town, struggling to stay hidden from the Towers and survive. Were they sticking together? Were they safe? Were they hurt? I didn't know, but it was too dangerous to go looking for them. They were likely better off without my help.

With a groan, I turned the key, bringing the car to life with a guttural growl of the engine. I was up to my eyeballs in elf problems, Tower problems, and family problems. I didn't have much hope of protecting five runaways. Besides, they had each other. They had to be in better shape than I was when I left the Towers nearly ten years ago. *God, I hoped they were in better shape . . .*

Shoving that errant thought aside, I drove to the Strausse Haus Restaurant and Bier Garden near Asylum. It was the first place I had met Reave and I figured that it was the best place to start looking for the Svartálfar. I was hoping that he was still in town if he was planning to pass along the rest of the information to Robert. After that, I was sure the little fucker would be next to impossible to locate. He had to know that the Towers were searching for him and would be keeping his head down until he had gotten his payment. Though how he ever expected to live in peace after this was beyond my comprehension.

It was shortly after three when I arrived at the restaurant and their lunch rush was winding down.

The seating hostess smiled at me and picked up a menu as I walked in. "Hey, Gage. It's been a while since you last stopped in."

I smiled at her before continuing to scan the restaurant for my target. I had stopped going to the Strausse Haus when I discovered that it was one of Reave's favorite haunts. It was bad enough that Bronx and I were forced to work for him; I didn't want to eat somewhere that I might run into him as well.

"Is it just you for lunch?" she continued, trying to catch my attention.

"I'm not staying. I'm looking for someone," I said, my gaze tripping over the faces I could see lining the bar just past the entrance.

"You know, I heard you were dating that Trixie person who works for you," the hostess said, dragging my eyes back to her. "I should have known you'd go for someone like that."

I chuckled, my smile stretching into something genuine for the first time. Lynnette was pretty in an exotic, dangerous sort of way, with almond-shaped brown eyes that she lined with black makeup, and dark brown hair. She had those big pouty lips that held all kinds of dirty promises. It was the kind of mouth that my friend Parker referred to as DSL—dick-sucking lips. But then, Parker was an incubus and I was sure that he was well acquainted with mouths like that. My thoughts stopped there, though. Lynnette was a siren and sirens were their own basket of troubles. Not to mention I was quite happy with Trixie.

"I'd watch it, Lynn. I'd hate for Trixie to find out that you've been saying bad things about her."

Lynnette made a noise in the back of her throat as she rolled her eyes at me. "Like I'm scared of her."

My grin never wavered. "And here I always thought you were smarter than that." Her lovely mouth popped open on a gasp, her tanned cheeks flushing red in her anger. I continued before she could unleash whatever tirade was forming in her brain. "Have you seen Reave?"

The color immediately drained from her face and her mouth snapped shut with an audible click of her teeth. "Mr. Roundtree hasn't been in recently," she said quickly, her voice barely above a whisper.

"When did you last see Mr. Roundtree?" I demanded, unable to keep the sneer out of my tone.

"It—it's been a while. I don't remember." She refused to look up at me, her eyes locked on the menu tightly clenched in her hands.

"Then I guess I'll have a look around."

As I started to walk away, Lynnette grabbed my arm in a tight grip. "Don't do this. You don't want to mess with him, Gage," she urged with wide eyes as she struggled to hold me back at the entrance to the restaurant. "He's dangerous."

Lynnette might have been aware of who Reave was, but she didn't appear to know that I was now involved with the bastard. Even better, she didn't know what I was. Reave might have used the restaurant as a headquarters. Hell, he might have owned the joint, but at least Lynnette had been kept out of his business ventures. I didn't know Lynnette very well, had only spoken to her a handful of times when I had come into the Strausse Haus or run into her at any of the local bars, but she seemed like a nice person. She needed to keep her distance from the dark elf.

I gently squeezed her hand before prying it loose from my arm. "I know what I'm doing."

Frowning, she pulled her hand from mine and stepped back, returning to her place behind the hostess booth. She seemed to shrink inside of herself, her shoulders slumped and pulled in as if to protect herself from Reave and maybe even from her own dark thoughts. The fear in her eyes was yet another reason that this area needed to be free of Reave.

With a mental shove, I pushed those worries down as I entered the main dining area of the restaurant. Lunchtime was never a particularly busy time for the Strausse Haus, as there weren't many businesses close by that would bring in patrons. For the bulk of the places in the immediate area, business came at dinner and later when people stopped by to drink and unwind. Looking around the restaurant, I found fewer than a dozen of the tables and booths containing guests, while there were only three people seated at the bar, nursing drinks.

I wound my way toward the back of the restaurant, where the light was a little dimmer and there was only one occupied table. My eyes briefly fell on the semicircular booth where I had first met Reave, but it was empty. I had a feeling that the booth was kept vacant, available only to Reave.

Out of the corner of my eye, I saw something large rise from the one occupied booth near me. Jerking around, I swallowed a curse as the tension immediately eased from my frame when my eyes fell on Freddie "the Moose" Bukowski. He worked as muscle for Reave, and wasn't the brightest guy I'd ever met. He didn't seem the type to hurt a fly, but somehow he had gotten sucked into Reave's employment.

"Hi, Gage! It's good to see ya," Freddie said with a fast and eager grin. The mountain of a man reminded me of an overgrown St.

Bernard puppy who was convinced that he was a lapdog. He leaned a little closer. "It's good to see you not looking so beat up," he added in a stage whisper that most of the restaurant could hear. No matter how hard you tried, you couldn't stay mad at Freddie.

"Good to see you too, Freddie," I said, unable to stop my smile as I extended my hand to the man. It was immediately engulfed in his large paw and he pumped it vigorously in his excitement, threatening to dislocate my arm.

"How you been doin'? I've been meaning to stop down to see you, but Mr. Reave has been keepin' me busy."

"Been better," I muttered, following Freddie back to his table. As the large man returned to his seat in the booth, I got a look at the men he was sitting with, bringing a fresh grin to my face. One man scowled at me while the other seated next to him carefully kept his eyes on his plate. "Jack! It's been a dog's age since I last saw you," I exclaimed louder than necessary.

His companion snorted as he tried to hold in his laughter, which quickly changed to coughing as he reached for his mug of beer. Jack glared at his pack mate for a second before turning his black look on me.

"Not long enough," he growled. I could imagine he felt that way. A couple months back, I had wandered through his pack's territory and refused to pay a toll. Jack attempted to jump me, and I turned him into a Chihuahua. It didn't hurt him, but he was stuck like that until the next full moon when his werewolf side permitted him to shift. If he'd quit nursing his bruised ego, he'd realize that I'd let him off easy. Any other warlock would have killed him and his entire pack on the spot.

I slid into the booth next to Freddie. Jack opened his mouth as if he wanted to stop me, but gave up with a grunt as he dug back into his plate. In the center of the table there were bowls filled with mashed potatoes, sauerkraut, and large sausages along with a large pitcher of beer.

"I'm surprised that your pack hasn't stopped by for some new ink," I said, watching the men refill their plates. "When we first met, it didn't look like your pack had its own tag."

Jack sneered at me. "What do we need a tag for? My pack is the only one in Low Town."

I shrugged, slouching in the booth. "You're the only werewolf pack in Low Town, but you're not the only shifters. I thought you'd want a little something to proudly proclaim that you and your members are of the local wolf pack. Anyway, you'd need it if you ever traveled into another's territory."

Jack made some noncommittal noise, not looking up at me, but the other werewolf was watching me now. I vaguely remembered him as Jack's caretaker when the alpha had been indisposed. He was probably Jack's second in command.

"What kind of ink were you thinking?" he asked hesitantly.

At the same time a server approached, placing a fresh bowl of sausages on the table before setting a plate, silverware wrapped in a linen napkin, and a frosted mug in front of me. I hadn't planned to stay for food and I wasn't a big fan of German fare. The smell from the bowls in front of me was starting to make my stomach growl. It was getting late in the day and I had yet to eat anything.

"You got a pen I can borrow?" I asked, looking up at the server.

She smiled at me as she dug in her pocket and pulled out a black ballpoint. "Anything else?"

"Nope. Thanks."

Spreading out my napkin over my empty plate, I clicked the pen and started sketching as fast as my brain could work. In the center, I created a stylized *L* and *T*, then placed it within a large tree that had its branches and roots spread about a larger circle. "Being the Low Town pack and proud of that, you definitely need an *L* and *T* within the tattoo. Personally, if I see one more werewolf with a full moon or wolf howling as his pack tattoo, I think I'll puke. It's old, predictable, and been done to fucking death. What I'd like to see you do is have the letters carved into a large oak tree. The oak is a symbol of strength, power, and virility. Kings are associated with the oak. The roots would represent your long, proud history, and the limbs represent your strength and your reach across Low Town."

As I finished the description, I lifted the napkin and turned it around on the plate so that Jack and his pack mate could see it clearly. It wasn't my best work, but it wasn't bad for a quick sketch on a linen napkin. Freddie even leaned forward a little to look at it.

"And you don't put this on your chest or arm," I said, dragging their eyes back to me. "It goes on the side of your neck. That way everyone can see it at all times. Everyone knows that you're a member of the Low Town Pack."

"That's pretty cool," said the pack member, his gaze dancing over the design.

Jack's frown returned and he focused back on his plate, digging into the food with more force. "No."

"But—"

"Drop it, Dave," Jack snapped. "You know we can't."

I folded the napkin and placed it next to the werewolf called Dave. Grabbing my fork, I stabbed one of the sausages and took a bite. It tasted fantastic, going a long way toward settling the complaints of my stomach. "Who could stop you?" I asked around bites.

Dave directed his attention to his food. Jack paused before looking up at me. Hatred blazed in his brown eyes that held a hint of yellow from the line of werewolf flowing through his veins. For the first time, I didn't think that anger and hatred were directed at me.

"Reave," I said softly. Jack gave a grunt as he grabbed his mug and drained it. To my surprise, he picked up the pitcher and filled my mug before refilling his own. "Why?"

The silence stretched for a couple minutes, until I was sure that I wasn't going to get an answer, but Jack unclenched his jaw and spoke.

"I might be the alpha, but Reave considers the pack his. He has for as long as he's been in Low Town. A long time ago, he killed off the pack members that had tags and declared there would be no more clan tagging in Low Town. I think he's afraid that the tag would mean that our loyalty belongs to something other than him."

Finishing off my sausage, I stabbed another and munched on it as I sat back, thinking. "So, if Reave wasn't around . . ." I said, letting my voice drift off.

Jack let out a bark of laughter, the last of the anger leaving his face. "Yeah, when pigs fly. It's a nice thought, but you've got to remember, we know your secret, magic man. You can't use your hocus-pocus on him or us, and that's the only way you're going to get rid of someone like Reave."

I leaned across the table, an evil grin spreading across my face. "Can't, huh? How'd that work out for you?"

The laughter left Jack's eyes and he glared at me again. "Yeah, well, I doubt turning Reave into an ankle-biter is going to get rid of him."

I sat back, finishing off my second sausage while debating taking a third. Freddie turned to look at me, a worried expression across his ugly face.

"You can't do that to Mr. Reave, Gage," Freddie warned. "He said the Towers would kill you if you use magic. Mr. Reave also has a lot of protection like ogres and trolls and that dark elf magic."

"It's okay, Freddie," I said, patting him on the shoulder, trying to reassure him. "We're just talking. That's all. It's just talk."

"Yeah, Freddie, we don't mean anything by it," Dave added. Some of his long brown hair slid over one shoulder to cast his friendly face in shadow.

"Head up to the bar, Moose," Jack snapped, dropping his fork on his plate with a loud clatter. "We need some fresh drinks. Get some steins of Dunkle."

Freddie nodded, a smile on his face again. I slid out of the booth, letting Freddie out.

When I returned to the booth, Jack sat back, watching the large man walk away. "Freddie's a good guy, but he doesn't know how to keep his fucking mouth shut. The Dunkle will keep him busy for at least ten minutes. What are you thinking, warlock?"

I arched a brow at him. "How can I trust you? You said Reave owns your pack."

Jack shrugged, his thick arms folded over his chest. "The pack does what it's told and he ain't said nothing about keeping you in line. Reave's handling that personally along with his trolls. What's changed that you suddenly feel free to use your magical mojo?"

"All bets are off now that the Towers are pissed and Reave's behind it."

Jack straightened and even David was watching me intently now. "What are you talking about? Indianapolis?" Jack demanded in a low voice.

I nodded. "Reave has something they want and they're going to do a lot worse than Indianapolis if they don't get it back soon. If they find out he's in Low Town, the city and everyone in it are going to be dust."

Both men looked ill as they sat staring at me. Dave recovered first. "Where does that leave you? Are you going to use Reave to get back into the Towers?"

"I have no intention of ever going back there, but I can do without Reave. This whole town could do without that bastard." Shifting my gaze to Jack, I smirked. "The pack could too."

"Yeah," Jack muttered, staring at his half-empty mug. "What do you need?"

"Where's Reave hiding?"

Jack and Dave exchanged a look, leaving the second in command giving a small shrug. The alpha turned back to me, glaring at me through narrowed eyes. "If Reave's gone, where does that leave the pack?"

"Firmly in your hands, for all I care. I want out of this mess. Bronx too."

"Fine with me," Jack said with a careless wave of his hand. "He's hiding out on the west side. He's got a few warehouses out there. The old paper mill is his current hiding spot, up in the second-floor office. All the windows are blacked out because he's keeping a whole horde of ogres and trolls out there with him. I got the impression that he's waiting for something."

"Sounds like a party," I said as I started to slide out of the bench.

"Wait!" Jack's sharp command stopped me before I could reach my feet. The werewolf leaned across the table, lines of worry and stress digging into his face. "You finish this. If you don't, it's only going to take Reave one conversation with Freddie to find out where you got his location and the whole pack is done. I don't give a damn about myself, but I've got family in Low Town. A younger brother and two sisters along with a grandmother too sick to be dragged out if the Towers come here. You finish this."

"I will."

I shoved out of the booth and marched through the restaurant toward the front, my stomach starting to roil around the sausages I had inhaled minutes earlier. They tasted good going down, but the worry over the coming fight and the fear of the Towers was unsettling my stomach. As I passed by the bar, Freddie turned toward me, holding four large steins filled with a beer that looked as dark and thick as molasses.

"You leavin', Gage? I got your beer," he said, looking more than a little worried.

"Sorry, Moose," I said, forcing a smile on my mouth as I patted his shoulder. "I just got an important call and I've got to go. Can you drink it for me?"

His expression immediately brightened. "Sure, Gage. Thanks!"

I chuckled as I waved at Freddie before turning and heading for the door. There was something that I envied about Moose. For him, the great worries of the world were left to smarter men. He was content to shuffle along, following others. Freddie didn't seem to worry about more than his next meal, his next beer, and his bed at end of the day. I could have been wrong about him, but his deep thoughts never showed and the worries that scrunched up his face always faded with a reassuring word from someone he counted as a friend.

If only everything could be that simple. Or maybe not. Life would certainly be less of a headache, but a lot more boring. While I wasn't looking forward to the fight that Reave was offering, there was a part of me that welcomed it. I should have taken care of the dark elf months ago, but fear of the Towers had held me back. Now I was simply more afraid of what the Towers would do if I didn't act.

15

THE WEST SIDE of Low Town wasn't the prettiest part of town. Crowded with warehouses, steel mills, giant rusting buildings, large courtyards surrounded by metal fences topped with barbed wire, and smoke-belching stacks, the west side was the blue-collar, industrial side of town, while downtown and the east side catered to the corporate side of the city. If my childhood had been spent in Low Town, I would have lived on the east side, but I would have had my fun on the west side.

I knew the Boons & Mills paper plant that Jack had mentioned. The company had moved out of Low Town more than a decade ago and left the city with roughly a thousand fewer jobs. Parked a block from the building, I quickly discovered that many of the workers had shown their anger at the company by spray-painting some not-so-nice things on the sides of the structure and along some of the signs that still lined the sagging metal fence. The windows on the first and second floor had been boarded up. That was likely Reave's doing if he was keeping trolls with him during the daylight hours.

Glancing up as I approached the main gate, I smiled to see the sun shining bright and clear above my head without a cloud in sight. That could come in handy. My target was Reave, but if it came down to his thugs and the safety of Low Town, I'd take the fuckers down.

As I neared the gate, an ogre approached, a bloodstained meat cleaver clenched in his right fist at his side.

"Go away!" he barked.

"I need to see Reave," I said, keeping one eye on the meat cleaver.

"He's not here. Go away."

I stared at the ogre for a couple seconds, weighing my options. Threatening his comrades in the building was a waste of time, as ogres didn't much care for anyone else beyond themselves and the person who paid them. In fact, ogres didn't respond much to threats in the first place. They needed action.

Unfortunately, ogres were only slightly smaller than trolls, and the asshole in front of me wasn't exactly on the sickly side. I wouldn't be able to overpower him on my best day, particularly with a fence separating us. I'd have to use magic, which I preferred not to use. Of course, if hell hadn't fallen on my head over the little scuffle with William a couple hours ago, I figured I had a little time before Gideon beat my ass. Or so I hoped.

Smiling, I stepped forward and wrapped my fingers around the wide mesh of the chain-link fence. I started whispering a river of words that had the ogre frowning and taking a step backward. He watched intently as the metal beneath my fingertips started to drip and run as if it were melting. Within a couple seconds, large holes started to appear in the fence. I stopped whispering and gave the fence in my hands a hard jerk. The barrier ripped apart, the section collapsing to the ground with a cheery ring like tiny bells hitting concrete.

The ogre recovered from his bespelled wonder and charged me with a roar, raising his meat cleaver high. Heart pumping, I quickly shifted, sidestepping him at the last second so that he flew past me through the opening. I jumped inside the paper yard and waved my hands up in the air. The remains of the fence mended in a flash and wrapped around the ogre, trapping him in a steel net. He fell over with an angry shout, his arms locked against his body as he thrashed about.

Leaning over him, I reached through the chain-link fence and pressed two fingers to the head of the meat cleaver, repeating the words I had uttered before. The metal blade melted like ice cream on a summer sidewalk, soaking into his pants. Sure, he was still far from harmless, but at least he wasn't waving a meat cleaver around like some demented butcher. I could do without any fresh nightmares to haunt me—I already had plenty.

Footsteps across the gravel-covered pavement drew my attention away from my prisoner. His mad-cow bellowing had drawn his companions. Three more ogres were running in my direction, knives drawn. As I desperately scrambled for another defensive spell, my eyes lit on a patch of dirt and fine gravel a couple feet away from me. Running to the patch, I slid beside it, falling to my knees. I scooped up a handful, my short fingernails scraping against the concrete. Muttering another spell that I had never had the chance to work before, I held my hand open before my mouth and blew out a steady stream of air. The wind kicked up at my back, sweeping down across the ground before lifting up into the chests of the approaching ogres.

They slowed as they lifted their arms to shield their eyes. I squeezed my own eyes shut, straining to hear their footsteps over the wind that grew in its ferocity. The spell wasn't strong enough to generate a wind that could stop the ogres, but then I wasn't trying to do that. The scuff of feet on concrete sounded close, but it also sounded as if they were approaching much slower. Someone cursed in a gruff voice before something large hit the ground. Holding my breath, I waited, body tensed. They were damn close. I could hear the rustle of their clothes as they moved. A part of me was waiting to feel the ripping of flesh as a knife dug deep.

It wasn't until I heard two more heavy thuds hit the ground near me that I breathed a sigh of relief. I murmured a few words and lowered my hands to the ground as if I was pressing the air to the earth. The wind slowed and died down.

Lifting the collar of my T-shirt, I ducked my face inside, wiping my eyes with the interior of the shirt before daring to open them. Two ogres lay on the ground less than three feet away, their snores reverberating through the silent air. The third one was a little farther away, curled up into a ball on his side, while the ass wrapped in the fence had even dozed off. It had been a little closer than I would have liked, but it worked, and so far, no one had been killed.

The spell was called Sandman's Kiss, and I had never worked it before. However, I had used other sleep spells before so I knew the theory behind it. I was also pretty decent at manipulating the weather. It was only a matter of combining a few things to get the Sandman's Kiss working. The dirt on the ground was twisted into a sleep agent and the wind was the delivery method to get it into their eyes. The only problem was that I was fucked if I was stupid enough to get it in my eyes.

With a grunt, I rose back to my feet and brushed off my hands on my jeans. The sleep spell lasted roughly an hour on humans and like-size creatures. I was hoping that it would last at least half as long on something the size of an ogre. I couldn't imagine that it would take me that long to locate and deal with Reave. My best chance for handling the dark elf was to catch him by surprise.

Unfortunately, it looked like the shouting ogre had ruined that for me. A heavy metal door screeched as it was pushed open and an ogre leaned out to look around. Spotting me, he frowned, his large brow furrowing so that his eyes were cast in shadow. My steps slowed as I warily approached the building while he watched me.

"You Gage?" he said almost in a grunt.

"Yeah," I called, stopping several feet away with my hands out to my sides, waiting for the attack to come.

The ogre grunted again. "Reave's waiting for you." He moved back into the building but one hand held the edge of the door, propping it open for me. Yeah, I wasn't so comfortable with that. When I entered the dark building, I would be at a disadvantage as my eyes struggled to adjust from the bright sunlight I was currently standing in.

Spreading my legs wide, I reached out with both hands, feeling the power filling my frame as I magically grasped the edge of the door. With a jerk, I pulled it free of both the ogre's grip and the doorframe. The metal door groaned and shrieked as it jumped from the building and flew across the empty yard. The ogre lurched back and I could hear shouting from inside the old paper mill as sunlight poured unexpectedly into its entrance.

I waved one hand at the guard and he stepped back into the shadows as I approached. Pausing just over the threshold, I waited for my eyes to adjust to the darkness, trying desperately to discern more than vague shapes of large creatures moving around in the shadows. An increase in the sound of shuffling feet on gritty concrete nearly had me taking a step back in to the yard, but I couldn't backpedal. I needed to take out Reave, or at the very least hand him over to the Towers so that they would stop their madness.

Using the same spell I had called up to rip the door off its hinges, I pushed outward through the building. Sounds of stumbling filled the silence. Large crates fell over and crashed to the ground, and still I pushed until the energy reached the outer walls. Wood creaked and groaned before one board after another flew off the large windows that lined the walls. Loud guttural shouts echoed through the empty building as large squares of light shot through the air to land in regular patches on the floor. The shadows receded, but then so did the dark figures that had been looming in the blackness, waiting for me.

As I stepped onto the main floor of the mill, I found that I was alone except for the ogre who had held the door open. There was some shuffling coming from the deeper shadows near the back of the warehouse and behind some of the large machinery that had never been taken from the building. I didn't see any new giant-size lawn ornaments, to my relief. Apparently none of the trolls had been caught by the light. I didn't mind beating the shit out of these assholes, but I was trying to avoid killing anyone if I could help it. Well, anyone but Reave.

Loud clapping jerked my head up to a second-floor catwalk that looked down on the main floor. Reave was standing overhead, a twisted grin on his thin lips. "Well, this is a surprise. Someone isn't too worried about the Towers, now, is he?"

"Why should I worry about the Towers when you're determined to destroy us all?" I shouted, tapping down the urge to rip him off the catwalk with a surge of energy. I didn't need to. With a hiss, Reave vaulted over the rusted metal railing and landed lightly on his toes right in front of me.

"That's just it. None of us should feel the need to worry about how the Towers will react," he snarled. "You're all power-hungry monsters determined to wipe us from the earth. You need to be stopped."

"Yes, they need to be stopped." I sidestepped him, trying to keep a comfortable distance between us as we circled each other. "But whatever you've got planned is going to get everyone killed when a new war breaks out. That's what you're driving us toward. Not freedom. Just death." I was unarmed except for my magic and Reave was fucking fast. The meat cleaver I melted earlier was starting to look pretty damn good.

"You're afraid—"

"Of course I'm fucking scared! You're threatening my family and friends. You're threatening millions of people who have never done a damned thing to you."

Reave sprang at me, swinging his fist at my face. I ducked away at the last second, but it was close enough that I could feel the breeze against the tip of my nose. I threw a couple punches at him but never connected. The bastard was too fast.

Large beefy arms wrapped around my chest from behind, pinning my arms to my sides. The arms squeezed my chest, making it difficult to draw a deep breath. I had forgotten about the ogre who had opened the door for me. He'd snuck up on me while I was busy with Reave.

The dark elf laughed as he came closer, watching me struggle. I kicked out with both feet, hitting Reave in the chest with enough force to send him stumbling backward onto his ass. At the same time I jerked my head back, breaking the ogre's nose when it crashed into his face. The ogre dropped me on a howl of pain as he backpedaled.

Landing easily, I turned in a circle on my toes, waving my arms in the air as I called together large amounts of magical energy. The air crackled and my skin tingled against the charge as I was gathering. This wasn't so much a spell as it was me forcibly moving around energy. Regardless, Gideon was going to put my ass in a sling any second now, but I couldn't stop. As I turned to face the ogre on my second turn, I pushed the energy outward, knocking him on his back and thrusting him out of the building through the open doorway. I continued to spin, turning back to face Reave in time to see him rise to his feet. Throwing my arms out to my sides, I shoved the trolls gathered in the shadows against the wall, leaving me alone to deal with the Svartálfar.

"I want the names of the people you plan to sell the information to," I demanded, taking a step toward the dark elf.

"Information? What information?" he replied with a grin.

"The locations of the Towers. How many do you know?" I didn't care that the trolls and ogres in the area could probably hear me. I would take them all out, destroy the entire building if I had to in hopes of protecting the people of Low Town. And to do that, I had to stop the information that Reave was trying to traffic.

The dark elf's voice was low and cold when he spoke. "All of them. All seven."

I kept my face blank, but inside I breathed a sigh of relief. He was still missing one. Unfortunately, knowledge of even one Tower location was one too many.

With a wave of my hand, I shoved some raw energy at Reave, pushing him across the floor until his back was pressed against a support beam in the middle of the warehouse. His arms were pinned to his sides. Gritting his teeth, he struggled against the spell that held him captive, but he was trapped as long as I could concentrate on holding him to the beam.

"Who are the people trying to buy the information?" I asked again.

"And why should I tell you?"

"Because this has to end. These people trying to directly assault the Towers need to be stopped before they kill us all in another war."

"You're right. This does have to end, but it's the Towers that need to fall. The people of this world won't continue to bow to their whims. We're done," he said with a low growl.

"I understand your frustration and hatred, but—"

"You understand?" Reave tipped his head back and laughed, the horrible and slightly mad sound echoing through the large room. "You understand nothing. You're one of them. You're only trying to protect your own interests in hopes that they'll let you into their exclusive club again."

"Not if I can help it." I reached back with my right fist and plowed it into his face, hitting him across the cheekbone and snapping his head back so that it bonged off the metal support beam. "Tell me their names!"

"No," Reave grunted. "The Towers need to be stopped."

I fisted my hand again to hit him but didn't. Beating Reave senseless wasn't going to get the information out of him and I wasn't skilled enough with the kind of enchantment spells I would need to go digging around in his brain for the information. He needed to be handed over to the Towers so that they could pry out the information and stop the chaos that was swirling around the world.

"Fine," I said, dropping my hand back to my side. Reave watched me through narrowed eyes, waiting for me to attack again. "You're the only one who knows all the locations. The information has been contained. I'll hand you over to the Towers. They'll kill you and stop hurting the rest of the world in an effort to protect themselves."

The Svartálfar gave a low chuckle that made my skin crawl. I took a step back, glaring at him, as his laughing ground to a halt. "That's where you're wrong, warlock."

"What are you talking about?"

"After the destruction of Indianapolis, I had a feeling that you'd come knocking on my door and I needed a little insurance." Reave paused and licked his lips as he watched me like I was a bug under a magnifying glass. I was hardly breathing, waiting to find out who else he had blessed with this damning information, but I was afraid that I already knew. "Dear Robert has been such a valuable employee and he has such a hatred for the Towers that I knew he'd want to help. So I pulled him aside and helped him memorize each location. Now he'll spit out the information to anyone who asks and he won't be able to stop himself."

I sucked in a harsh breath as I stumbled a step backward. That was where my brother had disappeared yesterday. It wasn't about getting a change of clothes. He was checking in with Reave.

I cursed, suddenly sick to my stomach. If I took Reave to the Towers now, they would pull loose the information on Robert as well. They would demand his life along with Reave's. My mind scrambled, trying to find a way to hand over Reave without trapping Robert as well but I couldn't think of anything. If I killed Reave myself, I wasn't sure that I'd be able to convince the council that the threat had been taken care of. I needed the Svartálfar alive with his mind intact to hand over to the Towers if we were to survive this mess.

Stunned by Reave's revelation, I forgot about the binding spell. Reave leaped at me, plowing a fist into my gut before I could react.

I stumbled but caught myself before I could fall on my ass. Rage pumped in my veins, burning a new hole through my soul. Reave had endangered my brother's life with his plans. He endangered us all. I'd put this asshole on ice somewhere until I could find a way to protect Robert and then I'd hand him over for torture in the Towers.

"You wanted to take on a warlock. Well, now you've got one," I growled.

A wide grin slithered across Reave's face as he palmed a long, curved blade that had been hanging at his side. "You? You're no warlock." He chuckled. "You're some kid who couldn't cut it with the other grown-ups, so you ran. And now I'm going to cut you down." The dark elf took a step, slicing at me with the curved blade in his right hand. I dodged it in time, watching the knife swing wide of me, but it was the unseen blade in his left hand that got me, digging into my side before I could react.

I groaned, my body clenching and stiffening as the pain exploded out from my side. Reave jerked the blade free, twisting it as he pulled. I clapped my hand over the wound, struggling to slow the bleeding as I scrambled for a new spell that would knock Reave unconscious without taking his head off in the process. Subtle spells weren't my specialty.

Grinning, Reave slashed with both knives, backing me up. This was fucking ridiculous. I was trying to fight him with magic when I didn't need to. Releasing my side, I dodged one blade while blocking his other arm with mine as it attempted to slash across my neck. My side screamed and my back throbbed, but I ignored the pain as I lifted my leg and kicked him in the knee. Reave moved at the last second and I only clipped it at an angle, but it was enough to get the dark elf to warily back off while favoring that leg.

"I think we've had enough fun for one day, boy," he said. "You've got more to worry about than just me." The bastard came at me fast. I dodged and blocked what I could, but the pain in my side and steady loss of blood was slowing me down. In the end, it was a foot in the sternum that put me on my back in the dusty warehouse. I jerked upright again with a groan, but all I caught was a glimpse of Reave's back as he sprinted out of the open doorway, disappearing into the bright midday glare of the fenced-in courtyard.

Another groan slipped past my clenched teeth as I got to my feet and ran to the doorway, grasping my side with my left hand. My feet skidded through the dirt and gravel as I stopped in the open area and looked for Reave, but he was already gone. The ogres I had knocked out were still lying on the ground, but the one who opened the door was missing. He shouldn't have been able to get away that fast, but I had a feeling he had sprinted to wherever Reave's car was stashed and started it in the event that the Svartálfar would need a fast getaway.

"Fuck!" I shouted. I shuffled across the courtyard, holding my side, grumbling about Reave, the Towers, and my own stupidity. I even paused long enough to kick one of the sleeping ogres in the head. He snorted once and rolled over before continuing to sleep, undisturbed.

When I reached my SUV, I stood next to the front grille and lifted my shirt to look at the cut. It didn't look that big, but the bleeding hadn't slowed. A good portion of my shirt and the left side of my jeans were soaked. Swearing again, I pulled the wound closed with my left hand while whispering a quick healing spell. I used just enough magic to knit the interior wounds and close the skin. I didn't want to waste the energy on the blood or the pain.

With a sigh, I leaned against the grille and glared at the old paper mill. This trip had been a disaster. Reave had fled and I had no idea if he was even going to remain in the area now. Robert had the information, making him a massive target. I was hoping my brother thought he still needed me. Strangling Reave sounded so good, but a living Reave with brain intact was the only thing that was going to stop the Towers. But now that seemed impossible since I didn't have a clue as to where he had gone.

As I stood there, trying to pull together the energy to move, I heard a strange, leathery, flapping noise. Wincing, I pushed back to my feet and twisted around, looking for the source of the noise. I didn't think it was Reave—the bastard had to be at the edge of town by now—and it wasn't the sort of noise that would come from an ogre. As the sound got closer, I looked up to see something I had never expected to see within the confines of Low Town.

The creature pulled its batlike wings in, swooped down toward me, and then threw its wings back out again so that it stopped barely a foot from my face. I lurched away, slamming my back into my SUV. The hobgoblin cackled with mischievous glee, his little face split with a wide grin while his almond-shaped black eyes flashed at me. Collapsing his wings a second time to his back, the hobgoblin dropped to the ground and landed lightly on all four limbs like a cat.

He quickly scurried over and climbed up the front of the car until he was seated on the hood. Hobgoblins were strange little fey creatures that were never seen within the city limits, as they preferred deep, undisturbed woods. This one was the first one I had seen up close. I had caught a glimpse of a couple over the years while camping and that was enough to give me nightmares. While prone to playing silly pranks when the mood hit them, they were rarely dangerous.

It was their appearance that I found frightening. Between their large leathery wings, the small horns on their heads, enormous pointed ears, and the pumpkin-orange scaly skin, they looked like demons escaped from an underworld amusement park. This one sat on the end of my hood, his legs crossed in front of him while his long, pointed tail idly swung from side to side.

"You Gage?" the hobgoblin asked. His voice was low and earnest as he leaned forward a bit.

"Yeah." The word came out slowly as I tensed, waiting for something new to attack me. It had been one of those days when someone was always waiting around the corner to remove my head or turn me into a magpie.

The hobgoblin tipped backward, his little feet kicking up in the air as he laughed and clapped his hands. "Ha ha! I told her I would find you! She had her doubts, but I knew I could!"

"Who? The queen?" The queen of the Summer Court was the only person I could think of who might have dealings with a hobgoblin, let alone had the ability to get them to complete a task. According to most textbooks, they didn't much care to obey anyone.

He instantly stopped laughing, but was still smiling broadly at me. "Oh, no." He then said something in this high, squeaky voice, but I shook my head, not understanding. "Her," he said, and then the two-foot-high hobgoblin disappeared and was replaced by a three-inch-tall violet pixie hovering in the air as her little dragonfly wings beat a mile a minute. A second later, the pixie was gone and the hobgoblin was back to sitting on the hood of my car.

"Her? The pixie?" I asked, and he nodded. "She was at that fix house, right?"

"Yes, she said you rescued her. Saved her life."

"Okay, but why did you need to find me?" The little devil wasn't making any sense, but he seemed pleased with himself over something.

"She was worried over you. She thought you'd be in trouble with that Svartálfar. I told her that I'd find you, keep an eye on you."

"Why?"

"To help her clear her debt with you. She's a good friend."

"And you're doing this out of the kindness of your heart?" I said, looking down at the hobgoblin through narrowed eyes.

The little fey grabbed his long tail in both hands and looked away from me, seeming almost embarrassed. "Well, she said you were a warlock and that you were taking on a Svartálfar alone. I thought you must be a lot of fun, so I wanted to tag along for a bit."

What he meant was that he thought I was a one-man wrecking

crew, causing chaos and mayhem wherever I went, and he wanted to watch the destruction, particularly if it involved a Svartálfar.

I sighed and roughly scrubbed my hand over my face. I didn't need this. "Look . . ."

"Duff. I'm Duff," he supplied with a grin.

"Look, Duff, it's been a rough day. I had a little powwow with the Svartálfar and it didn't go so great."

"I saw." It was the first time that he didn't sound like he was about to burst out laughing.

I sat down on the bumper beside him and groaned. "And now I haven't a clue as to how I'm going to find the bastard," I said, talking mostly to myself.

The little hobgoblin giggled and pounded on the hood with his two small hands. I jerked, turning to look at him as he exclaimed, "We can find him for you!"

"What?"

Duff leaned in and grabbed my cheeks in both hands, his fingers pinching my flesh in his growing excitement. "Reave. The Svartálfar. We can find him. You need him? We can find him."

I stood, pulling my face out of his grip. "I don't understand."

"I can get the pixies and some of my people! We can find him, track him. It'll be fun. We'll find him for you so my friend can clear her debt. Right? It will clear her debt?"

"You and your friends can do it safely?" Hope started to form in my chest. I might have a way out of this mess.

He nodded eagerly, a grin spreading across his face with a wicked delight. "We can find him for you. We'll watch from a distance and be safe."

I stared at him for a second, trying to think of some other option, but I was drawing a blank. "And you have no problem helping me?"

He held up his hand like he was trying to balance a set of scales. "Don't like the Towers. They killed so many fey. On the other hand, you don't seem evil. You saved my friend and many others. Also, you seem . . . different. Better. Funner."

I nodded. "All right. If you and your companions can find and follow him safely, then I'd appreciate your help. You can find me at my tattoo parlor when he settles in one location. I'll come and get him. He won't escape a second time."

The hobgoblin gave a happy shout as he launched himself off the car, his wings thrown wide as he took to the air. He gave me a little salute before darting off. I tried to watch him go but he was surprisingly fast, disappearing around some buildings.

I pushed off the grille of the car and rose with a groan. My side was killing me as it healed, and my clothes were rough and scratchy from all the dried blood. I was hurt, tired, and pissed from today's adventure. Reave got away, which was the one thing that I couldn't let happen if I was going to have any hope of saving Low Town and stopping the coming war. But at least I now knew that Robert was in deep shit. Well, deeper than since we last spoke.

For now, Reave was on hold until Duff could get back to me with his location. I would have to turn my focus to protecting Robert and finding a way to get Trixie safely back with her people. If I couldn't save Low Town, then I could at least make sure she had somewhere safe that I could stash her for a little while. It wasn't much, but right now I'd be happy with one thing going my way.

DAYLIGHT WAS WASTING away and there was still too much that I needed to get done. I reached Robert on his cell and convinced him to barricade himself in my apartment until I could get him into the parlor for a tattoo. In the meantime, I needed to stop by Chang's while I figured out what to do to protect my brother.

Despite the fact that the world dangled on the cusp of total destruction, nothing appeared to have changed at the entrance to Chang's. I cut through Diamond Dolls, barely aware of the exotic dancers as they made their turns around the silver pole in the middle of the stage while customers lounged in battered chairs, sucking down beers. Ducking into the white room near the back of the strip club, I found the two Doberman pinschers waiting for me. Everything normal. Yet, when we stepped into the elevator, the canine pushed the button to the first floor of the subbasement rather than the third, where I always met the old man, causing a fresh rush of tension to gather in my shoulders.

As the doors slid open with a soft hiss, I waited for one dog to lead the way as it always did, but neither moved. I looked down at the dogs, but both were staring straight ahead.

"Come along, Gage," Chang called, his disembodied voice dancing down the hallway.

Frowning, I stepped off the elevator and walked down the dimly lit white hall before turning a corner to enter the main room. My mouth fell open as my eyes struggled to take in the enormous garden spread before me. Much like the third floor of the warehouse that I always visited with him, the first floor appeared to be an enormous room with two-story ceilings. Yet instead of the usual assortment of tables and shelves filled with rare items, the room housed an enormous garden that would have put Versailles to shame. It somehow looked organized and elegant as well as wild and untamed all at the same time. Lush flowers bloomed around trees that stretched up to the ceiling. But the most spectacular thing was the light. I couldn't see a single bulb overhead, but the room was as bright as midday despite the fact that we were several feet underground.

It was only when I felt a small hand pat me on the arm that I pulled my eyes away from the garden to look down at Chang. The wily old Chinese man looked older than the Cairo pyramids, but there was a twinkle in his brown eyes that reminded me that appearances could be so deceiving. He raised a large metal watering can and I took it without thinking.

"Come, help me," he said with a wave of his hand before he started down a winding gravel path that disappeared into the garden. I followed him, parting the limbs of a weeping willow that hung over the path. The light that cast the room in a golden glow dimmed as we walked deeper into the garden, coming under the shade of so many massive trees.

"It looks like you've been busy," I said, struggling to keep one eye on the little old man with the cane while my attention kept getting drawn to the garden.

Chang gave a little chuckle and shook his head. "I have had this garden for years. It is very relaxing to wander here."

"Yes, but with everything going on topside, I didn't think I'd find you here."

The little old man paused and looked up at me. "The world is falling apart. Indianapolis has disappeared like Atlantis and Pompeii. Where would you be if you fear it is your last moments?"

I looked around, taking in the general serenity of the place. Except for the sound of water flowing past the banks of some distant stream that was cutting through the room, it was silent. The air was thick and heavy with humidity and the scent of flowers. It was as if the outside world had ceased to exist beyond Chang's private Eden.

I looked down at the old man and gave him a weak smile. "I understand."

"You were always a smart boy, Gage," he said with a wink. He continued walking with me, following a couple paces behind until he paused before an outcropping of what looked to be limestone. He pointed to several beds of light violet-colored flowers huddled near the rocks. "Give those flowers a drink for me."

With a nod, I walked over and watered them with the can he handed me. As I stood there, I peered closer at the flowers, taking in their thick leaves and delicate buds. Raising the watering can, I jerked around to Chang, who was watching me with a look of expectation.

"These are Cry Pansies, aren't they?" I demanded. Chang nodded, his smile growing. Putting the can on the ground, I knelt down for a closer look. "These are extinct." I barely controlled the urge to reach out and touch one of the blooms. "Not even the Towers have these in their greenhouses."

"Of course not," Chang snapped, drawing my gaze up to him again. He waved his hand at the flowers. "No magic or potion value. The Towers only save what they can use."

I pushed to my feet again and dusted my hands off before picking up the watering can. "Thank you, Chang, for showing me this. They are beautiful."

"It's my way of ensuring that certain plants do not disappear from this earth," he said with a shrug, but his face quickly brightened with a new thought. "I have a small section of my garden dedicated to Saint Helena. That island lost so many plants. I rescued an olive, ebony, and heliotrope."

I walked back over to the little old man and followed him as he continued to wander through the garden.

"I'm surprised that you recognized the Cry Pansy," he said, breaking the growing silence.

I paused, staring at a deep red bloom that appeared to be the extinct Cosmo Atrosanguineus. There was supposedly a clone in a Tower greenhouse, but the original was long gone from the earth. Except maybe for the one that I was now looking at. "A long time ago when I was studying, I discovered that I was pretty good at remembering the various uses for plants as well as their growing requirements. I thought when I got older I would spend a chunk of my life working in one of the Tower greenhouses. I always imagined that it would be peaceful and safe." My voice died off as I stared at the flower. I had never gotten to the greenhouse in Dresden, or more important, the massive exotics greenhouse at the Antarctica Tower. I was too busy trying to escape.

A sigh rose up in my chest and it was hard to hold it in. The greenhouses were just one example of the good the Towers could do. They preserved rare and nearly extinct plants and flowers, which could be used to heal wounds and cure diseases. But the warlocks and the witches weren't interested in saving the people of the world. Just themselves.

The sound of Chang's feet steadily moving down the gravel path tore me from my thoughts and I followed him until he sat on a carved wooden bench under an ancient oak tree. He gave a relieved sigh as he settled on the bench and stretched his thin legs out in front of him. Setting the watering can by the side of the bench, I sat next to Chang and looked out across the garden. I hadn't realized it as we walked, but we had moved uphill, so that we now looked over a large section that was spread out in a vast explosion of color. For just a moment the world had slipped away from us and there were no threats from the Towers or the Summer Court or Reave. It was just Chang and me, lost in nature.

"I've heard rumors," Chang started, his voice soft and almost hesitant. "I've heard the Towers are looking for something stolen from them."

Looking down at the old man, I arched one eyebrow and frowned. "Do you have a guilty conscience? Is there something you would like to confess?"

Chang scowled at me but didn't speak. My composure cracked and I smiled. "I can't imagine that your conscience would ever prick you. At least not when it comes to the Ivory Towers." The brief humor slipped from me and the weight of the situation descended on my shoulders again. "But the rumors are true in a way. They are looking for something they protect, but you can rest easy in that it's not anything that you've recently procured. Well, I certainly hope that you're not attempting to purchase this item."

The old man stopped scowling, but didn't lose his dark expression as he looked straight ahead again. "There are many interesting things that the warlocks and witches guard, but most . . . most are hidden within the Towers and can be accessed by only another witch or warlock. And seeing how you are the only warlock that I do business with . . ."

"We both know I have enough problems. I'm not fetching you new baubles from the Towers to add to your collection."

Chang didn't even blink an eye at my comment. Today was the first time either one of us had vocalized what I was sure he had always known. We didn't speak of my past with the Towers and I never asked how he knew. Chang knew things—that was how he had become the best at acquiring the exotic.

There was a tightness around his eyes as he stared at some distant point. He was turning something over in his mind. When he spoke, his words were slow, as if he was choosing them very carefully. "The destruction of Indianapolis. Nasty business and very visible. The

Towers do not handle problems in their own house like that, and if they were all hunting you . . ." Chang paused and looked me over in such a way that I could almost hear the calculator in his head. "If they were hunting you, you would have already been dead. No, I think they lost the one thing that we can actually steal from them."

"Chang," I warned, trying to force the wheels in his brain to stop.

"The locations."

My shoulders slumped and a headache started to throb in my temples. The old man was too smart for his own good. That or . . . "I pray by all that's holy you're not the buyer."

Chang cackled, slapping the bench armrest on his right in his amusement. It was the first time he seemed to slip back into his usual mood. Since I had stepped into his garden, he had seemed subdued and almost melancholy. But then, no one in Low Town was in a good mood at the moment.

"You're so funny, Gage," he said as his laughing died down. "Do you think I don't know where all the Towers are located?"

"How many?"

Chang's grin became positively evil as he held up eight fingers.

I slapped my hands over my ears and hunched over, trying to shrink into the other side of the bench. "Stop, Chang! I don't want to hear it! I've got enough fucking problems." Despite having my ears covered, I could hear him laughing at me, and I deserved it. If I stopped for one minute and thought about it, really thought about it, I knew that Chang already knew the locations of the Ivory Towers. The man had his hands on every interesting artifact, treasure, and doodad that had ever been created. Of course, he knew the locations! I just didn't want to know about him knowing.

I dropped my hands from the sides of my head and let them dangle between my legs as I stared at the ground, feeling as if I were worn down to the bone. Chang stopped laughing and grew silent beside me. He shifted on the bench and leaned forward to look at my face.

"Is that why you are here? Someone knows and you think I am buying the information?"

I sighed. "In all honesty, the thought didn't cross my mind until a minute ago. A different problem has brought me here today."

The old black-market seller clapped me on the back. "Gage, you can't afford another problem."

"No shit," I muttered. With a grunt, I sat back against the bench and stretched out my legs in front of me. The peace of the garden was starting to seep into my soul, easing away some of the tension. I pushed aside thoughts of the Towers and their wayward secret. I suppressed worries of Reave and the havoc he could wreak on this world. Arianna's problem was what had dragged me to Chang's doorstep. I was focused on the Summer Court and would deal with the rest when I heard from Duff.

"What do you know about impregnating elves?" I asked.

For the first time since I had met him, Chang looked dumbfounded. His little face wrinkled up and his mouth hung slightly open as if he was struggling to formulate a good answer. I came to Chang when I needed something to undo a curse, some magical protection, or maybe just a little bit of weirdness for a tattoo. This subject was not a comfort zone for either of us.

"I've not made any elf pregnant!" he finally exclaimed.

A deep chuckle rolled from my chest before I could stop it. "Not accusing you," I said with a grin. Draping my right arm over the back of the bench, I turned slightly so that I was facing him. "My latest problem is with the elves. Particularly the Summer Court, though I wouldn't be surprised if they were all having this problem."

"Are you trying to have a baby with an elf?" Chang shook his head, looking worried. "This is not a good time, Gage. Maybe you should wait."

"What? No! No, I'm not trying to have a kid." I jerked back from him like I had been stung. "I've agreed to help the Summer Court. They're having problems reproducing."

"Oh!" Chang laughed with a clap of his hands, looking more than a little relieved as he slumped on the bench. I was with him on that one. I definitely didn't need a kid when hell was breaking loose all around us.

"I've got Trixie checking with the Hearth Women for some herbal remedies," I continued, now that his mind was with me. "But I'm willing to bet they've tried most of that already. I've got a couple potions that I use to help keep people from getting pregnant, but I don't know any fertility potions or even spells. I was wondering if you had some kind of charmed item that might have been owned or created by some long-dead fertility god. Or how about a colored egg created by the Eostre? She was the goddess of fertility, right?"

"Yes, but that is not what you need." Chang frowned at me. "Creating children isn't easy business."

I arched a questioning brow that stopped him, causing him to think about what he just said.

"Bah!" He waved one hand at me in irritation. "Humans breed like rabbits because they are so fragile. I mean creating children isn't easy when magic gets involved."

"Why?"

He placed his scratched wooden cane in front of him and rested both hands on the curved end before looking at me. "Birth, babies . . . it's all a matter of old magic. Not that stuff those Towers use. *Real* old magic."

"You're talking the big bang, start of the cosmos, fabric of time, and breath of life magic," I said softly. Chang nodded and I heaved a heavy sigh. This was stuff that I didn't mess around with. No one did.

"Is it just one person who is having trouble or all of the elves?" he asked.

"It's one person that I'm trying to help, but it sounds like all the elves are having issues."

Chang scratched the top of his head, leaving some of his hair standing on end. "One Eostre egg isn't going to fix things. Not long term. Sounds like a spell. Bad spell."

"But what kind of a spell could do this? It didn't hit them all at once. It seems like they've gradually lost the ability to have children. Spells don't work that way. When one attacks a group, it's either all or nothing." I pushed off the bench and paced away a few feet with my hands shoved in my pockets as I fought against the growing frustration and nervous energy. "Besides, if it's a spell, I'm screwed. I'd have to find the person who created the spell if I hoped to unravel it. That takes time; time I don't have."

"Just because it's inconvenient doesn't stop it from being the truth," Chang said, stopping my pacing.

He was right. I might not like the answer, but that didn't keep it from being the truth. Unless Trixie found some strange change in the habits of her people, it made logical sense that the elves had been hit with some kind of infertility spell. Unfortunately, I wasn't skilled enough to know how to fix it. I needed a stronger witch or warlock or a big stack of spell books written by someone other than me. Gideon was out because he was too busy to bother with me. That only left Sofie, but since she was stuck as a cat, I wasn't sure how well she could instruct me in the construction of a fertility spell. And spell books were out. I didn't see the council letting me stop by to raid their library so I could perform magic I've already been forbidden to perform.

"I'm screwed," I grumbled, rubbing my hand roughly over my face as I tried to think of a way out of this hole.

"Maybe not," Chang said thoughtfully.

I looked up at the old man, trying to shove down the hope that was swelling in my chest. Whatever he thought of wasn't going to be cheap. Or easy for that matter. "You've got something? A little relic that knocks up women at fifty paces?"

"Not quite." Chang frowned at me, as if debating whether to tell me. "She doesn't like visitors. You must be respectful. If she says she can't help, you leave. No arguing. Do you understand?"

I nodded. "Sure. Of course. Who are you sending me to?"

Using his cane, Chang slowly rose from the bench and then withdrew his old leather wallet from the back pocket of his stained and patched brown pants. I watched as he opened it with slightly trembling hands and flipped through a pile of cards and folded bits of paper before he came to what he was looking for. He held out a white card to me while he shoved his wallet back into his pocket.

Flipping the card over, there was only one word: GAIA. Arching one eyebrow, I looked at Chang as he settled himself back on the bench.

"You're kidding, right?" I said before I could stop myself.

Chang extended a hand toward me. "If you don't want . . ."

I jerked the card back and even stepped away from him, which only caused the little old man to chortle. I wasn't sure that I quite believed in the existence of Gaia, but if Chang thought this woman could help me, then I wasn't willing to throw away the opportunity.

In truth, I didn't believe in the gods and goddess. I had a feeling that most were just powerful beings such as a witch or warlock, but not quite of god status. Or at least what I thought of as a god.

"So you're suggesting that I pay ol' Mother Nature a visit?" I said, turning over the card between my fingers. There was no address, no phone number, no Web site listed (not that I actually expected this Gaia to have a Web site, but you never know).

Chang grinned at me. "Can you think of anyone who might know more about life and birth?" He paused as if thinking of something and then gave a little shrug as he corrected himself. "Well, anyone you can actually talk to for answers?"

"Look, at this point, I'm open to trying anything. If you think she'll give me a hand with this, I'll pay her a visit."

Chang shook his head. "I didn't say that she'd help you. I just know that if anyone can fix it, she can."

"Fantastic," I muttered. Mother Nature would know how to help the elves, but it was all a matter of getting the old girl to give me a hand. This was certainly turning into one of those days when it would have been better if I didn't bother to crawl out of bed.

But it was a start. It was a direction to go in rather than spinning my wheels and wasting time that I didn't have. I sucked in a deep breath and straightened my shoulders. I could do this. Holding up the card toward Chang, I said, "There's no address. How am I to find her?"

"When you're ready to see her, she'll reach out to you."

"And what do I owe you for this?"

Chang's grin turned evil as it spread across his face and his eyes narrowed to thin slits. I suppressed a shiver as I looked at him, trying to remind myself that he was always fair. Of course, the little wrinkled man knew that I was desperate.

"Styx," he said.

I frowned, my stomach clenching. I told myself that it could have been worse, but I wasn't thrilled. A couple months ago I hanged myself so I could get to the underworld and obtain some of the water from the five rivers. Desperation had already forced me to trade Chang the water from Phlegethon, the river of fire, for a protection amulet—which I promptly lost. The River Styx was not only the river of hate, but it was also the river of death, as it was the main gateway to the other side. I wasn't yet willing to part with the Styx water.

Shaking my head, I shoved the card in my front pocket. "You've given me information rather than an item. Pointed me in a potential direction rather than given me a cure. The best I can offer is Cocytus."

"Cocytus? River of lamentation?"

"The water is supposed to be angel tears," I added, hoping this would entice him.

Chang gave a snort. "We both know how well using something from an angel worked for you," he said a bit snidely. I flushed but kept my mouth shut. You make one girl immortal using an angelic relic, and no one lets you forget about it. Of course, the entire ordeal had been a disaster, forcing me to commit suicide to get the Styx water in the first place so that her immortality could be cured. I'd learned my lesson and was now steering clear of anything angelic. "Cocytus and Acheron," the old man countered.

"Cocytus and Lethe," I challenged. Something about Acheron, the river of sorrow, made me nervous after seeing the swamp-like area while in Charon's ferry. I wasn't ready to hand that one over just yet either. Lethe represented forgetfulness, and while dangerous, it didn't send a chill through me like the Styx or Acheron did.

"Done!" Chang said with a thump of his cane on the ground.

"Can I drop it off in a few days? I don't exactly carry the waters with me."

Chang smiled at me and waved one hand as he pushed to his feet again. "I trust you. You'll drop it off. You're a good boy, Gage."

I followed as the little old man started back down the path that we had taken to the bench. Looking around, I couldn't tell how long I had been in his garden. This was no change in the intensity or slant of the light. Time seemed frozen here, and despite the garden's overwhelming beauty and tranquillity, I was ready to leave. But it was always like that when I visited Chang. He was an amusing little man, with a wicked grin and a gleam in his eye, but if you thought too long about it, you started to realize that he was probably the most dangerous thing on the planet and I didn't have a fucking clue as to what he really was.

Chang paused when the hallway came into view from the edge of the path. He turned and looked up at me thoughtfully. "It really is for the best," he said.

"What is?"

"You leaving your Tower," he said, leaning close as if he were whispering a secret. "You never would have been happy in a greenhouse. You have too much mischief in your soul." He reached up and lightly tapped a knuckle on the center of my chest as if he were knocking on my soul.

I smiled down at him. "Thanks." The small sadness I had felt earlier when I thought of the life I had left behind drifted away. I stepped around him as I continued toward the elevator and his two guard dogs. I never told Chang what I was or where I came from. The man seemed to always know, though it was only recently that he openly spoke of it. But then, I wasn't really surprised that he knew. The man knew everything and owned a little piece of everything. I figured that as long as I stayed on his good side, I didn't have to worry. If Chang was pissed, the whole world was going to burn.

I paused at the doorway and looked back at the lush greenery and blooming flowers stretching out as far as the eye could see. Chang was right about me. I wouldn't have been happy for long in the greenhouse. When I was a child, I think I clung to it simply because it represented a safe haven away from Simon Thorn and the bleakness of my apprenticeship. Now I had a different kind of haven in the world, and it needed my protection.

But the first thing I needed to do was check in with a special cat to see if she could offer any insight on the elf procreation problem. If I knew it was caused by a spell, it would mean I could give this Mother Nature/Gaia something more to work with.

Two months ago, I discovered there was a Grim Reapers' union. Now? A real Mother Nature. I hoped this world didn't get any fucking stranger than it already was. My brain couldn't take much more.

17

I PAUSED OUTSIDE of Diamond Dolls and glanced up at the sky. It was early evening, but it felt like it should have been later after the time I'd passed in Chang's private garden. A woman gave me a dirty look as she walked past me, her narrowed eyes jumping from my face to the front of the strip club. I fought the urge to flip her off as I shoved my hands in my pockets and trudged down the street.

Yes, Diamond Dolls was one of the sleaziest, dirtiest, most run-down strip joints in the city, but it also happened to be the easiest entrance into Chang's. I might not be fond of the place, but I looked far less conspicuous walking into Diamond Dolls than through the other entrance in the dressing rooms at Layla's Bridal Boutique.

With Gaia's card tucked in my back pocket, I tried to relax with the reassurance that I had a lead on how to fix the elves' little problem. Unfortunately, Chang's promise that the goddess would know when I was ready was gnawing on my ass. I was pretty damn ready now. Arianna's warning that time was running out had me worried. I wasn't in the mood to wait on Mother Nature when I had other problems weighing on me.

Traffic was starting to pick up as kids got off school and first-shift workers started heading home. I couldn't find any parking near Diamond Dolls, so I slid into a nearby lot about a block away. I didn't mind the short walk in the warm early-evening air, as it gave me a little time to think.

As I reached the corner and started to turn down the next block, an explosion rocked the area. The earth shifted beneath my feet and the concussive force slammed into my back, knocking me to the ground. I tried to catch myself, skinning my palms and banging my knees in the process.

There was a ringing in my ears and my body protested this constant abuse. As the ringing faded, I could make out the sound of screaming and desperate shouting down the street behind me. Turning to look the way I'd come as I got to my feet, I was thinking that it had to have been a gas leak at one of the shops. Or maybe a meteor fell from the sky. Clearly, I was in denial.

My heart jumped into my throat when I spotted the two witches and the warlock strolling down the street through the billowing smoke. They all held wands in their hands. With a quick flick of the wrist or a broad swing of the arm, a building would burst into flames. I backed up, ducking behind the corner of the nearest building so that I wasn't in their line of sight. Cars were overturned or simply stopped in the middle of the street, as the occupants preferred to beat a hasty retreat on foot, hoping to provide a smaller target for the magic users.

People tried hiding in the various stores along the street, which had worked in the past, but the deadly trio was blowing out windows, tearing off roofs, and setting structures on fire as they slowly progressed. A man darted out of one of the stores before it could be torn apart. He tripped and fell hard to his knees in front of one of the witches. Grabbing up her cloak in one hand, she gleefully kicked him in the head while the warlock landed a kick to his stomach.

Swearing a blue streak, I pushed away from my hiding spot. I didn't have my wand, but I had to do something. They wouldn't be permitted to continue causing this carnage unchecked through the city. Before I could step into view, a hand clamped down on my shoulder and swung me around until my back hit the wall I had been hiding behind.

I blinked in shock and found myself staring at Gideon. He was looking a little more pulled together than he'd been at our last meeting, but with him standing so close, I noticed that his tie had been pulled loose as if he were having a tough day at the office.

"What the f—" I started to shout, but Gideon cut me off.

"Shut up and keep hidden!" he ordered. I tried to push away from the wall as he leaned over toward the main street to get a better view of the carnage, but he immediately put a hand in the middle of my chest and pushed me back. "Stay here."

"Why? What the fuck is going on?"

"They're searching for you."

My blood ran cold in my veins with those words and I leaned against the wall for support. "Why?"

Gideon frowned at me for a second before he dropped his hand. "William Rosenblum came looking for you and he never returned to the Towers. Judging by your appearance, I'd say it's a safe wager that he found you but didn't survive the encounter."

I nodded. In truth, I was a bloody, ragged mess because of Reave, but that was beside the point. Wild Bill had come looking for me and got to chew on the front bumper of a truck for his troubles.

"Rosenblum dies in Low Town, so these assholes decide to come to town and tear shit apart. What the hell!"

The warlock shook his head as he peeked around the corner. Whatever he saw made him pale, but he came back to me with his face wiped clean of expression and roughly grabbed my arm. He pulled me down the block until we could duck down another alley, farther away from where the trio was destroying the shops.

Gideon released me when we were far enough from the view of

the witches and the warlock. He shoved one hand through his dark hair as he paced away from me. "Things are bad in the Towers. We haven't gotten a lead on the elf and there are a number of occupants screaming to destroy another city."

I pushed aside the twinge of unease and guilt and focused on the rampaging assholes. "But no one here knows what the Towers are looking for! Hell, people don't understand why this is happening at all. How can they help if they don't know?"

"Help? You think people would turn in the person who knows the locations of the Towers?" Gideon stopped his pacing and pointed back toward the street. "Those people are going to protect that elf and raise him up as a hero. And then they're going to take that information and try to destroy the Towers."

"But they can't. No one has the power to destroy the Towers."

He closed his eyes for a second and he looked ten years older. This life was wearing him down to an angry nub, leaving him with nothing. "I know that, but they can't let themselves believe it. You convince those people of it and you will have taken away their last hope."

"Fuck," I said as I turned to stare down the alley, back the way we had come. "Fine. So the Towers are terrified that people will find their secret locations and do . . . something. Why come to Low Town and wreak havoc?"

"They have to blame someone. They don't know where the elf is, but several members of the Towers have been able to figure out that you're in Low Town."

"And they thought that by killing a bunch of people, they'd draw me out?"

"It's working," Gideon said in a low voice, his eyes narrowed on me. "You nearly charged out to meet them, unarmed. Since we've been talking in this alley, you've edged back down toward the street and I doubt you're even aware of it."

I looked around as he spoke to discover that I was now standing near the mouth of the alley, several feet away from where we had stopped just moments earlier. Smoke was clogging the air and darkening the sky. I could still hear the screaming mingled with the high-pitched cries of terrified and hurt children. There was a slight tingle of magic in the air, but I couldn't tell if the warlock and the witches were still in the area or if they had left to search for me elsewhere.

"I'm supposed to just hide back here? Let those people die for me? That's bullshit!" I shouted before I turned and started to walk out of the alley. I didn't know what the hell I was going to do if I did encounter the trio, but it was going to be more than just hiding in some goddamn alley like a coward while the people of the Low Town suffered for my presence.

Gideon's quick footsteps echoed off the pavement a second before he grabbed my shoulder. His fingers tried to dig deep but I shrugged him off. He wasn't using magic and I could only assume that the reason for it was that he was afraid of catching the attention to the assholes one block over.

"What are you thinking?" Gideon demanded in a harsh voice, sounding like he was straining not to shout. "You're going to march out there and let them kill you. What's that going to solve?"

"It's going to stop them from killing anyone else," I said, turning back to face him.

"No, it's not! You die and they might continue killing people in Low Town. Nothing's solved. We both know they're going to kill people in the future because that's what the Towers do. Only thing that would be accomplished would be that you're dead."

"Then go out there with me. Between the two of us, we can take them."

Gideon's earnest expression disappeared and he straightened, his spine becoming a steel rod before my eyes. "No."

"What?"

"No. It's too risky."

"What do you mean? We can take them. End this."

He shook his head. "And what if one of them escapes before we can kill them? The Towers will know that I'm helping you. I'm dead. There will be no one to protect my family. I won't leave them defenseless. Not for a bunch of strangers."

"Gideon—"

"No. I'm sorry people are dying, but I'm not willing to risk the lives of my family for them. At least, not how you're willing to risk Trixie's life."

"What are you talking about?" I snarled, balling up my fist at my side.

"If you throw your life away on this trio, who is going to protect your girlfriend? And your brother? And your friends? Does she mean that little to you?"

I shouted, rage pouring through me. I was angry at the Towers, angry at the deaths occurring just yards from me that I could do nothing about, angry that I was so helpless in this horrible world despite all my abilities. I swung my fist at Gideon. The warlock wasn't quite fast enough and I clipped the edge of his jaw. Pivoting on the balls of my feet, I shifted, throwing my weight behind another swing, but something had changed in his expression. His head was turned away from me and slightly tilted as if he were listening to something. I froze, watching him as my billowing fury deflated.

"They're gone, aren't they?" I said numbly.

He nodded and a part of me hated him. He'd pulled me away, hidden me, and then distracted me when I was determined to run to my death.

"You're going out there," he said in a low voice, but I think he meant it as a question.

"Yeah."

"Don't use magic, even if it is to help them. They won't see you as a savior. You'll just be another warlock."

I turned to look over at him, to tell him to fuck off, but he was already gone. With stomach churning, I walked down the alley and headed down the short block until I came to the street that contained Diamond Dolls. Closing my eyes, I swore softly, hating myself a little.

In less than five minutes, two witches and one warlock had turned the little commercial district into a war zone. The windows in every building had been shattered and most of the buildings were burning. Cars were overturned and a few trees had been uprooted so they could be thrown into storefronts.

Diamond Dolls was split open like a festering wound and was smoldering as whoever remained behind struggled to put out the flames. I briefly thought of Chang, but pushed the thought aside. The old man knew how to take care of himself. There was no way he was ever going to be caught by the Towers.

Bodies littered the area, broken and torn. Blind eyes stared up at the darkening sky while blood spread steadily across the fractured pavement. Old and young. Human and other. The spell weavers had killed indiscriminately, striving to cause as much damage as possible.

Scanning the area, my eyes lit on a little girl in a dirty dress, sitting in the middle of the street next to the dead body of a woman. The child's face was streaked with tears as her little hand smoothed the hair back from the woman's face. I started to walk toward her, but I stopped myself after two steps. How could I comfort this child when it was my fault that her mother was now dead? If I had come out to face the killers, would they have stopped? Would most of the victims at least have escaped this brutal death?

Maybe Gideon was right. Dying today would not have fixed anything. It wouldn't have saved these people. The attack on Low Town was only the start. The warlocks and the witches of the Ivory Towers were going to keep coming, tearing apart the world until they located the person who had breached their defenses. People were going to be violently tortured and killed. Cities were going to be destroyed while others were starved. No one would be left until they had what they wanted.

If I wanted to help the tear-streaked little girl, I had to find Reave and stop him before a new war ripped this world apart.

Emergency vehicles screamed, announcing their approach to the scene. People who could offer more immediate help were coming to put out fires, mend broken bodies, and gather up the dead.

Swallowing back the bile that had risen in my throat, I forced myself to turn back and start walking toward my car. I hadn't been alive during the Great War, hadn't witnessed it firsthand, but the destruction of this little block was only a faint glimpse of what was coming. I knew the image of the little girl and her mother was going to haunt me for the rest of my life. Things had to change. If my world was going to survive, things had to change. I just didn't have a clue as to how that was going to happen.

18

WHEN I GOT back to Asylum after leaving the bloody mess outside of Diamond Dolls, I wasn't thinking clearly. I had lost Reave, who was threatening the entire world with his scheme, and he'd deftly thrown my brother in front of the bus that was the Towers. It seemed as if every step I took created a bigger mess rather than fixing things. And now I was relying on the help of a creature who might think itself to be Mother Nature, to help the elves so that Trixie could have a safe place to hide when all hell broke loose, while I watched the Towers tear the world apart in their search.

Slamming the front door behind me, I stomped through the lobby and into the back tattooing room. Trixie was rising from her chair when I entered, a worried look on her face. But it wasn't *her* face. She had opened the shop and I hadn't bothered to activate the antiglamour spell in the lobby, so I was now looking at the heart-shaped-face, brunette version of Trixie.

"What happened?" she demanded as soon as I rounded the corner. Her eyes widened and she gasped as her gaze dropped down to the blood-soaked side of my shirt and pants. Dropping the little white book she had been holding on to the counter, she closed the distance between us. She jerked up the shirt and leaned down to inspect my side, which now held an angry red line smeared with dried blood. It hurt like hell when I moved, but the worst of it had healed. I wasn't sure if the scars on my soul would ever heal. "Who did this?"

"The guy with the information," I bit out. "Things didn't go so well."

"I guessed as much." She let the shirt fall back into place as she straightened, a frown on her lips. She opened her mouth to say something else, but I caught it in my own mouth as I roughly kissed her. Something had snapped in the back of my brain. Maybe it was her closeness. Her smell. The softness of her lips or her voice. Or maybe it was the thought that I was close to losing her. I don't know. I needed to kiss her more than I needed anything else in this world. She hesitated for only a second before she kissed me back, her tongue tangling with mine as she wrapped her arms around my neck.

My hands drifted down, cupping her ass as I pressed her against me. It was almost painful how quickly I got hard. I kept her against me, grinding against her softness until she moaned in my mouth. Sliding my hands down to the back of her thighs, I tried to spread her legs so that I could step between them while trapping her against the counter, but she was still wearing the skirt from earlier and it was restricting her movement. With a grunt of frustration, I stepped back enough to start pulling up her skirt so that it was gathered about her waist.

"Gage," she said in a half gasp, half moan. "The shop is still open. Anyone could walk in."

Clenching my teeth, I released her with my right hand. Summoning up some energy, I waved my hand toward the lobby. A click of the dead bolt falling into place echoed through the quiet shop while all the lights blinked out. The place now looked closed. Sunlight seeped around the shade over the window in the tattooing room, allowing me to clearly see the woman in my arms.

"Lose the glamour," I said harshly while putting my right hand on her upper thigh again. Trixie closed her eyes and gave a little sigh before I found myself once again holding the beautiful blonde that I loved. It wasn't that I found the blond version more attractive than the brunette. It was that I felt like I was cheating on Trixie when I kissed the brunette. It also didn't feel real, and right now I needed real.

When she opened her eyes and smiled at me, I kissed her with the same urgency that I'd felt when I started this. I pulled her legs apart enough that I could step between them, pressing my own raging erection against her. Trixie groaned, threading the fingers of one hand through my short hair while the fingernails of her other hand scratched along my back. Pinned as she was between the counter and my groin, I leaned away and unbuttoned the tiny white buttons of her blouse. A grin lifted the corners of my mouth as I dipped my head down, kissing along the tops of her breasts until I could pull the cups of her bra down and take one pert nipple in my mouth. She arched her back, her hand tightening in my hair.

My sanity was going up in flames, faster and faster with each soft moan, arch of her back, and bite of her nails. I needed to be inside her, losing myself in her before I lost my mind. We were rushing headlong into an explosion. Not wanting to cheat Trixie, I wanted to slow down, but I was nearly beyond rational thought and gentleness.

With one hand kneading an ass cheek, I reached between us, brushing against the soft mound between her legs with my knuckles. Her whole body jerked, pulling muscles bowstring taut. A soft whimper escaped her and it was music. I smiled as I pushed aside her delicate silk panties.

"Oh God, tell me you're wet for me," I murmured. She let out a broken cry as I slid two fingers between her fleshy folds and circled her clit. She was drenched, making me impossibly hard. I played with the throbbing little nub before sliding one finger inside of her, earning me a deep moan. "Is that what you want? Or maybe this?" I pulled out one finger and slid in two. She moved on my hand, pleasuring herself. "You're so wet. I could slide right inside you." I pulled my hand back, returning to her swollen clit. Trixie moaned at the loss, bucking against me. The torture was exquisite and I was so ready, but I wanted her as mindless as I was.

"Tell me what you want," I whispered in a rough voice I barely recognized.

Trixie's eyes popped open and she looked at me. Her face was beautifully flushed and her breathing was quick. "Fuck me, Gage. I need you inside me now."

Cupping her ass, I picked her up while she wrapped both arms around my neck and I dropped her on the nearest tattooing chair. I stepped back and looked at her a second. She was a vision of pure sexual temptation. Her skirt was bunched around her waist while her shirt was open, revealing the loveliest pair of breasts I'd ever seen. Her face was flushed and her wet lips were slightly parted in anticipation.

"If you don't want those ruined, I'd remove your panties," I said while undoing my own jeans and shoving them down as I straddled the chair. To my surprise, Trixie simply smiled at me while raising her arms above her head to grip the back of the chair. I smiled back as one hand drifted down to stroke my erection once. Trixie licked her lips, her eyes following my hand. This woman was making me lose my mind.

Unable to prolong the moment any longer for either of us, I reached down and ripped her panties with one hard jerk. Cupping her ass in both hands, I lifted her before plunging deep inside her wet, tight body. We both groaned as I pushed deep, filling her. She felt so wonderful that I didn't ever want to leave this spot. I held still for a couple seconds, soaking in the amazing sensations before I set off on a mindless rhythm.

There was no more thought. I was moving on pure instinct, my body pistoning into hers. I could see the muscles in her arms tighten as she gripped the back of the chair for support while arching her body into mine, trying to get as close as possible. I pounded into her, filling her and stretching her while trying to keep in contact with her clit, giving her as much pleasure as I could while I lost what remained of my mind. Time no longer made sense.

And then she screamed as her orgasm ripped through her. Her entire body tightened and clenched. I immediately followed, shouting nonsense as every nerve ending in my body exploded in the most perfect sensation. The pleasure was so sharp it was painful. I kept pounding into her through both our orgasms until there was nothing left of me.

Releasing her, I leaned forward, holding myself up on shaking arms with the back of the chair she was reclining in. Her own arms flopped down at her sides, her breathing coming in short, violent pants. I looked down to find her watching me with a lopsided smile on her lips.

"I don't know which one of us needed that more," she announced.

A laugh jumped from me, knocking my head back as my eyes closed. I was alive and happy. I didn't deserve to be after all those people had died, but alive meant that I could keep others from dying at the end of a wand.

Leaning down, I kissed her lips, giving her the gentleness that I couldn't earlier. I pushed off the chair and straightened, pulling from her body with some regret. I noticed her wince as she pulled her legs back together and readjusted her skirt. A sharp flash of guilt tore through me. "Did I hurt you?" I asked while tucking myself back into my jeans before refastening them.

Trixie gave me a wry little grin while fixing her bra and shirt. "I'm a little stiff and sore," she admitted.

"I'm sorry." Coming to stand beside the chair, I gently scooped her up before I sat down where she had been. I settled her in my lap, wrapping my arms around her. "I wasn't thinking too clearly. I—"

Trixie placed a finger over my mouth, stopping my apology. "I'm stiff and sore, but I loved every second of it and wouldn't change a thing."

I breathed a sigh of relief, tightening my hold on her. She laid her head on my shoulder while wrapping her arms around my body. We sat in silence for several minutes. I closed my eyes, listening to her breathing slow and even out as I did everything within my power to keep from thinking, halting the inevitable review of the events of the day.

"Feeling any better?" she asked.

I smiled, but it felt uneven, as if the muscles in my face were suddenly too tired to obey my commands. "Yes, but I think I should be in mourning. Many brain cells were lost in the creation of that orgasm."

Trixie chuckled. "I appreciate their sacrifice."

I pressed a kiss to the top of her head. "Anything for you." And I meant it. I would do anything for Trixie to keep her safe, to make her happy.

She leaned back to look up at me, her expression turning serious. "Considering the mood that you arrived in, I'm guessing that your errand didn't go well."

The last of the happiness that was bubbling throughout my body evaporated and I could feel the tension creeping back into my muscles. It was time to return to reality. This little break had helped keep the horrors at bay, but I couldn't put the world on hold forever.

"Yes and no," I said. Reave was on the run and the Towers were determined to set the world on fire while they searched for him. On the other hand, I had a possible way of contacting a somewhat mythical being who *might* be able to help the elves. Chang was pretty damn reliable, but this one felt like a stretch. "How was your day?" I quickly demanded, trying to evade any questions that might lead to a conversation about Reave.

Bracing her arm on the back of the chair past my shoulder,

Trixie twisted around and grabbed a piece of paper off the counter. She handed it to me with a look of disgust. There were three things written on it:

Lower average birth weight
Shorter average gestation
Mushroom decrease Black Forest

"I've read almost the entire book Arianna gave me and these are the only anomalies that were noted during the few times that our women gave birth," she said, sounding more than a little frustrated.

"The lower birth weight makes sense if babies are being born earlier," I murmured, handing back the paper, which she dropped onto the counter before settling against me. It didn't feel as if there was anything to go on with that, but I could at least mention it to Gaia when I saw her. "We need to know why the women were having trouble conceiving. Any note of an increase in miscarriage?"

"Nope. If we can get pregnant, then we keep the baby."

"What about that mushroom line?"

"Oh, that," she said with a blush. "That was a note mostly for myself. The last time the Summer Court passed through the Black Forest a few decades back, there was a note that there was a significant decrease in the mushrooms found. The ones that grow in the Black Forest are something of a delicacy and everyone was disappointed."

A smile pricked at the corners of my mouth as I stared at her. A part of me wondered how much she missed her old life with her people, but I smothered the thought as soon as it formed. If she missed it too much, she might feel the need to return home and not come back to Asylum.

"Did the Hearth Women tell you anything interesting?"

Trixie shifted her shoulders against me in a shrug. "Nothing too helpful. They were very sympathetic and concerned when I told them the problem. They gave me an entire list of herbal remedies and warnings, but most of them look familiar, so I'm sure we've tried them. They also gave me a few potions to be burned that are supposed to cleanse the air of evil intent and emotions. We don't exactly believe in that sort of thing."

"I can't imagine that it would hurt to try. Anything else?"

Trixie was silent for a moment before she spoke again in a low voice. "They also believe that I'm quite fertile right now."

I stiffened beneath her and my breath became trapped in my lungs as my mind scrambled, replaying that sentence as I tried to read her tone of voice. Was she scared? Hopeful? Excited? Worried? She was centuries old. She might be old enough to hear the biological clock ticking down. Did she want a baby? Even if it was mine. I was at that age when normal human males were supposed to be thinking about settling down and having a family. Unfortunately, my life looked like a war zone set in a natural disaster. Not a good time for a baby. Even if things weren't a disaster, did I want a baby?

Trixie leaned back so she could look at my face. Laughter filled her vibrant green eyes. "Breathe, Gage. Breathe. I was teasing. I want kids, but right now isn't a good time."

I tightened my arms around her, pulling her against my chest as I sighed with relief and closed my eyes.

"Besides," she continued in a blasé voice, "I'm not sure you'd be my first choice for a father." I knew she felt me instantly stiffen at her words because she started laughing.

"Woman," I growled, "you're going to be the death of me."

"You worry too much," she murmured against my chest. Her fingers ran along my shoulders, soothing away some of the tension. A part of me longed to close my eyes and drift away in a dreamless sleep for a couple hours, but there wasn't time and this wasn't the place.

"Since this isn't a good time, I'm guessing that we're protected against today's bit of madness," I said, forcing my eyes open.

"Yes, we're safe," she said evenly, but I could still feel the laughter in her.

My gaze darted over to the one window in the room. The light coming in through the shade had dimmed significantly, casting deeper shadows about the room. The sun was setting and Bronx would be in the shop soon. This stolen private time was coming to an end and we needed to go back to the reality.

I captured Trixie's mouth in another gentle but searing kiss that left her sighing before I rose from the chair with her in my arms. Putting her back in the chair, I ran one hand absently through my hair and tried to focus my thoughts.

"Gage, about this afternoon and Demoiselle Noire . . ." Her lovely voice drifted off as she brought up the one topic that I wanted to permanently purge from my mind.

I clenched my eyes shut and held up one hand, halting any additional words. Muscles tightened and spasmed throughout my body as my mind flashed images of Noire while recalling her cold touch, that intoxicating scent, and the lush curves of her frame as she enticed me. I wanted to be sick, vomit up everything within me until I was free of her memory, but it doesn't work that way. I was stuck with her in my head.

"Please," I said when I could speak past the lump in my throat. "I know we have to talk about it, but not yet. I'm not ready yet."

"Okay."

"I can say that nothing happened."

"Gage . . ."

I took a deep breath and opened my eyes when I could turn my thoughts back to the parlor and the waning light. "Bronx will be in soon. I'll light some candles and open the shop again."

Trixie flashed me a devilish grin as she pushed back to her feet. "I'll get the bleach."

I shook my head as I headed to the lobby. This was the first time we had had sex in Asylum. I had mentally sworn that we wouldn't, but then I hadn't been thinking clearly when I had arrived. My promise to myself to keep business and personal separate wasn't working out too well, but I wasn't willing to throw all my efforts out the window. This was a small stumble. I'd do better the next time. *Yeah, fucking right.*

"Where's Sofie?" I asked once the parlor was set back to normal and the air now smelled of burned matches, lilacs, apples, and pumpkin pie as a result of the strange collection of candles kept in the shop. Trixie was just stepping out of the bathroom after discreetly tidying up after our interlude. She once again looked fresh and delicate, as if nothing had occurred.

She sat on her little tattooing stool again, the little white book Arianna had given her in her lap. "Upstairs watching TV."

"Should I hope that she had it turned loud enough that she didn't hear anything?"

"Doubtful. Of course, it wouldn't be the first time she heard us."

I frowned. It was yet another thing I didn't want to think about. Sofie was something of a mother figure for me and I didn't want to think about her overhearing my sexual escapades with Trixie.

My discomfort was quickly replaced with confusion as a new thought slammed through my somewhat foggy brain. "Where'd the TV come from?" I had left behind a little furniture when I'd moved out of the second-floor apartment, but no TV.

"Bronx dropped it off yesterday for her," Trixie said. "She says she likes to be close, but she doesn't like missing her afternoon and evening programs."

"That cat is turning into a couch potato."

"I think she could use a boyfriend. Do you know any warlocks who are cats?"

I shook my head. "You're insane. You've already got a witch and a warlock in your life and now you're asking for more. Simply insane."

Trixie waved one hand absently at me. "Well, the ones I know aren't so bad."

"We're the strange exceptions to the rule, I promise." I grabbed her hand and gave it a squeeze before I started toward the back room. "I've got to ask her something. I should be back down before Bronx gets in."

"Be nice, Gage. She told me what happened at your place. She hasn't been in a very good mood."

I nodded and headed to the second-floor apartment. I couldn't blame Sofie for being in a foul mood. She'd been attacked because of her association with me. If it had been possible for her to be safe by disassociating herself from me, I think she would have left. But then it was too late for things like that. If anyone knew that she talked to me, they'd kill her regardless of whether she'd turned her back on me or not. They'd torture her for information.

And in truth, I doubted that the danger was just a result of knowing me. She was an old, powerful witch. If she had still been human, her attackers would never have been able to harm her. Trapped as a cat, she was vulnerable. She could access a few spells, but nothing particularly powerful. Knowing me could get her killed, but staying near me now could keep her alive. Trapped as she was as a cat and trapped as my friend, Sofie's luck had pretty much run out.

19

THE LARGE RUSSIAN BLUE was stretched out across the battered sofa, her eyes half closed as she watched what appeared to be a talk show. A female goblin, a dwarf, and two human-looking females that I believed to be a vampire and a succubus sat around a table on some cozy soundstage animatedly talking. A window was open, allowing a breeze to sweep through the stuffy apartment.

"Shhh . . . They're talking about makeup tips and new uses for panty hose," Sofie hissed as I shut the door.

"Sof, you don't wear panty hose or makeup." I plopped down on the one cushion that she wasn't stretched across and propped my feet up on the table.

"I know, but if Gideon comes through, I'm going to need to know this stuff."

I smiled down at her. "You're a witch. You don't need makeup. You can use glamour or an enchantment. If my memory is accurate, you don't need makeup or panty hose anyway."

Sofie's head popped up and she stared at me through narrowed yellow eyes. "Gideon hit your head today?" I shook my head, still smiling. She took a quick sniff of the air and rolled her eyes at me. "Oh, got some, did you? That would explain your silliness. You know, if you weren't a warlock, I'd tell you that you need to make an honest woman of that poor girl. But then, I guess it's better this way."

My smile disappeared and I leaned my head back against the sofa as reality came crashing back down on me with a sickening thud. "Thanks for the reminder, Sof."

The cat stood, alternating between arching her back and stretching each leg so that long claws extended. "Sorry, Gage. I didn't mean anything by that comment. I guess I'm in a grumpy mood."

"I know. It's been a rough few days for everyone. It doesn't seem like anything is going right."

Sofie paused beside the TV remote and stepped on the red button, turning off the TV, before she walked over and curled up in my lap. I scratched the top of her head, getting her to start purring. If she was going to act like a cat, I was going to treat her like a cat. I'd deal with all the repercussions and complications if she was ever returned to her natural state.

"Trixie told me about your visit to see the queen of the Summer Court and their . . . difficulties," she said, her voice so soft that I could barely make out her words. She had stopped purring and moved her head away from my hand as she rested it on my stomach.

"That's what I was hoping to talk to you about." Placing my elbow on the arm of the couch, I leaned my head against my hand. "I've listened to the queen's story and what Trixie told me about the advice from the Hearth Women, but something seems off. Something about this whole thing seems like the elves are suffering under the effects of a spell. Everything I've been taught says that it's not possible because spells aren't this artfully selective or gradual, but my gut screams spell. What do you think?"

Sofie was silent for several seconds. She was so still that I thought she might have even stopped breathing. When she spoke, her voice was extremely soft and low.

"I've done many horrible things in my lifetime and I don't regret a single damn one of them. It was our culture. It was about protection. It was about being the strongest species. I believed it all . . . until now."

I lifted my head and stared down at the cat, my heart skipping in my chest. "What are you talking about?"

"The elves. They're barren . . . and it's my fault. It *is* a spell. I crafted it at the request of the council years ago. I had forgotten about it until I met Trixie."

My breathing was shattered as I sat on the couch with my thoughts colliding into one another before spinning off in another direction. My first instinct was to push her off me so I could pace around the room.

It was a spell. Sofie had created the spell that was slowly destroying the elves. The cat I was protecting—hell, the cat *Trixie* was protecting—was responsible for keeping Trixie's people from having children, leaving them stuck on a one-way train for extinction.

"Sofie," I breathed, my voice rough as I tried to order my thoughts.

"I'm so sorry, Gage. We always worried about the elves and their ability to find the Towers through the glamour. We were afraid that if we attacked them, they would go into hiding, making it impossible to find them. The spell was designed to attack more and more of their kind with each passing decade until none of them could have children."

"Well, it's nearly succeeded," I snapped before roughly running my hand through my hair. "The king and queen of the Summer Court can't have kids, and if they don't have an heir soon, the Winter Court or the Svartálfar could soon attack in hopes of conquering the Summer Court."

"I never meant to hurt Trixie. I like her. She's sweet and funny. I never wanted to hurt her."

"I know. The elves were a faceless people to you and all the Towers, but the fact remains that there are people that are being hurt. It has to stop. How do I unravel the spell?"

Sofie stood and walked over to the far cushion on the couch, where she sat down, wrapping her long tail around her body. She hung her head, staring at the floor. "You can't."

"What do you mean?" I shifted on the couch, moving to sit on the edge so that I could try to see her expression. "All spells can be fixed or unraveled."

"You can't. It's the nature of this spell. You can only start to unravel it after it's reached its natural end."

"Which is?" I prompted when she fell silent.

Sofie sighed and looked up at me. "When they're all barren. When not one female elf can have a child, then you can start to unwind it. But even then it can only be done slowly, working at the same speed in reverse."

Shoving off the couch, I paced the living room, moving between the sofa and the kitchen. "You know, if this wasn't absolutely horrible, I'd say that the spell was brilliant. It sounds impossibly complicated and yet exquisitely elegant. I can't even begin to figure out how you did it," I said, half talking to myself. I threw my arms up as I spun to face her. "But what the hell! How am I supposed to fix this?"

"I'm sorry."

"I'm not the one you need to apologize to," I snarled, pacing away again. I didn't mean to make her feel worse, but I was standing in the same room with the witch who had figured out the most elegant way of killing off an entire race without them realizing that they were being attacked. Neither the queen nor Trixie suspected a spell. They thought their barrenness was a result of something they had done.

"You can think of no way to stop the spell or reverse it?" I demanded, stopping when I was standing in front of her.

"No. I didn't worry about it because I didn't think I would ever want to undo the spell."

"Well, start thinking. We've got to figure something out and fast."

Whatever nervous energy had filled me seconds ago fled my body, leaving me feeling so tired that I was afraid my legs were going to buckle beneath me. Collapsing on the sofa, I leaned my head back and closed my eyes. I was exhausted in both body and soul. Between my struggles to protect my loved ones, to protect Low Town, and to hide from the Towers, I didn't think I had it in me to move again even if a warlock suddenly appeared in the room. But I had to move and think and do.

"I'm sorry, Sofie," I said. Cracking one eye open, I reached for her, holding one hand out toward her. "I didn't mean to be an asshole. I'm tired. Every step forward is accompanied by two steps back."

Sofie stood and walked over to me, rubbing her head against my hand. I scratched behind her ear and along the side of her head until she curled up next to me.

"We've changed, haven't we?" she whispered, sounding as tired as I felt and maybe even a little frightened.

"Yeah," I agreed with a little laugh. "We've changed, but I think for the better."

"We can't go back, even if we wanted to."

My shoulders slumped and I frowned at her words. *We can't go back.* What she meant was that even if she resumed her human form, she couldn't go back because she wasn't like the witches and warlocks any longer. She valued life. Or rather, she valued the lives of others. Even if the Towers could overlook the fact that she was one of my supporters, they would see this new outlook of hers as a weakness. They'd kill her rather than let her spread the softer mentality that Gideon and his movement were trying to foster.

Until this moment, I think Sofie had always harbored the small hope that she could go back and resume her former life when she became human again. But at some point during her exile, she had changed, and she now had no hope of going home even if she was human.

And that sudden knowledge hurt. I understood that. I hated Simon Thorn and all the other witches and warlocks who tormented me while I was an apprentice. But I loved magic. I loved studying it and using it. I loved getting lost in the enormous old tomes, learning the philosophy and art of what seemed to tingle at my fingertips. I tolerated Simon and the others for as long as I could so I could study, but in the end I had to leave. There wasn't a day that went by when I didn't miss the study of magic, but I couldn't live that life.

"Maybe that's all we need to do. Force everyone in the Towers to live among the unwashed masses for a few decades. That'll make them come to their senses," I said, trying to lighten both our moods.

Sofie made a noise in the back of her throat that sort of sounded like a strangled laugh. "That or get everyone killed."

"True."

We sat in silence for several minutes. Sofie was curled up against me and I was mindlessly stroking her soft fur, trying to calm both our nerves while desperately searching for some kind of solution to this latest dilemma.

"Are you going to tell her?" Sofie asked, jerking my attention back to her.

"Huh?"

"Trixie. Are you going to tell her?"

I stopped petting her and sighed. "I have to. I've kept way too many secrets from Trixie for too long. I'm trying to be more open with her. She deserves it."

"Please, don't," she pleaded. Sofie stood and climbed into my lap so that she was standing with her front paws on my chest as she stared into my eyes. "I love Trixie. She's my friend and I don't want to lose that. If it takes the rest of my life, I'll make it up to her. To her and her people. Please, don't tell her."

Clenching my teeth, I frowned at the cat who had become as dear to me over the past several years as Trixie and Bronx. She made a mistake. A horrible, ugly, painful mistake, but a mistake all the same and she regretted it. I knew what that was like well enough and I wasn't about to start casting stones.

"I have to tell her it was a spell," I started, and then groaned, inwardly cursing myself and my stupid soft heart for talking cats. "But I'll keep it to myself as to who created it. I'll leave that for you to handle."

"Thank you," she said around a loud purr. She bumped the top of her head against my chin, rubbing against me with relief. I rubbed her back one last time before picking her up and putting her on the cushion beside me.

"Don't make me regret this," I said as I shoved to my feet. Putting my hands into my jeans pockets, I grimaced as one hand ran over material roughened by my dried blood. I needed to change into clean clothes. Maybe I'd even try food and a shower while I was at it. You know, act like a normal, civilized creature who understood the basics of good hygiene and nutrition.

"I'm going to head home after Bronx gets in. Are you good to head home with Trixie tonight?"

"That's fine. Are you okay?" she asked, motioning with her head toward the side of me that was covered in dried blood.

"Yeah. Just a little scuffle."

"That's good."

I had walked to the door and grasped the knob when a thought occurred to me. "I've got a meeting soon, I think. Someone a friend thinks might be able to help with the elf problem."

"I don't know of anyone who can help with it," Sofie murmured. "You on good terms with another witch or warlock?"

"No, this is . . . something else," I said, and then paused for a second. I shook my head, pushing aside other worries and doubts. "I don't have high hopes, but it's worth a try. This friend has never steered me wrong. Anyway, if I don't show up tomorrow, I want you to promise me that you'll at least tell Gideon what you told me. Someone else needs to know what's going on. I know he's got a lot on his plate right now, but if things ever get quiet again, maybe you and he can start working on a counterspell."

"I will, I promise. Where's this meeting at?"

"No idea."

"Who are you meeting?"

I gave her a sly little smirk as I pulled the door open. "Mother Nature."

Sofie's mouth hung open for a full two seconds before she snapped it closed. "You're kidding, right?"

I snorted. "I wish."

Slipping out of the apartment, I closed the door behind me and suppressed a groan. By all that was sacred and holy, I wished I was kidding. I was putting all my hopes on a creature that thought it was the essence of life and the earth. If anything, I prayed that she didn't have a grudge against the Towers as well or I was in for a very short visit.

SOMEONE WAS HUMMING.

It was my first conscious thought the next morning. I lay in bed, trying to place the voice, since I knew it wasn't Trixie and there should have been no other woman in my apartment. The night before, I had stumbled into my place, where I ate and showered then settled down on the sofa with a large sketch pad. My brother sat on the other end of the couch, watching a movie while I made plans. I had an idea of how I would save Robert, but the tattoo would be complicated. Around midnight, I stumbled to my bed and was asleep before I could finish pulling up my blankets.

But now I could hear humming, close and clear. It wasn't coming through an open window because I never slept with an open window. They were too hard to put protective spells over. I didn't recognize the tune, but it sounded like it belonged in a Disney cartoon.

Rubbing my eyes with one hand, I lifted my head and looked around, half expecting to see that I had forgotten to shut a window before falling asleep. Instead, I found a woman dressed in what appeared to be a Victorian maid's uniform standing at the end of my bed, folding my underwear.

I jerked upright, pulling my blanket up to my chin like some flustered virgin. "What the fuck?" I blurted in a sleep-roughened voice.

The woman's face popped up and she smiled brightly, her lovely blue eyes twinkling in the sunlight that was pouring through my open blinds. "Good morning, Master Powell," she greeted cheerfully as she dipped into a quick curtsy. She sounded so damn chipper that I half expected to see little blue birds fluttering about her, singing some goddamn melody to shred the bits of my brain still clinging to sleep. I've said it before and I'll say it again, I am NOT a morning person.

"I am dreadfully sorry to disturb you, but we must get going soon," she continued, resuming the task of folding the pair of boxers in her hand.

"Going? Going where? No!" I said, holding up one hand as she opened her mouth to answer. I dropped my blanket to my lap, somewhat grateful that I had chosen not to sleep in the nude. "First, who are you? What are you doing in my apartment?"

"Oh, terribly sorry," she murmured with a blush staining her plump, round cheeks. "My name is Holly and her ladyship sent me to fetch you. You have an appointment with her this afternoon."

"Her ladyship?" I repeated dully. I wasn't particularly sharp upon waking either. "You mean Gaia?"

Holly nodded as she carried a stack of my underwear over and placed it in one of the bureau drawers as if she had done so a thousand times before.

"Fine. Then why are you folding my underwear?"

"Oh, that," she said with a dismissive wave of her hand and a giggle. "I arrived a while ago, but I wasn't sure when you'd wake up, so I passed the time tidying up. You had quite a bit of dirty laundry that needed doing."

At her words, I looked around the room. The enormous mound of dirty clothes in the corner and scattered around the room was missing. Hell, it even looked as if she had vacuumed my floor. The garbage and dirty glasses on the bedside table were missing. The door was open to my closet and I could see that not only had all my dirty clothes been cleaned and hung, but she had organized the clothes according to type and color. I flopped back on my pillows and covered my face with both hands.

"How long have you been here?"

"Mmm . . . only four hours."

I dropped my hands and stared at her. "Why didn't you wake me up?"

She giggled once more and shook her head as she came to stand at the foot of my bed again. "I couldn't do that, silly. You were exhausted and you're going to need energy for today."

I wanted to pursue that comment, but my brain was too sluggish. I might have been awake, but it was unlikely that profound thought was going to start happening until I had my first cup of coffee.

"Fine," I said. "When do we have to leave?"

Holly tilted the little watch pinned to her blouse toward her face, squinting slightly at the time. Dropping it back down over her heart, she smiled at me. "Five minutes."

I bolted upright in bed. "What?"

"We must leave in five minutes," she repeated with the same effervescent charm.

"Then get out of here, woman!" I barked, throwing back the covers, no longer caring what the hell she saw. "I've got to get dressed."

The strange woman giggled as she scurried out of the room, closing the door behind her as I darted to the closet and started pulling out clothes. I didn't know what you wore to a meeting with Gaia, but I was hoping that she wasn't picky. My escort hadn't thought to give me time to properly prepare. I simply grabbed my one black polo shirt that didn't have a hole in it and my dark blue jeans that had a hole in the back pocket. If I survived all this fucking chaos, I needed to look into a couple new shirts and pants. At my current rate, I was throwing out more clothes at the end of the day than I was keeping.

Grabbing shoes and socks, I ran to the bathroom, where I brushed my teeth and pissed at the same time while trying to ignore the fact that everything gleamed brightly. I leaned against the wall as I pulled on socks and boots. A quick glance in the mirror revealed that my hair was a mess, but at least my shirt was right side out. I also needed to shave, but there was no time. Mother Nature was going to have to deal with it.

Holly was waiting in the living room next to the front door when I left the bathroom. She clapped her hands and gave a little bounce when she saw me. "Very good. You're right on time," she cheered.

My gaze skimmed over the rest of the apartment only to find it in immaculate condition. I dreaded having to explain this one to Trixie if she happened to stop over before I could return it to its usual slovenly state. However, I was grateful to see that Holly had even patched the enormous hole in the ceiling. Overall, I was having trouble believing what she had accomplished while I was apparently dead to the world.

Robert was sprawled on the couch, one leg up on the back while the other was dangling off the end. A blanket was pulled half over him and he was snoring softly. He was dead to the world, oblivious to the fact that a perky woman had been cleaning around him for roughly four hours.

As I looked toward the kitchen, my eyes caught on the clock hanging on the wall.

"It's only eight in the morning!" I said, struggling to keep my voice at a whisper. I was never up before noon if I could help it. Consciousness at this hour of the day was . . . it was just unhealthy.

"Yes."

"And you've been here for four hours?"

"Yes." Her cheerfulness never wavered.

I shook my head, forcing my brain to stop trying to understand her. It wasn't possible. "Let me grab my keys. I'm guessing you're driving . . . or do you want me to?"

"No need." Holly placed her hand on my shoulder and the world went black for a second before I found myself standing near a large red barn at the edge of a vast green field bathed in golden sunlight. The air was cool and crisp without being uncomfortable.

There had been none of the usual sense of movement across space that typically accompanied a teleportation spell. This had been soft and subtle like a whisper, making it extremely frightening. I was dealing with some powerful creatures, and by all appearances, Holly was only a servant.

"'Bout time you got here," announced a gruff voice. We both turned to see a man stomp out of the darkness of the barn in a pair of worn overalls and mud-caked work boots. A straw hat was pulled low on his head, casting his dark eyes in shadow as he frowned at me.

Beside me, Holly checked her little watch again and then turned a scowl on the man. "We're right on time and you know it!" she argued, but the sour mood faded like a flicker of lightning as she turned to look at me. "We are on time, but Rocky likes to be contrary. You'll be helping him today. Good luck." She gave me what I'm sure she thought was a reassuring pat on the shoulder and then stepped back before disappearing completely.

I had opened my mouth to ask her what the hell she was talking about, but it was too late. Frowning, I looked over at the man who was watching me with a grim expression. He didn't look like he was going to be too helpful, but he was all I had. Standing in the barnyard, I realized that I didn't know where the hell I was, and while I was sure that I could get myself home, I had a feeling that leaving would not get me one step closer to talking to Gaia.

"Well, I guess we better get at it. We're wasting daylight," the man grumbled before turning back to reenter the barn. With a shake of my head, I followed after him, but paused just past the threshold, blinking as my eyes struggled to adjust from the bright sunlight to the darkened barn. As the world came into focus, I could make out various pieces of farm equipment, stacks of hay bales, and a few stalls. By the sounds of shuffling and heavy breathing, they were occupied by horses.

"Here," Rocky said, throwing clothing at me. I attempted to catch it, but wasn't fast enough. One boot and half of the overalls remained in my arms while the other boot bounced off my chest and hit the wooden floor. "Put that on so you won't get your fancy clothes dirty, city boy."

"Wait!" I snapped, letting everything fall to the ground. "What are you talking about? Why am I going to get dirty?"

Rocky sneered at me, his face becoming a mass of wrinkles and weathered skin. "You want your meeting with Ma, don't you?"

"Ma? You mean Mother Nature?"

The man gave a little snort. "You're not too quick in the morning, are you? Yeah, I mean Mother Nature. You want your meeting or not?"

"Yes."

"Then you work. If you're lucky enough to get a meeting with the old girl, you have to earn your way in to see her. You work hard enough, the faster you see her. You get me?"

My shoulders slumped but I nodded. "Yeah, I got it." I should have known getting in to see Gaia wasn't going to be that easy. This certainly wasn't the way I had expected to spend my morning, but I could put in a few hours of hard labor if it meant helping the elves.

Bending down, I picked up the clothes that he threw at me. The overalls were big enough to go over the clothes I was already wearing, but I had to sit on a bale of hay to switch out my scuffed up boots for a pair of worn, dirt-encrusted boots.

"Come on, slowpoke," Rocky called as soon as I finished lacing the second boot.

Clomping through the barn in the heavy shoes, I trailed after the older man and headed across the large field. I didn't try to talk to him, or even ask him where we were. Rocky didn't strike me as the talkative type. As Holly said, he was a contrary kind of person and I had a feeling he'd refuse to answer to spite me.

We walked in silence for nearly fifteen minutes until we crossed a split-rail fence and came up to another barn. This one was twice the size of the first and painted white. The scent of manure filled the air, threatening to make me gag, but I kept my comments to myself.

Rocky pulled back the door and gave me a shove inside. The interior was brightly lit, but I still found myself blinking at the two neat rows of black-and-white cows sedately chewing on hay. My companion walked over to the side of the barn and picked something up. When he returned, he thrust a stool and a metal pail into my hands.

"When the pail gets full, there are some large containers at the back of the barn. Pour the milk in there. When you're done with the cow, she'll know to go on out into the yard," Rocky informed me.

"You want me to milk all these cows?" I demanded, unable to keep the shock out of my voice.

He chuckled. "Quick one, aren't you? Milk them, and when you're done, I'll be back." Rocky started to turn around and walk out of the barn when something occurred to him, causing him to turn back toward me. "Oh, and a little advice: I wouldn't use any of your hocus-pocus." He was laughing to himself when he ambled out of the barn, heading back over the hill we had walked up.

I hadn't yet thought of using magic. My brain was still trying to comprehend the idea of milking cows. I mean, they had machines for this sort of thing, didn't they? Even as desperate as I was, I knew not to use magic. Besides being afraid of ripping the udders off the cows with a poorly woven spell, I had a feeling that if I used magic, I would either be whisked back to my apartment without seeing Gaia or I'd be forced to start completely over until I did it right.

Tightly clutching the stool and pail to my chest, I stared at the closest cow, feeling somewhat grateful that it completely ignored me as it focused on the pile of hay directly in front of its face. I could only hope that it stayed that way throughout this ordeal, because I didn't have a fucking clue as to what I was doing. Oh, I knew the basic idea. Put the pail under the udders, sit on the stool, and squeeze the teats until milk squirted out, but then I was worried that there was more to the job than basic theory. Hell, the closest I had ever been to a living cow was an almost-raw steak smothered in onions and mushrooms from the local steakhouse.

Muttering to myself, I decided to start with theory and adjust from there. I didn't have a watch on me, but I knew that it took the better part of thirty minutes for me to even start to get the hang of it and then another thirty minutes to squeeze the cow dry. But as Rocky said, as soon as she was empty, the cow slowly trotted out of the barn while I emptied the pail.

I moved to the next cow, finding that it got easier with each one that I finished, but I tried not to think about the fact that there had to be at least fifty cows in that barn. By the time the first row was done, I could barely open and close my hands, they had become so sore. At the three-quarters point, my back ached, my knees were throbbing, and I was pretty sure I'd never drink milk again. I had thought I was in good shape. I might have slowed down in my trips to the gym, but I hadn't lost all my muscle. There was something about this work that left me with the realization that there were entire muscle groups that I had never used, and they were screaming now.

As the last cow trotted out of the barn, which I could no longer smell, I groaned, holding my sore hands out in front of me. I wasn't sure I had the energy to move; my body was aching too badly.

Warm laughter jerked my head up to see a man and woman walking into the barn. Both were smiling, which was an improvement over Rocky. They wore overalls as well, but they didn't look as worn or grumpy as my last companion. In fact, they both appeared to be in their early twenties with the fresh faces of health and youth.

"Nice job," the woman said, her arm around the man's back. "I knew you'd figure it out."

The man slid away from the woman and stood before me. "Here, I'll get that for you," he offered, bending over to grab the full pail I had yet to empty.

"No," I said sharply, wincing as I stood. My whole body protested the movement. "Thank you, but I can get it." I started to bend over and grab the handle, but the woman placed a restraining hand on my shoulder.

"It's okay. It won't count against you," she whispered. Her wide brown eyes were soft and sympathetic. I sighed and nodded, slowly straightening my body again. The man chuckled as he grabbed the pail and quickly tipped the contents into one of the containers at the end of the room.

When he rejoined us, he clapped me hard on the back, nearly knocking me forward. "Let's get you cleaned up. Some cold water will help relieve some of the pain in your hands."

Wordlessly, I followed him out to the front of the barn and over to an old water pump. He grabbed the handle and gave it a few hard pumps before water started pouring out. I dipped my hands into the ice-cold water and sighed in relief. The chill coursed through my body, seeming to wash away the aches. I rubbed the liquid up my arms and then splashed some on my face, instantly feeling refreshed.

"Is Rocky coming back for me?" I asked, shaking off the excess water.

"He's busy mucking out some stalls, so he sent us," the woman said. "It's nearly noon. I thought you'd like to grab some lunch and then help us in the orchard. That is, unless you'd rather help Rocky muck out the stalls?"

I couldn't stop from grimacing at the idea. I didn't know what might be worse, shoveling out horseshit or spending more quality time with Rocky. It definitely sounded worse than lunch and work in an orchard. Unfortunately, I didn't know which one would gain me more points with Gaia, though I had a feeling it was going to be horseshit and Rocky.

"Brook!" The man laughed, wrapping one arm around the woman's shoulders. He looked at me, smiling. Something about his expression made me think that he knew exactly what had been crossing my mind. "You have to excuse her. She's teasing you. Join us for lunch and then we'll be picking apples."

After milking the cows and the threat of mucking stalls, the idea of picking apples sounded frighteningly easy. Of course, so did lunch. I was wondering if I would have to cook it when the man laughed again. Yeah, he was definitely reading my thoughts.

"My name's Ox," he said, extending his hand toward me. I shook it, finding myself smiling as well. "And this rascal is Brook," he finished, indicating the woman pressed close to him.

"Nice to meet you, Mr. Powell," Brook said with a little wave. "Let's grab lunch. I'm starving."

I walked with the pair back across the field in what I thought was the same direction I had come from with Rocky, but as we crested another hill I was faced with a quiet pond and a vast apple orchard instead of the red barn. We chatted about the nice weather, the peace and quiet of nature, and the random sightings of rabbits and butterflies as we walked toward the pond. I had been tempted to question them about Gaia, as both seemed far more willing to talk than Rocky, but even as the questions formed in my brain, they drifted away again on the breeze.

At the edge of the pond was a large picnic basket with a folded blanket draped over it. While Ox and I set about spreading the blanket, Brook started unloading containers of food. We knelt beside her and set out cheese, butter, bread, ham, chicken, potato salad, coleslaw, pickles, olives, fruit, and three different kinds of pie. More food came out of the basket than I thought possible, but I was reaching the point where I stopped questioning things in this strange place.

I gratefully accepted the enormously mounded plate of food from Brook and offered to help fill hers. Oddly enough, I didn't even balk when Ox poured me a large glass of cold milk. We ate in companionable silence, soaking in the sounds of frogs and dragonflies around the pond. The food tasted as if it had all been made fresh that day and probably was. As we finished, we reclined on the blanket and talked about memories of growing up.

During a lull in the conversation, I thought about asking them about the farm and Gaia, but the question slipped away again and I laughed at a comment Ox made. There was something comfortable about the couple that left me feeling like I had known them my entire life. Relaxing in the shade of a large tree with a full stomach, I was content. Even the grumpy Rocky and his fifty dairy cows didn't seem so bad anymore. The work had been hard and backbreaking, but it was good, honest work that had filled me with a sense of accomplishment. I felt as if I fit into something larger that my mind couldn't quite define yet.

It wasn't much longer before Ox declared that it was time to get back to work. I helped them clean up and repack the picnic basket. Brook folded the blanket and placed it over the basket as if we had never touched it. I followed them into the orchard, where I found three wooden ladders and fifty large baskets.

To my surprise, Ox and Brook didn't leave me alone in the orchard, but each grabbed a ladder and a wicker basket before heading off to a tree. I did the same and picked a tree near them. The next few hours were filled with easy conversation and laughter as we placed ripe apples in our baskets. The work was steady and tiring, but the buzz of the bees and the scent of blossoms on the breeze seemed to keep the worst of the fatigue away.

As I filled the last basket, I stood on the ladder and looked across the rolling landscape. I knew that I was there with the sole purpose of seeing Gaia. I completed each task set before me with the idea that it was getting me closer to meeting her. But as I worked and the day wore on toward sunset, the urgency I felt melted away. I clearly remembered why I needed to see her—to save the elves, to save Trixie—but the emotional turbulence that accompanied that idea had dimmed. There was only the peace and splendor of the world living and thriving before me.

I climbed down the ladder and carried my full basket over to the others. Yet Ox and Brook were nowhere to be found. Instead, Rocky was standing near the baskets, holding my boots. While his expression and manner weren't as gruff as when we first met, he wasn't as cheery as my other companions.

Without a word, I pulled off the overalls and changed back into my boots, leaving the others next to the baskets. I followed Rocky back through the field and over the rise. As we reached the top, a large white farmhouse came into view. When we were a few feet from the worn, wooden, front-porch steps, the screen door creaked open and a lovely woman in a soft white skirt stepped out. Rocky stopped at the bottom of the steps and clapped me on the back. I looked over at him to find that he was smiling at me. Somehow I had earned the man's approval.

"Thank you, Rocky," the woman said, sending the most amazing feeling through me. In that split second, I felt warmth, and peace, and the most overwhelming longing for home. When I gazed up at her, she extended her hand toward me. "Hello, Gage. I'm Skye. We have one last thing for you to do."

Taking her hand, I let her lead me past a living room filled with comfortable furniture and walls covered with framed photographs of smiling people. She took me up the creaking steps and down the hall. Looking over her shoulder, she smiled and squeezed my hand before pushing open the white door to reveal a nursery.

I took in the pale blue walls, the white lace curtains that danced in the breeze skipping through the open window, and the little dresser covered in stuffed animals. She led me over to an old-fashioned crank swing that held a baby in a blue outfit. Pale blond hair curled from his head and he watched me with wide blue eyes as he tightly held a soft rattle.

Skye released my hand and bent down to pick up the baby. She cooed at him as she settled him in her arms, but he continued to watch me the entire time. She pressed a kiss to his head and then handed him to me. I was awkward with the infant, as I couldn't remember the last time I had held one, but Skye remained close. She helped comfortably position the boy in my arms until I felt as if I had done it a hundred times before.

With one arm across my back and the other cupping the back of the baby's head, Skye leaned close. "This is your last task," she said in a near whisper. "You have to put him down for a nap."

"That's it?" I whispered, arching one eyebrow at her.

Skye smiled and nodded at me. She pressed one last kiss to the side of the baby's head and then leaned up on her tiptoes to kiss my cheek. "You'll be great, I know it," she murmured before releasing us both.

I turned as she reached the door, holding the little boy against my chest. "What's his name?"

She leaned her head against the edge of the door, her green-gray eyes twinkling at me. "What do you think it should be?"

I looked down at the little boy and his bright blue eyes. He had one fist in his mouth as he sucked on it thoughtfully. "Squall," I said before looking up at her.

Her smile grew a little wider. "Good choice." And then she left us alone, gently closing the door behind her.

A little tremor of fear slipped through me as I stood alone in the middle of the room with the little boy. I wasn't sure if I had ever held a baby and I knew I had never tried to put one down for a nap. While I was grateful that the little guy wasn't screaming his head off the moment Skye disappeared, I still didn't know what to do to get him to sleep.

Turning around, I spotted a large white rocking chair in one corner near the crib. My mom had kept one in my sister's room when she had been a baby. She said that it had been handed down over a few generations and that she used to rock us to sleep when we were fussy.

Sitting on the thick cushion, I settled the little guy against my shoulder while I rubbed my hand over his tiny back in a slow, circular motion. He shifted and drew in a deep breath, pressing his little chest against mine before he wrapped one arm around my neck and put his head on my shoulder. Slowly rocking the chair, I hummed a nameless tune that had no beginning and no end. I didn't know the song. I kept humming as his breathing evened out.

It had only taken him a few minutes to doze off, but still I rocked him, humming what I was sure was a lullaby. I turned my head toward him and the soft scent of soap and baby powder hit my nose. But there was more there, something I didn't have a word for. It wasn't so much a smell, but something from that tiny body that drove down into my chest, as if it were mending things broken there. All the weight that had rested on my shoulders slipped off to be replaced by this little head. The aches in my back, hands, and knees dissolved with the sound of his breathing. The pound of his heart against my chest soothed so many echoes of pains from my past.

Reluctantly, I stood and turned toward his white-and-blue crib. Closing my eyes, I pressed a kiss to his temple before I laid him on his stomach on the mattress. I continued to rub my hand on his back while he shifted once and yawned before settling into a deep sleep. My fingers drifted up to thread through his soft blond curls, reminding me of how I looked in my own baby pictures taken a lifetime ago.

A gentle hand moved across my back in the same motion that I had been using on Squall, helping to ease an ache that had grown and letting the peace seep back in, so it no longer hurt to breathe. I looked over to find a little old woman standing beside me, her snowy-white hair pulled up into a loose bun on the top of her head. She looked up at me with fathomless green-gray eyes and smiled.

"I knew you could do it, my boy," she said in a low voice that seemed to hold me in an embrace that nearly brought tears to my eyes. "You've done wonderfully, but then you understand this so much better than those who tried to teach you."

"Understand what?" I asked in a wavering voice.

She reached down and took my hand in her old one. She held it out so that my open palm hovered over Squall's sleeping form. "Life. Nature. The ebb and flow of all things."

As she spoke, I could feel a subtle throb of energy emanating from the baby's body. She pulled her hand away and I could feel more. There was the energy from the earth seeping up through the house and in through the open windows. There was my own energy and the energy from all the animals nearby. While the woman next to me produced no energy of her own, she brought all the energy around me into instant balance, so that it was one harmonious song. The same song I had been mindlessly humming to Squall.

I pulled my hand back to grip the railing of the crib. I felt as if I should be afraid or anxious, but the emotions drained away before they could fully form. I was at peace, standing in this room next to the old woman because she brought everything into balance. She stepped a couple feet away, dropping her hand from my back, but the feeling of peace didn't wane as I had expected.

"You know, you can stay here if you want," she offered. "Your life would be exactly what you experienced today. You would be wrapped in the earth and life. It would be hard and simple, but also satisfying and peaceful."

I looked down at Squall as he slept soundly before me, trusting and happy. I closed my eyes, but my head was filled with the sounds of remembered laughter and twinkling green-gray eyes. Everything fit so wonderfully. I fit so perfectly here, as if I had finally found the puzzle to which I belonged. It was so tempting. So perfect . . .

My eyes snapped open and I looked at the old woman. "You're not one of them, are you?" I demanded, referring to the people I had met around the farm. "You're Mother Nature. You're Gaia. And none of this is real." I couldn't keep the sadness from my voice as I looked down at the baby. I wanted all of it to be real. For a second the world I lived in and had left behind that morning came screaming back with all its harsh edges and dirty light, and I needed this to be real so that I could draw my next breath.

"Chang warned me you were a smart boy," the woman said, drawing my gaze back to her face. She took my hand again and held it over Squall. "Does that not feel real? You know, Gage, that there is more to this world than what our eyes show us. But if you need it, this is all real and just for you."

I nodded, struggling to swallow past the lump that had grown in my throat. All the emotions that had left me were surging back, leaving me feeling raw and ragged.

Gaia squeezed my hand. "You don't have to leave."

"I can't stay." My voice was rough and choked, but I didn't care. "If I leave, will I ever be able to return?"

She cocked her head to the side for a second as she stared at me. Her smile dimmed a little. "If you leave, you will have one more chance to return. But only one." She released my hand and slid her arm around my back, starting to steer me away from the bed. "Come. Let's get some lemonade before Holly adds too much sugar."

I paused, looking back into the crib. I could feel a slight tearing in my chest as I tried to move away from the little boy with the blond curls. It was becoming harder to breathe and my heart was pounding as if I had run five miles. "Squall?"

Gaia gave a soft chuckle as she stepped in front of me. Her old, wrinkled hands came up and cupped my cheeks. It was only when her thumbs brushed aside tears that I realized that I was crying. "He'll be waiting for you, I promise. He'll wait."

I gave a jerky nod. "Let's get some lemonade," I said, trying to smile.

Gaia led the way out of the nursery, but I paused at the crib and looked down at the sleeping baby, trying to memorize the feel of the little soul that, somehow, I knew would one day be my son.

WHEN I STEPPED out of the old white farmhouse behind Gaia, we were faced with a giant, lush garden rather than the rolling field I had walked across minutes earlier. I stood at the bottom of the stairs, taking in the rich array of blooming flowers, the green trees with branches spread wide overhead, and the thick carpet of grass that looked soft underfoot. But as I stood there, soaking in the beauty, I knew that what I saw wasn't real. It wasn't there. Oh, I could see it, feel it, smell it, and taste it only because there was a part of my mind that needed to find a way to comprehend this strange place.

Gaia's home was a place of energy and life. It was either the source of or a crossroads for all the living things of the world: plant, animal, and other. Gaia tried to keep life in balance, but it wasn't the easiest of tasks with creatures eating away at the domains of nature and the Towers unbalancing everything with their magic. Yet despite it all, she had this place of perfect harmony and I didn't want to leave.

The old woman placed her hand on my arm and I let her lead me around through the garden to where a small table and a pair of cushioned chairs had been set up under a copse of trees. As soon as Gaia was comfortably settled, Holly carried over a tray that she placed on the table before us. She flashed me a smile as she poured us glasses of lemonade and then wordlessly headed back in the direction of the house.

"Careful," Gaia warned as I picked up my glass. "She tends to make overly sweet lemonade. I think she may have lived as a hummingbird for a time."

I took a tentative sip to find that it was perfect, like everything in this place. "Who are these people that live here with you?" I asked as I put down the glass.

"Souls wander in every once in a while, looking for something that they couldn't find in other lives they had." Her voice was like the soothing murmur of a woodland stream. "They stay and I give them something to do. After a time, they find what they were looking for and they move on to something else. There are never more than seven here at any time, but usually fewer."

"Are they all dead, then?"

She smiled at me as she folded her hands over her stomach. "Do they seem dead to you?" Before I could answer, she chuckled at me. "This is just a different place from where you live. Nothing more."

I relaxed in my chair, stretching my legs out in front of me. From within the copse of trees, I could no longer tell what time of day it was. There were little shafts of light filtering between the leaves, casting the world in a medley of gold and shadow. "I've met everyone but the seventh so far."

"That's because there is no seventh at the moment."

My gaze snapped back to her wrinkled face and I frowned. "Were you expecting me to become your seventh?"

She gave a little shrug, her smile never wavering. "Not at first, but you seemed to settle in while at the pond. I could see you aligning yourself to this world, and so much faster than the others that came before you. I would never have offered for you to stay if I didn't think you would fit."

"I can't stay," I said firmly, but there was no denying the cry of pain somewhere in my soul. I wanted to stay, but I had to go back to my life. I had to help Trixie and Bronx. I had to protect my brother. I had to stop the Towers from destroying everything. Gaia was offering me an escape, but the people I loved would be trapped if I accepted it.

"I know. Your love of your friends and family is a good thing to honor and cling to. This place is a temporary thing. They all go back eventually."

I nodded, letting the pain in my chest ease a little as I sat in the quiet of the garden. There was something about Gaia's manner that reminded me of my maternal grandmother, something in her eyes and the way she smiled knowingly at me, a wonderful mix of amusement and pride.

"Chang told me that you were coming because you needed my help with something," she said, pulling my thoughts at last to the real reason for my presence in her domain. While my body and soul felt at peace, there was now a discordant note in my brain, as if it existed in two separate spaces: Gaia's world and mine. "I'm sorry to say that I rarely visit your world and I try to avoid having any dealings with it. I probably won't be able to help you."

"I understand, but the elves are in danger and you're the only person I can think of that will be able to help."

Both white eyebrows raised and she sat up a little. "The elves? They've always been quite good at managing on their own."

"Until the Ivory Towers became involved."

For the first time, a dark scowl crossed her face, deepening the lines there. The breeze increased to a stiff wind and a couple large clouds rolled across the sky. "Curse those Towers and all those arrogant sots," she complained. "They've spent centuries mucking up all my work. They take pleasure in tangling things up and leaving it for others to fix. I've seen two-year-olds exhibit more care with their toys than they do for the world they must inhabit."

"Unfortunately, a witch from the Towers has made a great tangle of the elves," I said with a sigh. "I've discovered that she cast a spell over all the elves that is slowly but surely destroying their ability to procreate year after year. I can't undo the spell. To my knowledge, no witch or warlock can until it has run its course and all the elves are barren. I'm afraid that if we are forced to wait, we won't be able to save the elves from extinction. Furthermore, if the queen of the Summer Court doesn't have a child soon, there's going to be a war, which will only expedite their extinction."

A sympathetic look crossed her face as she looked at me. "Sometimes that is the way of things. Before you were born, creatures lived and died on that planet. Now not a one is left. Their time is over and they had to leave to make room for the rise of others."

My heart slammed in my chest and I shifted to the edge of my seat, leaning closer to her. "Yes, I understand that, but this isn't about natural selection or some Darwinian survival of the fittest. This is the work of one person who is destroying an entire race. It can't be allowed to happen."

"But that is exactly what it is," she said with the same sad little smile. "It's nothing more than one race encroaching on the territory of another. The Towers have found a way to eliminate their rivals for their space."

"No!" Shoving out of my chair, I paced away from Gaia. My hands clenched my hair as I struggled to order my thoughts into a convincing argument that would sway her into action to stop this horrible event that she was so calmly accepting. The peace I had found here had completely slipped away. The feeling of balance that had soothed my soul was gone, so that I now felt like a small island being pounded by the waves of the ocean.

When I looked around, the garden looked a little less idyllic. The colors weren't quite so bright and the air seemed a little less fragrant. But the world hadn't changed; I had. I had fallen out of sync with it, and it hurt.

Pushing the feeling of loss down, I looked at Gaia. "It can't be allowed to happen. The world needs the elves. With you away and maintaining a hands-off approach to my world, it threatens to fall completely out of balance. The elves help keep the energies there on an even keel. I don't understand their magic, but the world . . . life is better when they are there." I held my hands out to her, trying to persuade her, but it didn't look as if my words were changing her mind. "It was all a mistake," I whispered. "The witch . . . she's sorry now."

Gaia moved then, a little jerk of her head, so that she was staring at me through narrowed eyes. "You know who did this horrible thing?"

"Yes." My hands dropped to my sides. "She's a friend. A witch who's a cat now. I found out what she did. She didn't think . . . or rather didn't care what the spell would do. She thought she was protecting the Towers, but she regrets her actions now."

Mother Nature gave a little snort and crossed her arms over her chest with a frown. "Sorry? I've never heard of a witch or warlock that was ever sorry about anything, regardless of who was hurt."

"I am."

She seemed caught off guard by my comment. She knew I was from the Towers and that I was a warlock, but I think she had forgotten about my past. Her angry frown immediately melted into a look of sadness. I knelt before her and captured one of her hands in both of mine. "I'm sorry every time I make some stupid mistake with a potion that gets someone hurt. I'm sorry that my family was hurt by the fact that I was born a warlock. I'm sorry that my friends are in constant danger because they know me."

Gaia squeezed my hands, then placed one of hers against my cheek. "Oh, Gage, you're not one of them."

"But I am and you know it," I pressed, praying that I had something that might change her mind. "I am a warlock and I lived in the Towers. I am one of them, but I'm not like them. And I'm not the only one. Sofie, the witch who made this mess . . . she's changed. She's sorry. She lives with an elf now and she lives in horrible fear of how that elf will react when she discovers the truth. She loves that elf and doesn't want to hurt her. She's sorry, but she can't fix this. You can."

She stared at me for a long time, gazing deep into my eyes. I didn't know if she was reading my mind to determine that I was telling the truth or if she was looking inside herself. I could easily imagine that she had spent a very long lifetime fighting to right the messes caused by the Towers and she had to be tired of what was becoming a futile act. I couldn't blame her for wanting to step away from the world and remain closeted here, where peace seeped so deeply into your soul. But I needed her to act.

"Chang also warned me that you are a sneaky devil," she said with a slight frown.

A sigh of relief burst from my chest and my shoulders slumped. She was going to help. On an impulse, I leaned forward and pressed a kiss to her soft cheek. "Thank you."

"Ah! Just a minute!" she said sharply as I pushed to my feet. She pointed a thin finger at me. "Even in this world, you can't get something for nothing. If I help the elves, what will you give me in return?"

I was so excited that I nearly opened my mouth and said, *Anything!* but I caught myself at the last second. Unfortunately, I had a feeling that she heard that thought because her smile grew. But then, if she had been reading my mind, she knew that she had me. I would do anything to get Trixie safely back with her people. If I couldn't stop the Towers, I needed some place for her to go that would be hidden, and the elves knew how to hide.

"It's amazing what we do for love, isn't it?" Gaia said, looking at me speculatively. "A little while ago, I said that you would have a second chance to come back here. Would you trade that for the elves? For your Trixie's safety?"

The thought hurt, but I didn't hesitate. "Yes, I'll trade it."

"Would you trade Squall for Trixie?"

My heart jerked in my chest and it felt as if my skin had become cold and clammy. I stumbled a step backward as if I could run from her question. "Trade him?" My voice was coarse like gravel. "Would . . . would he be safe and happy if he didn't come to me?"

Gaia gave a little shrug, closely watching me. "The future is always an unknown thing. Maybe yes, maybe no."

Thoughts collided with raging emotion until everything was simply a dark whirlpool sucking down into nothing. Trade Squall for Trixie? Just seconds ago I had thought I would trade anything, but now I couldn't say the words. I had known him for only a few minutes as I held his fragile body in my arms, but I knew with every fiber of my being that he was *mine.* Yet, by the same token, I loved Trixie and she was mine as well. I needed her safe if I was to have a hope of staying sane. How could I trade one person for another?

I never saw her move, but Gaia was suddenly standing in front of me, her hand on my arm. There was a lump in my throat and I was struggling against the overwhelming fear that I had gotten so close to my goal and it was now slipping through my fingers. I was failing because I couldn't let go of my son to save not only my girlfriend but all her people.

"Shhh," she said softly. Peace started to ease back into my chest, slowing my heart and shrinking the lump in my throat. "Breathe easy, Gage. It was a trick question. You can't trade one loved one for another. You end up destroying three lives and saving none."

"I offer everything that I am and everything I have, but I can't . . . can't choose." My voice was rough and a part of me was angry that I couldn't control my emotions. There was something about this place. Everything was so raw and fresh here, more vibrant and alive, that emotions usually so easily under my control veered wildly out of my hands.

Gaia smiled brightly at me, looking as if tears were gathering in her own eyes. "You don't have to. What you've offered me is enough. I'll fix the elves' procreation problem."

My heart lurched and my body tensed. My emotions were a fucking roller coaster here and I was beginning to think that it was well past time for me to leave. "What do you mean? What's the trade?"

"You gave me the truth. As painful as it was, pulled straight from your heart, you gave me the truth. It's a very rare thing in the world and I highly value that gift. Thank you."

I nodded jerkily, no longer trusting my voice. I was feeling wrung out under the weight of my relief.

Gaia stepped back, but she held both of my hands in hers. "Now, it's getting late and I need to send you back. I will visit with Arianna tomorrow, I promise, and will see about setting things right for the elves. You warn that little witch that she needs to stop messing in my domain."

"I will. She is sorry," I said, giving her hands a squeeze. "Could you tell everyone I said good-bye?"

Gaia arched a mocking eyebrow at me. "Even Rocky?"

I smirked back at her, starting to feel a little more like my usual self. "Especially Rocky."

"Of course."

I drew in a deep breath, feeling my smirk slip from my mouth. "Hug Squall for me?"

"Every day and twice on Sunday."

"Thank you . . . for everything."

Her smile grew a little wider, sending a tear skidding down her cheek. "Good luck and I'm sorry about this."

I wanted to ask what she meant by her last comment, but I didn't get the chance. In an instant, the world went dark and her hands slipped from mine. It lasted only a second. I blinked and Gaia's garden had been replaced with the parking lot behind my apartment building. It took me only a breath to realize why she had apologized. With me in the parking lot were three warlocks and a witch. The same witch I should have killed when she attacked me the first time. Damn. This was going to get ugly.

22

WE ALL STOOD there stunned. I was confused as hell as to what they were doing in my parking lot and they were confused as hell as to where I had come from. Common sense said that they had been preparing another attack on my apartment, but the panic screaming through my brain was drowning out any common sense I had left. I didn't have my wand, I didn't have the keys to my car, and I didn't have a clue as to what the fuck I could do to get out of this mess.

"That was nice of you to come to us," said one warlock, drawing my gaze to his face. He looked vaguely familiar, but then I had met few other magic users while I had lived in the Towers ten years ago. Those that I had met outside of my mentor, Simon, had been on . . . *Oh, fuck.*

"You're on the council," I said, talking mostly to myself as I took a step backward. "Fox. Henry Fox?"

"Correct," Henry said with a grim smile. The bastard had argued for my immediate execution when I had been brought up on charges. Apparently, he was still against the idea of me breathing.

My gaze swept around the parking lot, searching for an escape. After they had gotten over their momentary shock, the quartet had spread out, leaving me without an exit. The one potential weak spot was the bitch that I should have killed the first time. It made sense that my mistake would come back to haunt me in a big fucking way. I hated when Gideon was right. After dumping her in a net at the bottom of the ocean off the North Shore, I could only imagine that she was most eager to get rid of me.

"Warlocks who visit Low Town have been disappearing recently," Henry said pleasantly, his voice crawling across my skin like fire ants dragging razor blades. After my time in Gaia's garden, the whole world seemed to be washed in a dull gray light despite the fact that the setting sun was painting the sky in shades of pink and orange. Sounds and smells clashed together in a discordant fashion like a toddler pounding on a piano, leaving me flinching as my mind tried to make sense of Henry's words. "First Master Thorn goes missing two months ago, and now in a matter of days, Masters Rosenblum and Wilson disappear."

"Low Town can be a dangerous place if you're not prepared," I said between clenched teeth. Without moving a muscle, I started drawing small amounts of energy to me, swirling it around my hands and letting it seep into my skin. The cacophonous feel of the world eased so that it was no longer sliding along my brain like a cheese grater. No one flinched or moved. I didn't think anyone had noticed the shift yet, but then they could have been busy doing the same thing as I was doing.

Looking at my opponents, I figured that the one thing that I could count on was that they wouldn't all attack at once. That took teamwork and planning if they didn't want to risk ripping an ally inside out, and the occupants of the Towers did not play well together. The only thing they generally rallied together for was a type of us-versus-the-world mentality. Using magic in a single, concerted effort against one target was the domain of the guardians—the enforcers of the Towers did the dirty work. Henry Fox was a council member, not a guardian, and Useless Clod was an apprentice. That only left the other two unknown warlocks. They could have been guardians, but they were more likely lackeys of Fox.

This was one of the moments when I wished I had stuck it out in the Towers for a few more years, learned a few more tricks that could keep me alive. Just a couple more years and I would have been damn good at teleporting. Oh, I could do the spell now, but it wasn't safe for me to attempt it with so many warlocks watching me. I couldn't protect myself and teleport at the same time, and I didn't think Henry and his friends were going to wait politely. My only hope was for a wave of death and incapacitation to hit them.

As I turned, trying to keep as many of them in my line of sight as possible, Henry gave a little nod. The brown-haired, nameless warlock stepped forward, but it was only a distraction because at the same time I felt a surge of energy jump from the warlock with greasy blond hair and saggy jowls. An energy ball jumped from his fingertips, but I was ready, the shield in place, so that the spell was harmlessly deflected back toward him. Brown Hair joined him, throwing his own energy ball at me. But it didn't deflect as it should have. It splat like a tacky ball of electric-green slime and quickly started to spread around me, growing over the shield as if it were algae. My pulse raced. The slime was blocking my vision of my attackers, nearly covering me.

With a curse, I dropped my shield, as my attackers had expected. The green slime disappeared with a faint crackle. Energy jumped in the air. I dropped to my knees and rolled toward the witch, missing the two energy balls that smashed into the fractured concrete where I had been standing a second ago. Pushing to my feet, I found myself standing only a foot from Master Wilson's apprentice, a stunned look on her plain, pale face as if she was surprised to be standing so close to me. It was almost funny.

Slamming my fist into her face was funny. I didn't believe in hitting women. If my father had seen me, he would have tanned my ass, regardless of my age. But since she was trying to kill me, I figured I could make an exception. She cried out, falling backward onto her ass, covering her face with both her hands.

Confident that she was preoccupied for a minute, I turned back to where the others stood, summoning up great gulps of energy like a whale sucking down plankton. There was no subtlety or sneakiness this time, but we were past that, right?

Greasy came at me with a wave of fire, which was kind of surprising. If I hadn't properly blocked it with a blast of cold air, the flames would have cooked me and the witch behind me. He obviously wasn't concerned for her well-being in this fight, but then he didn't strike me as a particularly strong magic user either. He was sloppy and lacked imagination—two things that made a poor magic weaver. Definitely one of Fox's lackeys.

Brown Hair worried me, though. The strange energy ball that glommed onto my shield was a new twist. He was smart, sneaky, and dangerous.

What was worse, Fox had yet to move. He cast no spells, issued no commands beyond his initial head nod. You didn't get to be on the council without being very powerful. I didn't know what Fox was waiting for, but the anticipation was eating a hole in my stomach.

With the wind still in hand, I swirled it up into the sky, stirring the clouds. I immediately released it, hoping that I sent enough energy up in that direction that the momentum of the shifting weather took over. Over the years, I had become good at two types of spells: defensive and weather. I had had to learn to be good at conjuring defensive spells at the drop of a hat if I was going to outlive Simon. They could be tricky because the very art of magic was tricky. Most offensive spells were curses and they had to be deflected or unwound with very specific countercurses. Fear of Simon had taught me to recognize a spell before it left the fingers of the caster.

I had gotten good at weather spells because turbulent weather generated more energy in the area that a warlock or a witch could use. Not all warlocks or witches could tap that energy, but there were enough that I was potentially helping one of my opponents as much as I was trying to help myself.

At my left, I felt a new spell creeping toward me, a soft whisper of words on the edge of the energy that caused me to instantly stiffen with fear. Brownie was working a binding spell, but I couldn't tell if it was a physical or a magic binding spell. Gideon had used a physical binding spell on me every once in a while to gain my undivided attention. The words of a countercurse flared to life in my mind, but I tweaked the spell, sweeping my hands through an intricate pattern before my chest. You couldn't immediately unravel a binding spell once it was started. The countercurse always sent it back at the spell caster, but I knew this bastard would be prepared for such a thing.

On my right, Greasy shouted, his pale face growing unattractively red and splotchy. The binding spell had swept past me and hammered against him, leaving him waving his hands in the air harmlessly. There was a dead zone of energy surrounding him. Judging by the mixture of fear and rage radiating off it, the binding spell was a damn powerful one.

I sighed in relief, my right hand trembling and tingling slightly. It had been a close thing. I felt drained, and only one of the four was out of magical commission for now. A chuckle was rising in my chest when I felt the swell of energy at my back. The bitch had gotten her second wind. Unfortunately, my brain was moving too slowly under the temporary fatigue and the icy spell crashed through my defense like a rhino through wet tissue paper, throwing me to the ground. My back slammed against the gravel-strewn concrete and my head followed, lighting up a white glare before my eyes. My breath burst from my chest and I sucked in before I could stop myself. The air froze in my lungs like I had swallowed Freon, locking up my chest so I couldn't breathe.

Panic swarmed over me, painfully tensing my muscles. Cold chills racked my body, making it nearly impossible to think. It felt as if the bitch had dipped me in water and dropped me naked in the middle of the Antarctic. I had to think of the countercurse, but the biting cold was making it impossible to concentrate. The words scattered within my brain, darting off in a thousand different directions.

Someone was shouting. It wasn't me because I couldn't draw a breath, but I could hear it over the pounding of my blood in my ears. Twisting on my side, I looked up to find Fox pointing at me while he shouted at the witch. A small swell of energy washed over my chest and I could suddenly breathe. The absolute wretched cold didn't disappear, but I wasn't going to suffocate.

"You idiot!" Fox screamed. "I need him alive! He's useless to me dead!" A long knife flashed in his right hand from out of thin air as he moved in front of the woman. I could no longer see her, his larger body was blocking my view, but I saw his right hand reach back again and again. A sick, squishing and sucking sound echoed against the unnatural silence of the early evening as the blade sank into her chest with each thrust. No one moved except Fox as he stabbed the woman repeatedly.

Anger spent, he stepped back from her, letting the body crumple to the ground, a lifeless sack of chopped meat. I was pushing to my feet when he turned to look at me. A twisted light shone in his blue eyes while blood soaked into his shirt and slacks. It dripped from his face while more rained from the fist tightly gripping the knife. He might need me alive, but the insanity dancing in his eyes said that he wanted to carve me up like a Thanksgiving turkey and dig for the wishbone with his fat hands.

"And now you know I'm serious," Henry Fox said, breaking the thick silence.

I forced myself to smirk because fear was shredding what was left of my self-control, making it hard to grab a lungful of air. "Never doubted your seriousness, old boy."

Fox flinched at my familiar tone, his hand tightening on the knife, so that fresh blood dripped to the ground. "Good. Then I'll give you a choice. You can come willingly and submit to questioning, or we kill you. I will then raise you and you will tell me anything I want. I'm sure you can guess my preference."

Yeah, I knew the sadist's preference, but he would avoid it if he could. I'm sure he thought he could raise me from the dead, but we both knew that zombies were notorious for giving incorrect and incomplete information. The mind deteriorated way too fast after death because the soul couldn't be anchored in the body. And I was pretty sure that with Lilith holding a chunk of my soul, the underworld bitch wasn't going to let me be called back unless she could gain from the bargain. Henry Fox wasn't going to raise me, no matter how powerful he was.

Unfortunately, my other option was pretty shitty too. Questioning always equaled torture, and I was not going to let this bastard touch me. Particularly since he was going to kill me after.

If I was going to get out of this, I needed to change tactics. I couldn't remain on the defensive because they were going to wear me down until I made a mistake. But I wasn't a full-fledged, trained warlock like they were. I knew most of the spells that they could attack with, but I couldn't perform them with the same speed or strength. Most would be batted away before I finished. I had to stick with my strengths, the common, seemingly useless spells I could work reflexively. They weren't curses, but types of enchantments—easier to unravel but much harder to predict.

Widening my stance to keep my balance, I blanked my mind while shoving down the nausea rising in my stomach. Adrenaline bubbled in my veins until it felt like my hair was standing on end. In a breath, I pulled up a swell of energy, and I slammed it into Greasy and Fox. I couldn't manage all three at once. Greasy was a nuisance and Fox was dangerous. Brownie was somewhere in the middle.

Narrowing my eyes, I could feel Brownie summoning up a shield, but it wouldn't work. With only the smallest push, I directed the energy toward him but my only thought was of peeling an apple. I was vaguely aware of him jerking one arm sharply and twisting, looking around for whatever was attacking him. His face was a mask of confusion as he stubbornly held on to his magical barrier while straining to figure out what I was doing. A second later, his scream rang out, sending shards of glass cutting through my soul. His body twisted and writhed in pain. I tapped down the revulsion while my brain locked on the vision of a small paring knife sliding around a bright red apple as it cut away the skin in a single, long coil.

With the spell in place, I turned to find Greasy staring in horror. He seemed to have forgotten about me. I lifted one hand and extended one finger, pointed down. I slowly spun it in place, imagining that I was stirring a cup of coffee. The warlock gave a surprised shout as he began to spin in place as well, but his shouts and flailing arms were quickly replaced with pain-filled shrieks. When I took the time to magically stir my coffee, I also heated it.

I should have been feeling horror, revulsion. I should have been throwing up the contents of my stomach, but I felt detached and numb as I killed them. My mind desperately clung to the images of an apple and coffee because if I thought about what I was doing, I'd go mad.

I started to turn to look for Fox when I heard a voice directly behind me.

"Interesting approach," he said as if he was admiring an artist's use of light in a bucolic landscape painting.

Before I could move, pain exploded behind my eyes, blacking out the world. A sense of falling overcame me, but I couldn't recall ever hitting the ground. My last thought was that I should have used the spell I'd perfected to debone fish on Henry Fox.

THE WIND WAS blowing, but I couldn't feel it. Tall grasses were swaying and the thick wall of trees in the distance was dancing in the strong breeze, but I felt nothing. I had no sense of time because the sky was a heavy gray as if a storm had moved in but had yet to dump its load of rain. Fingers twined with mine on my left and I looked over to find Lilith standing next to me. The sickly, gray cast to her pale skin made her look almost dead, but a frightening light danced in her dark eyes.

"Where are we?" I asked.

With a jerk of her chin, she motioned toward her left. I looked to find that we were standing a few yards from an enormous tower made of white marble. It gleamed against the dark sky like a spotlight shooting up toward the heavens. The Ivory Tower was one of eight that dotted the earth, housing the witches and the warlocks of the world.

I tried to step away from her, but she tightened her fingers around mine. "Why are we here?" I didn't want to be anywhere around the monster that was clinging to a piece of my soul.

Lilith smiled and my blood turned to sludge in my veins. She was the queen of the underworld in a way. When a creature had to spend a year dead to pay a debt to magic, Lilith was the one who watched over him. When I passed through the underworld a few months ago, she had begged me to help her escape. And with my one-year debt and a portion of my soul, Lilith was positively itching to get me back into her domain.

"Help me escape, Gage," she whispered in a silky, sinuous voice that coiled around my brain. "We can set everything right. Just you and I." She raised her free hand toward the Ivory Tower before us, and in a rush, it was engulfed in flames. Behind it, one after another, trees burst into flames. Fire broke out of slender windows in the Tower followed by thick ropes of black smoke. The front double doors were flung open and people in black robes ran out as flames danced on their flailing limbs. Screams rose in the night to accompany the crackling of the fire and the thick scent of smoke that perfumed the air.

"I'm more powerful that any warlock or witch," she said. Her low, breathy voice brushed against my ear, sending a chill across my flesh. "With you helping me, we can destroy the Towers. We can make this world new."

I couldn't tear my eyes off the people streaming out of the Tower, dying wretched, pain-filled deaths. People ran free of the building, engulfed in flames, only to drop to the ground and roll in an attempt to escape, but the fire didn't stop until they were dead. Lying lifeless in the tall grasses that curled and blackened in the flames, the bodies sizzled and hissed like bacon on a cast-iron skillet. The witches and the warlocks were mostly horrible creatures, and maybe they deserved a horrible death for the atrocities they committed, but it wasn't my place to decide.

"Would your reign in this world be any different than theirs?" I asked.

Her laugh was like someone had shoved fat needles into my skin. "Of course." Yes. It would be different. The world would be far worse than its current fractured state with her running loose. The vision of the Tower burning was only the start. Lilith would bring hell to earth.

Unlike my dream of Bryce in which I woke up on a scream, this dream slipped away quietly and I slowly eased back into consciousness. Lilith was taunting me. Time was running out and I had yet to think of a way to escape her.

It hurt to think. It felt as if every stray thought bouncing through my head came armed with a sledgehammer and a sadist grin. I was vaguely aware that my body ached, but it was nothing compared to the gut-wrenching, soul-searing pain filling my head. I could feel the bones cradling my brain sliding around, sloshing fluids and pinching tissue as they tried to settle into their respective spots.

Sucking in pained breaths through clenched teeth, I cracked one eye open to find a witch bent over me. Her fingers were pressed against my head, but I could barely feel it. She was staring down at me with chocolate-brown eyes, but by her grim expression of concentration, I wasn't sure if she saw me.

"Take slow, deep breaths," she directed in a low voice. "It will help."

I tried, but it wasn't easy, as I started to get light-headed. My eyes fell shut again and I could feel her move her fingertips to another location on my head. As my breathing evened out, the pain was starting to ebb and I could feel the soothing flow of magic through my body. She was using a healing spell, fixing whatever Fox had done to my head.

"Why are you healing me?" I asked, my voice rough. I opened my eyes to see her frowning, but this time she was looking at me.

"Master Fox can't question you if you're in a coma." She released my head and took a step back.

I sighed with relief. A killer headache was still banging against the back of my skull, but it was significantly weaker than what I had been feeling. "Thanks."

The witch's face twisted with ugly rage. Lurching forward, she reached between my legs and grabbed my balls in a grip that had me screaming. Fresh pain lanced through my body, bowing it off the bed I was lying on while all the air rushed from my lungs. "Thank me again, traitor, and I'll rip your balls off with my bare hands and feed them to you!" she snarled. She gave them a quick twist before releasing them and stomping out of the room. I was vaguely aware of the door slamming and locking behind her, but I could barely hear the sounds over my own moaning.

I tried to roll on my side, wanting to pull my body into a fetal position, but my arms and legs were tied to the posts of the narrow twin bed. There was no mattress below me, only a metal web of hooks that were now digging into my back and squeaking as I shifted. The pain eased, but I was ready to throttle the bitch. Shoot me, stab me, or set me on fire . . . that was fine. Just don't grab my goddamn balls!

I took a deep breath and willed my heart to slow back down as I assessed the damage. My head and balls hurt like a motherfucker, but the rest of me seemed fine. I wiggled my fingers and rolled my ankles, checking to make sure that blood was reaching all my extremities. Well, if I could get loose, there was a good shot at me moving. The problem was getting loose and getting out.

Looking around, I found that I was in a small, windowless room with white walls and bare wood floors. The single door held a slight blue glow that I could pick out from the corner of my eye, indicating that it wasn't just locked but also guarded by magic. Shit. Bunch of sneaky bastards. They couldn't just put a guard outside the door to keep an eye on me?

Of course, I had a feeling there was a guard outside the door as well. A shudder ran through me as fractured memories from the parking lot seeped back into my consciousness. I had shut down when I hit Brownie and Greasy with those spells. I couldn't let myself remember because I was afraid I would start screaming and never stop. It was one thing to kill for survival, to protect yourself and those you love. It was a completely different matter to subject your prey to a slow, painful death.

Sadly, I was certain I wouldn't be penalized two years for killing them with magic because you couldn't die from having your skin peeled off. You died from shock and blood loss. It was a technicality, but for some reason, the fates and balance of powers observed it. And Greasy wouldn't die from being spun and heated. No, it was more likely that his feverish fat ass fell once the spell wore off and he died of splitting his head on the ground. I couldn't dare owe Lilith a second year. Not after her most recent dream visit. A second death caused by magic would mean that I'd have to fight her for two years, and I doubted my resourcefulness when it came to such a task.

For a moment I wasn't sure if it was sadder that those men had died because of what I did or because Fox had done nothing to save them. I banged my head against the springs beneath me in frustration and winced as fresh pain bloomed behind my eyes. Fox had hit me on the back of the head, cracking my skull and giving me a serious concussion. *Asshole.*

It could have been worse, but I was sure that it was only a matter of time before Fox came back to put me in some real pain, in the name of extracting information. *Fantastic.* Considering the comment from the witch, I figured he either suspected that I had released the locations of the Towers or he was going to torture me until I confessed to doing it so he could have an excuse to kill me. I had to get out of here. Even if I handed over Reave's name, it wouldn't save me. I needed to strike a bargain with the Towers if I was going to get them to back off.

Looking up at where my right wrist was tied to the bedpost, I twisted my arm, testing the strength of the knot. It was tight, but as long as I didn't mind a little rope burn and blood, I was pretty sure I could work it loose. I knew a spell to unravel the knot, but I didn't want to use it. If there was a single brain in the building that held me, they would have set a spell to alert them if I used magic. I had to sneak out of here the old-fashioned way.

With my teeth clenched, I pulled and jerked, twisting the rope and stretching it as much as possible so that it slid over my hand. Blood was streaking down my arm and it hurt like hell, but this was nothing if I didn't get moving. Carefully turning to my left so that I didn't make any noise, I untied the knot and freed my hand before bending down to free my ankles.

It took me nearly a full minute to sit up and put my feet on the floor. As I shifted my weight on the springs, they screeched loudly. My breath caught in my chest as I waited for my guard to charge into the room before I was ready, but he never did. I moved each hand and ankle, one at a time, making sure that circulation was flowing back into my extremities and everything was working properly.

Standing, I paused to wipe my blood from the bed with my shirt and pocket the ropes that had absorbed my blood. If I escaped, I didn't want anyone using it to find me again . . . or worse. There was an old belief that if you knew a person's real name, you had power over them. It was bullshit. Blood, on the other hand, was a great way to get at a person.

I crossed the bare wood floor slowly, rolling my feet with each step to try to reduce any creaks and groans. Stopping a couple feet from the door, I got down on my hands and knees to gaze under the opening beneath the door while praying that I didn't cast a shadow. At an angle, I could see a pair of shoes. It looked as if someone with big feet was seated outside the door. A man, or rather, a warlock.

Pushing to my knees, I inched a little closer to the door but was careful not to touch it. The spell was a simple one designed to keep me from using magic to pick the lock, which was also quite simple and old. By the age of the wood beneath me, the style of the door, and the old-fashioned iron doorknob with lock, I could easily guess that this was not a newly constructed house, which meant that the floors would creak and groan when I moved. Doorknobs would jiggle and rattle. Doors would moan when opened. In short, this was going to be a noisy fucking house for me to sneak out of.

But I didn't need to get far. Just out of the house. *Without* being detected. If I could escape to a quiet location that was hidden, I could teleport. If I tried it in the house, not only would they know I used magic, but they'd be able to trace the spell to my final destination. Sure, I was going back to Low Town, assuming I wasn't in Low Town at the moment, but I wasn't going to my apartment. I needed to hit the parlor if these fuckers were going to continue to play rough.

But first things first. I had to take care of the asshole guarding my door. Standing, I soundlessly backed up until I was sure that I wouldn't be trapped behind the door if he threw it open, but stayed as close as I could so I could jump on him when he came in.

I drew in a deep breath and closed my eyes for a second, willing the twisting and knots in my stomach to ease. My heart was pounding, increasing the pain in my brain, but I was barely aware of it. I had to get this right. If an alarm was sounded, I knew Fox would be here in a heartbeat.

Fisting my hands tightly at my sides, I raised my voice to a frantic scream. "Oh God! No! God! No! Help! Oh God! No! Help! Stop it!" Over my desperate, hysterical shouting, I could hear the scrape of a chair and the pounding of footsteps heading toward the door. I kept shouting as the key was inserted and the door unlocked. As I had expected, the warlock threw the door open wide as he stepped inside, ready to take out whatever monster had apparently snuck into my room from the closet. Jumping across the distance before he noticed me, I gripped his short blond hair in one fist and slammed his head against the doorjamb as hard as I could.

His large body became deadweight as he was knocked unconscious. I grabbed his sweater with both hands and silently lowered him to the floor in hopes of not making more noise than I already had. If anyone had heard me, I was hoping that my shouts had been generic enough for them to think that my guard had stepped in to torment me. Sweat ran down the side of my face as I grabbed his feet and pulled him into the room before closing the door.

The big oaf was out cold. There was a smear of blood on the wall, but a pool hadn't immediately started to gather on the floor, so he wasn't hurt that bad. Kneeling next to him, I pocketed the old skeleton key he had used to unlock the door and then grabbed the wand he had dropped. I turned it over in my hand, testing the feel and gauging the energy inside of it before cursing my luck. It was made of yew.

I stood and glared down at the warlock before giving him a swift kick in the ribs. What was this asshole doing with a yew wand? Yew branches were strong in death magic, which was nasty business. I could use the wand, but I wouldn't have the same kind of control over my spells that I did when I used my hands and I was a hell of a lot more likely to accidentally kill someone with a spell using this wand.

Regardless of my desperation, I wasn't going to use the yew wand. I was better off with my hands. Of course, I wasn't going to give this asshole the chance to use the wand should he wake up before I could escape. With a grin, I broke the wand over my knee. I dropped one half in front of him and shoved the other half in my back pocket without the hole. I'd burn the wand later. He wouldn't recover the magic from this one.

Stomping down the swelling of relief that I had gotten at least this far without being caught, I moved to the door and listened for the sounds of voices or footsteps, but all was silent. I briefly peeked out to find the hallway empty before slipping out and closing the door behind me. I locked the bastard in and put the key in my front pocket. With any luck, the spell on the door would keep him busy for a little while.

The hallway was narrow and dark, more white walls and bare wood floors. There was more light coming from the far end of the hall and what looked to be a set of stairs leading down. There were three more doors on either side of the hall, leading to either bathrooms or bedrooms, but all were closed. No noises came from the other side of the doors. I was itching to look out a window to figure out what time of day it was or even try to learn where the hell I was, but I didn't want to risk opening a door to an occupied room.

Frowning, I edged down the short hall, trying to make as little noise as possible. The floor creaked here and there, but I was hoping anyone who heard shrugged it off as noises that the house made as it settled. It was a struggle to swallow, my mouth had grown so dry, and I found myself clenching and unclenching my fists at my sides as anxiety ate away at me. I had made a ton of noise with the guard. Had no one heard me? Was there no one else in the house? Someone should have already stormed up the stairs.

At the end of the hall, I peered around the corner and looked down the stairs only to find another landing and more stairs. Fuck, I was on the third floor. How big was this place? Of course, if everyone was on the ground floor, they might not have heard the racket I was making. Praying that was the case, I eased down the stairs, sliding along the wall while trying to keep an eye out both above and below me.

Just as I neared the landing on the second floor, a door was thrown open and the witch that had twisted my nuts in her fist stomped out, frowning. She was wearing the same wrinkled blue blouse and black slacks I had seen her in a while ago, but her dark hair was now down around her shoulder instead of in a neat bun. She looked to be in her early forties, but her constant frowns and glares were putting years on her face. The witch walked to the stairs leading to the first floor and I crouched down, trying to stay out of sight while keeping an eye on her.

"Marceau, what's going on down there?" she shouted. We both waited, but there was no response. The witch made an angry sound in the back of her throat before turning back to the bedroom she had exited. Instead of going inside, she leaned in and said something to the darkness before heading down the stairs. A couple seconds later, a warlock emerged, tucking his shirt into his pants as he followed her down the stairs.

I couldn't stop the smirk that twisted my lips. The prevailing rule was that witches and warlocks weren't supposed to have physical relationships, but while no one openly admitted to it, I had little doubt that it was happening.

I waited until I could hear his footsteps moving away on the ground floor, before I followed behind him. I didn't know what had drawn the duo to the first floor, but I was hoping that it would work in my favor. If I was lucky, everyone would be gathered in one part of the house and I could sneak out another.

Before hitting the main floor, I peered through the railing to find that the stairs ended near what appeared to be the living room. Bright sunlight was streaming through the windows. It had to be near midday, but which day? Was it the same day I had been attacked, but we were in another part of the world? Or was it the next day or even later than that?

There was no one I could see in the living room. Only old plaid furniture and spindly tables covered with magazines. I looked around and my eyes caught on the front door. Freedom! So close. Even better, I could see no spells on the door. Nothing to alert them if I walked right out of the house and down the driveway or street or wherever the fuck I was.

But I was too slow. Just as I started to straighten my body and head down the stairs, fast footsteps approached. I reached into my pockets and found only the skeleton key I had taken off the guard. The witch turned the corner, one hand on the large wooden banister, as I reached the last step. She looked up, her mouth dropping open in surprise to find me standing in front of her. With the end of the key clenched in my fist, I shoved it into her throat, crunching through flesh and her trachea. She gasped, but the sound was more like a bloody gargle. Her hands fluttered helplessly around her throat as she started to crumple to her knees. Grabbing her shoulders, I spun her around and laid her on her back on the stairs. She wouldn't be visible until someone tried to go to the second floor.

At the back of the house, I heard a brief scuffle and then nothing. By my guess, there were at least two more people in the house, the warlock from the second-floor bedroom and Marceau. If I was careful, I could take both out and then escape, which might buy me more time. If I left someone behind alive, they could alert Fox. But if they were all dead or unconscious, Fox might not find out for a little while.

Carefully heading down the main hall on the first floor, I approached the source of the noise. Common sense said to stay hidden, but the sight in the tiny kitchen stopped me cold. The two men I had been concerned about were lying on the white linoleum floor in a spreading pool of blood. Over them stood . . . kids. Kids holding wands. Except for one. A girl between the age of twelve and fifteen stood over one man holding a blood-splattered baseball bat.

I must have made some noise because all eyes swung to me at the same time while wands were raised in my direction. I knew in that second I was fucked because nothing in this world could get me to attack a kid, let alone kill one to save my own life.

"Gage!" the girl with the baseball bat said with an exuberant laugh. "We were just coming to rescue you!"

I could feel the blood draining from my face at that announcement as my eyes skimmed over each young face. There were five kids gathered in that little kitchen, faces smudged with dirt but all looking at me with an expression of joyous expectation and wariness. Five kids with wands.

Oh God, the runaways had found me.

I SAT AT the wobbly folding card table with my head in my hands. The throbbing in my temples had returned with a vengeance at the sight of the five kids determined to "rescue me" when I had been doing my damnedest to make sure our paths never crossed. After checking to make sure that the two warlocks were still breathing, I ushered the kids back outside to a secluded location in what turned out to be the Austrian countryside before we used a teleport spell to return to their secret hideout. The crumbling, abandoned house had no electricity, no running water, and no heat. While a quick look around revealed that it was relatively clean, I knew that they couldn't stay here, but I wasn't sure what to do with them.

Lifting my head, I found the oldest of the group and proclaimed leader, Étienne, frowning at me. From what I could get out of him, the seventeen-year-old French teen had escaped from the Tower in Brazil with Paola and Anthony. They had hidden out in Texas for a short time before coming to Low Town, where they were later joined by the baseball-bat-wielding Alice and her brother, James, from the Tower in upstate New York.

For now, we were waiting. It was about an hour before dawn. Luckily, Fox and his cohorts had had me for only a few hours rather than days. If I planned carefully, I could still get Trixie to contact the elves about Gaia and then I could turn my attention to my brother and Reave. Yet, I first had to do something about this little band, and I needed help for that. With some reluctance, I used magic to send a message to Sofie, who was supposed to locate Gideon and send him to me. From what I could tell, neither Étienne nor Paola was fond of my plan. Anthony, or Tony, as he preferred to be called, seemed to smile and roll with it all, while Alice busied herself with tidying the small house and making me a sandwich from their meager pantry. Her younger brother, James, remained silent and close to her at all times.

He was the one who worried me the most. His thin face and large eyes held dark shadows, as if he was constantly haunted by the memories of the Towers. James needed somewhere safe to live. He didn't need to spend every second of his life looking over his shoulder and flinching at every sound. The others seemed stronger, more pulled together, but every once in a while I'd catch a ghost float through their eyes, find a crack in their armor. No child should have to live in hiding like this.

"How did you even find me?" I demanded, dropping my hands to the slightly sticky surface of the table as I tried to turn my mind away from their future and focus more on the present.

Étienne's lips pressed into a hard, thin line and the muscles in his jaw flexed. The kid was taller than me, but he was too thin, his T-shirt hanging on him so that he looked like a scarecrow. His handsome face was smudged with dirt and his blond hair was becoming long and shaggy, and yet he managed an almost regal bearing. I didn't know if it was a defense mechanism or if it was a French thing. I didn't take it personally. He took the safety of his companions very seriously and he didn't trust me.

Tony laughed from where he stood next to Étienne. "We'd been keeping an eye on your place for the past couple of weeks, trying to figure out a way to approach you. We saw the fight. Paola was afraid they'd take you, and we wouldn't be able to follow. James came up with the idea to hit you with a spitball, seeing as he'd be able to track his spit with a spell." He laughed again and nudged Étienne with his elbow. The older boy tried to maintain his frown, but was struggling. There was something infectious about Tony's laughter.

"Disgusting," Alice muttered from across the room with her crisp British accent. She and her brother were from the United Kingdom, while Paola was from Italy. Tony sounded as if he was from somewhere in the South like Alabama or Mississippi, which added to his charm.

A part of me wanted to laugh with Tony because the trick was quite simple and ingenious. With all the chaos going on, I doubted anyone would have noticed a spitball hitting me. But I was equally sickened by the thought that these kids had witnessed the brutality and ugliness of that fight. I was going to have nightmares for years, and I was supposed to be the fucking adult in the room.

"I appreciate you trying to rescue me, but why?" I flopped back in the folding chair and stared at Étienne. I knew the ultimate decision had come from him. He had put these kids in danger coming after me, knowing that I was being held by members of the Towers. "You know the Towers are going to be watching me and harassing me. We can't be seen together. We can't help each other. It's too dangerous."

"We will not be bullied by the Ivory Towers." Étienne's low voice was strong as his French accent curled around each word. He narrowed his bright blue eyes on me and leaned forward. "We have been beaten, starved, tortured, and frightened from the moment we were stolen from our homes. We escaped because we will not be treated like that. We know we cannot go home to our families, but we will not let them kill another like us. Another who has stood up against them and said no."

I frowned, taking in his quiet fervor. Something had bothered me from the moment I saw him with the others. Listening to him, I finally knew what it was. He reminded me of myself, but worse. I left the Towers because I hated what they were and I tried to secretly protect others from the witches and the warlocks when I could. The big difference, though, was that when I was his age, I only had myself to look out for. Étienne had four kids depending on him to make good decisions. That was going to wear him down fast.

"I understand," I said with a nod. Étienne sat back, looking confused and skeptical, so I pressed on. "I do understand and that's why you were going to talk to me. You knew that if anyone could understand what you're going through, I could. I've been in this spot before, ten years ago. I know what you're risking and why you're doing it. Because of that, you have to believe me when I say it's time to stop. Things have to change."

The young man stiffened and even the easygoing Tony was now frowning. The room had gotten extremely quiet as they all waited for Étienne's decision.

A hard knock banged against the wooden front door. We all jumped at the sound. Wands appeared a heartbeat later, sending me surging to my feet to stop any kind of preemptive attack. I was hoping it was Gideon, and he didn't much care for having spells slung at him. The kids needed his help and pissing him off before getting him inside wasn't a good first step.

"Whoa! Whoa! Whoa!" I said in a harsh whisper, holding my hands up while sliding in front of the door. "We're going for inconspicuous here. Wands down. Let's aim for normal and then go from there."

It was with a great deal of reluctance that the wands were lowered, but no one put their wand away. Maybe I was jealous that they had their wands on hand. Gods knew that I was dying to hold mine, but I would have to make do until I got back to my apartment.

I lifted my right hand and held it in front of the door, pulling up a spell to tell me exactly how many people stood on the other side of the door. When the spell revealed only one person, I sighed with relief. One I could handle.

"Who's there?" I called.

"Gideon," the cold, familiar voice snapped back. "Open the damn door."

As I grasped the doorknob, I looked back at the kids. Alice had stepped in front of James, while the rest were spread about the room. All had matching grim expressions. They didn't trust Gideon, and I couldn't blame them. He was a member of the Towers to them. Opening the door, I stepped back so Gideon could enter. He didn't get far. The warlock took one step forward, his eyes immediately landing on the kids spread about the small, dingy room.

"Shit," he whispered, his shoulders slumping. Yeah, that was pretty much my thought. A second later, Gideon wrapped his fists in my polo shirt and threw me against the nearest wall. He held me pinned there, his lean face twisted with rage. "You promised me you weren't talking to them! You said you would stay away!"

I opened my mouth to start shouting back at him when the point of a wand dug into Gideon's cheek. "Release him," Étienne said in a voice stripped of all emotion. I had little doubt that he'd remove Gideon's head without a hint of remorse if he failed to obey. Unfortunately, I could see the anger in Gideon's eyes being transferred from me to Étienne, which wouldn't do the young man any good. I had spent the past several years putting up with Gideon's abuse. I could take it. Étienne didn't need it.

As soon as Gideon released me, I slid between him and Étienne, holding them apart. "Étienne, put your wand away," I ordered. The teen hesitated, glaring at Gideon. "Do it! You're not helping anyone. Gideon isn't going to kill me." *Yet.* I had a feeling that the warlock was positively itching to strangle me with his bare hands, but he'd wait for now. When Étienne grudgingly lowered his wand, Gideon took a step back, putting some space between him and his opponent.

A low meow broke the tense silence. I looked down to see Sofie slide through the open front door. She padded in, rubbing against my pants leg and then Gideon's as her keen eyes darted about the room.

"Oh! What a lovely kitty cat!" Alice squealed. She rushed forward, scooped up the large Russian-blue cat, and held her pressed against her chest.

"Put me down, child!" the cat shouted, startling Alice, but she didn't drop her. Instead, she looked up at Gideon, while brushing her cheeks lovingly against Sofie's head. It was all I could do not to snicker.

"Is the cat your familiar? I was told we don't have familiars."

"I am *not* a familiar!" Sofie cried indignantly, starting to squirm. I was grateful she hadn't started using her claws yet.

Reaching over, I pushed the door closed and locked it. "Sofie's a witch that has been turned into a cat."

Alice gave a little shout and dropped the cat as if it had suddenly burst into flames. The girl backed up, moving in front of her brother. In fact, everyone in the room seemed a little tenser, knowing that they were now faced with a witch and a warlock.

Looking over at Gideon, I frowned. "You had to bring Sofie with you?"

The warlock made a scoffing noise in the back of his throat. "It wasn't about bringing her. It was more like I didn't want to waste the time on a spell to stop her from following."

"Gage Powell!" Sofie said shrilly, walking over to sit in front of me. "You disappear from the face of the earth for an entire day and then send a short message for me to fetch Gideon with no explanation. Did you honestly expect me to sit back and hope that everything was well? Trixie would have been furious if I had stayed behind."

More likely, curiosity has been driving Sofie crazy, so she decided to tag along. Regardless of her usual grumpiness, Sofie's life had become infinitely more interesting since she had come to live with Trixie, and the cat was enjoying it.

I let the comment go and turned back to Gideon, who was looking about the room. The kids were closely watching him, their wands in their hands. "To answer your earlier question, I did stay away. They found me." When the warlock regarded me again, I gave him a brief summary of the attack at my apartment and the escape from the house in Austria. He grew paler as I spoke.

"It's been getting worse," he said, but then shook his head as if to push the thought away. "You should have left immediately. It's too dangerous for you and them."

"Look at this place! You want me to ignore this? I can't leave them like this!" I shouted, throwing my arms out to encompass the poor living conditions. "This isn't a home and they aren't safe here."

"They made the choice to leave the Towers. They have to accept their fate," he said coldly.

"I know you're not this much of a bastard. *You* can't be."

Gideon ground his teeth together, barely keeping his anger in check at the veiled mention of his hidden wife and child. "It is because of my situation that I am a bastard. I have to protect them first. With chaos threatening to consume the Towers, I think the kids' problem is the least of our concerns."

"I can take care of the Towers, but I need to try to settle things here first," I said softly. If things didn't go well with Reave and the council, I was afraid that the Towers weren't going to give me a second chance to help these kids.

"You know?" His voice was so soft and haunted that I almost looked around for a ghost passing through the room. "You know the person . . ." For a second time that morning, Gideon gripped my shirt and slammed me against the wall. The air crackled with barely controlled energy, but I did nothing to defend myself. Terror held sway over Gideon's mind. "Give me the bastard, Gage!"

"I can't. Listen, if you or someone else turns him in, it's not going to stop them from coming after me. They realize that I am a potential threat. I have to remove that thought from their minds, and to do that I have to be the one to take him to the council."

Gideon released me and stepped back. "You want to make a deal?"

"I'm going to try." My heart was pounding in my chest like a thing gone mad. Gideon was dangerous, and it wasn't because he was a powerful warlock. It was because he knew me, knew what I was capable of. He had spent years watching over me. The only advantage I had over the other warlocks and witches I had fought was that they always underestimated me. Gideon wouldn't make that mistake, and I wouldn't have a chance in hell against him.

All the energy drained out of the room, as well as poured out of Gideon. The man's large, narrow shoulders slumped and he almost seemed to sway on his feet as a look of hopelessness crossed his face. He knew I could bring the culprit before the Towers. He wasn't expecting me to survive the encounter. I couldn't blame him. I didn't have high hopes myself.

Taking him by the shoulders, I gently turned him around and ushered him to the chair I had vacated minutes ago. Étienne returned to his seat to watch both me and Gideon.

"A favor, Gideon?" The warlock arched one eyebrow at me, looking skeptical, and I smiled. I couldn't blame him. He'd already done a lot of favors for me. "The kids don't have a lot of food on hand. You mind . . ." I trailed off, giving a little wave of my hand like I was holding a wand.

"Oh," he said, sitting up and looking around again as if taking in his surroundings. "Oh, yes, of course." He didn't bother to pull out his wand, but waved his hand over the table. In a second, piles of fluffy pancakes, waffles, sausages, bacon, eggs, and freshly chopped fruit appeared in platters, along with clean plates, flatware, and white linen napkins. My eyes caught on the large silver container in the center surrounded by empty mugs. Coffee. Glorious, wonderful, caffeine-filled coffee.

The kids held back, almost painful looks filling their faces as they gazed at the food. They were afraid to trust Gideon. They might have been able to create the same spell, but they were trying not to use magic for fear of being tracked. I popped a piece of bacon into my mouth before reaching for the coffee. It was like a green light at a racetrack. The kids fell on the table, piling a mountain of food on their plates in an explosion of excited chatter. Even James seemed to come alive with the promise of a warm meal.

Only Étienne held back, watching Gideon through narrowed eyes. I clapped the younger man on the back and smiled. "I know it's hard to believe, but he is one of the good guys. Eat." When the boy didn't move, I turned my back on Gideon and leaned down. "He's got his own wife and kid to protect," I whispered for only Étienne to hear. The young man's eyes widened as he looked up at me. He understood the risk Gideon was taking, the rules he was breaking.

"Oh, Gideon!" Sofie scoffed, jumping into the warlock's lap. "Pancakes with sugary syrup? You should have made something healthy. These children need oatmeal."

Gideon stared at Étienne and smiled. "Bridgette loves my chocolate chip pancakes," he said before dropping a piece of fruit into his mouth. Étienne gave a small nod, a smile toying with the corners of his mouth as he picked up a plate and started filling it.

While the kids scattered around the room, digging into their food and getting lost in happy conversation, I leaned against the wall near Gideon and discussed both William Rosenblum's attack and Henry Fox's kidnapping attempt. Apparently, things were deteriorating in the Towers faster than either of us had expected. I needed to get my hands on Reave before they decided to wipe out another city in order to shake up the masses.

Gideon set his empty mug on the table and looked around the room. Kids were lounging on the floor, soft groans of fullness slipping from them as they settled into their own personal food comas. It sounded nice. I had picked a little, but my head ached and I had too much on my mind to try to put food in my stomach.

"I agree that they can't continue to live like this," Gideon started, sounding more than a little weary. "But I'm not sure what we can do. We can't keep coming back here. It may attract attention and these kids need to slip away without notice."

"They need homes. They need to go to school. They need to be around other people. Normal people with no magic," I said, pushing off the wall to put my nearly empty mug on the table. Being around nonmagic users would teach them how to blend better. Right now every time they were startled, they grabbed their wands, which only drew attention to them.

"They can't go home," Gideon said firmly.

I nodded. "It's the first place anyone would look. Their families are probably being watched already."

"I will not endanger *mia famiglia,*" Paola said, lifting her chin, proving that despite the appearance of being in a carb-induced stupor, the kids were intently listening to our conversation. Others nodded at Paola's statement, looking sad.

"I know," I murmured, trying to smile at them before looking at Gideon again. "But I was thinking maybe a family or two that you might know could be willing to help."

Gideon frowned at me. He knew what I was asking. I wanted him to contact other members of his little movement, see if anyone was willing to take the kids in and protect them. "I don't think anyone I know could take all five."

"You want to separate us? You can't separate us!" The cry went up, followed by a dozen others as all the kids were now on their feet and decidedly against being separated.

I held up my hands and silence settled back over the room. "It's for the best. The Towers are looking for five kids. Not one or two kids in a single household. You'll be better protected if you're separated."

Just as the arguments started again, Étienne said, "He is right."

They fell silent, but I saw Alice's hand tighten on James's. She hadn't escaped with Étienne. She had gotten out of the New York Tower on her own with her brother. There was something mutinous in her stare. The warm, bubbly girl wielding the baseball bat had melted into a young woman of hardened determination. I had a feeling that she had been willing to follow Étienne because it meant there was someone else to help protect James, but she would run if someone tried to separate her from her younger brother.

I smiled at her and gave a little nod. Some of the tension eased from around her eyes. I'd talk to Gideon. James and Alice needed each other. They had escaped together, been through a similar horror.

"It's going to take me a little while. I need to talk to some people. They may need to strengthen defenses and such," Gideon said, seeming to talk more to himself than to me.

"I want them to continue their training," I added.

"Are you insane?" He jerked out of his chair, standing a couple feet away from me. "They left—"

"And they're still being hunted. They need to be able to defend themselves, as well as have excellent control—the whole reason for being taken to the Towers in the first place." Gideon's mouth thinned to a hard line, but he didn't argue. He knew I was right, but I was asking a lot. The families that took them in would need increased security. Training the kids would demand even more protective spells to cloak the activity.

I shrugged at Gideon. "We could find someplace and meet once or twice a month for a few hours. Just some defensive spells."

The warlock made a sound of disgust and shook his head as he returned to his seat. "Are you going to be the one to train them?"

My smile slipped. "You think that's wise?"

"I don't think any of this is wise, but it needs to be done," he said. "I'll get started. If you survive the next few days, I'll get back to you when something has been decided."

"Sounds good." I pushed away from the wall and stood in front of Étienne, who rose from his chair. "Can you keep things under control here for a little while longer?"

He nodded stiffly. "Of course."

I was impressed with the young man. Not once had he argued about putting the kids in families, or about me stepping in to take control. They may have been his responsibility, but he knew that the group couldn't continue as they were indefinitely.

"If there's an emergency, you know where to find me," I said, a part of me hating to leave them unprotected and vulnerable.

"Yes."

I extended my hand to him and he shook it.

Gideon shook his hand before we turned toward the door. The warlock paused and looked at me with a frown. "You are going to take care of the other little problem first?"

"Very soon. I'm waiting for some information from a very resourceful hobgoblin."

He rolled his eyes and left the house without another word. I think Gideon had had all he could stand from me for one morning. Smiling, I turned to find Sofie curled up on Paola's lap as the girl stroked her fur. Alice was scratching her head.

"Sof, are you staying or going with me?" I asked with a chuckle.

The cat rolled off the girl's lap and stretched her entire body before walking over to me. Picking her up, I paused at the door and said good-bye to my would-be saviors. I didn't know if my plan was going to work. I didn't know if these kids were going to have something that resembled a normal life or if I was putting more people in danger. But they deserved a shot at it. We all deserved a chance at normal.

25

HELL BROKE LOOSE when I stepped out the door. I didn't think to scan the area to see if anyone else was about. Gideon had left less than a minute before me, and I was sure it was safe. I could use a thousand excuses like I was exhausted and distracted and worried, but it all came down to the fact that I didn't check the area before I stepped outside.

As I pulled the door closed behind me, I looked up to see Gideon standing at the edge of the yard talking to a witch and two warlocks in low, tense tones. Of the faces that I could see, no one looked happy. And then they looked up at me, shock filling their expressions. Apparently Gideon hadn't been telling them that I was inside with the runaways. Of course, I didn't doubt Gideon for a second. He could act like a bastard at times, but he wouldn't get rid of me like that. Not when I'd given him so many other opportunities over the years.

Gideon turned sideways to look over his shoulder at me. For a moment he looked sad, but the expression disappeared in a second and the hardness I was accustomed to seeing filled his eyes, wiping his face of any emotion. When he turned back, he was already reaching in his sleeve for his wand. None of the others saw it because all their attention was on me. A bright green flash hit one of the warlocks, throwing him across the street. His limp body bounced on the concrete once before he continued to roll until he hit the curb.

Taking advantage of the distraction, I dropped Sofie as I pulled the door shut and whispered a quick locking spell. I wasn't sure who I was barring, but I didn't need the Towers getting into the house and I definitely didn't need the kids coming out to help. The locking spell wouldn't keep anyone tied up, but it would buy Gideon and me some time while we dealt with this new problem.

The remaining witch and warlock were getting over their shock when I hit the weed-choked yard in a roll. Jumping back to my feet, I snatched up an old rust-laced shovel that was laying off to the side. The witch was squared off against Gideon in the middle of the empty street, her body partially blocking the unconscious warlock. The remaining warlock was approaching me with his wand drawn.

Holding the shovel in both hands like a bow staff, I smiled at my opponent. "I'm sorry. Were you looking for me?" *Damn, why the hell did I travel without my wand?* This world was getting just too dangerous for an ex-warlock to go about without a little protection.

"Master Fox wants a word with you," the warlock replied in a heavily accented voice. His accent reminded me of some Brazilians I had met years ago, but his expression didn't indicate that he wanted to swap stories about his former home.

"Yeah, I'm gonna have to decline that honor."

The warlock nodded with a grunt a second before whipping his wand in my direction. The conversation had given me enough time to summon up the energy for the defensive shield that popped into existence as the blue flash surged toward me. As I had hoped, the fucker had shot a stun spell at me. Fox was still trying to get his hands on my living body. Zombies were a bitch to interrogate.

As he lowered his wand, his mind searching for a new spell, I lunged forward and swung the shovel at his head. The asshole raised one arm, deftly blocking the weapon before he swept under it. Moving like flowing water, he spun and kicked out one leg at me. I jerked away at the last second so that the bottom of his shoe scraped lightly across my upper arm.

We both stepped back, taking stock. The warlock grinned at me and shoved his wand back into the holder up his sleeve. Not only was this asshole Brazilian, but he apparently was well versed in something, possibly Brazilian jujitsu. I was fucked because I was a beginner when it came to most fighting styles and he was obviously looking forward to knocking the crap out of me.

The warlock was on me before I could think of a way of dealing with him. He threw an intense combination of punches and kicks in my direction that kept me retreating across the yard if I didn't want to get my head knocked off. I couldn't spare a glance in Gideon's direction, though I was aware of the continuous tingle of magic in the air. He was dealing with the witch and would be forced to keep an eye on the other warlock. All I knew was that the trio couldn't be permitted to live. If they escaped, Gideon was dead. I was dead. The runaways were dead.

I dodged punches as best I could, and those I couldn't avoid were at least reduced to glancing blows that would leave me sore later in the day if I survived that long. He was coming at me so fast I couldn't catch a break to cast an attack spell that would buy me a little breathing room. I waited, just trying to stay on my feet with the shovel handle clenched in my fists. I was praying for an opening.

Unfortunately, the opening came from an angle I wasn't expecting and didn't welcome. Brazil pulled back from his last punch, but froze for a second when something off to his left caught his attention. I heard the movement, but I didn't dare look. Tightly gripping the shovel, I swung it as hard as I could, slamming the metal spade against the side of his head. He went down like a sack of wet noodles.

"Gage! Watch out!" a young girl's voice shouted. I twisted to see

Alice and the other kids racing around the side of the small ramshackle house. They had gone around my locked door.

Time slowed down to a crawl. Alice sharply halted several yards away from me and swung her wand, sending out a bolt of red energy across the yard. A blast of bright white energy was already streaking across the street from the now-conscious warlock. But the white light wasn't coming at me as it should have been. The energy hit Alice square in the chest and her small, thin body was thrown backward. Her long blond hair flared out from her in a pale cascade before she hit the ground with a lifeless thud.

"No!" I screamed. The warlock should have been aiming for me. He should have attacked me. But instead, he killed a kid.

The world grew dark as I turned to face the warlock who had killed Alice. Energy snapped and crackled like a downed power line. Black clouds churned and lightning jumped across the sky followed by the angry rumble of thunder. I wasn't conscious of drawing the energy together, but I welcomed it. It danced along my skin while all the fine hairs on my body stood on end. There was so much energy in the air, I felt like I could pull the world apart.

The warlock looked nervously up at the sky and then took a step back as his eyes darted to me. Holding the handle in both hands, I snapped it near the spade over my knee with the help of a little magic. I dropped the metal spade with a thud and then drove the spike through the chest of the warlock I had knocked out only seconds before. He never stirred, never cried out, as I plunged the spike through his heart.

The other bastard snarled something at me, but I couldn't make it out. Stepping on the dead warlock's chest, I pulled the spike out and held it in my right hand like a bloody spear.

The warlock hurled a nasty attack spell at me, aiming to rip my flesh off, but I batted it away with a thick wave of energy. At the same time I threw a fireball at him with my left hand. A smile curled on my lips as I watched him predictably raise his hands in the proper countercurse to protect himself. Hefting my spear, I threw it at him with all my strength and the bulk of the energy shifting in the air. The broken handle hit him hard enough to plunge through his chest and throw him backward. The point of the spear slammed into a telephone pole behind him, pinning the bastard to the thick wooden beam.

The man weakly groaned, his hands loosely clasping the spear in the middle of his chest as the last of his life drained out of his body. Blood soaked his clothes and ran like a river down to the sidewalk.

I started to march across the street to make sure this kid-killing fucker died in as much pain as humanly possible, but Gideon stepped in front of me. I tried to shove him away, energy arcing between us. Gideon shoved me back and then backhanded me hard enough to make me stumble.

"Pull yourself together!" he said in a low, harsh voice.

"He killed Alice," I snarled. Blind with rage and pain, I was ready to take him apart.

"I know, but you need to get a grip. You've got enough magic gathered to kill us all." I rubbed my sore jaw, staring at him through narrowed eyes as his words slowly sank in. "Pull it together, for the kids."

"The witch?" I asked, trying to breathe around the fury licking at my brain. My tight grip on the magic energy in the air started to loosen. The charge slackened and the air grew less dense as I packed my emotions away in a box in the back of my mind.

"Dead," Gideon replied, motioning toward the bloody heap in the middle of the street. "You okay?"

I nodded, looking anywhere but at him. Standing in the middle of the street on that early morning, I understood for the first time why the Towers forbid warlocks and witches from marrying and having children. It wasn't because they were afraid of them being distracted from their studies or some elitist idea of sullying themselves. It was simply too dangerous for us to form emotional attachments. We were brought to the Towers to learn control, but in a moment of rage and pain, all that control was thrown out the window and we became a deadly force of nature.

I couldn't bear the idea of a child being killed by a warlock, especially a child I knew and respected. Yet standing there, struggling to bury the horror, I had a feeling that if it had been Trixie or Bronx instead of Alice, Gideon would not have been able to stop me without killing me.

"How'd they find us?" I asked, trying to push my thoughts to more important matters.

"They said something about blood."

My head snapped up to look at Gideon. "Mine? I thought I—"

"No, one of the dead warlocks guarding you," he said, cutting me off. "I think one of the kids stepped in the blood and tracked it here. They followed the trail."

I cursed in a low voice, squeezing my eyes shut. I hadn't thought of that. I should have thought of that. Should have thought of some protection spells to hide the kids better. Should have done something . . . more.

Turning, we walked over to where the kids were standing in a small semicircle. Paola was pressed against Étienne, softly sobbing, while Tony stood on the other side of his friend as silent tears slid down his dark brown cheeks. James was on his knees beside his sister, holding her hand in both of his, staring blindly. He wasn't crying, but it would come as the numbness wore off.

As we drew close, Étienne glared at us and raised his wand. "He led them to us." Paola raised a haunted expression to me, filled with fear that more fighting and dying would come. Tony looked as if he was about to shatter before my eyes, his mind unable to accept that I might have betrayed him through Gideon.

"No!" I said sharply as I stepped in front of Gideon. "They followed the blood on the baseball bat." I wasn't sure if that was it, but

I didn't want to risk any of them looking at their shoes, wondering if they had brought the attackers and Alice's death.

Étienne's face twisted in pain and confusion as he turned over the idea. "But—"

"Gideon risked his life to protect you. He risked his family to protect you. He didn't betray us."

The anger drained from their expressions to be replaced with pain. I stepped over and gently grabbed Paola's elbow, pulling her away from Étienne. She looked at me with wide, sad eyes. "I need you to help James. Please."

She nodded woodenly and moved over to the little boy's side. Very carefully, she pulled him away from his dead sister and into her arms. He stood with his face buried in her side, his breathing growing heavy as the first sobs started to hit him.

Gideon swept in and knelt where James had been, spreading his black cloak on the ground. He gathered up the girl and lovingly laid her on the material. Folding her arms on her stomach, he wrapped her up in the cloak. I looked away when I saw the tears streaking down his pale cheeks, knowing he was thinking of his own daughter.

Turning my attention to Étienne, I cleared my throat so I could speak past the lump. "We need to get out of here. Do you know of another safe place to hide?"

"Yes."

"Go inside now. Get everything you need and then leave out the back door. When you're sure you're safely hidden, send a message to me at my parlor," I instructed in a hard, even voice, hoping the tone was drilling into his head past the pain and self-doubts.

"Yes, but . . ." His words immediately drifted off as he motioned toward Gideon; the warlock lifted the body in his arms.

"Gideon will see that she gets a proper burial. You need to get these kids to safety. It might be a little while, but eventually the Towers are going to come investigate this fight. You need to be gone."

Étienne nodded and then quickly urged the others back into the house. They wordlessly followed his orders and I was grateful for that. I turned to find Gideon standing a couple feet away, the cloak-enshrouded Alice held in his arms with the same gentleness he would show any sleeping child. Tears still streaked his cheeks, but there was a coldness to his eyes that made me glad that he was on my side.

"We will end this," he said in a low voice, and then he disappeared.

A chill swept over me as I stood there alone in the silence. I had a feeling that the *this* that Gideon was referring to was the Towers' reign of terror. I hoped he was right, but I was afraid that we wouldn't live to see the fruits of our labors.

A soft meow drew my attention to the ground to find Sofie stepping out of some thick bushes near the front porch. I had completely forgotten that she had been in my arms as I left the house. I couldn't blame her for hiding, as there wasn't much she could have done in that fight besides die. As I bent down toward the ground, she ran over to me and let me gather her up in my arms.

We stood guard at the side of the dilapidated old house as the kids gathered their meager belongings. I rubbed Sofie's head, but she never purred. I stared off into space, concentrating on using a quiet spell that tracked all magic in the area, but no other witches or warlocks appeared.

When the remaining kids had run from the house and disappeared to some unknown location, I used another small spell to dissipate any lingering traces of magic spells in the area. With any luck, when the Towers came to check out the dead, they would assume that I was the only one who had been found. They would have no proof that the runaways had ever been there.

Holding Sofie against my chest, I teleported, wishing I had never left Gaia's world.

I WANTED TO go back to Trixie's apartment with Sofie. I wanted to crawl into bed with the blond elf and pull her tight against my body while mentally blocking out the world. But I didn't. After grabbing my wand from my apartment, I went to the tattoo parlor and prepared for the end.

Spells were put into place to alert me if someone decided to unexpectedly pop in. I grabbed my wand, tucking it in my back pocket, so that I wouldn't feel quite so naked. I had no idea if Henry Fox was going to make another grab for me or if he was going to send yet another group of witches and warlocks to be slaughtered. He had come at me with three other magic users. He held me in a house with others magic users. He had sent three more hunting for me after my escape, and still I slipped from his grasp. I was hoping that he was going to be more cautious. It would buy me time, which is what I needed most because I was sure that I wasn't going to escape again.

With my defense in place, I spent the morning on the phone, draining my bank account and trading in favors to get things done quickly and quietly. Plans were finalized. This business had put me in contact with more than my fair share of shady characters. I had always hoped that I would never contact them, but that never stopped me from secreting away their phone numbers against the day when I would need them.

By late afternoon when Trixie walked through the door for her shift, I was done and was waiting for my target. I felt numb and I was grateful for it. If I had felt anything else, I wouldn't have been able to continue.

Trixie stepped close, placing her hand against my cheek as her wide eyes searched my face. "Are you okay?" she asked. There was an ache to her voice as if she already knew the answer to her question. "Sofie told me what happened."

I pulled her into my arms, holding her tightly. Her head rested against my shoulder with her face pressed against my neck. "I'm okay," I whispered. We stood that way for several seconds, barely breathing. I could have stayed like that forever, but time was slipping away from me and things needed to be said.

Stepping back, I leaned against the counter in the tattooing room. "I have one client coming in today and I'll be with him for several hours. I've canceled all my other appointments, but could you tell everyone else that I'm not in today?"

She nodded, worry starting to fill her face.

"I don't think the Towers are going to strike here, but I've taken precautions in case. I've got spells in place for warnings. If they come, I need you to do as I say when I say it without question. Can you?"

"I can," she agreed, far too easily for Trixie. "Is there anything I can do to help?"

"With the Towers, no," I said with a shake of my head. "But you can finish things with the Summer Court for me. Someone is supposed to visit with the queen and king today. She should fix the baby problem. You will need to tattoo them when it's over."

"Who is visiting?"

"Gaia."

Trixie's face brightened and her mouth formed a silent O in surprise. "You spoke to her?"

"Yes. It was an . . . interesting experience." A swell of longing rose with the memory of my time in Gaia's garden, threatening to choke me. It hurt to think about the place I had walked away from—that perfect place where I fit. The place that held my son. But if I had stayed, I would have never looked down on Trixie's smile again and I didn't want to face a world devoid of that beautiful sight.

"She's agreed to help, but you need to make sure everything is mended with the king and queen. You won't be hunted any longer."

She leaned into me, grabbing me in a fierce hug. "Thank you, Gage!"

The little bell on the front door sounded, indicating that someone had come into the shop, and Trixie moved away from me. She started to go to the lobby, but I grabbed her arm, stopping her. I had already seen the person on the monitor, and I had been expecting him.

"I've got it," I said as I walked past her. I paused before the entrance and cleared my throat, pushing back the lump while wiping my face clean of worry and sadness. Stepping into the lobby, I pushed a grim smile on my lips as I looked at my brother, Robert.

"You ready for this?" I asked, drawing his gaze to me. He was looking haggard. His eyes were underlined with dark shadows and his cheeks were hollowed out as if he'd been eaten away by worry.

"Yeah, let's get this over with." His voice was rough and low as he looked over the shop, searching for some hidden assassin. "I haven't heard from Reave in a while, but I'm guessing that plans haven't changed. I need to make the delivery tomorrow."

"Good. Let's go." I turned and he followed me wordlessly to the back room, where I had made all my preparations. I closed and locked the door behind him then set a spell over it to ward against anyone trying to come through with magical means.

Robert slipped off his jacket and tossed it over a spare chair in the corner while I grabbed a piece of paper and pencil. "Give me your driver's license. I need to make a record for TAPSS," I said.

He crossed his arms over his thick chest and glared at me. "Reave said no records."

"I have to put down who I tattoo. I just won't put down what I really did," I said.

When he grudgingly handed me his wallet, I handed him a piece of blank paper and pencil. "While I'm doing this, I need you to write down the coordinates. I'll turn them into code from that."

We worked in silence for several moments before he handed me back the paper. I didn't give him his wallet. A quick glance revealed that the coordinates were genuine. I didn't know the actual coordinates like Robert did, but there was a resonance in those numbers. Something in my gut screamed that these were the locations of the Towers, the thing that could bring destruction down on all our heads.

I stood, staring at the paper, fighting the urge to blast this information out across the world just like Reave wanted. After the threats to me, the threats to Trixie, and Alice's death, I was ready to see the Towers fall. If I thought for a second that this information could free the world without causing it to burn first, I would have let Reave proceed with his plan. But the world couldn't beat the Towers. At least not yet.

I put the paper down on the table with a grunt and walked over to the counter before the cabinet of supplies. I poured some weak tea from the little kettle into a mug and offered it to him. "It's going to take a few hours to tattoo these on you. Drink this. It will help dull the pain."

Robert stepped back from the mug. "I don't need it."

I frowned and took a step toward him. "The tattoo is going on your side along your ribs. It's going to hurt like hell, I promise. Drink it. The painkiller is as much for me as you. The more pain you're in, the harder it's going to be to tattoo you because you're going to squirm. Let's get this done."

"I don't trust you." The words sliced through me, cutting deep. It must have shown because he cursed. "I don't trust you not to try to save me. You have to do this."

"I know. We're trapped. If I don't tattoo you, Reave will have you killed," I said, anger rising in my voice. "Fine. I'll tattoo you, but I can at least reduce the pain. That's all this is."

Robert grimaced, but took the mug and drained its contents. My brother had been right not to trust me. I had been lying through my teeth since he walked through the door. Reave wasn't going to kill him if he wasn't tattooed because I was going to take care of Reave. Unfortunately, Robert was still a target for the Towers and that was why I was going to tattoo him.

"Take off your shirt and lie on your side on the table," I said as I took the mug back from him. He nodded, following my directions while I grabbed the paper with the coordinates and settled on the little stool beside the table as he got comfortable. There was no outline to put on his body. I was working purely from memory. But I wasn't worried. I wouldn't screw this up. If I wanted to save my brother's life, the tattoo would be perfect.

I prepped the area where I would be working, shaving away the little hairs while slathering some petroleum jelly on his side. Snapping on a pair of gloves, I took up the tattooing gun in my right hand while positioning the pedal under my toe.

"I was thinking of stopping by to see Mom and Dad soon," I said, holding the needle poised over his skin.

"I think they'd like that." Each word was slow and slurred as he started to drift off to sleep.

"Good. I'll tell them you said hi."

"Thanks," he murmured, the word nearly lost in an expelled breath. "Don't try to save me, Gage. I'm the older brother. It's my job . . . to save . . . you."

A couple seconds later, a soft snoring tumbled from him as the sleeping potion took effect. Keeping Robert asleep throughout this process would make it easier for me to work the various spells and potions I was attempting.

Swallowing past the lump in my throat, I stepped on the pedal and drew my first line. The world slipped away from me so that I was no longer aware of the shop or Robert's snoring. There was only the steady buzz of the tattooing machine and the stretch of living canvas spread before me.

Six hours later, I sat back against the wall, staring at the man on the table. It had taken me nearly three hours to complete the tattoo and another three to finish all the other spells. I was exhausted, drained to the bone, but I expected my plan to work. Robert had walked in with brown hair and eyes. The tattoo had changed that, giving him blond hair and green eyes. Pushing away from the wall, I walked over and leaned down to take a closer look at him. The stubble on his now-wider jaw had a reddish tint to it and his nose looked larger and crooked as if it had been broken. There were a couple scars on his arms and his neck that hadn't been there when he walked in. I thought they'd be a nice touch. No one would recognize him. Not our parents. And now not even Robert himself.

He shifted on the table, waking as the sleep potion wore off. I stepped back, turning toward the table where I had left his wallet with his new ID and credit cards as well as some extra cash from my own wallet.

"How you feeling, Chad?" I asked, raising my voice while pretending to look for something on the table. "You dropped off on me about halfway through. Trixie even poked her head in when she heard your snoring to make sure I hadn't fallen asleep." I forced a little chuckle as I turned back to him.

Robert, now turned Chad Lancaster, sat up and rubbed his head with the heel of his palm, looking somewhat dazed as his gaze drifted around the room. His memory was going to be foggy for a little while because his mind was trying to organize the holes where I had taken memories and to sort through the new ones I had put in their place. It wasn't a smooth process since I was forced to distort a lot of old ones rather than risk leaving him with no new memories.

"Yeah," he said. "Sorry about that."

"No problem. You warned me you were exhausted. You want to take a look at the tattoo?" I asked, motioning toward his ribs. He twisted in surprise and then winced as the pain reached his brain. Slipping off the table, he walked over to the mirror hanging on the wall.

"I liked your idea of doing two of your Chinese zodiac animals. It's a very powerful tattoo," I continued, trying to verbally reinforce the memories I had implanted about him coming into the parlor.

The tattoo was of a monkey and a wild boar wrestling, their bodies curled in such a way that they almost formed a circle. It was one of the best tattoos I had ever done. The colors, while sharp and vibrant, were soothing to the eye. The wild boar, or rather pig, represented the Chinese zodiac sign that Robert had been born under, while the monkey represented the person I was trying to change him into. In the tattoo, the monkey was winning the fight.

I didn't put much stock in astrology and the different zodiacs, but the animals of the Chinese zodiac had proven time and again that they were effective when it came to tweaking a person's outward appearance and sometimes personality. It was the reason I had used my own zodiac animal of the tiger to change my appearance when I had my back tattooed.

What Chad didn't see was the code for the Towers hidden within the lines of the tattoo. With luck, he would never see it. It wasn't meant for his eyes, but for his protection.

"It looks fantastic," Chad said, twisting to the left and then right to take in the whole design.

"Glad you like it. Let's get it bandaged up so you don't miss your flight tonight." I walked over to a table, holding a pile of gauze and tape. Chad nodded and quietly let me bandage him up while giving him proper care instructions.

When I was finished and he was dressed again, I handed back his wallet. "Oh, here. A courier dropped off your bag and plane ticket while you were out. Good luck in California." Bending down, I grabbed a large black bag filled with clothes I had created while he was sleeping and handed it to him. I couldn't risk letting him have any of his former possessions for fear of them triggering an old memory.

"Thanks. I think it's time for a change of scenery and California sounds good to me. I was passing through Low Town when I heard about your shop."

Inside, I breathed a sigh of relief. He had pulled up a thought I had placed in his brain and used it, sounding comfortable and accepting of the idea. My words and actions were matching the memories he had, so he was willing to go with it.

A knock on the door nearly had me jumping out of my skin.

"Taxi's here," Trixie called through the door. Her footsteps echoed through the hall as she walked toward the tattooing room.

"Great! Thanks!" Chad said, shouldering his bag. I stepped in front of him, quietly unlocking the door before he could notice and held it open. He walked out of the room and gave a wave to Trixie and Bronx before stepping into the lobby. Trixie followed him with wide eyes, but she said nothing.

As he opened the front door to leave, I stepped in front of him and extended my hand. "Take care of yourself, please," I said, struggling to keep the waver out of my voice.

Chad gave a little smile, clearly confused by my sudden shift in emotion. I knew I was acting strange when he had no memory of us meeting before today, but I couldn't hold it back. This was going to be the last time I ever looked at my brother, ever talked to him.

He took my hand in a firm grasp and shook it. "I will. You too. Thanks again for the great tattoo."

And then he was gone.

I don't know how long I stood at the front window, staring out at the empty street where his taxi had been before Trixie joined me in the lobby. Her long arms wrapped around my waist and she pressed her head against my shoulder. She didn't ask any questions. Just stood there, leaning against me.

"When I left home the last time, I knew I wouldn't ever see my parents, brother, or sister again, and somehow it didn't hurt as bad as it does now," I said in a rough whisper. "For the past couple days, he's been at my apartment when I got home. We ate pizza, drank beer, laughed at movies we never got to watch together until now. In the span of a couple hours, he went back to being the best friend I ever had. I think I let myself dream that we could have this friendship now that I was away from the Towers. But he shook my hand, looked at me, but didn't see me. He doesn't remember me and he never will again."

"Is he safe now?" Trixie asked, her arms tightening around me.

"Safer now than if he stayed and remembered."

"Then it's for the best."

She was right, but it did little to ease the pain. I was clinging to the hope that handing Reave over to the Ivory Tower council would help with the pain. The bastard was going to pay for touching my family, for destroying lives.

A SOFT SCRATCHING sound on glass rose over the fading chords of a Perfect Circle song playing through the speakers. I looked up as Trixie stepped away from me, also searching for the source of the sound. We turned toward the front door to see a little demonic face peering through the glass at the top. Duff was hanging upside down, clinging to the top of the door as he stared at us with his impish grin.

Bronx stepped into the lobby as I opened the door to let the hobgoblin in. Extending his leathery wings, he caught the wind as he dropped so that he could easily glide into the shop. He circled the lobby once, wagging his fingers at Trixie before lightly landing on the glass case that served as a counter. Duff puffed up his little chest and threw his wings out wide as if trying to warn off Bronx before he took a couple sniffs of the air.

"You got a cat in here?" he asked, cocking his head at me.

"No cat," I said as I shut the door.

"You sure about the cat? I can smell a cat here." He scuttled around the case, gazing over the edge and down through the glass, searching for Sofie.

"I'm sure. The cat's not in the shop today," I reassured him. He nodded, sitting down on the case with his wings gathered behind his back. Unfortunately, I didn't have time to let him rest. "Did you find him?"

"We almost lost him a couple times, but he's not sneaky enough," he said with an evil chuckle.

"Where is he?"

"Home."

My stomach did a sickening little flop at that single word, but I pushed the feeling down and clenched my hands into fists along the end of the case. "He's hoping for a little safety in numbers to work in his favor. Where are they now?"

"That's the strange thing," he said with a shake of his head. "They're close. The Svartálfar are never near when another Court is close, and I know that the Summer Court is in the immediate area."

Trixie's hand grabbed my wrist, her nails biting into my flesh, drawing my gaze to her stricken face. I covered her hand with my free one. "I'm sure they're only in town to stir up trouble, but we both know that their problems have already been taken care of."

She nodded stiffly, forcing out a breath, but her grip didn't immediately ease on my wrist. I had a feeling she wasn't going to relax until she knew the Svartálfar had left the area or that the throne of the Summer Court was secure. With any luck, the queen and king were already working on that.

"Was he tracking the one who has the information?" Trixie inquired. I nodded.

"Reave?" Bronx's deep voice swept through the room. He was frowning, a look of worry in his eyes.

I nodded. "He was using my brother as a delivery boy for the info, but I made a slight change of plans in hopes of protecting him. I'm going after Reave next."

"What do you mean you're going after him?" Trixie snapped. Using her grip on my wrist, she pulled me so that I was forced to turn and look at her. Fear clouded her lovely eyes and cut lines of worry around her mouth. "If you know where he's at, can't you send some message to the Towers telling them? Let them handle it."

"You know that won't work. Do you think the Towers would bother to sort out who knew what? No. They'd exterminate every dark elf in the area."

"You say that like it's a bad thing," she said in a low, hard voice.

"You don't mean that." She looked away from me, but I put my hand against her cheek and turned her face back to me. "I won't let them exterminate another group. And even if they did, it wouldn't stop them from coming after me later. I need to deliver Reave to the Towers personally."

"You're going back?" She whispered her question so softly that I barely heard it, but there was no missing the horror in her expression. "You can't go back. They'll kill you. There has to be another way."

"If I don't go, they'll kill me. They're going to question Reave before he's killed. My name and my brother's are going to come up. I have to try to control the damage if I'm going to have any chance of saving either of our lives. I have to go," I said, hating myself for the pain I was causing her.

Her voice drifted to me, weak and thready. "There has to be another way." She sounded as if she were being haunted by visions of my dead body. Unfortunately, she had already seen that once. I'd prefer it if she'd never have to repeat that experience.

"There's not," I said firmly, then looked up at Bronx, who was watching with his usual unreadable, stoic expression. "If things go badly and I don't come back right away, I've left a copy of my will in the back room. It can't be executed until I've been missing for eighteen months, but it contains all the information and passwords you might need to keep the shop going. I'm leaving everything to you and Trixie."

Pain exploded across my cheek, jerking my head around to look down at Trixie's tear-streaked face. "How can you talk so calmly of dying? If you go after Reave, I'm not sticking around here, waiting to hear whether you've been killed or not. I can't do it."

The pain tearing through my heart was infinitely worse than the temporary pain in my cheek. But I pushed it back, keeping my tone hard and even. "That's fine. You've got somewhere safe to go now."

She gasped, taking an unsteady step away from me. "You've planned this all along. It's the reason you've helped the elves."

"When I started, it was about making sure you could stay here with me, but recently, yes, I needed somewhere you could hide safely if I failed."

A bitter smile twisted on her mouth. "Well, you succeeded in that, because I'm not waiting here for news of your death. I can't. Not again." Trixie turned sharply on her heel and stalked out of the room, sliding past Bronx and into the back. I could hear her heels pounding on the floor until she reached the back room and slammed the door behind her. Duff stood and glared at me for a second before shape-shifting into a pixie so that he could easily dart off through the parlor after Trixie.

"She's scared," Bronx said, and I nodded in a jerky motion. "But you know she'll be here when you get back. We both will be."

I narrowed my eyes at the troll. "Why aren't you asking to come with me?"

"Would you let me?"

"No."

The troll raised both eyebrows at me and gave a little smirk. "And that would be why." He shrugged his massive shoulders as he laid his hands on the countertop. "Seems like it's a magic users' party anyway and we trolls aren't so strong at magic." His light expression slipped away and he frowned at me. "I would go with you, though. I'd take on the Svartálfar and go with you to the Ivory Towers."

"I know. I'd choose you guarding my back over a hundred warlocks anytime."

"Thank you."

I smiled weakly. "Watch over Trixie for me."

"Of course."

There was nothing left to say. I was merely wasting time because I didn't want to go charging after Reave into the heart of the Svartálfar nation. I didn't want to risk my life to capture him, only to take my life in my hands again when I delivered him to the Towers. Despite all my planning, this wasn't going to end well. It couldn't. But I had to keep moving. The longer I delayed, the more people were going to be hurt.

Pulling my wand out of my back pocket, I turned and opened the front door, sending a little electronic chime through the shop. As I expected, the hobgoblin darted from the back of the shop. He settled on my shoulder, one small arm resting on the top of my head while his long tail wrapped around my biceps. He had to give me some directions to Reave's location. We stepped out into the cool night air, ready to hunt down a dark elf.

THE DARKNESS SEEMED impossibly thick around us despite a velvet sky full of stars and a half-moon hanging overhead. As my eyes soaked in what little light there was, I started to pick out a thick swath of trees surrounding us. There was a feeling of empty space directly in front of me, as if the earth suddenly fell away. I decided to trust the feeling and not step forward.

I had used a teleportation spell to take the hobgoblin and myself across more than a hundred miles, leaving us close to where the dark elves were huddled. Duff had given me the mental image of the spot, promising that it was a safe distance from where he had last seen them.

I needed to get my bearings before we started out. I had no idea where the hobgoblin had taken me, just that it had been south of Low Town and my shop. Cupping my hands in front of my face, I blew a slow, steady breath into them as if trying to warm them. The air curled around my palms, brushing against my fingers as I willed it to form an almost solid ball. Closing my eyes and turning my head away, I gave one more push of energy into the ball of warm air before tossing it up into the sky. When I looked back, a ball of energy hovered a few feet above me, casting the area in a soft, white glow.

Shadows lunged and thickened where they tightly clasped to trees and in deep hollows. There was a drop-off directly in front of me. I couldn't tell how deep it was, but I wasn't willing to find out the hard way. I could see a path leading off to my right that seemed to snake through the forest. The trees were heavy with leaves and the brush was thick on the ground, hiding all sorts of predators, but then I wasn't counting on sneaking up on the Svartálfar. No one snuck up on an elf on its home turf, not even a warlock.

Turning around, I saw a stone formation rise up behind me. The glowing orb ducked in closer at my command, showing that two openings had been cut into what would have been a rock wall. A rush of anger flooded my veins and I silently cursed the dark elves for ever stepping foot in this place.

"Angel Windows," I said, my eyes dancing over the rock formation. "They had to come here."

Duff shifted on my shoulder, one tiny fist tightening in my hair. "That's what the humans call this place. You know where we are?"

I nodded, turning toward the path, the glowing orb shooting out in front of me. It hovered high so my night vision wasn't destroyed, but cast enough light to keep me from walking off the edge of a cliff. "Yeah, I used to camp here. We're in Red River Gorge, but the dark elves aren't supposed to be here. This is part of a national park. The government set up massive swaths of land for the fey to live undisturbed, but they aren't supposed to be living in the parks."

Duff's chuckle was soft, as if he was afraid of drawing attention to us. "The elves go where the earth calls. The boundaries of the government are just lines on a piece of paper. If the elves choose to hide in the forest, do you think anyone can find them to evict them from the land?"

A sigh slipped from me, knowing he was right, but it made me feel uneasy knowing how many times I had come camping down here alone. Red River Gorge was part of Daniel Boone National

Park, and was lined with some of the best hiking trails I had ever found. The sandstone that filled the park had been worn away over thousands of years to leave dozens of amazing formations such as natural bridges. I had wandered down most of the trails, and yet I found something new and beautiful on each trip. Angel Windows was a favorite formation of mine. I always tried to visit it as well as Princess Arch and Rock Bridge when I was in the park.

The only problem with Red River Gorge was that it was not a place you wanted to walk through in the dark. The entire park was a series of valleys and peaks. If you weren't one hundred percent sure that you were in a valley, there was a very good chance that you were going to walk off the end of a cliff and fall down into a steep ravine. Every year, several people died in the park from falls. I was hoping not to be one of them as I picked along the narrow path that led to the main road.

As we came to flatter ground, Duff flew off my shoulder and zipped up ahead of me. Slipping past the reaches of my meager light, he disappeared into the trees as if he were made of them. I was hoping that he was going to scout out ahead and get our bearings before we were faced with the Svartálfar. I wasn't worried about him betraying me to Reave, simply because the bastard had attempted to kill his friend for her organs. As a warlock, I wasn't much of an improvement, but at least I hadn't tried to kill the pixie. That had to put a point or two in my favor.

The darkness eased back as I stepped into a gravel parking lot at the head of the trail. Duff darted back to me, keeping a wide distance from the glowing orb.

"He's where I last saw him. It's another rock formation, like the opening of a cave at the top of a steep rise. I don't know the human name for the place. Gage, why must humans name everything?"

A small smile lifted one corner of my mouth. "I don't know. Maybe it gives them a sense of ownership."

He gave a little snort as he grabbed his tail and twisted it between his two hands. "You said 'them.' Aren't you human?"

His question made me stop. I hadn't even noticed my choice of words. When I had lived in the Ivory Tower, Simon had taught me that I was no longer human, but after I left, I felt sure that he was wrong. I wasn't so sure anymore. Maybe it was all the magic I had been using lately, the power coursing through my body, or even the echo of memories from Gaia's garden, but I didn't feel as if I belonged to that race any longer.

"I don't think so," I whispered. "I think it's the same way that a vampire or lycanthrope is no longer human. They may have started out human, but in the end, they're not."

"Does that make you sad?"

I shrugged. My sense of identity was the least of my concerns. "It is what it is. Was Reave alone at this cave?" I abruptly changed the subject back to the reason I was standing in the middle of a gravel parking lot in Red River Gorge during the blackest part of the night. I didn't want to think about my humanity, or the lack of it, when I was in the middle of hunting down another living creature.

"The bulk of his people have gathered there. Maybe you should wait. We can hide among the trees and wait until he is alone before attacking."

"Can't. He's not going to leave his people. Right now he's confident that I'm the only one who knows he's the one with the information. He thinks that I won't hunt him down while he's surrounded by other Svartálfar." Reave was almost right. Facing the dark elf nation alone was suicidal. They were warriors, born and bred. If the world didn't stand on the brink of war, I might have considered Duff's suggestion. But I couldn't wait. Time was slipping away from me.

I did have one thing in my favor. The Svartálfar were fantastic liars and deceivers, Reave being among the worst. I was hoping to use that fact against him.

"Time for you to head back to your own people. I need to handle this alone."

Duff's face crumpled as he looked over his shoulder, back the way he'd come, and then at me. He was debating following me. Hobgoblins were sneaky little devils that could get in and out of most places using a mixture of magic and cunning.

"If anyone has a good shot at capturing you, it's the Svartálfar and we both know it," I said with a frown. "I won't be able to help you if things get ugly. Even if I survive this, I won't be the only warlock in the area. Get out of here. Tell your friend that we're even now."

Duff nodded. Lifting higher into the air, he gave me a little wave with a sad look before disappearing into the woods.

I was alone in the darkness, which now seemed to crowd closer despite the glowing orb hanging overhead. The wind ruffled the leaves and the sound of chirping crickets and frogs could be heard, but the world I knew slipped away from me. There was no rush of cars, no electric hum of appliances, no shuffling of people's footsteps or the brush of fabric. I was a warlock alone in the domain of the elves.

Tapping down the fear clawing at my heart, I took a deep breath and drew in a swell of the energy circling around me. The spell was a simple one. I had been to this cave on more than one occasion, but I had always walked the long trail back to it. That, I would not survive tonight. The path was a narrow one, with a steep mountain on one side of it and a sharp drop-off on the other side. The trail ended in a type of bowl as you stepped into the cradled embrace of a wall of rock on three sides and a thick copse of trees directly behind you. While the trail was long and winding, the worst part was the climb up to the cave I had always called Rock Coliseum, as the ascent was a steep bank of broken rocks that slid out from underfoot as you climbed. There weren't many places that were worse for a fight with a dark elf in Red River Gorge.

I released the energy with a word. It swirled around me before plunging through my chest. The glowing orb went out and darkness consumed the world. A second later, I was speeding through the trees, but I couldn't feel the biting wind or the sharp brush of tree branches as I passed. I was reduced to little more than energy as I flew to my destination almost as fast as a thought.

My flight came to a screeching halt and my feet settled on a large flat stone at the bottom of the sharp rise to the cave. Again, I raised my cupped hands to my face and blew, creating another light orb, but this time, when I flung it out into the sky, it multiplied until more than a dozen hung in the air, lighting the area. The dark elves stepped silently out from behind trees and stood in the black mouth of the opening in the rocks that formed the cave.

"Hear me, King of the Svartálfar, I have no quarrel with your people. Send out Reave and I will leave without striking at them," I shouted. My voice bounced off the high rock walls and echoed back toward me before becoming tangled in the line of trees at my back. For nearly a minute, there was only the sound of the wind in the trees. I could see the dark elves within the shadows created by my orbs, but no one made a sound. They waited to hear the decision of their leader.

"Quite brave of you, warlock, to come to our home alone," one Svartálfar called down to me from the edge of the opening. He was a large man with a shock of white running through his long black hair. His voice wasn't soft and melodious like Reave's, but rough and coarse like a piece of splintered wood. "While I'm sure you're powerful, we do have you outnumbered. You may kill some of us, but you won't kill all of us before we get you."

With a wave of my hands, I rose in the air until I was eye level with the old king, but hovering in open air. "I have no wish to slaughter your people. I want only Reave."

"Ah . . . but as much as I hate to admit it at times, Reave is one of my people. He's proven to be useful, so I find myself reluctant to hand him over to you." The king's face was sharp and angular, lined with deep scars. One long scar slashed down through his left eye, leaving it a blind milky white. Unlike those of the Summer and Winter Courts, the kings and queens of the Svartálfar weren't born to their roles. To rule the dark elves, you took the position by force and you defended it until another stole it from you.

"Would you give him in trade for a service rendered?" I asked.

The question gave the old king pause as he stared at me skeptically. "What service would you offer?"

"It has come to my attention that the elves have been cursed with a rather nasty spell over the past several decades, long before even the start of the Great War. I'm sure you've noticed."

The king was perfectly still, as if he was made of marble, but there was a tension in that stillness that said I definitely had his attention. There was movement deep in the shadows behind him and I had a feeling that it was Reave, but I couldn't see the figure clearly.

"You've been having trouble bearing children," I continued in an even voice as if I were trying to put him in a trance. "More and more years pass between the birth of offspring. Your people are dying, going extinct *without* the need for a long, bloody war. The Ivory Towers will wipe all the elves from this world without needing to fight you."

I cocked my head to the side as I stared at him, a new thought coming to my mind. "That's why you've risked coming so close to the Summer Court. You're desperate for children, so you've decided what? Steal members from the Summer Court to bear children? That must have been a hard decision, to willingly mix your bloodlines."

"I don't see how we've been left with any other choice." The king's voice was low, but there was a strong undercurrent of anger and hate boiling among his words. Despite the close relation between the three courts, there was no love between them. "As you've already said, great warlock, my people are fading away with no offspring to fill these woods. So, what's your service? You've come to break the curse you set upon my people."

"Unfortunately, because of the nature of the spell, I can't undo it," I admitted with a shrug. "However, I've spoken with someone who can. She's already unraveled the curse and your people are free to repopulate the earth without being forced to sully your bloodline." I was hoping that I was telling the truth. Gaia had said that she would meet with the Summer Court elves today and undo the spell. I was hoping that she could not only fix it in one day, but that she was going to help all the elves, including the dark elves. The only thing that was working in my favor was that the leader of the Svartálfar couldn't immediately prove me a liar.

The king laughed, a cold sound that scraped along my arms and sent chills down my back. "Seeing as you are fixing a mess that your people made, I don't see how I should feel obligated to give you anything."

"My goal was to help the Summer Court. I didn't have to help the Svartálfar, but I have."

"And now you expect payment."

I clenched my teeth. He was right and I felt like shit trying to force him into handing over Reave for fixing a curse that his people didn't deserve in the first place. "I'm trying to give you an amicable solution to our problem."

"It appears that you are the only one with a problem here, warlock, seeing as you've so kindly solved ours." He chuckled, but there was nothing happy in that noise. "I'm feeling generous tonight. Leave now and we won't kill you where you . . . float." He finished with a wave of his hand.

"I can't do that," I said with a snarl. I didn't want to kill the dark elves gathered around me, but I'd do it to get to Reave. "I can't leave here without Reave. You hand him over to me now or you will find this valley flooded with warlocks and witches before you can even signal your people to attack me."

"So you've moved from bribery to threats," he said, sounding as if he were bored with the entire conversation.

"It's no threat. Just a statement of fact. I can't leave without him, and if you keep him, you risk the life of every last Svartálfar. The Towers are searching for an elf. They don't yet know the elf they seek is Svartálfar. If I were to tell them, they would kill every dark elf on the planet rather than bother to search out their true target. You know this."

I smiled at the king, a grim, cold thing as he glared at me. My voice dipped a little lower so that I was nearly whispering but everyone in the valley could hear me. "Or did Reave not tell you the true reason for his return to the bosom of his people? Didn't you know that he's the reason Indianapolis was destroyed?"

"Noooo!" The scream echoed throughout the cave before flying free into the night air. A tall, lithe body ran past the king and jumped from the edge of the cliff. There was no time to react as my mind struggled to accept that fact that Reave had thrown himself at me. I noticed the knife clenched in his fist a half second before his body crashed into mine. I grabbed his wrist and arm with both hands to stop him from plunging it into my chest, but I had no way to compensate for his hitting me. We flew backward into the darkness, smashing into tree branches as we fell to the earth in a tangle of struggling limbs. Pain exploded across my back as we hit a tree, while more pain slashed across my face as we passed branches. We had moved out of the light I had created, so I could no longer see Reave, but I had my hands on him, holding him away from me.

The impact of hitting hard earth and rocks threw us apart. Grinding my teeth against the pain, I rolled to my feet, eyes searching the woods for a sign of the damn dark elf. My heart pounded like mad and my breath was coming in shattered gasps. Pain seared through my chest with each inhale, making me think that one or more ribs were broken, but I couldn't worry about it. I wasn't sure if Reave would run or come at me again. He certainly had an advantage in fighting me in the woods, but it would be next to impossible to spot him if he ran.

The wind shifted and I twisted around to see a shadow lunging at me. The knife winked briefly in a shaft of light as he attempted to plunge it in my stomach. I sidestepped the blow, but Reave only turned and slashed the knife through the air. I raised my right hand to block his arm, but I wasn't fast enough. The knife sliced through my wand, sending a massive jolt through my body. Breaking your wand sucked in the worst way, but you never wanted to be holding it when it happened. Any energy accumulated in that little instrument instantly shot back through the wielder.

I dropped the remains of the wand as everything became numb from my fingertips to my right shoulder. With my arm hanging limp at my side, I swung my left fist, hitting Reave on the side of the face with enough force to cause him to stumble past me. The deadweight was throwing me off balance and there was a buzzing in my head that wasn't great for my concentration, but I was keeping a close eye on Reave now that I had him in sight again.

The dark elf turned toward me, knife raised. Everything in me screamed to cast a protective spell, but the jolt from the broken wand felt like it had fried a few circuits in my brain. I was worried that I'd only do more damage if I tried something before the buzzing passed, or worse, that nothing would happen.

Reave slashed at me with the knife, pushing me backward until I was pressed against a tree. He lunged again and overextended himself when he missed me and embedded the knife in the tree trunk beside my head. With a grunt, I kicked him in the stomach, sending him wheeling. As he tried to regain his balance, he tripped over a half-buried log and fell into the small clearing blanketed with golden light.

I followed after him into the light. The elf easily rolled to his feet and squared off against me. He didn't look armed, but I wasn't willing to stake my life on it. His black eyes were narrowed at me and spittle was running down his chin. Fear and anger were making him careless. It was the only reason that I was still alive after a hand-to-hand fight with a dark elf.

"Come on, warlock. Kill me," he growled. "Or did you not reach that part in your training?"

"Don't worry. They teach us how to skin a Svartálfar the first day," I said with a mocking smile.

With a guttural cry, he charged me. My right arm was dead to me and my buzzing brain was like a hive of honey bees. I didn't have a lot of options. As he drew close, I dropped into a baseball slide so that my foot slammed into his knees. The dark elf screamed in pain as he was thrown off balance. He flew through the air over me and landed on his face in the rocks and dirt several feet away. Reave rolled until his body crashed into another tree. His moans echoed through the silence. If I had hit him right, at least one knee was now hyperextended, leaving it completely useless. It also looked like he'd broken his nose and maybe an arm from that impact.

A part of me wanted to laugh. I'd spent the past few years studying different forms of martial arts, and it turned out to be my six years of playing interspecies softball that saved my life.

Pushing to my feet with my left hand, I remained in the middle of the circle of light, watching Reave's ragged breathing. With a sigh, I drew in a trickle of energy and was instantly relieved to find that the buzzing steadily dimmed. The magic in my brain had rebalanced itself, so that I felt safe casting spells. Feeling was starting to come back into my right arm, but I didn't welcome it because pain was replacing the numbness.

Lifting my left hand above my head, I sent a quick summon spell out into the ether before turning my full attention to Reave. I cast a second spell that lifted the elf out of the brush and held him above the ground before me. Blood poured down his face from his swollen nose and an array of scratches. His breathing was rough and shallow while his eyes remained unfocused, lost in the grips of severe pain.

Lightning forked and spiderwebbed across the sky, followed by a loud boom of thunder. The elves I could see jerked and stared at the sky, missing the sudden appearance of Gideon at my side. There was a sharp gasp when they noticed him. They shrank back into the shadows. Only the king remained standing in the open at the mouth of the cave.

"You look like hell." Gideon's eyes swept over my torn shirt and dirty jeans. He then looked briefly at Reave and gave a shrug. "Well, better than him at least."

"Always a pleasure, Gideon," I said sarcastically, feeling both exhausted and nervous. Step one of my plan was complete: capture Reave. The hard part was coming next: survive a meeting with the council.

"I need you to do me a favor," I said, pulling my thoughts free of my growing fears. "Call an emergency meeting of the council." Gideon didn't move a muscle. I was asking a lot. I was putting his life at risk because he was supposed to be the one policing me. "It's okay. You're taking me . . . with him."

The warlock's eyes darted to Reave, who was starting to sweat despite the chill in the air. "He's the one?"

"Yeah."

For a second, rage filled Gideon's cold, gray eyes but the rest of his face was like stone. He turned those hard eyes on me. "Are you sure?"

He wasn't asking if I was sure Reave was the culprit. He was wondering about my decision to go before the council. I shrugged. "We both know I don't have a choice."

"Do you have your wand on you?"

A sigh escaped me as I looked over my shoulder at the dark woods. I was half tempted to call the broken pieces to me, but there was no point. The magic from the wand had already discharged back into my body. The only thing resting on the forest floor was a pair of broken sticks. "No. No wand."

"Good." Gideon reached over and placed a hand on my shoulder, preparing to teleport both me and Reave to whichever Tower was going to hold the meeting. By now, the information would have come back to Gideon. I could have done it myself, but I was afraid that if I announced that I was coming to the Towers, they'd ambush me and kill me on sight.

"Wait!" I shouted, and stepped away from Gideon while staring up at where the king was watching us. "I'm taking Reave and I will be sure the Towers know he acted alone, but . . ." I frowned, feeling helpless. "Well, it's the Towers we're talking about. If I were you, I'd move my people tonight."

The king nodded, then stepped away from the edge of the cliff and disappeared into the shadows of the cave. He would move his people, disappearing deep into the forestlands of the surrounding area to protect them from any potential retaliation from the Towers. I was praying the council would be content with Reave's life. And potentially mine.

I walked back over to Gideon and nodded. The warlock placed a firm hand on my shoulder, giving it a slight squeeze before the world went dark as we crossed a vast distance in a heartbeat. I said a silent prayer to Lady Luck that she might see me through this nightmare. I was doing the one thing that I swore I would never do. I was willingly walking back into the lion's den after I'd barely escaped with my life the first time. Letting the Svartálfar kill me was starting to sound pretty damn good right about now.

THE WIND WAS bitter cold as it swept across the black field, and I wouldn't have been surprised if snowflakes started drifting down from the sky. Based on the fact that it was still night and fucking cold, I knew we were standing outside the upstate New York Tower. The gleaming white monolith rose up toward the heavens. It should have looked like a beacon of hope to the world, but the world couldn't see this structure because of the thick web of protective spells that stretched around the area. Of course, if the world could see the Tower, they would have viewed it as a giant bony middle finger. They would have been right.

Gideon pointed his wand, his face expressionless as he motioned for me to lead the way through the wood-and-iron-banded door in front of me. A giant could have walked through the massive opening without needing to duck his head down. I never understood why they had made it so big since everyone who entered walked on two human feet. I guess it was made to intimidate, but sadly warlocks and witches didn't intimidate easily.

This was my first visit to the New York Tower, but all the Towers looked the same. The exterior was a mix of white marble and pale granite, while the interior halls were covered in red-veined black marble. The individual rooms were customized to the tastes of the inhabiting witch or warlock, ranging from the spartan to the extravagant.

It was after midnight and the halls of the Tower were nearly silent, but then the Towers were rarely ever noisy, as if idle conversation had been forbidden by the council. A few people paused as they passed through the halls to stop and stare. Lips curled with disgust at the sight of a beaten and bleeding dark elf, but eyes narrowed speculatively when they spotted me. I doubted anyone would recognize me. Oh, all the people of the Towers knew my name, but few had ever seen me and even fewer knew of my altered appearance.

We moved silently down the hall to a large opening. There was no elevator car as you would expect, just an empty shaft that ran from the top of the tower to several floors below the earth. Without hesitating, I stepped into the emptiness, my feet finding an invisible platform. Gideon and Reave were immediately behind me.

"Council chambers," Gideon said in a strong voice.

The invisible floor fell away and we dropped into the darkness, my stomach instantly becoming swept away. Reave screamed, the horrible sound echoing throughout the shaft, so that everyone within the Tower could hear it. I closed my eyes and clamped my mouth shut, willing myself to trust the magic despite my own desire to scream. The worst had always been when a new apprentice was brought to the Tower. The child's screams could be heard for weeks echoing through the building until the apprentice grew accustomed to this mode of travel.

Just when you were sure you would slam into the earth, breaking every bone in your body, a gentle force surrounded you, slowing your descent so you landed softly on another platform at your desired floor. I opened my eyes to find us on the bottom floor. Torchlight danced along the walls of the narrow hallway that ended in another set of enormous black doors. The walls and floor were black. The wall sconces were black iron. The only color was the flickering flames.

I stepped out of the shaft first with Reave floating just above the ground behind me. Gideon hadn't bothered to heal his knee and kept him in a physical binding spell. There was no reason to heal him so long as he could talk and scream. As we walked down the hall, the doors automatically opened to reveal a room almost as big as the entire Tower was round. When we entered, it was like walking into a wall of noise after passing through so many silent halls. A quick glance revealed that all twelve members of the council were present. Only one seat was vacant, but then a new member had yet to be elected following Peter's death. They were all dressed in the classic black robes, but in place of their wands were long wooden staves topped with different-colored orbs.

The twelve council members were on a dais so that they could easily look down on the supplicants and accused. Before them was an open floor that was a strange mix of a courtroom floor and an arena for gladiators. At the opposite end of the room were several rows of seats for people to watch the proceedings. To my displeasure, every seat in the place was taken. I had prayed that due to the lateness of the hour, I would come before only the council members, but I had a feeling that because of the high stress caused by recent events, everyone was waiting for news with bated breath.

As we neared the center of the room, one of the council warlocks pounded his staff on the floor twice. A moment later, the double door banged closed, sending a horrible echo through my chest. *Please, let those doors open for me again.*

"Mr. Powell, this is an unexpected visit," Henry Fox called down to me. I clenched my jaw, fighting the urge to make a snide remark. These assholes weren't going to make it easy on me, but starting a fight with the council would not help me see daylight again. "And you even dressed for the occasion."

I stood, stiff and sore, staring straight ahead at the cold, black stone wall that made up the front of their dais, refusing to acknowledge Fox's comments. I knew as soon as I said one word to the prick, he'd bring up the fact that I'd used forbidden magic in a fight that he witnessed—getting both myself and Gideon in trouble. Sure, that fucking asshole started the fight, but I wasn't sure there were many in the room who would care about this technicality.

"Master Toussaint," one witch on the council started a bit wearily. I nearly looked around to see who she was addressing when it dawned on me that she was talking to Gideon. I knew his last name, but I hadn't heard it used in a long time. "It seems that Mr. Powell has finally given you a reason to bring him before us. It's a shame it couldn't wait for a more agreeable hour."

There was a soft rustle of material behind me, making me think that Gideon had bowed to the council. "I am sorry about the lateness of the hour, but I felt that due to the urgency of our current situation, it would be best if this were handled as soon as possible."

It was a struggle not to roll my eyes. The warlock could be as smooth as silk when he wanted to be, not that he ever wasted it on me. He was diplomatic, with only the faintest touch of lips to ass to keep all the feathers unruffled. It was yet another reason why I couldn't survive in the Towers.

"Really?" another warlock said.

"Yeah, I heard that the Towers were in a bit of a fix," I said, my gaze darting up to the sour faces glaring down at me.

"And how would you know about the concerns of the Towers?" the same warlock demanded, his voice growing stiffer as he straightened in his high-backed wooden chair. You'd think if they were going to be stuck in those chairs for hours on end, they'd make them out of something more comfortable, but then I guess a cushioned recliner didn't look as intimidating.

"Well, having Indianapolis destroyed was kind of a giveaway," I said with a shrug and a grin. "But then, you hear things when you're living among the puny mortals. Things I'm sure you don't want the masses to know, but one way or another, those whispers find their way to my ear."

No one spoke for several seconds as the members looked at one another. Their faces were blank, but the buzz of energy in the air grew. A couple orbs at the end of the staves held by the council members glowed, tying a fresh knot in my stomach. The light indicated when a witch or warlock was drawing energy to her- or himself. The council members weren't necessarily starting to cast a spell. High emotions also tended to draw and excite the energy in the air, but a glowing orb was rarely a good sign.

The council chamber was supposed to be a magic-free zone in the hopes that people could speak freely there without the fear of being vaporized. It didn't exactly work out that way, but it was a nice idea. The room was black because it was intimidating, but I had a feeling that its designers had also chosen the color because it didn't immediately reveal spilled blood.

"Why are the problems of the Towers your concern?" a witch asked. It was the same one who had addressed Gideon with such a tired voice. Her black hair was pulled back into a severe bun with a few thick streaks of gray threading through it. Her skin was the color of rich mahogany and she looked as if she'd be pretty if she smiled, but there was something about the lines surrounding her dark eyes that said the witch didn't smile much.

"I guess because I would rather not see the town I'm living in wiped from the map," I said with a little more bite than I had meant to use. Frowning, I walked over to Reave and grabbed a handful of the back of his torn and bloody shirt. "Let's cut the crap. Someone found out the locations of the Towers. *Seven of them.* With my usual rotten luck, I tripped over the bastard who wormed through your glamour spells and I've brought him to you." As I spoke, I gave Reave a little shake. The dark elf snarled at me, trying to twist around so that he could hurt me, but Gideon's binding spell was holding him in place.

"Now, that is extremely generous of you, Mr. Powell," commented a warlock with a heavy dose of sarcasm. Somehow, he managed to lounge in his chair, looking as if he were nine months pregnant and proud of it. He had been at my hearing ten years ago, but I couldn't recall his name. He had been an asshole then too. Funny, that.

"Yes, well, since I've had a few witches and warlocks appear recently looking for my head because of this fiasco, I thought it would be in my best interest to clean up this mess for you."

A little less insulting, if you don't mind, Gideon growled in my head. *I'd like to live through this nightmare.*

I wanted to telepathically tell Gideon to fuck off, but I had a feeling that I was being very closely monitored—the council members would know if I was secretly speaking to my warden.

Instead, I clenched my teeth and pushed down my anger. Sure, I was the one being unjustifiably hunted and had a right to be pissed, but Gideon's fate was largely tied to my own. If I fell tonight, there was a good chance Gideon would fall as well. Against my better judgment, I was starting to like the asshole and didn't want to be the reason he was roasted.

"I think many who came knocking on your door felt their arrival was justified since you most likely supplied the information about the Towers' locations," Henry Fox said blandly.

I smiled at Fox, but it was little more than a baring of my teeth, like a dog guarding a bone against an unwelcome guest. "I may have not wanted to be a part of your club, Master Fox, but we all know that I wouldn't betray the secrets of the Towers. That would help no one."

Fox grinned back, a cold, evil thing. "I don't think anyone would put betrayal past you following the death of Master Thorn."

"When I left, I retained the right to defend myself against attack. Simon Thorn came hunting for me when he wasn't supposed to know where I was. The bastard got what he deserved. I struggle to believe you're mourning his death considering that he kicked your magical ass on more than one occasion."

A low wave of noise crashed behind me, a mix of gasps, chuckles, and angry words that rippled through the room. Gideon even swore under his breath and I knew he was longing to punch me, but he held it in. Henry Fox jumped to his feet, the orb on the end of his staff glowing bright red in his rage. Everything in me screamed to gather up some energy for a defensive shield, but I was afraid that if I tried to do this, the council wouldn't look too kindly on it. I had a right to defend myself, but I was already skating on thin ice, no reason to punch through to a frigid death.

"Master Fox!" snapped the black witch, causing his head to jerk around and look down the row to her. The orb on her staff glowed an icy, bluish white. Her slender body was extremely rigid as she stared down at him. "Sit," she said with a hiss that silenced everyone in the chamber. Henry glared at her for several seconds before resuming his seat. The red glow dimmed at the end of his staff, but didn't completely fade.

I won't do that again. Curb your tongue or I'll cut it out myself. The words drifted through my brain, cold and sharp as if someone had shoved a knife through my temple. The witch who was glaring at Fox never looked directly at me when she sent the message, but I knew she was the one who sent it.

My gut told me that she was part of the same movement as Gideon and Peter, but I wasn't willing to bet my life on it. She may have just been concerned about determining the source of the information leak and would have been happy to see me impaled on my own wand at a later time.

"Back to the issue at hand," Pregnant drawled as if bored by the whole affair, but I had seen his smile at my dig at Fox. I wasn't stupid enough to think that he was on my side. He was only amused at Fox's embarrassment. "I'm assuming this thing that has been dragged before us is the one who located the Towers. Do you even know how he managed it?"

"Gage did it!" Reave shouted. He had been silent for so long that

I had forgotten that he had the power of speech. "He told me where to find the Towers. Sent me to each location. He forced me!"

I lunged at Reave, hammering my fist into the side of his face with enough force to make him slump against the binding spell. He wasn't unconscious, but he was close. "You fucking liar!" I snarled. "You brought this on yourself. I won't let you drag me down with you."

Reave's mouth moved as if he were trying to smile. "I won't be the only one to die today."

I raised my fist to hit him again, but energy wrapped around me and I slid across the floor as Gideon drew me away from Reave. I wasn't helping my case.

"Read his mind," I said between clenched teeth as I glared at Reave. The Svartálfar was breathing in short gasps as if the pain was getting to him. Either that or it was a rising tide of panic pressing against his chest. My head snapped up to look at the council members. "Read his mind and see the truth," I said louder. They didn't look particularly pleased with my "request," but one after another, each orb glowed a neutral yellow as they cast the spell to read the dark elf's mind.

It was several seconds before anyone on the council spoke again. "Powell wasn't involved in the information leak," one warlock said, almost disappointed. He hadn't spoken since I entered the room and he didn't look particularly pleased with the revelation that I wasn't involved. Of course, I had a few other strikes against me.

"But he did work for the elf," murmured a witch at the far end of the row of council members. Her voice was soft and thoughtful, as if she were carefully considering the things she was seeing in Reave's mind.

"Not willingly," I said. "A daylight attack by Simon Thorn forced my secret out into the populace. Reave used blackmail to force me to work for him."

"So I saw." Her voice hardened. She didn't look at me when

she spoke, but was looking over my shoulder at Gideon. My heart pounded in my chest and a cold sweat broke out between my shoulder blades. If she was seeing Reave's anger about my activities at the fix house, then she was likely drawing some interesting conclusions about Gideon's failure to report what had occurred at the house to the council. *Fuck.*

"Reave is the one who discovered the secret locations," I said in a rush, pushing forward in hopes of distracting the rest of the council from whatever the witch had seen. "I humbly request that the Towers punish the Svartálfar called Reave and send a message to the leaders of the world that you've captured the enemy that brought destruction down on the world's people."

A low chuckle rippled over me, drawing my gaze down to the opposite end of the row of council members. A lean warlock sat back in his chair, watching me through dancing green eyes. He wore the same black robes as all the others and his staff wasn't much different from theirs, but when I looked at him, the only word that came to mind was *dandy.* Something in me wanted to believe he was harmless, which only set more alarm bells. No warlock or witch was harmless.

"I didn't think you knew such a term, Mr. Powell. *Humble,*" he said with another laugh.

I didn't recognize him, so I didn't think he had been at my hearing. Of course, the memory of my hearing was a terrified blur, so he could have been there.

"Can you be humble?" he asked with a grin.

I bowed to the council a bit stiffly, bending low at the waist. "Please, consider my request. Let people sleep easily in their beds again." I was looking at the shiny floor as I spoke, but they heard me. Bile rose up in my throat and I wanted to scream. Hatred and shame battled in my chest until I was nearly choking. I hated having to abase myself before these assholes, but if it kept everyone safe for a little while longer, I could swallow my pride.

When I straightened and gazed up at the council, they were all looking at each other but no one was speaking. The orbs had changed to an orangish glow as they used telepathy to deliberate silently with each other. If there was a consensus among them, they wouldn't bother to vote. If the council was widely divided, they'd vote verbally.

I swallowed hard, fighting the need to throw up as the tension roiled my stomach. The argument seemed cut-and-dry to me. Reave had found the locations of the Towers. He deserved to be punished for threatening the order of the world. I doubted there was a government in the world that would agree to punish him with a death sentence, but if a scapegoat could take the blame without risking more lives, they'd all hand him over without hesitation. It wasn't right, but it kept people alive.

Of course, I didn't know what else they had seen in Reave's mind and I was praying they didn't throw my name in with his so they could get rid of me.

"It's decided," the black witch announced, and my heart stopped for a second, waiting. "The elf will be executed for his violation of our sanctity." I waited but she stopped talking and no one said my name. I released my held breath in a rush. My head swam and my knees went weak. I was sure that I was going to fall on my ass in the middle of the chamber and I didn't care.

"I'm not the only one who knows!" Reave screamed in desperation.

"No," I said in a broken whisper before I could catch myself. If I thought it would have made a difference, I would have killed Reave in that second, but it was too late. The words had already hit the air. Apparently, the council members hadn't dug deeply enough to see Reave give the locations to my brother, but now they would know.

I closed my eyes against the swell of impotent rage and tears, but not before I saw the orbs snap to bright yellow as they dove back into Reave's mind, searching for the bit of information that they had missed.

"Robert Grant . . . your brother . . ." one of the council members said in surprise. I didn't know who had spoken, but the voice had been female, sounding almost sad, or at least pitying.

I took at deep breath and blinked back the tears before looking up at them. "It was Reave's way of ensuring my cooperation and protection against the Towers. He told the locations to my brother." My tone was quiet, almost as if I was dead inside, but I wasn't that lucky.

"And the location of this brother?" the dandy inquired.

It had been on the tip of my tongue to say that I killed him, but they would know the truth. They would search my brain until they found the memory of me murdering my brother. I couldn't lie to the council. I could stretch the truth, but not outright lie.

"He's gone."

The warlock smiled at me, trying to look as if he was my best friend in the world, but I wasn't buying it. "Where?"

"No."

The warlock's eyes widened, but otherwise there was no reaction on his lean face as he watched me. Out of the corner of my eye, I could see several orbs flare to bright red. Yeah, this was what I had been waiting for. You didn't refuse the council and you never struck bargains, but I was going to try to do both to save my brother's life.

I prepared to step out on the tightrope. The council members could try to read my mind like they had read Reave's, but they wouldn't be as successful because I was a warlock. I knew how to compartmentalize thoughts, hide them away so that a quick search would reveal nothing. Oh, they could eventually find the truth, but it wasn't going to be quick. They'd have to strip away each layer of my brain until there was nothing left of me. Normally, the council wouldn't have a problem with such a thing, other than that it took lots of valuable time. I had to give them a good reason not to destroy my mind.

"Reave told my brother, but I wiped the memory. Robert doesn't know the locations now; nor is he aware that he ever knew them."

The dandy flashed me an indulgent smile that I wanted to rip off his face with a rake. "Forgive us if we're not as confident as you. Memory wipes are quite tricky. I can't imagine that you've had a lot of practice at them." His smile widened as he waited for me to backpedal. Memory spells were not covered in my self-defense-only agreement and I was about to hang myself if I admitted a second time to using it.

My gaze never wavered from him. "As Simon Thorn could at one time attest, I am talented. My brother's memory has been wiped."

The murmur of conversation behind me picked up again for a couple seconds before one of the council members pounded his staff on the stone floor. The warlock who had spoken smiled at me, his grin nearly sharklike. He thought he had me, and he was probably right, but I wasn't done yet.

"My brother's memory has been wiped," I repeated, my voice rising strong and firm. "He has no memory of Reave, myself, or my family. I gave him a new name, appearance, and past that he doesn't question. He was sent from the city where he lived and I have no idea where he will settle."

"A very pretty attempt at protection," Henry Fox commented, sounding bored, but I knew better. His mind was already turning over the spells that he could use to track down Robert. It would take time, but he could do it.

I grinned at him, looking sharklike myself. "I also gave him insurance." Fox's satisfied look crumpled to a frown and even the dandy seemed to be paying closer attention now. "He has the coordinates tattooed on his body in code, though not currently visible to the naked eye. However, if he should die unexpectedly and there is even a hint of magic surrounding him at the time, not only will the tattooed coordinates appear on his body, but they will also appear on ten different people every day for the next ten years. And should they die in a similar manner, the spread will be amplified. There will be no stopping the spread of information if he is harmed. My brother will *not* be hunted."

The conversation in the chamber rose to a deafening roar as the gathered mass realized that the council had been outmaneuvered. No one did such a thing, and certainly not some rogue who had turned his back on the Towers. It took several minutes of pounding on the floor and few shouted threats to get the room back under control.

If I wasn't looking at my own death sentence, I would applaud your efforts, Gideon whispered telepathically. Surprisingly, he didn't sound angry. I was hoping that it was because he understood why I did what I did, and maybe knew he would have done the same thing to protect his family.

"Powell," the black witch said on a sigh when the silence had returned. She was frowning, looking as if she had aged ten years since I had entered the chamber. She probably wanted to smack me, and I couldn't blame her. "You're a devious bastard, which only makes it seem fitting that you wound up with Thorn since he was a devious bastard as well. Through your actions, you've handed yourself to us on a silver platter. You've broken the agreement not to use magic beyond self-defense, and yet I can't shake the feeling that you've still got one more card to play. Shall we get on with it?"

It was a struggle not to grin at her, but I managed, keeping my face empty. A wistful thought wandered through my brain: if she had been my mentor when I came to the Towers, I might have stuck around a little longer.

"You need me," I said, shoving my hands into the front pockets of my battered jeans.

Laughter exploded throughout the room, which helped to ease

some of the growing tension, but it crept back into the room as everyone slowly realized that I was completely serious. Seats creaked as people nervously shifted while the council members frowned.

"The information leak should have impressed upon you that the Towers are no longer in tune with the events occurring in the rest of the world," I continued when silence had returned. "The people of the world have gotten better at hiding their secrets from you because time has taught them your tricks. They fear you, that will never change, but they've found new ways to work around you. Reave's accumulation of information couldn't have happened overnight; it required the passage of weeks if not years. Yet the Towers didn't discover it until he had all the locations. Simply put, you're dangerously out of touch."

To my surprise, none of the orbs glowed red. Instead, faces turned red and some members shifted in their seats. They were uncomfortable. I wasn't telling them anything they hadn't already realized and had begun to worry about.

"We don't need you, traitor." The pregnant-looking warlock sneered, but he gave no other argument because he had none.

"In fear, members of the Towers destroyed an entire city to kill one person when it would have been more effective to have killed him quietly and secretly without arousing the suspicions of the world," I said, careful not to blame the destruction of Indianapolis on the council. "Now the world is wary. People have scattered like cockroaches with the light flipped on. They'll be harder to find, harder to kill." I smiled, letting an evil glint enter my expression. "You need me living among them, sifting through the rumors to protect the safety of the Towers."

"Why do you wish to protect the Towers?" the dandy asked. The mocking look had been wiped from his face and he seemed to be taking a new interest in me.

"I'd rather not see another city destroyed," I said, and then sighed, hating to admit something else, but it was the truth. "And despite our differing opinions on . . . Tower culture . . . I do believe in the dedicated study of the art. But that can't be done if you're constantly worrying about what the rest of the world is plotting."

"And you're offering your services as a spy?" The dandy looked supremely amused, barely holding back his laughter.

"In exchange for my life," I said with a small bow, hiding my face when I was sure I was going to be sick. I was trying to trade servitude to Reave for slavery to the Towers. Not an improvement. When I could breathe evenly, I straightened and smiled broadly. "Unless, of course, you want to leave the Towers to live among the people? Think you'll get many volunteers?"

Turning sharply around, I faced the wall of spectators and spread my hands out toward them in invitation. "Who among you will leave the Towers to live among the people? Who will pack up their wands and give up magic to live in a quiet suburban house or a cramped one-bedroom apartment where the floor creaks and the faucet leaks? Who will stand in line at the grocery, rub elbows at the local bar, and *get a job*?"

The silence was deafening. No one moved. Hell, I don't think anyone was breathing for fear that the council would volunteer them. I spun back to face the council, swallowing a shout of laughter.

"You've made your point, Mr. Powell," the black witch grumbled, causing the smile to be wiped off my face. She glanced down at her fellow council members, frowning. "We will consider your offer."

Now it was my turn to stop breathing. I had laid all my cards on the table, made my final move. There were no more tricks up my sleeve to save my life. It would either work, or I was going to end up dead along with Reave very shortly. I watched the orbs glowing orange as the council telepathically discussed everything that I had laid before them. While no one spoke, the mood seemed more animated this time, as warlocks and witches moved in their seats and facial expressions changed. Only the dandy on the end remained still, his expression never changing. He sat back in his chair, holding his staff with one hand while he stared unblinking at me.

Minutes ticked by one after another in an ever-thickening tension. I didn't know if it was a good sign or a bad one. If they decided too quickly, would it mean they had ruled against me? If it took too long, would they go to a verbal vote? I wasn't counting on a verbal vote ending in my favor, and a tie would be worse, as I would be imprisoned until the new council member cast the deciding vote.

When I was sure that I would explode from impatience, the glowing orbs dimmed and everyone straightened in their chairs. No one was smiling.

"You've left us with a quandary, Mr. Powell," the witch commented. "You've admitted to breaking your agreement and casting forbidden magic, but you've done the Towers a great favor and offered your services, which I'm sure you find quite distasteful." She paused, her frown deepening. "Killing you is the easy answer, but then we would feel as if we had been . . . ungrateful for your assistance. It may also show the rest of the Towers that we don't appreciate the vigilance of our fellow warlocks and witches in our protection. We have decided on leniency, this one time."

"Thank you." I sighed with relief as I bowed deeply to them.

"I would hold your appreciation until you've heard our terms," she sharply continued, causing an uneasy flutter in my chest. "We will accept your offer. You will become the eyes and ears of the council while living among the people. You will execute our edicts, punish those who threaten us, and deliver those who need to be questioned by the council."

I took a step back, frowning. "You make it sound as if I am to be included as a part of the guardians."

The guardians were the enforcement arm of the Towers. When the people shook in terror at the Towers, the guardians were the group they were usually thinking of. This was bad. I had been thinking of something less obtrusive and deeply hidden. The council's agreement meant that I was back to killing and torturing people for the Towers.

"That can't be because I'd have to be considered an inhabitant of the Towers to take on such a role," I said, shaking my head.

She said nothing. She stared at me with cold, dead eyes. I wanted to scream at them all, but I couldn't because I couldn't catch my breath. As the truth hit me, I started hyperventilating. To survive, I had to take their offer, which meant that I was a part of the Towers again. *I was one of them. I was back.*

Nearly a decade ago, I had fought my mentor, nearly killed him, and nearly died in the process to break free. I had survived a hearing before the council. I lost my family, survived repeated assassination attempts, and lay hidden, lying to the world for years. All of it to escape the Towers. And now I had to choose between death and willingly returning to the enemy's ranks. The killing I had sworn against doing would only be the tip of the iceberg once I was at the beck and call of the council. If they wanted me to live among the people, they wouldn't give away my secret, but I'd still have to look at myself in the mirror each day, remembering the lives I destroyed for them. *The life I had built was slipping through my fingers.*

I drew in a deep, fragmented breath, trying to stop my hyperventilating. I was on my knees on the cold, black floor, but I couldn't remember how I had gotten there. A cold sweat covered me and I was so light-headed that the room seemed to sway.

Gideon's dress shoes came into view. He couldn't touch me, offer any comfort without giving himself away, but knowing he was close kept me from feeling quite so alone in that ocean of cold, black stone. His presence was a silent reminder that he was a guardian and yet he maintained a secret life that was a place of love and happiness with a wife and daughter. He had found ways around the council's orders. He was quietly helping the runaways. Yes, he did horrible things for the Towers, but he also did positive things that were protecting lives—namely mine.

If I agreed to serve the council, I could help people like Gideon. I could do more than I was able to do now. I wasn't sure I'd be able to face myself at the end of the day. Sadly, as I sat there staring at the shine on Gideon's shoes, I knew I had already decided. I was sick with the thought, but the truth was that I was desperate to live.

When I spoke, the words were so ragged they sounded as if they had been torn from my chest. "If I accept, will I be reinstated to the full privileges of a Tower member?"

The silence stretched but I didn't look up. They were discussing my question among themselves. My question covered a multitude of sins, but my main concern was being permitted to use all forms of magic again, and they knew it.

The witch's voice washed over me, sounding less harsh than it had been earlier. "Not yet. This will be on a trial basis. If you prove yourself diligent and trustworthy, we will consider reinstating all your privileges. For now, you may use magic only in self-defense and in relation to a task done in service to the council."

I frowned. The door wasn't closed on the topic, but reinstatement to full privileges was looking unlikely. On the other hand, the witch had given me a nice amount of gray area to work in, definitely more breathing room than I had had before.

"Will I retain a warden?"

"Yes."

"Not Toussaint," I said sharply, trying to infuse as much anger and hatred into those two words as I could. I lifted my head and glared at the council. "He's been a knife in my side for nearly a decade and I've had enough. His constant abuse and attempts at entrapment have gone against our agreement of live and let live. I want someone else!" By the time I was finished, I was on my feet; I didn't have to fake the anger.

The "pregnant" warlock lounged in his chair and smiled broadly at me. "It seems Master Toussaint is doing an excellent job, so why should we relieve him of the task? He will remain your warden." He had spoken without consulting any of the other council members and none would disagree with his decision out loud, though several looked like they wanted to.

My attempt at reverse psychology had been clumsy and ham-fisted, but it was all I could think of. I was afraid that if someone else was assigned to watch over me, the Towers would simply kill Gideon for his failure to curb my magic use. Luckily, the warlock who had just spoken had been so eager to see me suffer that he didn't think about my possible motivations. I scowled at him, playing my part, but others didn't look so convinced.

"For your first assignment," the witch broke in, drawing my eyes back to her, "you will kill the dark elf for his attack on the Towers. And you will kill him with magic."

Panic surged through my frame for a second and I even saw Gideon stiffen beside me. I knew why they'd decided this. Punishment for outmaneuvering them. I'd lose a year of my life for killing Reave with magic, and not one of the crappy ones off the end. It could be one of the good years right out of the goddamn middle. But it wasn't losing a year of my life that bothered me. It was the fact that Lilith would have me in her clutches for two whole years since she was holding a chunk of my soul.

Of course, this was all assuming that my body would be preserved during the years I was dead. I couldn't come back if I didn't have a body to come back to.

I wanted to scream and rant at them. I wanted to tell them that they were handing me into the most dangerous being in existence—Lilith would use those two years to break free and I wouldn't be able to stop it. But I knew they wouldn't listen. They wouldn't believe me when I told them she really existed and they would never believe anyone could be more powerful than the Towers. There was nothing I could do.

Not trusting my voice, I gave a jerky nod and turned toward Reave, who was watching me. He'd known he was going to die when

Gideon and I brought him to the Towers. He'd had enough time to accept it. Hell, he'd probably known he was going to die the moment he embarked on this insane scheme. He was just disappointed that he didn't take me down with him.

"Release him," I barked. Gideon hesitated. I liked to think that he was mentally scrambling, trying to think of a way out for me, but in the end, the binding spell disappeared. There was no way out. If I didn't do as they asked, they'd kill me. If Gideon did it for me, they'd kill both of us.

Reave balanced on one leg, the toe of his injured one barely touching the floor. His bearing was straight and his head was high as he stared me in the eyes. He was in pain but you couldn't tell. I hated Reave. I hated him because he was behind the death of countless creatures. I hated him for tearing Robert out of my life. I hated him for all the harm he had done to Bronx. I hated him for helping to destroy the life I loved. But standing there as he was, with body straight and gaze unflinching, I had to respect him, and that was the only reason why I killed him as quickly as possible.

Gathering up a quick swell of energy, I thrust both my hands forward and Reave jerked as if I had plunged them through his chest. I clenched my fists together, gathering the energy around his heart, crushing it. The Svartálfar gasped, his eyes widening in pain, and then he collapsed, dead.

It took only seconds to kill him and it would cost me a year of my life. I could hear Lilith laughing maniacally in my head as she celebrated the second year I now owed her.

"Excellent," the witch said, jerking my attention back to the council. "An agreement has been reached. All is settled. This meeting is adjourned." She pounded her staff on the floor twice, signaling the end of the meeting. There was a low murmur of conversation as people either disappeared from the chamber or filed out of the room through one of the doors. The council members disappeared one after another. Except the dandy.

He smiled at me, sending a chill down my spine. "Next time you come before the council, you may want to consider dressing for the event, Master Powell." He dipped his staff toward me and I could feel a wash of magic run down my body like someone had poured a bucket of cold water over my head. I held his gaze, refusing to flinch, until he disappeared. When I looked down, I found myself wearing a suit identical to the one Gideon had on.

I wanted to scream, and cry, and burn the whole fucking place down. Instead, I looked over at Gideon to find him staring at the chair the dandy had sat in.

"Who was that?"

Gideon sighed, a sound that seemed to come up from the bottom of his soul. "Darius Courtland. You don't want his attention. You definitely don't want to be caught alone with him. He makes Thorn and Fox look like Boy Scouts."

"Figured as much," I muttered. That was about how my luck ran. There wasn't anyone on the council I particularly wanted to face off against, but there was something about Darius that made my blood run cold with fear.

"I think he's the one who killed Peter." Gideon's voice had dipped to a whisper, as if he was afraid that someone was listening, but we were now alone in the council chamber.

The warlock blinked and turned to face me. Sadness filled his eyes, making me feel uncomfortable, mostly because he was sad about the things I wasn't yet letting myself think about. If there was anyone who knew what the agreement I had just made cost me, it was Gideon. I had a feeling that in the deep dark of the night, when he had his arms wrapped tightly around the waist of his secret wife as they cuddled in bed, he wished he had gotten out like me.

"Welcome home," he said, a grim smile touching the corners of his mouth.

Oh God . . . I was back.

30

IT WAS NEARLY three in the afternoon and the sun was beating down from a clear blue sky as if it was trying to convince the inhabitants of Low Town that it was the middle of June rather than the start of October. Leaning against the side of my SUV, I tilted my face up and closed my eyes as I soaked in the warmth. The leaves had already started to change into a blend of red, yellow, and orange, and the smell in the air held echoes of fall, but today felt like summer with the warm air and the distant growl of lawn mowers gliding across lawns.

My birthday was only a few days away and we were hoping the nice weather would hold up. Trixie was planning a grill-out, complete with scorched meat, fireworks, and a plastic wading pool, because she was desperately trying to keep a smile on my face. She had even gone so far as to suggest that I invite Gideon and his family, though I wasn't expecting them to show. I hadn't been smiling much since my return from the Ivory Tower. Trixie hadn't asked what happened, and I hadn't volunteered any information, but the question was coming. For now, she waited and watched me with a worried look when she didn't think I could see her.

The Towers had made no demands of me yet, but that would come too. The world had fallen into a tense peace as people tried to return to their lives while holding their breath in anticipation. Few knew why the Towers had destroyed Indianapolis or attacked Low Town and most didn't think the attacks were over yet.

The sound of leathery wings flapping caught my attention. I lowered my face and opened my eyes as I turned toward the noise. Duff landed on the hood of the SUV, where he did a little dance, hopping from one foot to the other as his bare feet cooked on the hot metal. With a frown, I stepped close so that he could crawl up to perch half on my shoulder and half on my head while his long tail curled around my arm.

Duff weighed the same as a small dog, so this wasn't the most comfortable position, but for some reason, he liked to be close to me. In the few times he'd popped into the parlor, I'd never seen him try this with Bronx or Trixie.

"Were you waiting for me?" he asked with a chuckle.

"You know I was," I said as I leaned against the car again. "How're things at the shop?"

"Trixie just finished up with the queen's tattoo and it is so lovely," he said, excitement filling his voice. "The king was a gentleman the entire time. Your friend wasn't needed."

I kept my comments to myself. When I discovered that I couldn't be at the shop when Trixie tattooed the king and queen of the Summer Court, I'd asked my friend Parker Banton to hang out and keep an eye on the king. Parker was pretty good at taking care of himself and I knew he'd watch out for Trixie for me, but I had asked him because he was an incubus. It was a subtle threat. If the king gave Trixie any grief, Parker was going to use his unique charm on the queen. Considering the queen was now pregnant with the king's child, I thought that jealousy would keep him on his best behavior.

Of course, the king also knew what I was and that I considered Trixie mine. I didn't think the elf was stupid enough to piss me off more than he already had.

"You should have seen him," Duff continued. He pulled at my

hair with his little fingers as if he were playing with it. He paused and bent down so that his upside-down face was directly in front of mine. "He was so attentive to the queen. I think they are past their quarrel and are in love again."

I closed my eyes before they could cross and pushed his head up so that it was no longer in front of mine. Duff specialized in being ridiculous.

"How's your pixie friend?"

"Much happier now that the dark elf is gone." We stood there in companionable silence for another couple minutes before Duff tightened his fists in my hair and pulled until I looked up at him. "Well, you've had my report. No more stalling from you. Get in there. Once I see you inside, I have to report back to Trixie and then I am joining the pixies. They're starting their trip to Buenos Aires tomorrow. We're following the Summer Court to their next destination. I've also heard whispers from the Winter Court that they're planning an ice storm before All Hallows' Eve."

I pushed away from my SUV as Duff launched himself into the air. "Safe travels."

The hobgoblin settled on the low branch of an old oak tree and then pointed over my shoulder. He was right. I was stalling.

Taking a deep breath, I walked up the sidewalk to the red-brick ranch with the dark blue shutters I had been sitting outside of for nearly thirty minutes. The yard was neatly trimmed and two sedans sat in the driveway, baking in the afternoon sun. I got to the front porch before I started to lose my nerve. I wiped my sweaty palms down the legs of my brown cargo pants and over the edge of my navy polo shirt. They were the nicest clothes I owned besides the fucking dark suits that kept appearing in my closet. I shredded the first two only to have four appear the next morning. I wished it was Gideon's doing, but I knew it was Darius taunting me.

Cursing my cowardice, I punched the doorbell with my index finger before I could chicken out. I held my breath, listening to the sound of footsteps echoing through the house as one of the occupants approached the door. My heart pounded and my throat was threatening to close up on me. As the footsteps stopped by the door, I realized I didn't have a clue as to what I was going to say. I almost bolted when the door was pulled open.

My first thought was that she was shorter than I remembered, but then I realized that I must not have been done growing when I last saw her. Her hair was still pale blond, making it nearly impossible to pick out the gray hairs, and there were more lines around her eyes and mouth. It wasn't so much that they made her look older as that they softened her lovely face.

"Hello," she said in a voice that cut straight through my heart. There was no recognition in her eyes at first, but they immediately swept up for a closer inspection as if something had registered faintly in the back of her mind.

"I'm sorry to bother you," I started, my voice low and rough. My eyes darted away from hers, no longer able to hold her gaze as I frantically searched my mind for what to say next. What was I supposed to say? *Hi, I'm the middle child who ruined your lives.*

"Jason?" Her haunted whisper jerked my gaze back to her face. Tears were filling her eyes. My entire body tensed painfully. I licked my lips and tried to say something, anything, but I couldn't make a sound past the lump in my throat. I finally settled on a nod.

My mother gave a harsh cry before she threw both of her thin arms around my neck, holding me in an impossibly tight embrace. Her fragile body was racked with violent sobs as she held me in her arms. I hugged her, wrapping my arms around her.

From the back of the house, I heard heavy footsteps rushing toward us, and the tension that had started to ease returned. I took a step backward, pulling my mom with me as my father turned the final corner to enter the hallway. I was afraid of being rejected, of being blamed for their hardship. It was no less than I deserved, but that thought did nothing to protect me against the pain.

My father was still a tall, broad-shouldered man, but his brown hair had gone completely gray. Confused anger hardened his features as he looked from his crying wife to me standing in her tight embrace. "What's going on here?"

My mother pulled back enough so she could turn to look at him, but both of her hands were tightly fisted in my shirt as if she were afraid that I was going to disappear. "It's Jason. It's our baby Jason," she cried.

He held back, his eyes narrowed on me, searching my features. I wasn't sure what my mother had seen to convince her it was me, but it only took him a second to see it as well. His face crumpled in a blink and I found myself pulled roughly into the house by big hands before I was engulfed in a hug by my father.

I don't know how long we stood there, hugging and crying; somewhere between a heartbeat and forever, but I knew it would never be long enough. It was only when my mother laughed that we started to pull away.

"Goodness," she said, wiping away her tears with her right hand while her left hand was tightly clenched in my right. "The neighbors must think we're crazy, standing in the open doorway, crying like a bunch of loonies."

My father and I laughed, letting the last of the tension ease from my shoulders. My father reached past me and closed the door while my mom ushered me down the hall toward the living room. I stopped, my eyes falling on the wall filled with framed photographs. They were all family photographs taken over the years. Sadly, there were no pictures of me over the age of seven, and those were all of the blond-haired, blue-eyed boy I had been so long ago. I was surprised to find that I was on the wall. It was only when I was standing there staring at the pictures that I realized I hadn't expected them to be on the wall.

Something must have shown on my face, because Mom touched my cheek. "Jason, honey, what is it?"

"I didn't expect to see my picture here," I admitted softly before I thought about what I was saying.

Dad placed a hand on my shoulder from where he was standing directly behind me. "Of course your picture is here."

"I talked to Robert." My voice was rough with emotion. I wasn't angry. Just surprised. "He said you told everyone that I died. He said that I was the reason you were forced to move and come to Low Town. I figured when you started fresh here, there'd be no evidence of my existence."

Mom placed both her hands on my cheeks, forcing me to look down at her. "Oh, no, honey," she started, and then stopped, fresh tears spilling from her eyes. "I mean, yes, we did tell people you had died when you first left, but we were always so ashamed of that lie. We have never been ashamed of you and your wonderful gift. But they told us it would be easier if we told everyone you were dead. We never took your pictures down and we never denied that you are our son."

I folded my mother in a fierce hug. "I'm not angry. You did what everyone does, what you were supposed to do. I guess I'm surprised. I wasn't sure how you'd react to seeing me again. I'm sorry about what happened in Vermont. I'm so sorry I screwed up your lives."

"Jason Stephen Grant," Dad thundered behind me, causing me to flinch. I hadn't heard anyone use my entire real name since I was six and in trouble for covering the dog in green food coloring. "I don't ever want to hear you apologize for that nonsense. You have nothing to be sorry for or ashamed of. Like your mother said, we're proud of your gift and have no regrets. And the weather is much nicer here than in Vermont."

I laughed. I couldn't stop. If my father was anything, he was always practical.

We walked into the living room with its pale yellow walls and thick brown carpet. I sat on the end of the couch while Dad took the chair nearest to me. Mom hovered, offering to get drinks but seeming unable to let go of my hand. I squeezed hers and smiled. "I'll be here when you get back, I promise." She gave a jerky nod and then released my hand as she expelled a heavy breath before disappearing back down the hall.

Dad shifted to the edge of his chair, leaning close as he clapped his hand on my shoulder. "We're happy to see you, son, don't misunderstand me," he started softly so Mom couldn't overhear. "But the last time we saw you, you said you weren't coming back because it was too dangerous. I'm guessing something has changed."

I sighed. "Yes and no. There's some danger, but not like before. If you want, I'll leave. I can alter your memories. You'll never know I was here."

"No! No!" Dad said quickly, sitting back in his chair. "Damn glad you're here. Just wanted to make sure you were okay." He knew there was a lot I wasn't saying, and he wasn't going to ask for more information, but he felt that he needed to have a handle on the situation. As I said, Dad was practical. "Regardless of your hocus-pocus, you know you're not getting out of here before having Sunday dinner. It's not as fancy as when you were a kid, but your mom still makes a great pot roast."

Sunday dinner had been a tradition in my family. Throughout the week, all of us were constantly running for school, work, soccer practice, Little League games, and music lessons, but by some odd twist of fate, Sunday dinner seemed to be one time when we all managed to be in the house at the same time. Mom and Dad had taken turns each week making a large meal that we ate while sitting around the formal dining room table. When I had been taken by Simon to the Towers, it was the first thing I missed from my old life.

Mom quickly rejoined us with drinks and then took a seat next to me, her hand slipping back into mine. A part of me wanted to keep the conversation light, filled with silly stories and random incidents, but that wasn't why I had come to their house. Mom squeezed my hand and smiled at me, trying to look encouraging. She knew there was something, but then that was Mom. Dad was practical and Mom always knew when we were hurting like she had some kind of mystical sixth sense.

Slowly, I told them about Robert. I cleaned up the story as much as I could, but something in Dad's eyes told me he knew I was leaving bits out. The last thing I told them was that his final thoughts as Robert Grant had been about them. I never mentioned his new name or the direction I sent him in. I also didn't mention the deal I had made with the Towers to keep him safe.

We sat in silence for several minutes. I kept my eyes fixed on my untouched iced tea, the glass sweating on the coffee table while I listened to my mother cry.

"Is he safe now?" she asked, both her hands tightly gripping mine.

"As safe as I could have possibly made him."

She nodded. "Thank you. I don't know what it cost you to do it, but thank you for saving your brother."

I took a deep breath and launched into a brief and somewhat clean version of my life, trying to distract them as much as possible from the loss of yet another son. I knew they'd think about Robert and cry when I left, but for now we smiled and laughed over my bad relationships and tattooing adventures.

A comfortable lull in the conversation had Dad taking command again. "Was Robert the reason for this visit?"

"Part," I admitted with a blush. At least I had the decency to look embarrassed. "Part was because I didn't know you were in Low Town until I spoke to Robert and I wanted to see you. And part is because I need to ask a favor." I stopped, my mind struggling with how to broach the subject.

"It's okay, honey. We'll help you any way we can," Mom coaxed.

"I know, but it's a lot to ask."

"Then ask and see if we can help," Dad pushed, bringing a grin to my lips.

"A while ago, five kids escaped from the Towers much like I did," I started, and then paused, licking my lips. Good grief, I had to be out of my fucking mind to even think this was a good idea, but I plunged ahead. "They're young, between the ages of nine and seventeen. They can't go home because the Towers are searching for them and it's the first place they'd look. We've managed to find homes for some of them."

I paused again and sighed, shoving one hand through my hair as I fought to block out visions of Alice. "Look, when we first came up with the idea of finding a home for these kids, you were the first people I thought of. I don't know what it was, but you did something right with me. I got out of the Towers. I stuck to the ideas of right and wrong that you gave me. I clung to the belief that people were good. I'm afraid that if they don't find someone like you, they're going to end up like the monsters in the Towers despite having escaped. I won't lie to you. There is some risk, but we can take precautions to protect you and them. If expense is a problem, I can help. I have some money saved."

"Honey," Mom said, laying her hand against my cheek. I was babbling. I was afraid if I stopped talking, they'd say no. She smiled at me. "What are their names?"

"Étienne is seventeen and from France, but his English is excellent. Anthony is fourteen and American. They escaped together and are close like brothers. Something in my gut says it would be a bad idea to separate them. I—"

I instantly shut up again when Mom put her hand against my cheek again. She looked over at my father and said nothing. He smiled at her and said nothing. Maybe that's what came of thirty years of marriage. You didn't need words anymore to say the things that needed to be said.

When she looked back at me, she was smiling a secret little smile that came with being a mom. "When can they move in?"

I pulled Mom to me in a fierce hug as a shudder of relief ran through my body. "Thank you. Thank you so much. I will help you in any way I can, I promise," I said in a choked whispered.

Mom ran her hand over my back, soothing away the shaking. "We're proud of you, Jason," she murmured in my ear. "We always have been."

After a moment I pulled away and hugged Dad, who only laughed at my worry. I should have known they wouldn't hesitate to help the runaways.

At Mom's urging, we followed her into the kitchen so we could sit at the table and talk while she finished making dinner. Throughout the meal, she hit me with a mound of questions, pulling out all the information I had about Étienne and Tony. By the end of dinner, she had a legal pad beside her, making a list of all the things that she would need to get to make the house ready before they arrived. Dad smiled, happy to leave the planning in her hands. As I said, Dad was practical.

It was after eleven when I finally managed to step outside the house following a series of long hugs and promises to come back soon with the boys. Leaving that night was one of the hardest things I had ever done, but I promised myself that I'd be back soon. I promised myself that my parents would be safe.

As I reached the bottom step, I realized that I never told them that my name was now Gage Powell. I never explained why I looked different, but I let it go. It had been nice to spend one last night as Jason Grant, son of Lily and Jonathan Grant. For one last night, I hadn't been Gage Powell, a warlock who had killed for the first time at the age of thirteen. I wasn't the monster who had killed other witches and warlocks. I wasn't the one who'd traded another person's soul to Charon the ferryman. I wasn't the one who'd killed a dark elf to save his own life. I was just a guy trying to be something his parents could be proud of.

Turning away from the house, I spotted Gideon standing beside my SUV wearing a dark suit with his hands shoved into his trouser pockets. I hadn't seen him since we'd left the New York Tower together nearly a month ago. Of course, I hadn't been using any magic since then, so he wouldn't have shown up. I received one brief message stating that Paola was now living with his wife and daughter, while James was safe on a ranch in Montana living with a witch and warlock who had faked their deaths. He never gave me names and I didn't want to know. He only asked me for suggestions on where to place Étienne and Tony.

I couldn't stop the smile that rose when I reached him. "The boys will stay with my parents," I announced before he could ask.

Gideon gave a soft grunt and a nod, at least acknowledging that he heard me. His face was blank, but his eyes wouldn't meet mine.

"Paola okay?"

"Yes, fine." His words were clipped and terse, but I didn't get the impression that he was angry at me. When Gideon was pissed at me, there was no doubt about it. Of course, when he was pissed at me, I was usually in pain.

"You're not here about the boys, are you?" I asked as a deep uneasiness settled into my bones.

Gideon looked up at me, meeting my stare with his unblinking silvery-gray eyes. His expression was solemn and a little sad, but his voice never wavered. "You need to change. We have a job to do."

I nodded, fighting the urge to let my shoulders slump in resignation. I'd made my choice. I chose to go back to the Towers rather than face death. Now it was time to live up to my end of the bargain. I'd survived Simon Thorn's murder attempts. I'd survived Reave's attempts to plunge the world into another war. I'd survive this. I escaped the Towers once. I could do it again, and this time I was taking Gideon with me.

How hard could it be?